THE BONDS THAT BIND US
BOOK I

The Blood Princess

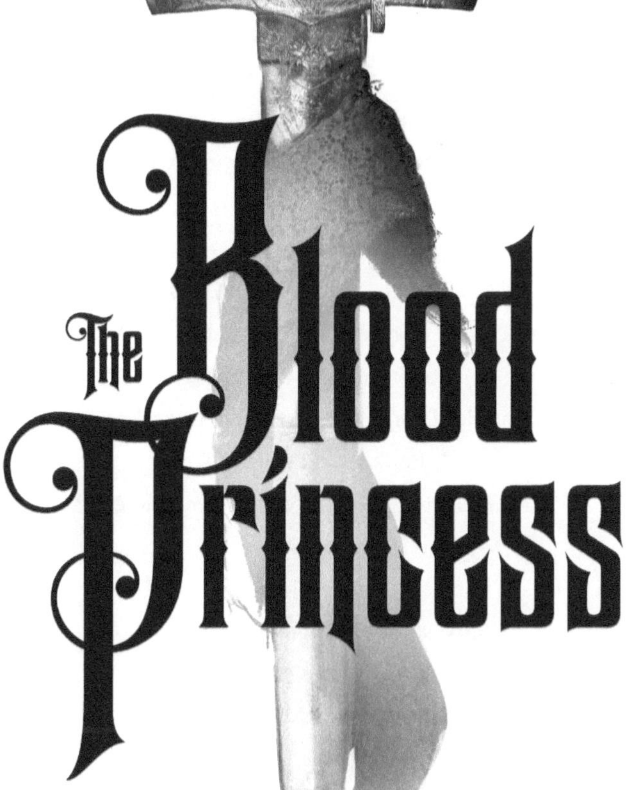

S.A. GONSALVES

GRENDEL PRESS

Trigger Warnings

This book contains subject matter that may be
triggering or unsuitable for those under sixteen
or with mental health illnesses.
Sensitive subject matter includes:

Graphic depictions of violence.
Allusion to sexual assault.
Self harm.
Refences to violence against minors.
Mention of cult like activities.

TO US

❧

This book is dedicated to me and you.
And to anyone who struggles to reach their dreams
while dealing with mental health illnesses.
We are not alone.
I see you.
And you can do it.

To Rita Lee-Goring
The most gangster person I've had the pleasure to meet.
May you rest in paradise.

ANTAC
ZILWU
PROELIUM TERRA
THE SOLUS
SYND
EQUES
VALENS
EMPIRE
ILLA
MACIL
MORTUI GEMMA
ANTIQUA
FLADE
TRANQUILLUM FOREST
ZYAID
XCANDA
MUUDAL
UHURU
ROWARK
THE
World of Vartugaul
YEWIN

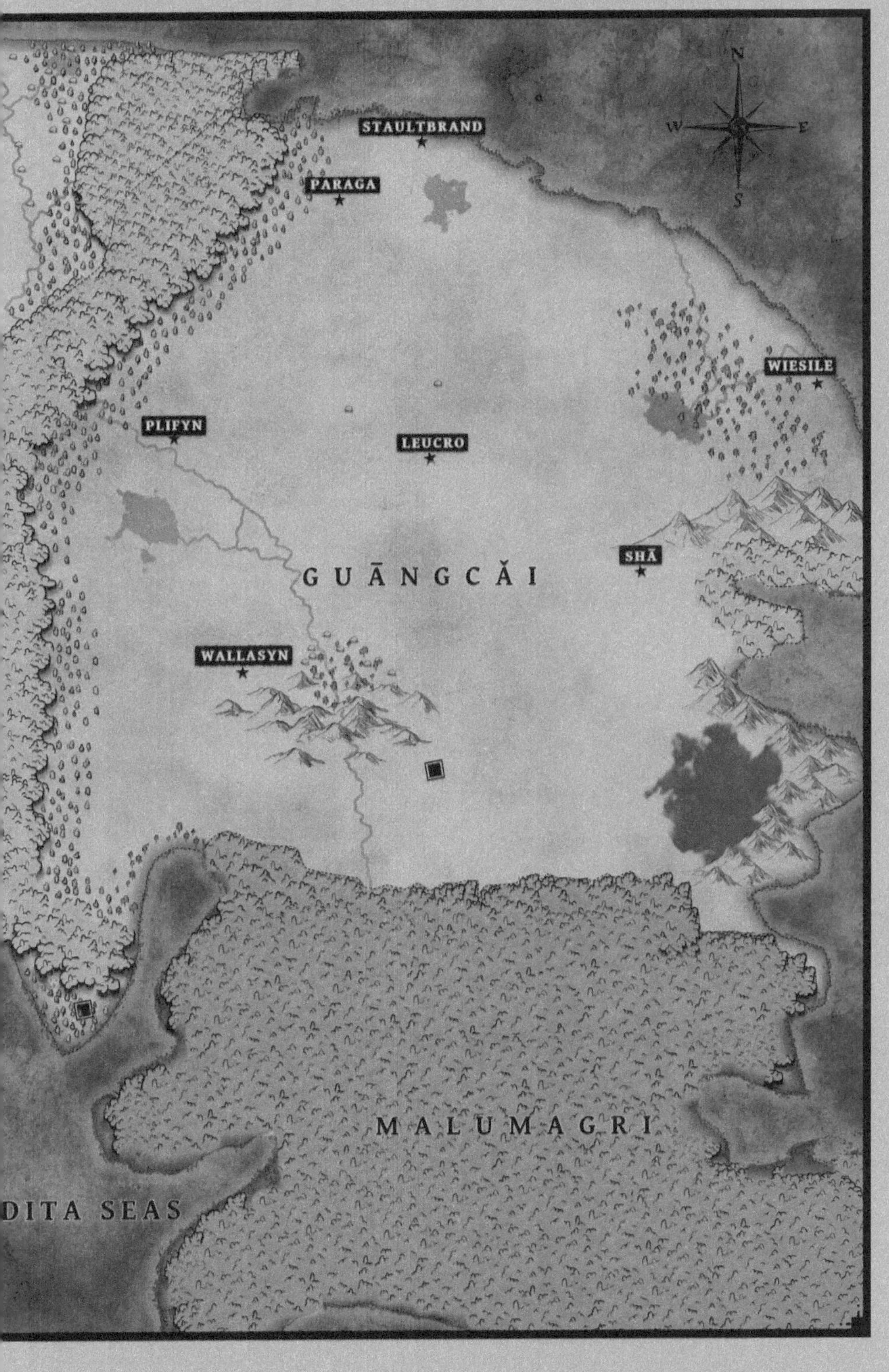

N
W
E
S
STAULTBRAND
PARAGA
WIESILE
PLIFYN
LEUCRO
SHĂ
GUĀNGCĂI
WALLASYN
MALUMAGRI
DITA SEAS

TABLE OF CONTENTS

The Star

| RAGHNALL |

RAGHNALL leaned against the tree trunk, the burning house no longer visible through the thicket of forest leaves. The wind was still and the night was preparing to break into dawn.

He looked down to rewrap the now sleeping infant. Both the burn on his neck and the burn on the baby's calf were roughly taken care of by his shoddy healing magic.

Raghnall took off the ash-covered swaddle, realizing the baby was a girl. "Well, look at that…" he mumbled in barely a whisper, the sun peeking over the edge of the horizon. He could see faint rays shine through the trees and laughed to himself as he picked her up, cradling her.

"I'm going to go ahead and assume you don't have a name," said Raghnall, shifting his position against the tree to look at the sunrise clearly. "The sun is always beautiful." He looked down at her sleeping soundly in his arms. "The sun is the biggest star, you know. Hmm, yes, I think that is fitting. Sulwyn—blessed sun."

I

Ascent & Descent

| WILKSON |

IT WAS PURE MADNESS.

Terror and fear filled the stone streets of the High City, but alongside it came shouts of glee and exhilaration. Wilkson kept to the ever-moving crowd, everyone huddled in dark cloaks, pushing and shoving. He looked to the distance—the beautiful stained-glass walls that lined the front of the Vitrail Palace were now shattered. Its tall dark walls loomed above them, the spires even sharper in this bloodstained darkness. A thick, long wooden post stood in the centre, reaching past the shattered window frames; something covered in black was bound to it. Though not a small man, Wilkson was shoved back and forth, a tangle of people pushing their way forward or trying to run away.

Fires burned around them and in the far distance. Homes and shops alike lined the path of destruction from their people, the Néosan that now marched their way along the sides. He knew he'd have to leave soon. The Néosan would start rounding everyone up within the fallen High City and sort through who was worthy and who was not.

Forced closer, he stumbled towards to the rainbow of shattered glass, the pole coming closer in view. Dawn was almost near, the sky brightening as if showering the spot in light.

People started to slow, unmoving, and Wilkson looked closer to see why. A man and a woman both stepped out from the broken walls and atop the shards of glass. The light from the rising sun illuminated them, making their presence that much more terrifying or elating, depending on whose side you were on.

"Finally!" roared the man before them. Thousands cheered but people somewhere behind him started to push and cry in terror, and Wilkson finally saw why. The man had turned around and slid the large black sheet off what was revealed to be the now dead king of the fallen High City. His long black hair was matted with blood, covering most of his face. Deep cuts, black bruises, and ripped skin decorated his naked body. His arms were missing, and his legs bent oddly, wrapping behind the pole. Wilkson's father and the last ruler of the Zalman clan, their last source of peace, hung dead before them.

Horror ran through him, paralyzing him at the sight.

Raghnall could continue gallivanting like the hero he was, but that wouldn't be enough. It had been six days since the man and woman before them had left the burning house to complete their coup. Six days since he last saw Raghnall. He hoped the bastard had managed to save the baby and get out of the house in time. The peace that Raghnall and the High City had maintained was shattered like the coloured glass crushed beneath these murderers' feet.

As if reading his mind the man continued, answering the yells. "Peace? What peace do you cry for? The Zalman clan and their descendants have been lying to you for years! Using their words and magic to influence you!" The man stepped forward, his dull green eyes sweeping the faces of excitement or terror. "Are you shocked? Are you surprised to hear my words? Devinal were born among them. They led us with their lies, using their power against us! But we! We broke free!" He pounded his chest, the roaring rising.

Wilkson's heart dropped.

Devinal were rare to begin with, and to his knowledge, he was one of the few Devinal born into the Zalman. No one knew this fact, not even his own family. And even though he was a powerful Devinal, he would not be able to stand against this. Nor would he want to, but it mattered not at this point. He watched as the Néosan began to capture and bind people around him. It was starting; he'd need to leave now. Slowly he stepped back just as the voice continued to ring over him.

"We have worked with all of you for many, many years. Showing you the way, the right way." Thousands cheered louder as the man smiled widely, his long black moustache and short beard moving with every word and every smile.

Wilkson could sense it. The people frozen in fear were now accepting their fate. Slowly they all started to listen to his words. They knew full well that if they didn't obey, they would be next. Another piece of broken glass added to the pile they stepped on.

"This ends the reign of the Zalman and of the High City! From now on, WE the people shall rule! We shall create this empire and walk together into a new future!" He raised his arms wide, the deep burgundy cloak blowing around him. Finally, the woman next to him moved. She stepped in front of the man and the dead king to speak; her hair was just as red as the blood that dripped down the wooden post.

"Just like you, we have suffered at the hands of the High City, from their ideals and what they believed peace to be. But where were they when I was left alone? As a mere child, my parents pushed me aside to survive, blinded by the High City and what they offered to maintain their hold on us!" Her clear voice cut across the chaos.

"Where were they when they stole Artaxiad's father from him, his mother from him?! They were here, building peace atop our sacrifices, pushing *us* to the side. Pushing you all out! We were nobody to the Zalman clan! All of us were pawns for their idea of peace! Subjects to use their filthy powers on!" she yelled, her light grey eyes piercing through everyone around her. Even Wilkson stopped again to listen to her.

"We are here to be *your* voice! We are here for you, the ones who have been tossed away for not meeting their ideals! And anyone who stands in our way stands against us. Just like my parents." The woman gestured to the side. Four Néosan brought forward an older man and woman, forcing them to kneel before the red woman. Both were taut with fear, their dark steel eyes full of tears and horror—eyes that were pleading for forgiveness, for mercy, for anything as they yelled into the cloth that silenced them.

Silently the man gave the woman a blade. She stared at her parents for just a moment, an expression of hatred etched in her face, before she slashed their throats. She nudged them to the side with the hilt of the blade, watching their bodies fall over and tremble their last breaths.

Ice flowed through Wilkson, watching the blood seep over the shattered glass. What madness had come before them? How were they any better than what they claimed the High City to be?

Someone fell near him, and a Néosan came forward, dragging the person away. He needed to leave, but his body didn't want to move. Dread enveloped him, keeping him in place. They were doomed anyway; what did it matter if they fought back? Even if he ran and hid, even if he faked his own death, they would find him. Somewhere in the back of his mind he hoped against hope that Raghnall would still be alive to fight. To do something, somehow.

The woman tossed the blade to the side, wiping her hands on a handkerchief and moving next to the expressionless man. The sounds of cheers reached Wilkson's ears, drowning out the yells of terror and fear.

The man took a deep breath, smiling wider still. "From this day forward, we will be the Empire that carries us into a stronger, better future." He opened his arms widely. "I, Artaxiad, as your king, and Pandora as your queen, will lead you all into the right direction—the best direction—are you with me?!" he yelled with power and might as even more cheered than before.

Artaxiad turned to Pandora, looking at her with triumph. Pandora smiled, looking into the crowd of their followers.

∾

| SULWYN |

Twenty-Three Years Later

This town was like any other; people walking quickly, hurrying to finish their business or the small amounts of work they could get their hands on, all while avoiding trouble. But if there was one thing that never really went away, it was curiosity.

Other than the monthly rotations from Artaxiad's Néosan, there wasn't much to see or do. Not without punishment, of course. So either out of fear, interest, or both, curiosity always lingered, making people keep their eyes and ears open for something like hope, that might give back a bit of the life they once had.

This moment was no different.

The small groups of men and women hurriedly scattered against the short building walls along the cobblestone path, a trail of men in tanned coloured uniforms running past. All armed, all part of Artaxiad's Néosan army. But it was who they were chasing that had everyone riled up. On-lookers stared openly, as with great speed an older man and younger wom-an dashed by, the Néosan not too far behind.

"Raghnall! Why did you stop me?" yelled the young woman, skirting a crowd of people, her face hidden beneath a black silk scarf, her face known only to those now dead. Her long black hair trailed behind her, shining with a purple sheen in the high noon sun.

"Kintana, look behind you!" yelled Raghnall. He turned towards her, never slowing. The woman he called Kintana turned to look as well. About fifteen of Artaxiad's Néosan had come behind them.

She narrowed her eyes, "Okay, fine. But originally there were only five," she retorted, catching up to Raghnall. "The rest had time to come because *you* were late!" She ran past him, weaving in and out between carts and people. Both ran directly out of the town gates towards two black horses.

"Don't let them get away!" yelled one of the men, but Kintana and Raghnall had already mounted the horses and were taking off at a gallop. Kintana looked back as they made space between them and the town, the sand kicking up around them. But she could see the Néosan getting horses as well. They would have to lose them in the trees of Tranquillum.

"Why were you late?" she asked, taking the scarf off her face and tuck-ing it away in a pocket of her black linen pants.

"It matters not why I was late, Sulwyn, I told you to stay low, and you didn't." She gave him an alarmed look, eyes wide. "They can't possibly hear me call you Sulwyn from here and your face is already uncovered." He hissed at her reaction.

Sulwyn just rolled her eyes. He was avoiding her question. "You've been up to something."

"I haven't been up to anything. Now ride faster so we can get out of their sight and into the cover of trees."

Raghnall took off, spurring the horse faster. She, too, picked up her pace, glancing back to the distant figures along the terrain. The bright yellows and blues marked the setting sun, hiding them farther in the forest.

After hours of travel within the lush forest of Tranquillum, no longer able to navigate through the thick trees, Raghnall let the stolen horses go back into the wild while they continued on foot through the river.

Sulwyn looked around. The vast forest on the edge of Antiqua was more home to her than anywhere else had been in a long time. The setting yellow and green sky could still be seen through the foliage of emerald and navy.

She observed Raghnall's back. His short silvery-white hair was a mess of leaves and twigs just like hers. Despite his age, he was still one of the best warriors anyone had ever seen. His slow steps through the water made no extra sounds; his posture was tense and alert. But something about him was nagging at her recently. However, the thought was brushed aside momentarily to address her wet, pruned feet.

"Three hours, Raghnall…" muttered Sulwyn, her boots tied together and strung across her neck, bumping her chest as she walked. Her feet took the blow of the cold water, uneven stones, and cuts.

Raghnall turned to look at her, his expression softening a little. "We're almost there. But don't let me remind you that we are shaking off the trail because you caused a scene."

"I will not stand by and watch their men beat a five-year-old for stealing their crumbs." Her voice raised.

Raghnall sighed. "Here looks good…" He bent under a low branch, stepping out of the water with grace and near silence. She followed just as quietly through the grass, sand, and mud of the forest. Within minutes Raghnall led her to an open clearing. She looked around carefully. As familiar as she was with Tranquillum, she had never come this far north. Raghnall led her past the brambles and thinning trees to a smaller clearing.

Sulwyn took the boots off her neck, and, throwing them against a tree, flopped down onto her stomach. She propped herself up on her elbows, crossing her legs behind her, watching.

"No, no, don't bother helping me set up camp," said Raghnall sarcastically, but Sulwyn only smirked.

"It's your punishment for coming late. We barely escaped this one." But she knew that wasn't true; they always escaped.

"I don't know. I thought you were doing fine on your own. You had most of the town's eyes on you."

Sulwyn smirked. "Well, I almost never have to buy myself a meal." She fluttered her eyelashes but stopped when Raghnall tossed a small loaf of bread at her.

"This was all we managed, then?" She sat up, crossing her legs. Her hair fell loosely around her, dusting parts of her pants with sand.

"Unfortunately, that town has already been raided by the Néosan, on top of the semiannual food collection." Sulwyn watched Raghnall take their bags, unpacking to settle for the night. Raghnall made short work of propping up the tent and finding wood to burn.

She bit into the slightly stale bread. They hadn't had anything solid in a few days, so this was a treat. Looking up she noticed the darkening of skin along the side of his face.

"Your burn is starting to show," said Sulwyn.

Raghnall reached up, touching the left side of his face and neck. "Hmm, I'll need to visit Wilkson soon for more of this cream," he huffed, reaching into his bag for a small glass jar. Opening it, he scooped up a small dab of white cream, rubbing it along the scarred skin. Instantly the large pink patch slowly faded away as if it had never existed.

"Weren't we just there a couple of weeks ago? Why didn't you refill it then?"

"Slipped my mind I guess." He re-pocketed the tiny, nearly empty jar and went back to tending the fire.

Sulwyn watched the fire roar, her cold, wet legs warming slowly from the heat. She looked at Raghnall carefully. He'd taught her everything she knew. He'd taught her how to fight, hunt, and survive, as well as how to feel remorse and warmth. How to think with both her mind and her heart. He accepted her choice to fight when he told her about her parents—the king and queen of Vartugaul—who had left her for dead in a burning house. He never dissuaded her from wanting to take it all back and instead tried to persuade her to live a modest life. She knew everything about him. But somehow today he was different. Something was off about him. And she couldn't place it.

"You were late today..." she pried one more time.

"Had I not been, you wouldn't have been able to save that boy," He didn't look at her, tending the fire.

"Had you not been, we wouldn't have been tailed for so long. They'll look for us forever, *oh great* Steel Warrior."

Raghnall looked up at her, distracted, as if he were not there. But then he chuckled deeply, his arctic blue eyes bright and aware. "All the more reason this is actually *your* fault, Kintana."

"This could have all been avoided if you had just let me fight them," she huffed. Raghnall smiled, taking a small metal pot out of one of the bags. He walked out of the clearing and gathered water from the river before bringing it back. Sulwyn finished her roll of bread, waiting patiently for her tea to come.

"You know that would have been bad. We're famous even in the small villages, Sulwyn. You've spread the name "Kintana" as much as my own "Steel Warrior." I think you surpassed your teacher a long time ago." Returning from the river, he looked at her carefully. Endearment crossed his face alongside another emotion she couldn't place. But she laughed all the same, her face flushed from the compliment.

"You know better than anyone. There is always something left to learn. I don't think I'm done yet."

"Well, this is true. Otherwise, we would not be in this mess, would we?" He was humouring her, and she knew it.

"But I wouldn't have had to interfere on my own had you been on time. Where did you go, anyway?" She pushed her luck further. It was rare for Raghnall to keep things from her and somehow a distant and uncomfortable feeling was forming in the back of her mind.

"Be thankful I was late, Sulwyn," he said with a note of finality. Sulwyn knew not to cross him, but she would find her chance and get it out of him later. With that, she pushed it to the back of her mind. Silence spread around them for a bit, as both watched the pot.

"How many men did you take out before I got to you?" The water came to a boil.

"All five? But they're like bugs. They didn't stay down and ran to get more men, and well, then you came, and we had to run. It's a good thing I haven't had a premonition in ages, otherwise I would have just passed out and died from being attacked, since you *abandoned* me." said Sulwyn dramatically. But Raghnall laughed. At least he was laughing now. His smile and his laugh were rarely shown to anyone but her.

He looked at her, his eyes slightly distorted through the smoke of the flames and steam. "I remember when I first found you; had to trek far to find a wet nurse. You know she almost killed me from the fever you got? Your premonitions are definitely curious just from the physical agony they put you through," he sighed. "You've come a long way from the little girl who cried for weeks after her first kill," he smiled bittersweetly.

"Well, it does help when the men of the Empire are scum and react to every woman they see," she huffed.

"Can't be helped. Use it to your advantage. A lot of them are weak to a unique woman like you. Wink at them or something, then cut their nuts off."

Sulwyn snorted with laughter. "Like you can flirt? I can't flirt. You didn't teach me that."

"Did we miss that lesson?" He chuckled, fiddling with his hand a bit. Slowly he removed the small, silver ring off his pinky finger. "Give me your hand, Sulwyn."

She raised her hand towards him without question, but he had that strange look again. His eyes seemed far away, but then he looked at her like she was the only person in existence.

He smiled gently, placing the ring on her left index finger. "You know I've had this ring for as long as I can remember. Take it with you and show it a world of peace." He looked up at her, nodding, his eyes oddly bright. He patted her hand, looking to the darkening sky. "We travelled for a few days. Now we rest, Sulwyn; the sun has set. I will take first watch."

Sulwyn didn't understand what had gotten into him but knew this ring was very precious. It had belonged to his mother, and she had given it to his wife. When he lost Amaya, it was the only thing he had left of them both. She couldn't explain it, but a sudden rush of sadness filled her heart. Her eyes started to sting, but she pushed the feelings back. She would consider it a graduation present to follow his earlier statement. Sulwyn looked at the old silver ring for a moment before drinking the rest of her tea. She kissed the top of Raghnall's head lightly, bidding him good night.

"Sulwyn..." whispered Raghnall urgently.

It took Sulwyn a moment to understand what was happening, her eyes adjusting to the darkness and faint moonlight. Softly, in the distance, she could hear the cracks of twigs and crunch of leaves. Somehow the Empire's men had caught up. Regular Néosan wouldn't have found them. Were they part of the Validus? She could never really tell them apart. They all looked the same in her eyes. To her understanding, the Validus were higher in rank than the Néosan. They travelled in smaller groups dealing with special assignments. But in her mind, they were just a higher rank in scum.

She stepped out of the tent, bringing everything out. Quickly, they both packed their belongings. Sulwyn broke apart the fire pit, scattering dirt and leaves across the ground. By the time they finished, the clearing looked just as it had before. Raghnall took off through the trees with Sulwyn following close behind. The men weren't that far from them. It was hard to track them, let alone find them. How did they get so close? What had they done wrong?

Caught in her thoughts, Sulwyn crashed into Raghnall.

"Raghnall? Why did you stop?" she hissed. The moonlight illuminated the small clearing before them.

Pounding feet were closer now. She looked behind her, waiting for the first sign of movement, but it came from ahead of her instead. She turned to look at Raghnall; his eyes were cold and distant with a look she had never seen directed towards her. His gaze was the reason why they called him the Steel Warrior.

She looked behind her as the Empire's guards came crashing through the trees, but they halted in front of her. Before she could fully turn to face Raghnall again, a cold, wet cloth came up from behind her, covering her nose and mouth.

A strong burning smell sent her mind reeling, burning her lungs in a poisoned heat. She tried desperately not to breathe, but she could not fight her way out of Raghnall's grip. He pulled her close against his chest. Her eyes widened, tears rising from panic and the lingering burn. She could feel her heart beat erratically alongside Raghnall's. But her mind began to fog; she couldn't think. Everything started to fade, the surrounding trees and ground melding into one. She watched the men form a circle around them, waiting.

Until she couldn't hold on any longer.

Sulwyn felt her knees hit the hard ground, her body weak and slack. The smell of dirt wafted up her nose before everything went black.

II

Thicker Than Blood

| RAGHNALL |

RAGHNALL let Sulwyn go, watching her fall limply onto the ground. He frowned, blinking furiously for a moment, before looking up at the men in front of him. He recognized the brown uniform of the Validus, darker in comparison to the tan clothes the Néosan wore. So, they had sent them to assist. That was fine. It made no difference to him.

"Lead the way," said Raghnall gruffly, bending down and picking Sulwyn up with ease. He slung her over his shoulder, her head bumping slightly against his back with every step. The Validus walked in silence in front of him, and he followed just as silently. He blinked rapidly again, pinching the bridge of his nose and rubbing his eyes slightly as they walked up a slope.

It had been years since he had been this close to the Empire, not since it was formally the High City. He smiled slightly, but it vanished as he concentrated on the task at hand.

By the time they reached the looming, black stone walls of the Empire, dusk was arriving. The sky in the distance shone in brilliant shards of pinks, yellows, and greens. Without question, a man-sized entrance opened within a corner of the stone doors, allowing them all to pass through. Raghnall could not focus on the details of the city around him, his mind a blur, keeping close to the Validus instead.

A little way in, the men stopped, saluting. Raghnall looked past them to see a hooded, lone figure make its way towards them from the distance, a tall man with his face hidden.

Soon the familiar sensation, like the buzz of a horde of bees, entered his mind. He blinked a few more times, focusing instead on the man a few meters away, willing the buzzing back. As quickly as it came, the buzzing started to seep away into the background. A whisper, almost like a chuckle, flitted through his thoughts. But the cloaked man was now in front of him distracting him further, and in an instant, he forgot about it.

"Thank you for your assistance," said the man, his voice low, tense, angry even. Raghnall couldn't tell. But he could feel some form of tension radiate off him.

Raghnall didn't acknowledge it. "Are we trading then?" he asked instead.

The man didn't speak but gestured for Raghnall to release Sulwyn to him. He grunted in compliance, taking Sulwyn off his shoulder and lowering her onto the cobblestone with a hard thump. Raghnall barely had time to register the intense hostility when a large bag of coins was shoved into his hands. Without a word the man bent down, picked up Sulwyn, and cradled her tightly to his chest.

"Your task is complete. The Validus will escort you elsewhere."

Raghnall looked up to the man as he stood upright. The rising sun flitted across his face, shining a light under his hood. Raghnall stared into the man's eyes, his own widening in recognition.

"I see…I bid you farewell," said Raghnall smiling faintly, his eyes never leaving the man's until he turned away, leaving with Sulwyn in his arms. The buzzing in Raghnall's mind cleared faster now, his thoughts a little less confused than they were before. Blinking a few times more he turned, tucking the coins into a pocket, and facing the Validus behind him. Silently, they led him towards a smaller Néosan base, away from the man walking toward the distant castle.

Raghnall walked with them, taking in his surroundings.

The Empire had changed on the outside since it had been the High City. Different structures rose in places they didn't used to be, newer and sturdier buildings either in stone or metal. Everything was in muted tones of red, black, and grey. In the far distance, he could see the mountain that held the Proelium Terra. Looking straight to where the man had come from, he could see that all the stained glass of the High City's Vitrail Palace had been replaced with the same hard, black stone that guarded the Empire borders; the castle now named Valens Muros. As they walked, he brought his attention to the small limestone base that appeared before him.

The Validus led him to a set of stairs and stood alongside it, one gesturing for him to go down. He did as he was told, taking the steps slowly. Here it was dark, wet, and surrounded by rough brick stones. With each step, his mind cleared more and more while his heart grew erratic.

He continued until he reached a large iron door, knocking on it once. A voice within called to enter and a manservant led him in and bowed himself out. The room itself was small, draped in red and black cloth. A small fire had been lit in the corner, making the room stuffier. He noticed a woman was sitting quietly atop a wooden desk in the corner, against the draped walls.

He smiled tightly. "Pandora."

"Well, well, well..." she purred. Most of her face was hidden in the dark shadows. But she sounded just as he remembered from all those years ago, her voice clear, slightly deep, and intense. She commanded millions with that voice, and none would dare question her. "It's been ages since I've last seen you, Raghnall. Age has taken its toll on you."

"But not on you at all, my queen."

She edged forward a bit, the light of the fire catching her crooked smile. "Flattery can get you far, dear Steel Warrior..."

Raghnall could sense it in her. She was a dangerous woman, far more than she used to be, and instantly he felt cautious. He watched her lean forward, the delicate folds of her navy blue dress ruffling about her legs and waist.

"I *have* been trained to survive, my queen."

She laughed a high, fake sort of laugh, her smile growing wicked. "Survive? Is that what you've been doing all these years, Raghnall? Gallivanting with the child, teaching her to survive? But look at you now! You've gone senile. You've brought her to *us*. Of your own accord. You made a deal *with us*." Pandora slid off the desk, coming entirely into the light.

Dark red hair fell about her, flowing gently down her back and past her waist. Her dress pulled lightly against the curves of her body. And her grey eyes, lighter than Sulwyn's, were full of poison. She was as beautiful as ever, and Raghnall laughed. Sulwyn would murder him if she knew he had just compared them. They were so strikingly similar in appearance.

Pandora's smirk faltered. "You dare laugh? In your situation?" She scoffed in bewilderment. "You didn't honestly believe I would let you walk free, did you?" She stepped toward him.

He should kill her; here and now he should kill her. But he couldn't. His will had not returned, and he had done all he could for now.

"I am senile after all. Everything seems a bit—funnier—when you're about to die, wouldn't you say?"

She looked at him, face expressionless, and her eyes dark, "I wouldn't know about such trivial things, Raghnall. I am the queen, after all. But I applaud you. You're quick on the uptake."

Raghnall saw it coming but didn't bother to block it, only shifting slightly as Pandora took a long dagger from the folds of her dress and plunged it into his chest. She pushed him hard, his back crashing against the door.

"I've missed your heart it seems…no matter, you will still die. Slowly, and in agony," she whispered in his ear, pressing her chest against his. Raghnall managed to laugh again, knowing full well it would anger her. She pushed on the dagger a little harder.

"You are a fool, Raghnall. A disgrace to your name. I looked up to you at one point, did you know that? The great Steel Warrior, back when the High

City still thrived, and you led their army. No one dared touch you. But then you disappeared. Hid. And we rose further. We rose to power and changed everything for the better." Pandora's manic energy was still present from the last time he saw her all those years ago. Tears shone in her eyes from the sheer pressure of it.

"The better? Do you still believe in that nonsense, then? The better..." He knew he shouldn't aggravate her further, but it was hard not to. He wanted to bring her pride out to its peak for this moment.

"Nonsense? We are at the top. It matters not how many we need to sit upon. The ones who deserve it are living in a world far better than the High City ever was."

"What will you do with Sulwyn? You've wanted her for ages now." He could feel his knees growing weaker by the second, sliding against the door. The beat of his heart slowed, the blood around his wound finally slowing as well.

"Sulwyn...That name is very like you... it doesn't matter what I want with her. She is young. We can paint her whatever colour we like."

"She won't be easy." He slid down fully, lying on the hard floor. His neck bent oddly against the door. Pandora stepped over him, sitting across his chest.

"Why, because you trained her?"

"No, because she's your daughter."

Pandora laughed, taking a finger and pressing it into his bleeding wound, pulling the dagger out altogether. She licked the blood off her finger. "Was she the replacement?" she asked casually.

Raghnall stared at her—she knew about that too?

"Don't look at me like that. She was, wasn't she? For the child you and Amaya never had. Such a sentimental idiot you are. Children are a burden."

"If you were going to want Sulwyn on your side, why did you abandon her in the first place? Why didn't you start the fire in her room instead of on the opposite side of the house? Did you think I wouldn't notice?"

Pandora's eyebrow twitched before she smirked. "Weakness. I needed to cut it out." She pushed on his wound with more force this time, digging her finger into it. He forced himself not to wince. He would not show pain to her.

"Hmm, your blood is slow and thick. Guess you can't run from age after all." She shrugged. "Sulwyn will be in good hands. We have many ways of persuasion." She smiled wider, staring at him, waiting for him to draw his last breath.

And breathing was difficult now, especially with her sitting astride him. He looked up at her. Her dark red lips were now tainted redder with his blood. His breaths were ragged; her eyes never left his. But still, he laughed. How could he have possibly gone through with all this madness? The buzzing in his mind left him entirely, finally leaving his thoughts clear, and all he could do now was laugh.

Pandora glared at him, coldness in her eyes. "You senile—do you think this is funny? You are dying! The end of the Steel Warrior is at my feet. The only hope for those wretched beggars is in my hands. Their great Kintana!" she sneered, standing and pacing. Somehow, she looked madder than he had ever seen her, a twisted smile and unfallen tears marring her face; uhinged.

"You knew about that as well? I forgot how well informed you've always been."

"Of course I did. You aren't the only one who has ears across Vartugaul. You are the past. The last of the past. And you are dying. We will show everyone what has happened to their great saviour. And Kintana will be gone. No one knows who she really is. Now there is no one left to give hope to those bastards that think we have wronged them. Well done, Raghnall. You've lost." She spat at him, just as his vision started to blur red. Raghnall watched Pandora knock on the door once, calling back the servant.

"Take him to the lower dungeons. Let him rot amongst his people." She tossed the dagger to the ground.

Her voice sounded more distant than she really was, but he didn't worry about that now.

He had gotten what he wanted.

Raghnall smiled to himself; the man hefted him up, forcing him to walk.

Maybe he had gone senile.

He could only pray that Sulwyn would fix the mess he'd created.

III

| SULWYN |

S HE couldn't look back.

She wouldn't.

Sulwyn danced through the trees, making her way across the brambles and roots. Though they did not harm her, she wouldn't stop; that was not the threat. A metallic sound followed her, like chains waiting to bind.

Why?

Why were chains chasing her?

Where was Raghnall?

"Raghnall!" yelled Sulwyn, sitting up, her heart erratic and her breath coming short. She kept her eyes closed. The echo of her yell rang around her. The scent of burning poison disoriented her, as the space around her spun in shades of black. But it was just the lingering smell from her face. She lay back down on the ground. What was the other smell?

"Dust…mould…" she said out loud to herself. No one responded. She must be alone. The air was cooler, dark, damp; underground. She passed a hand over the ground. Hard, rough dirt. With every deep breath the dizziness passed. Slowly she sat up. The poison lingered, but she could fight off this much. Opening her eyes, she saw long, iron bars in front of her.

"Dungeon or prison?" She sat quietly, eyes adjusting to a small bit of flickering light within the stone halls. She looked up, unable to see the ceiling. Around her, the cell itself was rather small. Stretching out her arm, she touched it. It was a rough, older stone. Carefully she stood, keeping her arms above her head. Even when she stood upright completely, she couldn't reach the top. She jumped a bit, her arms still outstretched, but felt nothing. Sulwyn leaned against the wall, steadying herself as waves of vertigo passed over her.

Where was Raghnall?

She slumped down against the stone wall, bits of it scratching her back, but she barely registered it. What was she missing?

"Forest...we were in Tranquillum. Going north. We ran north. And then he..." Coldness ran through her, her whispers echoing. "North? He never allowed me to go so far north..." she continued, looking up suddenly as if envisioning what was outside of the cell. Numbness spread through her.

She was in the Empire.

A heaviness formed in her heart, her breath tight in her throat.

Raghnall had betrayed her to the Empire?

No.

There was no way he would betray her...

He of all people had betrayed *her*.

How did she not see it? He had been acting strangely for months. But betrayal?

She clutched her chest, tightness seizing her. Needles stabbed her drying throat, a ball of metal sliding up and down as she gulped ragged breaths.

Panic? Was *she* panicking?

Sulwyn was in the Empire. She was their prisoner. Where? Where exactly was she? There were only two places they would put her. Either in the dungeons of Valens Muros itself or in the prison cells of the Solus.

Which was worse?

Raghnall had betrayed her.

࿇

She coughed, spluttering, cold water splashing over her. She looked around, startled. She was lying down again. Had she passed out? She raised a hand to her cheeks; the crust of dirt mixed tears stained them. She sat up ginger-ly, looking at the two men in front of her cell. One was tall and burly with a rather matted beard; the other short, stocky, and a little stupid looking.

"Look at her," said the taller of the two. Were they guards? They had the light tan uniform of the lesser Néosan, lowest of the rank, the scum. She hated them. Though the Empire no longer forced civilians to join the Néosan like when they first started their reign, others too weak to be on their own chose to work for the Empire in order to share in their gains. She watched them reproachfully.

"Oh, look at that *glare*…" said the shorter of the two.

"You've been a bad girl, yeah? Don't you think so?" The tall one nudged the short one. They were gruff, rugged, and slimy. Her disgust rose.

"You givin' us a bad look there for someone trapped like a mouse." She narrowed her gaze. They didn't know who she really was.

"You don't talk, sweetheart?" said the short one. He passed a knife over the iron bars. Over and over it clattered and echoed loudly. Comprehension dawned on her; they had been here before. Watching her as she lay there unconscious. The reason for her strange dreams. A shiver ran through her and she bent her knees to her chest. The cold was getting to her. But she felt it with each movement; she was weak.

"You've got quite the assets there, my pretty thing," said the taller one. He leered at her, and she deepened her glare hoping that they would get bored with her if she kept silent. But they were grating on her nerves.

"So, what you in here for?" said the short one.

"You know where you are?" said the tall one.

"I don't think she can *com-puur-hand* our words," the short one laughed.

"Are you going to keep ignoring us?" said the taller one, his voice raised. The other one quickened his pace with the knife. Back and forth, the sound of metal against metal grinding against her skin. She clenched her jaw.

"I said WHAT YOU IN FOR?!" yelled the taller one, pulling out his short sword, banging it loudly against the bars.

In unison, the men backed away as Sulwyn quickly stood up, shock in their eyes. But that didn't last long. Their short burst of fear turned into leers at the way her red tunic clung to her skin, outlining her frame.

They were too stupid to sense danger, it seemed. She eyed the knife in the short one's hand, deciding her next move.

"Blood…" She murmured. Keeping her gaze on the short one, eyes hooded, she slowly walked closer to the bars and pressed against them, her damp hair clinging to the sides of her face and neck. The bars pressed her wet clothes further onto her.

"Blood?" he grunted, entranced by her. He, too, stepped closer. She glanced at the other one watching them both with a hint of envy in his eyes. Sulwyn brought her hands out through the bars as if to embrace him, passing the back of her hand gently over his cheek.

"You look like fun…" he breathed. He raised his hands to hold her own against his cheek. She smiled sweetly, gazing at his dim, brown eyes. Swiftly she gripped the greasy hair from both sides of his head and with great force, twisted it, breaking his neck.

She didn't like to kill like this, but she didn't regret it. Not this one.

Sulwyn pulled back fast but not before she secretly grabbed his dagger. The short man crumpled to the floor. His faint expression of surprise still lingered on his face. The tall one rushed at her, banging the sword against the bars. She narrowed her eyes.

"You don't have the keys, then," said Sulwyn confidently. She swiftly tucked the small dagger into her boot unseen. The guard yelled angrily at her but finally registered some form of fear. He stomped away.

Sulwyn listened, hearing the loud groan of a heavy door. A smell like decay, mould, and blood, wafted in. Instantly she doubled over, her mouth salivating by the vomit threatening to come out. But as quickly as it came, it went, with the sound of the closing door. She breathed deeply, the smell gone, but the coldness of the dungeon sent shivers through her.

"There, Raghnall, I flirted. Happy?" She looked beside her, remembering she was alone. Sulwyn leaned out over the bars, pressing her face against them, looking as far right and left as she could. But she couldn't see any other cell, or anything at all for that matter, aside from the flicker of fire on stone walls. She shivered again, glancing at the dead man at her cell door.

She slumped down, sliding back to brace against the wall, settling with her knees to her chest. Sulwyn leaned her head back, thinking. What did she know?

Raghnall had betrayed her for some reason. No matter what she tried to think of, she couldn't really understand why. She put that thought in the back of her mind. It wouldn't do her any good now. She'd just have to beat it out of him later when she eventually got out of this place. What else was there? The guards were average, low-rank Néosan. This meant she wasn't in the Solus. But this was not the lower dungeons. She briefly remembered the smell and gagged a little.

Raghnall had told her about the High City before. They had built an upper and lower dungeon. But during their thousand-year reign, they had never had a need for it. It wasn't until the Empire came to be that the lower dungeons were used. It was all theory, but anyone put in the lower dungeons never left. This *would* explain the smell…

She gagged a bit more.

The men didn't know her. Which meant her capture and detainment were not yet public knowledge. Why? Why were they hiding it and not flaunting it? They could easily announce her capture. But did they know her as Sulwyn or as Kintana? If Raghnall betrayed her, then they would know both. But what would they do with that information?

Sulwyn slumped over, her line of vision sideways. She avoided looking at the dead man and looked to the walls instead. The fire flickering in the distance burned her eyes, causing her to fall asleep once more.

She was back in the forest, running from something unseen. But the sun was guiding her. She followed its rays through the trees. Brighter and brighter it became, the trees thinning. She ran faster, never stopping, never looking back. Suddenly she halted at the top of a mountain, below her were mounds and mounds of snow and rock. The wind blew stronger now; snow carried on it, sticking to her wet clothes.

"Hey…" said a whisper.

Her eyes opened slowly.

Now that she was awake, the coldness burned through her even more. She shivered, her eyes focusing in front of her.

The dead man had been removed. This time a cloaked person stood before her. Face hidden beneath the shadows of their hood, most likely a man.

She sat up. Her arms and legs ached from stiffness and cold, but she wrapped her arms tightly around her.

The person stayed quiet, watching her. He was tall, taller than her, taller than Raghnall even, his shoulders broad. Most of his body was covered by the cloak, but he wore heavy boots. It must be another Néosan. She looked back up to his head.

"Sulwyn…" the voice not too deep, a little husky. So, it was a man. A man of the Empire, higher in title than the two before. Much higher based on his style of dress and the fact that he knew who she really was. She continued to stare. Maybe she should feign ignorance just in case.

"Sulwyn?" she spoke, her voice louder than his. Somehow this startled him. He moved as if to shush her but decided against it.

"Listen to me. You will be visited soon," he kept his voice low, but she noted its urgency. Narrowing her gaze, she tried to will the firelight under his hood. He continued, "If you don't want to be tortured, I need you to say you'll trust me and follow my instruction."

"What?" she said incredulously, brows raised.

"Please, Sulwyn. Just give me your word, and I can get you out now…"

"Get me out first, and then I'll give you my word." She stretched her stiff legs. She was weaker than before. She wouldn't be able to fight him properly. But she was willing to test that. Slowly, she stood, forcing herself up without the aid of the wall.

"I can't do that."

"And you ask me to trust you? I don't know who taught you how to go about making deals, but you aren't doing it very well."

"We don't have time for this. I won't be able to stop the first visit."

"Where is Raghnall?" She stood straight, poised, ready to fight. She couldn't be sure, but he seemed like he had the key or at least had the means to get it. She stared at him, but he didn't answer. She stepped closer. "Where is he?" she raised her voice slightly, watching as he shifted restlessly. He turned to look right, towards the presumed door.

"Dead."

"What?" Somehow that thought hadn't occurred to her. How could he be dead?

"Dead. Raghnall was killed."

"Why? Where is he?"

The man tilted his head slightly. "Why are you asking about the whereabouts of someone who has betrayed you?" His tone changed. It was a little rougher, angrier. Why should *he* be angry?

"It's no business of yours. Who killed him and why?"

"Pandora. After the completion of his task." Sulwyn stared at him, rage rising within her alongside despair.

"Are you helping me?" asked Sulwyn, inching a bit closer. The man stayed in the same position.

"Yes..."

"Why?"

"I can't tell you that here." He turned to look at the door again.

"Let me see you then."

"I can't."

"You come here, asking me to trust you and you won't even show me your face? I don't know you. Why should I trust you?" She stepped closer still. But the man stiffened, standing straighter. She could feel it, his glare on her.

"You of all people should know it matters not how long you've known a person." He sighed, shaking his head a bit. He crossed the line with that.

"And you ask for my trust?" That one hurt her. But she was close enough now. With all her energy, she rushed forward, pushing her arms between the iron bars and banging her elbows in the process. But she didn't care.

He stepped back quickly. He was fast. Faster than her, or Raghnall even. But she achieved at least one part of her goal. The man turned to her, his hood knocked back and his face in full view.

She gasped.

His cheeks were rosy; flustered. Though his skin was otherwise smooth and pale. His face was slim, with high cheekbones and a square jaw. He seemed divine and bright. His tousled dark brown hair, a little long, was to his ears. But what held her attention were his eyes. His irises had three colours. From the outside a dark sea-blue bled into a slightly brighter violet, ending in scarlet before his pupil. However, this was not the first time she had seen these eyes.

These were eyes she would never forget.

"You...do you remember me?" Sulwyn stepped back, transfixed by his eyes. And he too watched her with unwavering attention. He remained silent. "I was six when you helped me in the square town. You stabbed one of the Néosan." She whispered. He looked down slightly, as if ashamed. "Why are you here?" she asked, quieter still.

"I can't tell you these things now." His voice maintained its urgency, but he avoided her gaze.

"Why are you here," she said louder, "when you had such fire in your eyes?"

"People change, Sulwyn..."

"Change? What? Did they entice you with the rich life? The food of the poor that they've stolen? The clothes and the warmth that is created by the bodies that they walk on?" Her voice rose higher. How could someone like that be here? How could someone like Raghnall bring her here? Her chest was hurting again. First Raghnall and now him?

"Do not speak about things you know nothing of!" he shouted. He glared at her with such intensity that she stepped back a bit more. "Damnit..." he cursed, running a hand through his hair. He shifted his gaze towards the door and stepped back.

A few moments after, the heavy iron doors opened. Sulwyn held her breath for a moment, expecting the smell, as the sound of footsteps met her ears; she counted two people. She breathed out slowly, waiting. The man moved to stand against the stone walls as *three* people stepped before her. She narrowed her eyes, staring at the two Néosan. She had heard them walk in. It was the man in the centre she had not. So, he specialized in stealth. Probably worked for years to attain that skill; impressive.

His hair was snow-white; and he looked slightly older than her and the other man. Thick-jawed, lanky, and taller than all of them. Unlike the uniformed Néosan, he wore his own clothes; a white sleeveless tunic and dark brown pants tucked into brown boots. Strangely, he had bandages wrapped up around his forearms and past his elbows. And his eyes were bright blue like thick ice, but she couldn't read them. Not at all.

"Well, Galahad, looks like you've come to visit before us. Of course, you did. Such a good little prince, aren't you?" His voice was slightly higher than Galahad's, echoing loudly around the stone walls. But Sulwyn only had eyes for the man named Galahad.

"Prince?" she asked. Galahad's face was impassive, but his gaze never left hers.

"Didn't you introduce yourself? Or are you upset that the Blood Princess is here? Do you feel threatened because you're not the blood heir? Though it wouldn't be much of a threat if they didn't have such a wasteful man as prince, don't you agree?" He looked at Galahad for a moment. "If we could call you a man at all..." He smirked. Sulwyn watched Galahad's jaw clench.

"Who are you then?" she snapped at him.

He turned to her smiling, though it didn't reach his eyes. He seemed full of pretenses and lies. "Caldwell, at your service, my lady. You are indeed as striking as I've heard." He bowed elaborately. Irritation rose in her.

"Galahad, are you staying or leaving? You have no purpose here, I assume? I have this, so I don't need your key." Caldwell held up the metallic handle to what Sulwyn realized was the end of a long whip. Sulwyn turned to Galahad, who looked down.

"I will be back later to check in. Don't get carried away, Caldwell. She is the princess." Galahad turned swiftly, his cloak swishing behind him as he left. Sulwyn held her breath again only to release it once the door closed.

"Now, princess, I am here to educate you. You have been raised in captivity all these years, learning all the wrong things." He spoke lightly yet the tone beneath was excited, and almost cruel. As soon as he finished speaking, he raised the whip before bringing it down. It slapped against her thigh, forcing her down to her knees immediately. But she could barely register the pain for shock. The whip had gone through the bars.

He held a finger to his lips. "Keep it a secret. You know how everyone is about magic and Devinal. But Queen Pandora has some connections for some select tools." He winked at her before raising it again, holding it up high. "Now then, princess...I'm surprised. You fell right away."

Sulwyn silently glared. This wasn't the first time she had been whipped. But she wouldn't admit it she was surprised too. She was much weaker than she had thought. She didn't even bother to stand back up. That would be a waste of energy. Caldwell observed her, the smile still playing along his lips. Something was off about him. More than anyone she'd ever encountered. His eyes and his expressions didn't match.

"Tell me, my lady, what is the Empire?"

"The poison of Vartu—" She was whipped before she could finish.

"Now, now...that is not the right answer."

☙❦

Cuts across her arms, back, and legs burned and pulled with every movement. But the cold wetness of her clothes dulled the pain, if only a little.

"Come now, princess, we've only gone through thirty questions. Though you got each one wrong. Shame..." She could visualize him crossing his arms and shaking his head. But she refused to move. The ground seemed a better place to stay.

"I didn't tell you another part of this wonderful whip, though I'm sure you must have noticed. It grows stronger with every hit. *Magical*, isn't it?"

She'd kill him. She'd definitely kill him.

"Now, who are Artaxiad and Pandora to the people?"

"The living embodiment of evil—" Whipped again. But she wouldn't scream for as long as she could help it. She had felt worse. And she knew others had felt even more. She could not afford to lose here. She could hear

Caldwell ask her something but couldn't focus on it. He whipped her again for lack of response, but her eyes were closed, mind blackening.

"I'll let you rest for now, princess. It's no fun if you stop responding," he spoke softly. His voice seemed far away, as if she were underwater. Her eyes rolled before she could open them, the putrid smell reaching her nose. Had she not been so weak she might have thrown up this time.

She stayed still for a moment, her mind clearing a little as all the pain rushed back to her. It was numbing. A throbbing that coursed through her entire being. A cut on the side of her face bled a little into her eyes and down the side of her nose. She couldn't think. As numb as her body was, her brain felt it too. She closed her eyes, darkness meeting her again.

"Sulwyn..." said a familiar voice.

She stirred, a new smell coming forward.

Food.

Her stomach cramped and tightened like knives. How long had it been since she last ate or drank anything? She struggled to raise herself up off her belly, her body stiff, cold, and heavy, like iron. Everything burned or itched. It seemed like years since she last had that bread and tea, the fire by her side. Eventually, she gave up, lying back onto the ground and turning her head. Her eyes adjusted, focusing on the person in front of her cell. Galahad was kneeling on the ground, a tray of food to the side of him.

"How many times?" Her voice was hoarse. She eyed the jug of water. Without looking away from her, he grabbed the jug, pouring water into a glass. Slowly, he put it within her cell as close to her as he could reach. She swallowed involuntarily, staring at it.

"It's not poisoned. As I'm sure you can detect, for the most part." She knew they wouldn't kill her yet, but she still looked at it apprehensively.

"How many times?" she asked again, still staring at the water.

"For what?"

"You didn't leave the dungeon when you said you did." She watched his mouth twitch a bit; was that a smirk?

"Thirty-five times. He left when you finally passed out."

"You stayed there and listened, then?"

Galahad stared at her, "I don't have much of a choice."

"I thought you'd have all the choice since you're their son, prince and all." She closed her eyes again, trying to ignore the food and water.

"Adopted."

"Is there a difference?" she asked weakly, but she could sense a rising hostility. She opened her eyes to look at him again, his face impassive.

"I'll warn you again not to speak of things you know nothing about." His tone was final.

"That's not how you get people to trust you, Galahad..." And she faded out of consciousness again.

☙◦☙

She screamed in surprise, searing pain flaring against her back. Her eyes shot wide open, and she struggled along the ground to put space between the cell door and herself. But the wall was only so far away. It took longer for her vision to come into focus. Caldwell was back, the food and water now within her cell in the corner. Cheater. Galahad had come in when she passed out.

"You should have eaten, princess. It's been six hours since I last came here. We need to go over those questions again." She closed her eyes slowly. This was getting harder.

"Are you ready, my lady? Please, do not hold it against me. It's just, we need to correct you."

"We?"

"Artaxiad and Pandora, of course."

"Where is Raghnall?"

"You shall be seeing him soon, I'm sure. Not in the way you expect though...now, I am not here to be questioned. You are. Let's start. Who were the Zalman clan?"

"A good and just—" The whip was harder this time. Much harder. And her back had already taken so many of the blows she decided to lie on it instead, her stomach the one to receive the hit. Instantly, all the pain from before flared up. And against her will, she screamed louder. Heat rose through her body and across her skin, turning into cold sweat.

"Did ya learn nothing?" He asked slightly exasperated. She gave herself over to the pain. His voice faded into the distance again.

"Raghnall! Raghnall?! Who is this?" squeaked a small, young girl in strange blue pants with a red dress. Her dark hair flitted in the wind as she ran through the grass and sand to the cool shade of the blue tree that Raghnall was under. She held up the old painting she had found back in the house while rummaging through bookcases, waving it back and forth.

"Sulwyn, I can't see what you are showing me if you hold it that close to my face." He took the yellowing, sun-stained canvas from her, his eyes widening in recognition and nostalgia. Sulwyn continued to wiggle happily, waiting for an answer.

"Come here, my love." He pulled Sulwyn towards him, sitting her on his lap, holding the painting in front of her. Even though it was a little worn and faded, the image was as clear as it was when first painted. Two women sat with their arms around each other. One older with long blonde hair tied behind her in a braid, the other younger with flowing, shoulder-length black hair. Both were wearing matching blue dresses and laughing.

"This one," he pointed to the blonde woman, "was my mother. The other was my wife, Amaya." He smiled tightly until he looked down to the sounds of sniffles. "Why, my child, are you crying?" He laughed, placing the painting down and standing her up. He turned Sulwyn to face him, tears streaming down her face.

"I'm sorry! I'm sorry! They were pretty! I wanted to know who they were! I didn't want to make you sad!" She began crying fully, her face becoming red and her nose running. Raghnall pulled her gently towards him, hugging her.

"Silly girl…yes, it is sad. But it's sad because of love. And because of love, even if it is a little hard sometimes, it's still okay. I know that they loved me, and they know that I loved them. Just as I love you. Alive or not, we will always be together." He let go of her, drawing her attention to his hand.

"Now this ring…"

"My lady, my visits will become more frequent if you cannot learn the right answers." Caldwell froze as Sulwyn sat up suddenly. She paused for only a moment to gather her senses, the memory fading and giving way to the pain that flared through her body and pounded through her head alongside vertigo. But with surprising vigour, she crawled towards the tray of food, tearing at the bread, taking slow sips of cold yellow soup and bites of soggy cheese, ignoring Caldwell and the other two men, who could only stare. From the corner of her eye, she noticed a shadow. Galahad was there too. She downed the jug of water, instantly feeling a little better if slightly sick. She could think a bit clearer now.

Maybe Raghnall did betray her. Really betray her. But knowing Raghnall, there was the possibility that there was more to it than that, and she wanted to believe in that fact. That was what she would hold on to for now. She looked at the ring on her index finger. This ring held everything about who he was in the past. She knew there had to be something more, and she would find out in time, but now there were other matters to deal with.

Raghnall had dropped her into the centre of the Empire; this was not an opportunity she could let slip by. Sulwyn turned to Caldwell, who was taken aback by her sudden energy and change.

"I like this." He smirked, "Good, princess. For that, I will reward you with a break while I go report. You will need to participate in something *quite* spectacular momentarily. I'd say you need your energy for it. And then after that, it's you and me. At least until I need to leave for an assignment. Be good." He winked, walking away and signalling the men to leave.

"Don't you have princely duties to attend to?" said Caldwell, somewhere past her line of vision. There was no answer, but the door opened. After a few moments, Galahad stepped forward.

Sulwyn watched him carefully. Now that she had eaten, she could see clearer and think faster, though she struggled to put the pain behind her, and it was still cold as hell.

"I don't like it when people are standing over me when I'm sitting," said Sulwyn, crossing her legs and leaning against the wall. She winced when her back touched the hard stone but took deep breaths to pass the pain.

Galahad considered her for a moment before he too sat in front of the cell cross-legged.

"Are you the only one with the keys then?" she asked immediately.

"What makes you think that?"

"Caldwell can't come in here. Otherwise, he wouldn't need that kind of whip. Those guards from before couldn't either. But Caldwell seems much higher in rank than them."

"Only I, Pandora, Artaxiad, and one other have the key to the cell doors." He answered quietly and without eye contact. She tilted her head to the side, observing him. She was missing something with him.

"Well, your rank is obviously highest, oh prince. What is Caldwell then? He isn't a normal Néosan. Validus?"

"Higher. Validus Uferor."

She was surprised to hear this. Raghnall had only gained a small amount of knowledge in what the Uferor were. All she knew was that they were highly skilled in combat, amongst other things. If they had anywhere to be it meant trouble. "Oh? Impressive. As what then? I couldn't hear him before…an assassin?"

Galahad nodded; his brow furrowed.

"What does the Empire need an assassin for anyway? Don't you all go open fire and burn whatever is in your way? I didn't think they knew any-thing about being *discreet*."

"The Empire has many enemies."

"I wonder why," muttered Sulwyn sarcastically. "What are you then? Besides their beloved prince." She caught that one; he twitched almost irritably. How much could she irritate him to make him open the cell door and come after her?

He looked at her carefully, and she was mildly distracted by his mul-ticoloured eyes. "Caldwell leads Uferor En. I lead Uferor San, but I have leadership over all the Uferor groups."

"Ah, so you're a show-off then?"

Galahad stared at her. "Caldwell is impressive, and I'm a show-off?" That was the first time he showed some form of emotion.

"Don't you have princely duties to attend to?" she quoted Caldwell, watching him close his eyes for patience. Their brilliance was as shocking as ever when he opened them.

"You're rather frustrating. It's no wonder..." he stopped himself, but Sulwyn understood where he was going.

"What? That's why I've been betrayed, is it?"

He breathed out, "Look at you. You needn't go through this torture if you will just agree to trust me."

"Let me out, and I'll trust you."

"I can't do that."

"What difference does it make if I agree before or after? Isn't it all the same thing?" asked Sulwyn, standing.

"I'll know when I have your word. That is the difference."

Sulwyn just laughed. "Why in the moon's name do you think I would trust the son of the Empire?"

"I've warned you, Sulwyn..." his tone was low as he too stood. She watched him closely. That was his trigger. And she was going to smash through with it.

"Warned me about what? What could possibly be worse than where I am right now? Than being betrayed by someone I loved most? As the son of the Empire, I wouldn't expect you to understand."

"Sulwyn."

"Stop saying my name with such familiarity. You aren't worthy of it. None of you are." Even though she was trying to irritate him, anger was rising within her. Sulwyn took a deep breath and stepped closer to the bars. She had glimpsed a set of keys under his cloak when he stood.

"Stop assuming things."

"Why? Am I not at liberty to do even that? Last I checked the Empire didn't control thoughts yet. Are you going to have me whipped for that too?"

"I am not having you whipped." His voice grew louder. Sulwyn moved closer. She could tell he was far more skilled than anyone she had met before. But she would try.

"You aren't stopping it either. What use is being the prince when an assassin under you seems to have more leverage than you?" She stepped closer. "At that rate you should have just stayed with your clan instead of becoming their son."

"Do NOT speak of things you know nothing about!" He yelled, and it was déjà vu. She rushed forward, quicker this time because of her new energy. She grabbed the keys off his waist, pulling them towards her and through the bars. She moved far back against the wall, but he made no move to try and stop her. Did he just let her grab the keys? But she was distracted. His cloak had folded back behind him. Underneath he wore black pants as most did. But his tunic was green.

"Green is banned. They banned it since the fall of the High City," said Sulwyn slowly, watching him. She tightened her grip around the ring of keys.

"Yes, it is." His voice was low. Sulwyn's eyes widened. A hint of the fire she had seen in them all those years ago flitted within his gaze. But it was gone as quickly as it came and his eyes were as impassive as before.

"Then how…"

"I cannot answer these questions here. The walls listen in the majority of this castle."

They stared at each other, silence passing between them for seconds. Then minutes. Nothing was making sense to her. What was she missing? She looked down to the keys. She'd just have to get it out of him. She studied the lock before carefully choosing a medium-sized, heavy iron key. Sulwyn moved to the door cautiously, watching Galahad. But Galahad never moved, only stared.

She put her arm through the bars, finding the hole and pushing the key into the lock. With a turn and a loud click the iron gate swung forward, open.

IV

Falling Star, Rising Blood

| SULWYN |

S ULWYN quickly pushed the cell door open, Galahad stepping back. She reached for the hidden dagger in her boot, rushing at him with the intention of cutting or stabbing him anywhere. This, she achieved.

Though still dizzy, she managed to shallowly stab his right arm. But what held her in place was that he made no move to block or protect himself. He stared at her, a dagger in his arm, but hadn't moved an inch.

Why? She stepped back. She hadn't anticipated this. Suddenly he moved forward, holding both arms out wide before pulling her into an embrace. Her eyes widened.

"What are you doing?" said Sulwyn, her voice muffled by his cloak and shoulder. Warmth spread through her immediately. Why? Because she had been cold? Of course, that was why. So why was she so flustered?

"I need you to know that I will never willingly hurt you, please know this…" He continued to hold her cautiously, with space between them. But shock made way for reason, and she pushed him away, pulling the dagger out from his upper arm and pressing it against his neck.

She pushed him back against the wall, his hands up. She looked up at him, her dark grey eyes reflected in his multicoloured ones. Somehow, she had no fear or wariness, so why was her heart racing? Adrenaline. It must be that. A sharp pain pounded through her head and she faltered momentarily, the blade nipping his neck. But still, he made no move to stop her.

Slowly he lowered his arms, placing his hands on her shoulders. The warmth spread through her again. She took the dagger back, watching him.

"Is this a trick? A ploy? Have Caldwell come here and abuse me? And then you come here to comfort and try to gain my trust? Like some sort of saviour?"

"I'm not trying to trick you. Sulwyn, I don't have much time. I need you to promise to trust me, and then I can be in charge of you."

"In charge of me? And do what? Have your way with me then? Enslave me?"

"You confuse me for the king," he said dangerously.

"Am I? Oh, son of the Empire. What makes you think you are so different? Am I out of this cell? Out of this dungeon?"

"I did not put you here."

"Well, you sure as hell haven't gotten me out."

"Sulwyn…"

"Where is Raghnall?"

"I've told you, Pandora killed him."

"And? Did they burn him then? Where is his body?"

"Why?"

"None of your concern. Fine, I will find him myself." Sulwyn moved towards the assumed door, but Galahad held her arm, stopping her.

"You cannot wander around like this!" he hissed, eyes wide.

"Why? Would you be in trouble? Would daddy punish you?" Suddenly her face tingled. The sound of a slap resonated within the empty stone halls. She glared at him, raising her hand to her cheek, watching him flex his fingers.

"I have been patient with you. I ask you not to speak with assumptions again," he ground out.

"Assumptions? Your actions are my answer." She stepped forward again but froze. The door opened. Instantly she held her breath, the shadow of five people dancing on the walls.

Five? Why were there more? She turned to Galahad, but he had taken his assumed position against the wall, his eyes something she couldn't read. She focused on Caldwell.

"Why, princess! So eager for this afternoon's show?" He looked from Galahad to Sulwyn, sighing. "Why you're the prince I'll never know…You must feel at peace if you can just let her out like this," said Caldwell.

Sulwyn turned back to Galahad and paused, blinking profusely. Was she seeing things? Galahad looked at her. The edges of the whites of his eyes appeared darker, black even. But only slightly. Then he blinked and it was gone. Wondering what it was she had just seen in Galahad's eyes, she was caught off guard by a pinch in her neck and her thoughts instantly slowed. Caldwell had plunged a syringe into her neck.

A gaggle of noise reached her ears.

So many voices and sounds; they disoriented her. But she kept her eyes closed, her lids as heavy as her body. There was a slight itch on her arms and around her collarbones. Sulwyn tried and failed to move her limbs in response. The noises were coming louder now, a gentle warmth bearing down on her. She was no longer cold or wet. But the ache of the lashings throbbed through her. And as the pain resurfaced, so did the rest of her senses. As if she were being pulled from the earth, she broke free, the sounds turning into thousands of voices.

She opened her eyes, squinting against the harsh light of the sun. It was noon, and a slight warm breeze greeted her skin. Sulwyn looked in the distance towards a mass of people, trees, and stone hills surrounding them. She was sitting in an elaborate wooden chair to the left of a precipice above the crowd of people. But she couldn't move.

She looked down. Someone had changed her. She was dressed in a crimson lace dress that bunched around her feet. The long sleeves covered all the scars, cuts, and bruises on her skin. Her legs and hands were bound to the chair in red rope, hidden. From afar no one could tell she was tied. She went to yell, but her voice wouldn't sound.

So, she took a deep breath.

It would do her no good to fall into panic here. Sulwyn continued to take deep breaths. She was too far back for anyone below to see her. So why was she here? Sulwyn looked around again. She had heard of this place before. A mass stadium carved out of a low mountain, for all the important events that took place on the outskirts of the Empire; the Proelium Terra.

Placed in front of her and in the centre were two ornate, empty golden chairs, and behind her was a gaping hole in the rock. Something was missing. What were they presenting?

"Sulwyn…" A whisper from behind, to her side. But she did not startle. She had been expecting it and was slightly surprised by this fact. She knew he'd be here. This was going to be something huge, something devastating. Galahad crouched beside her, staying unseen from the masses below.

"I was drugged, I'm assuming" croaked Sulwyn. "I can barely move. It wasn't even necessary to bind me." She could barely whisper these words. But he heard her all the same.

"I had no say in the matter."

"For someone who is the prince, you don't really seem to be *involved* in a lot of things."

He laughed bitterly, "I have been telling you this."

"Can you be here then?" She coughed. Whatever they had done to her was more annoying than anything. She hated this lethargic, foggy feeling.

"No, not yet. I came to warn you."

Sulwyn turned her head slightly, looking down at him. His tricoloured eyes were serious, urgency etched in his face. "Do not lose to them. No matter what you hear, no matter what you see…" He turned suddenly, looking somewhere she couldn't see. "Promise me. For your benefit, remember what I just said."

Galahad dashed away and she turned to the front. He needn't have told her that. She could sense it. Icy despair ran through her despite the warmth of the sun. She closed her eyes, waiting, the lace of the dress scratching her, the pins tying up her hair pulling at her scalp. She hated this kind of formal wear.

A gong resonated somewhere behind her.

Her heart stilled.

The voices silenced instantly.

Another gong rent the air.

It vibrated and echoed along the skies and land around them.

Another and another.

On the tenth gong, Sulwyn heard footsteps on the far right of her. She turned slowly to look, waiting. The steps louder and louder while the crowd below maintained silence.

She waited, but her intake of breath never came. She could only stare at the people who emerged from the top of the stairs. The crowd below erupted in cheers, calling their names.

For the first time in her life, she saw her birth father, King Artaxiad, and her birth mother, Queen Pandora. Maybe she would register this shock later, but no matter how much she tried, she couldn't bring herself to feel anything other than hate. She didn't view them as parents but as she always did, the enemy.

They waved, greeting their people below with smiles and poise. It was hard to tell that Artaxiad and Pandora had ended thousands of lives with the way these people screamed their names. The Privileged that lived within the Empire were the only ones who would ever cheer for them like this. Sulwyn wanted to turn away, but she couldn't.

Pandora was beautiful, stunning even. But her light grey eyes were cold, void of any feeling. Her dark red hair was tied low between her shoulders, flowing down her back and flitting in the wind, joining the many folds of her dark purple dress. Sulwyn was slightly taller, her body not as voluptuous as Pandora's. But Pandora never looked at her. And she was glad for it. However, Artaxiad had already turned his gaze towards Sulwyn, his dull green eyes piercing through her.

Artaxiad was a fit man, tall, with broad shoulders and a broad body. He was strong, and one of the best in swordsmanship. Even Raghnall admitted that Artaxiad was a hard man to beat. But he could still probably beat him, which meant Sulwyn could too. And she held onto this fact.

She continued to stare at them. Many of her features came from Pandora, but Sulwyn's black hair, with that special violet sheen, and olive skin had come from Artaxiad. Without a doubt, she was related to them.

Where was the dungeon? She wished to be facing its cold dark walls instead.

Another gong sounded at Artaxiad's raised arm. The people fell silent once again. He led Pandora to her seat and continued to stand overlooking the crowd, a broad smile on his face.

"My people!" The crowd cheered, but only for a moment before they quieted once again. This was a different perspective from what she was used to. She had been surrounded by hate and fear for Artaxiad but here he was loved. He was worshiped and revered. It sickened her.

"I have come to address these rumors that have been flitting about," he raised his right hand wiggling his fingers at the word "flitting." She rolled her eyes; dramatic. "A couple of days ago, we were shocked." He paused for effect. "Yes shocked…our long-lost daughter has been returned to us."

Sulwyn stared at Artaxiad, wide-eyed. How many more surprises were they going to throw at her? She looked towards what of the crowd she could see. They all looked as if some sort of miracle had befallen them.

"Yes, yes. Finally, our daughter has come home. And I am here to answer your unspoken questions. Twenty-three years ago, our daughter was taken from us. Some nights before we finally took the head of that vile High City king, she was stolen, a mere newborn! The enemy snuck through our defences during this difficult time. And I am ashamed to say we were bested. But we had an obligation to you, our people, and with a heavy heart we made one of our greatest sacrifices." He hung his head, the people below choked with emotion.

"After we managed to gain back the peace…we searched for years, trying to find her, searching high and low. But it was impossible." The Privileged booed, as if something could ever thwart them. "Yes, if our enemy wanted to stay hidden, she was as good as gone. And so, we finally accepted that fate. It brought pain to us, and as you know, Pandora was left barren, but we had you to give our hearts to, to give us strength. And so, we said our goodbyes in the hopes that our child was in a better place." He showed his back to the crowd. "Galahad, please come forward." Artaxiad waved his arm to the side.

Sulwyn watched Galahad come forth from the stairs, his face impassive as ever. But he did as he was told. It seemed an accepted fact that he was the sole person in Vartugaul who could get away with wearing green since its ban.

He was completely unarmed, clothes modest for the occasion with a simple dark green tunic and black linen pants, unlike Artaxiad, who wore a heavily gold-embroidered indigo jacket with all the matching accessories.

"Galahad came to us, slightly filling the void in our hearts. I know that he has always seemed difficult to you. And we must forgive him, for he too lost his family. But since he joined us, he has carried himself well." Galahad kept his hands behind his back, expression never changing, but Sulwyn could see the tick in his jaw.

"However, in more recent years a rumor began to grow and travelled to us. Finally, we learned of our daughter who had been hidden and abused in captivity. And finally, we caught the one responsible. But first let me introduce you to her."

Sulwyn started forward, her chair pushed by Néosan from behind, until she was centre and in front. She could see the mass of people that filled the terrain below her. But her back stiffened instinctively. Her chair was now a few feet in front of Artaxiad and Pandora, the unnerving feeling of threat behind her. She turned slightly to look at Galahad. Making eye contact briefly, he warned her silently and discreetly before looking back to the crowd.

She held her breath, sensing Artaxiad move behind her. Slowly he placed both hands over her shoulders, squeezing the right side tightly.

"Our child...has returned to us!" he roared. Stunned, the crowd was silent, until they broke into wild cheer and applause.

Sulwyn breathed slowly, in and out.

Their child? What crap. The only thing she could ever thank them for was bringing her into this world, but her notion of them as parents ended there.

There was no reason to be afraid.

This wasn't her family.

Blood didn't tie her to them.

She was nothing like them.

But as she thought this her hands grew cold. They were showy; why the big reveal?

"And with that comes our other news. This day is joyous, yes? But now we have carved another moment in history. It has not been easy, maintaining this righteous peace that we have all achieved. I am sure you have heard of the few who are wild and brash, foolish enough to stand against us. But none more so than the Steel Warrior and Kintana." The crowd booed and jeered at these names. Sulwyn clenched the edges of the chair arms weakly. Artaxiad's grip was still firm on her shoulder, but she refused to look up.

"These unworthy, uneducated people have been eradicated. Unfortunately, Kintana's corpse did not survive her punishment. But we have our main prize and trophy." One of Artaxiad's hands moved away from Sulwyn, letting her look back.

Rising slowly by ropes in the centre of the hole behind the golden chairs was a long, thick wooden pole covered by a black cloth. Slowly it rose, higher and higher, so that everyone below would be able to see it.

Pandora finally stood, looking at the people, before looking at Sulwyn. And Sulwyn never looked away despite the glare within Pandora's eyes. Against her will she felt a slight sting behind her eyes, emotions she couldn't comprehend rising in her. But she would not show it, and least of all to this woman. Sulwyn blinked, pushing down her thoughts, and watched Pandora turn, stepping behind the chairs to another rope, finally speaking.

"A thorn at our side has finally been removed, *personally*." She smiled, speaking clearly, pulling on the rope.

Time had slowed before her eyes, the black cloth falling away. Dropping and twisting in the light, warm breeze until it rippled to the ground.

But Sulwyn could feel none of that warmth.

Instead, she was plunged into suffocating ice, all energy within leaving her, her eyes on Raghnall's bruised and battered face, barely recognizable. His clothes were covered in blood, a large puddle of it at the centre of his chest. He hung there limply, tied to the pole. Hushed whispers rode the breeze, but even that was still to her. Her heart beat hard against her ribs, hurting her, the cold going deeper still as she stared at his swollen face. Her tears threatened to fall, but she would not show that to them. She blinked, continuing her deep breaths.

"Dead. By your queen's hand!" roared Artaxiad again, the crowd finally cheering in victory. "But that is not all. As luck would have it, this great warrior came to *us!* After keeping our child hostage, he had the gall to come and make a deal for coins. How dirty…how filthy…he even sold out his partner, Kintana. The revered Steel Warrior was nothing more than a sell-out, falling to the vices he claimed beneath him." Artaxiad's smile twisted, reveling in this thought. "But it matters not. Because he is dead. Kintana is dead. And our daughter is back with us."

Artaxiad smiled broadly, the crowd cheering louder still. Sulwyn couldn't take her eyes off Raghnall. A tangled mix of emotions ran through her, but one made itself very clear.

"Now, I do ask all of you to please treat my daughter kindly. Be patient and teach her our ways. She has been tortured and brainwashed and abused. But one day she will stand alongside and rule with us. And I hope that that day is soon. So, I extend my hand to you all to join us for a festival to coronate her as princess one week from today. And I ask that you please extend your cheers to Princess Sulwyn!"

The cheers erupted behind her, loudly and almost deafening. But she still wouldn't look away. Until Artaxiad stepped directly in front of her, blocking Raghnall's body from view. "Greet your people, Sulwyn," he whispered dangerously.

Sulwyn did not fear him. She looked directly at him, smirking even as her insides felt hollowed and scraped. "I will gladly do so, *father.*"

Sulwyn caught Galahad's eye, a slight smile playing along his lips at her words. She turned, facing the people before her. Thousands of the Privileged looked up at her, unable to see the torture the king and queen had caused, and unable to care. She loathed them all. But she understood it now. She saw the game they were playing and neither side had rules. Sulwyn looked back at Pandora, her gaze firm against Pandora's glare.

Facing the crowd again, she leaned back. If she weren't bound, she would have crossed a leg over her knee, but settled for smiling at the people below.

V

Grey Eyes In Chains
| SULWYN |

SULWYN shivered, waking from her sleep, a cool draft flitting by her. How she missed the warm fires of her camps. Of the outside sun.

She was back in the dungeon.

Her skin heavy.

They had drugged her again once the crowd cleared out, but she felt like the effects were wearing off faster. She mentally nodded to herself. That was the safest decision they could have made. She would have made a public scene otherwise.

Her skin itched with every movement. They had left her in the lace dress, something worse than the drug. She hated lace or constricting clothes in general. But she sighed, turning her head slowly to look sideways out the cell. Not surprisingly, Galahad was sitting just outside it, leaning against the wall, a leg raised to his chest. He looked relieved that she had awakened. It must have been some time since that announcement.

Every time she blinked, she could see Raghnall's body tied to the pole. Bile rose, burning her throat. She couldn't be sure since she saw him from a distance, but she wouldn't put it past them to have beaten his body after death. It looked fairly abused and rather odd now that she thought about it.

"What are they going to do to his body?" Her voice was hoarse. She would have to find his body and lay it to rest before they could do any more damage.

"Leave it there for the next three days for people to view their achievement. After that, they usually either return it to the lower dungeons or burn it. I'm not sure what they will do with his."

"They return it to the lower dungeons?" she said disgusted. "Aren't there…living people down there?"

"There are," he said tonelessly.

Sulwyn looked at him trying to read him, "So they saved you?" she asked quietly. She didn't know why she was asking. She was starting to see the real answer, but she needed to hear it. To see him. But he didn't answer. Instead, he watched her, his gaze concentrated. She found herself staring at his eyes. Despite their brilliance of colour, they were void. Empty of much else besides what? There was something there. But she couldn't read it even as it nagged at her.

"Sulwyn…I want to answer your questions. But I can't unless—"

"Unless I say I trust you? But why? Why do you need me to trust you? Aren't I a threat?"

He continued to look at her, and this time she registered something else in his eyes. Pleading? Was he *pleading* with her?

"To help you. With everything you are doing." He got up from the ground, dusting his pants off. She followed him with her eyes, her head tilting up. She felt a faint stab to her head and slowly lifted a hand to her hair, pulling out a hairpin. She looked at it for a moment, then to the lock in the cell door.

"Those pins won't work," said Galahad, smirking, to her annoyance. But his face became impassive once more. The door in the distance opened and closed with a smell and a thud.

"Ah, prin*cess*," jeered Caldwell, looking at Galahad, "and the Blood Princess is awake! Perfect!" He addressed her form on the ground. Sulwyn noted the whip in his hand and sighed. The drugs were starting to wear off and the pain from before was starting to come back.

"Did you request to keep me in this dress while you torture me?"

"Maybe." He winked. "And I would never torture you; I am reforming you. But you needn't be punished if you answer my questions properly.

Now, I will be going away tomorrow for an assignment, so why don't we try and limit the hits, hmm? Less pain for both of us." He smiled brightly, running his bandaged hands over the whip. His eyes were as icy as ever but this time Sulwyn could read them. There was regret.

"Where are you going, then?" asked Sulwyn conversationally. She couldn't get up, so she stayed exactly as she was, on her back.

"We have important matters to attend to in the north. Isn't that right?" He looked at Galahad, who resumed leaning against the shadowed walls.

Sulwyn suddenly looked up at him, her eyes wide. "As the Uferor? Are you going on a mission as the Validus Uferor?"

Caldwell stared at her a little nonplused. "Yes...it is kind of in our job descriptions and all."

"Let me come with you." Sulwyn forced herself up. Her arms shook with the effort, but she managed to sit up, slumping.

"What?" said Galahad, Caldwell staring between both.

"You said I am to learn the proper ways of the Empire. What better way than to experience how it is you all *correct* us. You can keep me chained. I don't mind."

"Excellent...what an excellent idea!" said Caldwell excitedly. "But I don't have the authority to say yes." He turned to Galahad, who was now standing next to him. Sulwyn looked at Galahad in silence. She watched him look at her before looking down and then to Caldwell.

"I will propose it to our king. But if he is to say yes, she will be useless to us beaten." Galahad held out his hand, gesturing at Caldwell. Caldwell looked like he wanted to say something more but decided against it, handing Galahad the whip.

"I will return once I've gotten the answer," said Galahad, glancing at Sulwyn before walking past Caldwell and the two Néosan. He paused somewhere near the door. "You are dismissed for now." The door opened and closed. Sulwyn held her breath but noticed that Caldwell did as well.

"Well, let's wait and see if you can accompany us. I promise it will be enlightening for you. I think this is a great idea." He smirked, but it didn't reach his eyes. Caldwell and the Néosan left. The door closed and silence was upon her once again. Sulwyn flopped back down onto the ground. Her body hurt more, the lace burning at her open wounds. Was this the right idea? She couldn't think of anything else to get her out of the cell. She needed to know what was happening outside of the Empire.

Artaxiad had announced Raghnall's death to the masses. Word would spread in time and fear would bury its way deeper. But they had also said Kintana was dead, and no one would dare question them, even if they didn't have a body. Sulwyn had to assume that they knew she was Kintana. They had to know. If they knew how to contact Raghnall, they would have seen her with him. It wouldn't do to reveal her being the princess. It would give false hope and cause an uprising. So they killed Kintana instead. It was a smart move on their part.

Sulwyn closed her eyes, her head overflowing with thoughts and confusion, and amongst it all was Raghnall's pale and bleeding face. She felt hot tears well up beneath her eyes before they flowed against her cheeks.

What nonsense was this really?

৵৽

Her hands passed over a warm comfortable softness that seeped into her. Over her, a gentle softness covered her body.

She must have died. She had to have.

Why else would she be in a real bed?

Sulwyn sat up suddenly, a white sheet falling off her torso.

She looked around her quickly, heart racing. She was in a small, plain, square room with light blue walls, illuminated by tiny torches in sconces. A little chair by the door to her right, and another door in the far left of the room, slightly ajar with another torch shining through. The bed was small and simple, made of dark wood and basic white linen. The bedding was stuffed with feathers and wool. It was nice. She hadn't slept in such a good quality bed in almost two years.

Slowly she swung her legs over, touching the floor. Lush midnight carpet greeted her feet.

"Am I still in this dress?" she exclaimed, tossing the rest of the sheet and standing. The room had no windows, and the door was locked with no doorknob. She huffed.

"We could just kick it down?" said Sulwyn, turning to look behind her. Only a flickering torch met her gaze. She really needed to remember she was alone. She stood in front of the door for a moment, touching it gently and pressing her ear to it.

Silence met her ears.

Whether it was because there was no one there or because they were just really quiet, she would never know. She left the door for now, walking over to the other door and sighing in relief; it was a real bathing room, and being in the Empire meant they had functioning toilets.

On the small toilet were her original red tunic and black pants and underclothes, laundered and dried. Sulwyn walked towards the tub, dipping her hand in the water. It was rather warm; someone had just drawn it. A little unsettled by this fact, she threw caution to the wind and rid herself of the red dress, immediately scratching every part of her. Then she kicked it to a corner. It was a lovely dress, but much too irritating.

She presumed she was still in the Empire, but if they had upgraded her room status, it must mean she was granted permission to go with them. Sulwyn closed the door to the bathing room, allowing herself this moment of peace.

๛

Sulwyn positioned the small wooden chair in front of the door, sitting, waiting, and staring. She had replaced the dress with her own clothes, but her boots, weapon belt, knives, and pouches were missing. She tapped her foot silently. Waiting and waiting. Her pain had eased after her bath, but she had nothing to treat her open wounds with. She hoped her red tunic would hide any blood but wouldn't hold out for it. She waited longer still.

Sulwyn had started to lose patience when finally, she could hear footsteps approaching. For a moment she considered using the chair as a weapon, but her fatigue decided against it; it would use up too much effort on her part.

Iron scraped iron before the door was pulled open. More light filtered in, casting the front of the person in shadows, but she knew it would be Galahad. He seemed to be the only one with keys in this place. The door closed behind him; the sound of iron scraping iron reached her again.

Just as she noticed the tray of food in his arms, the smell of food filled the room, and her stomach rumbled loudly in response. Heat crawled up her neck at his laugh.

"There's no table in this room," mumbled Galahad, looking around.

Sulwyn got off the wooden chair and sat on the floor in front of it.

"Table." She pointed to it. He smiled again. They were always small, fleeting smiles, but each time they weakened her heart a bit. She turned away from him and instead focused on the food. Last time she ate, her food had gone cold and lost taste. This time it was fresh and warm and light.

A bowl of onion soup accompanied by a small plate of mashed potatoes graced the tray, along with a small jug of water. It was more than enough for her. She reached to pick up the spoon when she stopped, turning to Galahad.

"I don't like people standing over me."

"Ahh, yes…" He looked mildly confused as to where to place himself. Sulwyn gestured to the bed. He hesitated for a moment but took a seat at the edge. Her back was to him, but she didn't feel threatened. Not that she was surprised by this fact. She had given him a lot of thought.

"When do we leave?" asked Sulwyn, bending forward to sniff at the soup and potatoes. Considering all her knowledge of poisons and drugs, it was hard to tell if her food had been laced or not. But she figured she'd try anyway. In the end, she started to eat.

"Soon. In a few hours' time."

"What is this trip for?"

"We don't know yet. There have been reports of disturbances."

"Disturbances…by the Néosan no doubt."

"There are other evils besides them," said Galahad quietly. She stayed silent, eating her soup. The taste was light but flavourful. In her haste, she burnt her tongue. Silence spread between them and with every passing moment, she felt it press on her.

What else could happen if she gave him her word? He said he wanted to help. And it was obvious there was more to him than she could ever guess. She was already in the Empire anyway. This was an opportune chance. And she had never forgotten his eyes from all those years ago either.

"Sulwyn…" He spoke softly just as she finished drinking water. She had anticipated it, let it happen, tasted it in the water. But that didn't stop her from panicking. The room started to spin around her. She watched him kneel in front of her closely, touching her shoulders gently. He spoke with urgency again, looking into her eyes. "Just trust me."

⤞⤝

She was starting to get a little tired of waking up in random places, but given her record, she really did understand the need to be drugged each time. She kept her eyes closed but knew she was outside, sensing the late afternoon sun. She moved her fingers over the wooden grooves beneath her. The sound of wheels crunching over rock and gravel and the clop of horses reached her ears. They were en route.

"Was it your choice to drug me this time?" Sulwyn asked to her surroundings. She didn't even need to look anymore, she was starting to learn how to sense his presence.

"No, that's not something I would opt for…I'm sorry," said Galahad, but she could hear the smile in his tone.

"Why are you smiling as you apologize?"

"Don't sit up so suddenly—"

But it was too late.

Sulwyn smacked her head against a metal bar of some kind. Falling back, she opened her eyes to see a small collection of spears overhead and tiny stars in her eyes.

Before she could register the pain, laughter reached instead. She turned on the floor to look up at Galahad. He sat across from her, head in between the laid-out spears and crates, smiling. He looked as if he hadn't laughed in ages.

"Your forehead is red..." he coughed, sliding forward. He reached his hand over her forehead, but she moved her head to the side. Tentatively, he tried again, looking at her carefully. His fingers were cool against her skin. The slight throb in her head began to dull almost instantly. He was healing her. She looked slowly at her hands and noted that the cuts seemed days old. Even the pain from the whipping and bruises had dulled. Had he healed those too? But this wasn't Devinal magic. And healing magic always cost the user. She narrowed her eyes.

"Your head is still a little red..." he said softly. Galahad removed his hand away from her skin, leaving it hotter than before. The carriage stopped suddenly, sliding her towards his feet, his back sliding to hit the walls of wood, instantly guarded. Sulwyn looked around, spotting the door. It was then she realized her wrists and ankles were chained.

Quickly she sat up, avoiding the spears, shifting towards the door. Galahad watched her in silence as she bent her legs up, one resting on the side of the carriage door, the other hovering in front of it. Hearing the latch open, she immediately kicked forward earning a surprised yell and a grunt of pain. She smiled slightly at Galahad's stifled laugh.

"Princess, please refrain from causing injury to the other men. We only have three others with us," said Caldwell, stepping forward to help the fallen Néosan.

"Isn't the Uferor the top of the top?" said Sulwyn, swinging her legs over the edge of the carriage. The chains jangled, putting weight on her ankles. She hated these things.

"You should still be asleep."

"I think you've already noticed that drugs don't last long on me," she smiled mischievously.

"I have actually—you are one of the few that grow immune, aren't you? And that's why you're chained." He smiled back. "We're taking a short break." He stepped back, gesturing for her to come out.

The other men stood stiffly around her. She looked around the familiar terrain of grass, sand, and wilderness. They were currently on a travelling road, the gravel and rocks hard from use. Sulwyn inhaled a deep breath of fresh air and hopped down from the carriage, her hair flowing around her. She tried to move it back, but her hands were bound too tightly. Quickly giving up, she shuffled away from the carriage and straight towards the copse of trees to her left. The other men moved to follow her, but Caldwell held his hand up, following her instead. Galahad remained in the carriage, watching.

She was thankful to have her boots again, but she wished she had the rest of her belongings. Within a few seconds, she found what she had heard. A small stream passed through the trees, continuing on for as far as she could see. Sulwyn stooped down, scooping water into her hands and drinking it.

"You shouldn't drink water straight from the river like that," said Caldwell behind her.

"I know which water is safe and which is not. Besides, the water you all keep giving me is drugged."

"We don't have to drug you anymore, so you shouldn't worry about that." He handed her an empty canteen.

"Thanks." She opened it, sniffing the inside. She dipped it into the stream, letting the cold water flow past her hands and fill the canteen.

"Are you excited?" asked Caldwell stooping to fill his as well.

"Anywhere is better than in a dungeon, no?" She turned to look at him and stared. It was there again, the regret in his eyes.

"That imprisonment was for your benefit, princess."

"Do you really believe that?"

"The Empire is a good place. We can't have you upsetting that." He smiled at her.

"I've been told you're the assassin, for lack of a better word. What do you do during these assignments?" She closed the canteen, sitting back onto the ground.

"That's a pretty word. I don't only assassinate. I kill openly too. Don't look at me like that, you kill as well."

"How did you come to the Empire?" She looked at him intently, watching his expression turn reminiscent.

"The Validus collected me. The Uferor didn't exist then. I was sold for food by the elders. And I went willingly. Everyone there was garbage. Fighting over everything, betraying everyone. It was shit, Sulwyn, the Empire saved me. I found purpose there."

"By killing other people?"

"I said it, didn't I? You kill people too. What difference does it make?"

"It makes a difference. I killed to protect people. What the Empire does is wrong. Everything about this is wrong." Her voice was a little higher now. She needed to pull this back. The whole point of her getting out was to learn the "ways" of the Empire. But Caldwell just chuckled.

"Different views, but at the end of the day killing is killing. I kill when I'm told to. I kill in defence like you did with that Néosan. I kill for sport and for revenge…and I like it. I won't deny that. I can't help it at this point."

Sulwyn stared at him, mouth agape. Everything he said didn't match what she saw in his eyes and expression. There was pain there, but he was smiling.

"Killing for fun is wrong."

"What is really different about your killings?" he asked, watching her stand.

"I regret every single one of them," said Sulwyn roughly as he too stood. He looked down at his bandaged arms and hands before he looked back at her.

"We aren't that different then." He smiled wider still and stepped closer to her. Sulwyn looked up. She had never seen someone whose eyes were so conflicted. They darted back and forth between her own as he came closer. Unintentionally she stepped back until she looked past him.

"We've been here for too long, Caldwell," said Galahad suddenly. Caldwell flinched, looking as though he still wanted to say more, but turned to face Galahad.

"Lead the way, princess," said Caldwell, smirking at Galahad without giving Sulwyn a second glance. But Sulwyn only looked at Galahad. She hadn't sensed him. Not at all. And given Caldwell's reaction, he hadn't sensed him either, which was even more surprising given his expertise.

"You should be careful around him." Galahad's voice was low and barely audible.

"You aren't an exception," said Sulwyn walking past him. He followed her quietly as she led the way out of the trees. When she stepped out from the shade and back in front of the carriage, she marched directly next to one of the horses.

"Let me ride. I promise I won't escape!" said Sulwyn innocently.

Galahad looked at her, then Caldwell. The other three men shuffled uneasily. She looked at them, who really knew she was Kintana? What did the rest even know about her?

"Tie those two horses together," said Galahad, pointing to the horse in front of her and the one off to one side. Caldwell glanced at Galahad but remained silent. He and another did as they were told. Galahad came to Sulwyn, bending down and unlocking the chains on her ankles.

"I feel like you could ride with them on but figured this would be easier?" He considered her for a moment, standing and wrapping the chains together.

Sulwyn smirked, "Not something I haven't done before, but it's maddening." She walked over to the horse and put her foot in the stirrup, hoisting herself up and sitting in the saddle. Ready and waiting.

Galahad tossed the chains in the carriage before mounting the horse tied to hers. Two of the other men had their own horses, while Caldwell and the other man sat in front of the carriage. Caldwell took off just as Galahad nudged her horse before his.

He kept their horses in line with each other in front, Caldwell and the others behind them. But Sulwyn was simply happy to be doing something other than being trapped within walls. She was on a horse again, the wind blowing past, ruffling her hair behind her. Even though she was chained, she felt free and clear. She looked up to the bright yellow and green sky. It seemed like a good day today.

As they rode, Caldwell called out to Galahad, "So what happened to Daijiro? Why did he send a replacement?"

Sulwyn looked between them. "He's leading Uferor Divi on another assignment," said Galahad a little stiffly.

"I guess it's about time they let him lead alone," said Caldwell shrugging, "but having all three of us on one assignment is overkill any-way." He smirked brightly, turning to Sulwyn. "Just relax, princess, and make sure to keep what you see in mind." He winked, urging the horses faster.

❧

It was nightfall the next day by the time they reached the outskirts of town, slowing to a light trot. Sulwyn stayed vigilant. It was strange for her to go anywhere with her face exposed. Not many people knew her as Sulwyn, and most definitely not this place. She hadn't been here with Raghnall be-fore; it was located too close to the Empire.

As they got closer, she saw the mandatory low brick walls that framed the town's allowed perimeter. It was located on the very north edge of Antiqua near the coast. She looked to her left, the snowy mountains of Mortui Gemma far in the distance. Sulwyn noticed Galahad glance there as well; an odd expression crossing his face before he looked forward again, the emotions gone. Sulwyn, too, looked back.

She noticed an old, wooden pole stuck in the ground which carried the flag that marked the town's symbol. Two triangles on their sides, the centre points meeting in the middle. To her knowledge, this place was Antac, the town responsible for shaping Neuore. It was no wonder they sent the Ufer-or. Neuore was one of the prime sources of heat and weaponry, gathered elsewhere in one of the four slave towns and forged into what was neces-sary here. This was an important town. They wouldn't harm the people here, or at least she didn't think so.

Reaching the edges of the walls, they waited by the massive wooden en-trance for cargo and large groups. Galahad jumped off his horse, walking in quick strides, his black cloak flitting around his legs. They watched as he knocked twice on a man-sized door before someone quickly opened it. Within a few moments, the large wooden doors swung forward for entry. Galahad returned, leading his and Sulwyn's horses forward.

Sulwyn was right about the importance of the town. This one was lively with many people living in it. Even though the sun had set, men and women could still be seen working or shopping. The babble of people, the tinkle of storefronts, and even light music from unknown sources played. The small brick and wooden shops were in good condition. The people were clean, with well-cared-for clothes. Even the cobblestone on the streets and sidewalks was clean. Sulwyn noted the lack of Néosan patrolling. There must be a break in the rotation.

"You've noticed?" asked Galahad quietly as she looked down at him. "This town shouldn't have any Néosan watching it for the next few weeks. But the disturbances don't seem to be from them or the civilians."

Sulwyn looked around her. It was true. Compared to the other towns and villages, this one was rather well-behaved. Her horse stopped alongside Galahad's. Caldwell, too, had stopped, getting off the carriage front.

"Now that we've let them know we are here, go back and set up camp outside the town. We will gather information then come back before sunrise," said Caldwell, the other men saluting him.

"What a pointless show of authority...they still seem like regular Néosan to me," said Sulwyn, gesturing to their retreating backs. Caldwell beckoned her down.

"One of them is, the one sent to fill in for Daijiro. The other two are Validus. You can tell them apart based on the uniform," started Galahad, taking the horse's reins and giving them to the innkeeper to tie. "Usually, it's heads of each Validus team and one of the Leaders that make a group of five for the Uferor. There are five groups of five. Caldwell, Daijiro, and I are Leaders alongside two others, Eurus and Tarak. However, the fact that they originally wanted three Leaders this time is a little odd." said Galahad, looking around.

The three of them stood off to the side. Sulwyn noted the civilians were starting to realize who they were, making a wide berth of space between them.

"We're already attracting a lot of attention despite coming so late," said Caldwell, crossing his arms, "probably because we have a woman with us." He smiled broadly.

"There are tons of women in your Empire," retorted Sulwyn hotly.

"But there are no women in any of the Validus Uferor...no one has applied," said Galahad, looking at the people and buildings. "What?" He turned to face Caldwell's stare.

"It's been a while since we've both been on the same assignment. Why is it that you are acting like the only Leader? You could go back with the other men," he demanded.

Galahad stared at him. "I wouldn't entrust the Lady Princess to you, and technically I lead all groups."

"Barely, and I'm an excellent teacher for the princess."

Galahad scowled. "We go to the bar first. Word will already have spread about our arrival."

He turned to walk forward, but Sulwyn grabbed his arm. "Wait, you can't leave me chained like this."

Caldwell looked at her a little skeptically, but she continued, "Look, I don't have any weapons on me. I won't get in the way. But I think part of the reason they're staring is because I'm chained. Artaxiad and Pandora took the time to bind me in red rope to match the dress at the reveal. I don't know about you, but if these people find out I'm the recently announced princess, don't you think it looks bad if I'm chained like this?" She held up her shackled wrists for Galahad. He considered her. "And even if they don't know who I am, a woman in chains will still bring tons of attention to us. Not to mention the sound." She jangled them dramatically.

Caldwell sighed impatiently, "Just unchain her. It's not like she can get away now. And she's right; it'll bring back bad rumours regardless. You know what Pandora is like. Besides, this is taking too long."

Sulwyn looked at him. Caldwell seemed a little uncomfortable, antsy even. She noticed Galahad looking at him a little apprehensively as well.

"Fine, but don't go anywhere we can't see you," Galahad took the keys, unlocked the chains from her wrist, and handed them to the innkeeper. Sulwyn rubbed her wrists gratefully.

Without waiting, Caldwell led the way to the centre of town, but Sulwyn pulled Galahad back as they walked.

"What's wrong with him?" she whispered, hoping he couldn't hear. He had been increasingly agitated the closer they got to the town.

"We used to go on assignments together before I was promoted to a Leader. But every time we were about to arrive, he'd get like this. He's been to more of these than I ever have."

"How many?"

"I think this makes around seventy?"

"Seventy-three, Galahad. If you're going to talk shit about me, at least get your information right." He looked back at them, pointing to a two-story brick building near them. Most sound and chatter emitted from here. But Caldwell seemed unaffected by their gossip and continued onwards. And soon they entered the bar.

It was a small, wooden cavern with low beams and thick posts, the air a little thick with soft smoke and the scent of cooked food. Workers could be seen leading guests up the stairs or bringing things back down. She assumed this was also an inn. The dark wood tables were old and used, but cleaned and regularly attended to. Despite everything, it seemed like a well-used and cozy place.

Instantly the sound, music, and chatter stopped; every single person turned to look at them. Sulwyn had seen this reaction before, but to have the eyes of hate and fear directed towards her was new. A few glasses clinked, and a chair scraped, the silence stretching.

A gangly older man with long brown hair and crinkled dark skin rapped the wooden counter of the bar, gaining their attention. Galahad approached him, and slowly the sounds, chatter, and music warily began to pick up again.

"We've received a complaint from someone in this town about the Néosan making a ruckus," said Galahad quietly to the barman.

"Is that news to you men?" called someone behind them. A round, robust sort of man looked at them skeptically. He looked dirty and tired; a Neuore handler. Sulwyn assumed most of the people here were getting a drink or some food to end the day of work. The chatter died down again, everyone on edge. Some of the men at his table looked away nervously.

"It is when they aren't scheduled to be here," said Galahad, slowly turning his attention to the man.

Sulwyn wasn't sure exactly what she was feeling. But whatever it was, this guy and everyone else felt it too. Galahad exerted a sort of authoritative pressure. It kept most of them quiet, but this man didn't want to back down despite the slight tremor she heard in his voice.

"Scheduled? Do you people even *have* rules? Besides the ones oppressing us, of course." His voice grew stronger with every word, and with it the confidence of everyone else in the room.

"We don't want to be recruited if that's why you're here!" yelled someone unseen to them. Others mumbled in agreement.

"If it didn't matter to them, we wouldn't be here on a report. And we are not here to bring anyone unnecessarily to the Empire," said Galahad stoically. He turned back to the barman. But the man wasn't done yet and stood up. Everyone froze, watching. The waiters and waitresses paused in their duties. Others held their breath, but it was Caldwell that spoke.

"What a useless town. If it weren't for the Neuore, you'd have lost all privileges." His body tensed, waiting for a fight.

"Bernt, be careful..." whispered one of the men at his table.

"Useless? You come in here, in our town, and call us useless? When we supply your shitty Empire with our hard work?"

"You all belong to the Empire! We all belong to the Empire," said Caldwell strongly, pounding his chest and stepping forward.

Sulwyn had planned to keep a low profile, but she rushed forward, putting herself between Caldwell and Bernt, holding out both arms just inches from their chests. Caldwell rubbed his thumb on the blunt edge of the axe he carried in his belt, and Bernt was reaching for a dagger.

"Caldwell..." warned Galahad, reaching for a small drawstring pouch in his pocket. Sulwyn could hear the coins rattle within. Bernt looked down at Sulwyn.

"We ain't ever heard of a woman with the Uferor." Sulwyn looked up at him. She put as much warning into her glare as she could, making him falter and step back.

"Sulwyn, please step back," said Galahad, and she immediately did as she was told, walking back to the bar. Caldwell did the same, coming back down to himself for just a moment.

"Sulwyn?" mumbled others, confused.

Sulwyn heard them whisper Caldwell's and Galahad's names as well. They seemed rather well known. She never did pay attention to titles or the uniforms (or lack thereof where Galahad and Caldwell were concerned) when they were travelling. All Néosan seemed the same to her. How wrong she was.

"What's your name?" asked Galahad, turning back to the barman.

"Azhar..."

"Tell me what you know, Azhar," said Galahad. Puzzled, the barman waved to the rest of the crowd to carry on their business. Caldwell continued to stay near, pacing in front of the counter.

"As you know, Antac has a three-month rotation break right now," said Azhar, his voice a little gravelly. He eyed Caldwell as he walked. "About a week after the Néosan group moved on, other set came and took up living space in a few of our homes by the coast. This was suspicious as the Néosan have lodgings elsewhere in town. No one knows what happened to the original tenants of these two houses. But they've been wreaking havoc ever since. I don't know who reported it, but they've been here for about a month. No one wants to fight them. Antac is important, so why is the Empire terrorizing us?" he spat out at the end, then trembled for fear of speaking too much.

Galahad only nodded, placing the pouch of coins on the counter. "You're the representative of this town, I presume? For your help." He slid the pouch directly in front of him. "It's up to you if you want to keep it for yourself or use it on the town."

"Uferor have never come to our town before. You're not too bad for an Empire man," said Azhar, eying the pouch. He stopped looking at Caldwell and looked at Sulwyn instead.

"We will take our leave. Which way to these houses?" asked Galahad, stepping back from the bar and towards the entrance.

Azhar pointed straight. "Continue all the way down, opposite where you came."

Galahad gave Azhar a curt nod before shoving Caldwell out of the bar. Sulwyn turned to follow as well but stopped when Bernt addressed her.

"What is a woman like you doing in the ranks of the Uferor?"

"Biding my time. I suggest you all keep your heads down," she replied, lowering her voice slightly. They didn't seem to know anything about her.

"Is that a threat?" asked Bernt apprehensively.

"A kind warning."

"Are you sure you don't want to leave them and stay here?" asked Azhar. "It would be more peaceful. We could hide you. Wouldn't be the first time."

Sulwyn smiled at the thought. "I would bring nothing but destruction upon your town. And the Empire needs you too much." She bowed in farewell before taking off out the door.

⤍⋄⤎

|AZHAR|

Azhar chuckled quietly, and Bernt stepped up to him, eyes lingering where Sulwyn had just been.

"You seem oddly calm, Azhar."

"Have you ever been rescued before?"

Bernt shook his head in confusion.

"When there is nothing else left, and a star comes before you, you would remember what it looked like, right?" Azhar picked up a dirty glass, wiping it down before dunking it in the sink full of water.

"I guess, it would be important."

Azhar chuckled again, "I'd never forget those grey eyes," he mumbled to himself.

VI

History Of A Name
| SULWYN |

"CALDWELL, do not act on your own!" hissed Galahad, following him. Caldwell immediately took off in the direction they had been told. Sulwyn ran after them.

In the time they had spent in the bar, the town had started to go to sleep. Sparse amounts of people were in the streets now despite not having a curfew like the Empire. As they walked along the stone road, stores became fewer, and small houses lined their path. They walked for a long while until a strong breeze reached them.

The air smelt and tasted like salt and stone as they neared the coast and the two houses in question. A large, lone, cloaked man went along, lighting the night torches that lined the path. Galahad glanced at him hobbling past, unaware of or uncaring who they were. Caldwell remained in front, a few paces ahead. Sounds of men and women chatting and screaming in delight reached their ears.

"Caldwell!" said Galahad louder. "Don't get carried away!"

"Galahad," said Sulwyn, gaining his attention. He seemed tense. "Let me go and check out one of the houses. I won't do anything I can't help. I swear."

Galahad's forehead was creased in worry, conflicted, "Sulwyn, if you make a mistake here—"

She grabbed his wrist, stopping him in his tracks. The multicoloured stars and fire lights reflected in his eyes, almost stunning her. "I will trust you. Not fully, but I will trust you, so trust me," she breathed out.

She meant it.

The entire time she had been thinking about it, her mind making way for her heart. She knew it when she first realized who he was.

Galahad's eyes were wide. He paused for just a moment, until he turned to the sound of Caldwell knocking both his axes together. Galahad pulled one of his short blades from his waist belt and handed it to her. Then he took off after Caldwell, heading for the house on the right.

Sulwyn crouched low, taking off towards the house on her left. Both houses were small and modest, with two floors built of wood and steel. Each had light flickering within the windows on the ground floor. Quickly she scanned her assigned house, spotting a slanted cellar door in the ground. She tore off towards it, looking back only once to see that Galahad and Caldwell had already disappeared.

She knelt in front of the wooden cellar doors and pulled. After some struggle, the wood cracked, and she pulled it open. Sulwyn stepped down the stairs and was immediately hit by waves of foreboding. A putrid smell reached her nose, similar but much weaker than the stench in the dungeon. Halting her descent, she reached for her canteen. Opening it, she poured some water into the cap, drinking the rest within.

"If only you'd let me learn more magic, Raghnall, not that I'm good for it…" whispered Sulwyn. A stab of pain fleeted in her chest at the thought. She was not born a Devinal, and thus had little right to wield magic. But Wilkson and Raghnall had shown her some minor but useful spells. While Wilkson spoke the Devinal tongue, she needed to use special words, phrases, and even poems. Anything that could be used to anchor the magic to words, since she couldn't anchor it to her body. Taking a deep breath, she recited, "Fluid and strong with might, turn this water into light."

The glow was faint, but the water illuminated in the metal cap. Enough for her eyes to adjust to her surroundings and continue her descent, the cap safe in her hands. Soon she hit even ground and stepped off the steps to walk forward. She could hear people above her now. Slowly, she continued until she stumbled, her foot caught on something that almost caused her to drop the cap of glowing water.

Five bodies lay on the ground before her, thrown unceremoniously. Resentment growing in her, Sulwyn placed the cap of light on flat ground before inspecting the bodies. All five had been bound and beaten, two burned. She could scarcely make out their faces, two men and three women, the wounds still apparent to her. They must have been killed shortly after the houses were taken.

Sulwyn crawled carefully between them, noticing a piece of paper in the fist of one of the men. Slowly and carefully, she pried it gently out of his hand. The sheet was rather long, with messy writing, most likely done after his capture:

> To whomever it is that finds this note, if you find this note, I hope that you bring justice in our name. These men claimed they were Néosan and took our home in the dead of night. They took my wife, children, and myself into our own cellar, locking us here. The back door is jammed, we are stuck. They are making a ton of noise above us. I believe they are robbing us. I just hope they leave.

Sulwyn noticed the note had become a short journal as the next few lines were spaced out with different content:

> They took my daughters. I could not stop them, neither could my son. They were stronger than I could have imagined. I don't think they're from the Empire, but I wouldn't be surprised if they were. My wife won't stop crying.
>
> My daughters won't speak again. I don't know how many days it has been since they were up there, but the sounds of their screams will never leave my heart. They took my son now. We are

both too weak. With no food or water, our souls have been broken. The image of my daughters will forever be burned into my mind.

My son too will never speak again. He was strong; he didn't want to scream, to let his mother hear. My wife and I have decided, before they come back, that if we are to die, it will be by our own hands. Hopefully, we can take the house with us.

Sulwyn folded the note carefully, placing it in her breast pocket, reaching to pick up the cap of light. Galahad's voice of warning was in the back of her mind, more blurred and distant with every step forward towards the stairs.

They had burned themselves alive, though their attempts were futile. She could see the fire was put out before it spread too far. It only lingered long enough to kill these two poor souls.

How desperate must they have been to do that? These thoughts ran furiously through her mind with every step up she took. Soon she faced a door.

The voices were clearer here. Sulwyn could hear a few men and women, joking and laughing. Their words were too muffled to hear, but she didn't care about what they said, only that they could. Their voices irritated her, grating on her skin. Sulwyn threw the cap of water down. The light diminished immediately as she kicked the door.

Instantly the voices stopped, listening.

Sulwyn waited and waited until they began to laugh nervously, thinking they had misheard. She kicked it again. She could hear as they picked up whatever weapons they had. Imagining faceless people standing guard, she kicked harder this time, rattling it. They would realize it was *this* door.

"I thought you killed the bastards?" said one muffled voice.

"Hey, last I checked they set themselves on fire. They can't be alive. They were dead when we put them out to keep the flames from spreading." Sulwyn gripped the short blade tightly in her hand. Galahad's voice was even farther away now.

"Well, you go check it out then."

"Yeah, yeah. You're such a puss." The voice laughed, sighing at the inconvenience

Sulwyn closed her eyes just as light flooded the basement. She aimed a hard kick forward, earning a yell of surprise and a grunt of pain. She opened her eyes slowly, letting her eyes adjust to the mass amounts of torchlight before the other men could realize what had happened.

She stepped forward, smashing her foot down into the gut of the fallen man, earning another yelp before kicking his head, knocking him out. Sulwyn looked around the once decent house. The place was ransacked. Scraps of garbage and waste scattered the old wooden floors, paintings destroyed, drawers and chests searched and tossed aside.

"What happened?!" yelled another man, coming from an open room. Sulwyn quickly stepped forward as he turned the corner, stabbing the man in his thigh. He hollered, falling to the ground. But Sulwyn walked on, grabbing a sword from his belt.

They weren't Néosan.

One thing she had learned about the Empire from Raghnall: Artaxiad and Pandora were proud. They spent money on their army. It was one of the reasons people joined, in the end. Though she had never really paid attention to the colours and rank, the uniforms these men wore were cheap imitations.

"Look at that, it almost makes it sound as if I had the same pride," muttered Sulwyn, walking into the room and assessing the scene. Two men stood by the window looking out, another half out of his seat. Three women sat in simple chairs all around a bright fire, food, and drinks. The echo of the dead family in the basement covered this room. Small paintings of the family, worn but delicate trinkets atop the mantelpiece. They had obviously worked hard to get where they were, and it was all erased on the whim of the people in front of her.

"Who are you?" asked the man, standing fully.

"I should ask you that. Isn't it against some law to impersonate the Néosan?"

"Impersonate? Who do you think you are, bitch? We could have you locked up in the Empire faster than—"

Faster than what, she didn't learn.

Sulwyn whipped the short blade straight at the man's chest. "I must not be feeling well. I missed your heart," she growled, stepping towards the man as he fell into the chair. She pulled the short blade out of his chest, grabbing his collar. His eyes rolled in and out of consciousness. But she shook him anyway, hefting him up with one hand and pointing the stolen sword towards the rest with the other.

"Don't move or I'll kill him. Now, who are you?"

"You—you heard him. We're from the Empire."

"Funny. I'm also from the Empire," said Sulwyn, looking at them and dropping the man back into the chair. "You three." She pointed the sword to the huddled woman. "What do you know about this house?"

"We don't know nothin'! They brought us here! Paid us!" said one with long, dark brown hair.

"Ah, you sold yourselves to them. How *businesslike* of you. Tell me, did you know that there are raped women in the basement? They're dead now though. You can thank your employers for that." The woman looked on in fear. Sulwyn sighed in irritation. "You fear me, but you don't fear these men?"

"You're pretty cocky for a woman," said another man, stepping away from the window. He pulled out his own sword, pointing it towards Sulwyn. The women got off the chairs and went behind the man, huddling further.

Sulwyn scoffed in disgust. The man inched his way closer but rage roared within her. She grabbed the man she had stabbed out of the chair, waking him from semiconsciousness and dragging him near the lit fireplace. The man cried out, freezing everyone in place.

"Now, I'm going to ask one more time. Who are you? Why did you come into this town, into this house, and kill these people?"

"It's...it's easy..." mumbled out the man near the window.

"Easy?"

"Everyone fears the Néosan. It was an easy job to take. Doing this gets us places, gives us rewards if we do well." He smiled weakly; the one with the sword shot him a warning glance.

Sulwyn narrowed her eyes, straining a little to lower the man closer to the fire; he whimpered more. "How many times have you done this?"

The men looked at each other. "About seven?"

Sulwyn let the man go.

His head landed in the grate and into the fire. Screaming loudly, he shuffled to escape but she held him there with her boot to his abdomen. She looked down at him, watching his hair and clothes catch fire before she took her foot away. The man screamed higher, flailing weakly around until he stopped, whimpering until he was forever still. The fire continued until it burned out.

"That's not even a fraction of the pain you cost those people and whoever else you have made your target," she spat, and turned her attention to the man who charged at her. Their swords clashed loudly, the women screaming. The other man came to his partner's aid, but Sulwyn blocked him with the short blade. Both men faltered, staring at her, but she left no space for hesitation. She pushed them forward, bringing their swords down before twisting, stabbing one in the arm.

"Sulwyn!" yelled Galahad from the basement.

Sulwyn groaned in annoyance. Galahad rushed to the sitting room, another short blade in his hand, eyes sweeping the scene. Sulwyn stopped, stabbing the last man in the knee. She would let them be taken prisoner. They'd wish she had killed them here and now instead.

"Sulwyn, stop," said Galahad softly, coming next to her. He looked down at the burnt corpse. His face showed no emotion to any of them. But then he looked at her in concern and warning.

Sulwyn dropped the stolen sword and gave Galahad his short blade. "They've been going around impersonating the Néosan. I don't know if this is a new movement or just these bastards. Take their whores too. They witnessed everything."

Galahad nodded, reaching into his pack, and pulling out a tightly bound bundle of rope. Sulwyn sat on the chair, her leg over the other, staring at the women with disdain.

"You're a terrible woman…" cried out one of the women as Galahad bound them all in a line.

Sulwyn smiled widely. "You and I are going the same way." The women whimpered, shuffling to the side. Galahad gave her a strange look, but she ignored it. "Caldwell?" she asked, watching him tie the men.

"I left him when I heard screaming. We need to get back to him. We've bound the men there too." He went out of the sitting room to tie the other two men.

Sulwyn nodded, getting up to help Galahad lead the men and women to the front entrance. She removed the locks and wood barring the door, opening it as they stepped back into the night. They made their way to the other house when they heard a loud cry of laughter.

Sulwyn turned to Galahad, taking back one of the short blades from his waist and running forward. She thought Galahad would protest but he followed instead, kicking the men to move forward. She bounded up the hill and through the door, crashing through the stone threshold.

Blood decorated the walls in every direction.

Carefully she walked in. This house mirrored the other one, and she quickly found her way to the sitting room. More men and women were here. Bound and gagged. But only three of the men were alive, the others stabbed. Sulwyn kept walking until she heard sounds from another room. On closer inspection, she reached a dark kitchen with a lone woman tied to a chair in the centre. Blood seeped through the stab wound on her chest as Caldwell stood in front of her. He turned to Sulwyn, and she froze at his gaze, his eyes oddly bright and his face smiling widely.

"You must bring luck, Sulwyn. Look at the job we got…" he whispered, smiling wider still, almost insane. He let go of the dagger in his hand and left the kitchen. It dropped to the floor with a clash, the excess blood splattering around it. Sulwyn looked at the woman and realized she had been crying, but a smile lingered on her lips.

Her hair was tied behind her; loose blonde strands pushed out around her face. A large tan birthmark ran along her collarbone, standing out against her sickly pale skin. Unlike the other women, she looked as if she had been imprisoned here for other reasons. Sulwyn stepped closer, pressing her hand to the woman's neck. She had no pulse, and her body only just started to grow cold. She had just been killed, so why did she look so content?

Sulwyn walked out of the kitchen, back to the sitting room, where their fire was burning out.

Caldwell forced the remaining men to stand and silently pushed them out of the house. Sulwyn followed wordlessly behind.

"Caldwell, there were five men and four women. What did you do when I left?" asked Galahad, but Caldwell let go of the men and marched right up to Galahad. Sulwyn ran after him, pausing to watch.

Caldwell was clearly on edge, stepping as close as he could to Galahad without touching him. He was slightly taller than Galahad, but Galahad did not back down, his glare intense. He stood straight and poised, making no move to harm Caldwell.

"Stop. Stop trying to control me, telling me what to do. I've been doing this a lot longer than you. It's only been a few years since you started to lead Uferor San and all the other groups. Uferor En was the first one. *I* was part of the first one. Remember that."

"My title gives me authority over you," mumbled Galahad reluctantly, but there was disgust in his eyes with each word.

"What, being prince? No one likes you. No matter what you've achieved in the past. You are nothing to the Empire. Your only purpose was to challenge their daughter." He scoffed, "What? Didn't think I knew about that? But that changed too! Now she's here, on their side. What's your purpose now?"

"I still hold a title you begged Artaxiad for and failed," said Galahad through clenched teeth. Sulwyn saw it now. The edges of the whites of Galahad's eyes seemed darker. But Caldwell didn't pay any attention to that.

"You know nothing, Galahad. Picked to be the prince? Do you know what it's like to struggle? I fought to get where I am!"

Galahad clenched his fists. "Don't speak to me of struggle." His voice was lower, and Sulwyn could sense danger.

"Both of you need to calm down. We came here to fulfil an assignment, and it's done," said Sulwyn loudly. Instantly Galahad unclenched his fists and looked at her as if he had never seen her before. He closed his eyes for a moment, breathing out, then opening them again. Sulwyn was sure she hadn't seen things. But the whites of his eyes were clear of any darkness. She narrowed her gaze, but he turned away.

"Walk," said Galahad to the women and men, pushing them forward.

Their prisoners walked together in misery. The night was finally asleep save for a few stragglers going home or closing shop. As they walked back down the way they came, silence spread between them. Azhar stepped out of his bar to sweep the front, looking up as they came by.

Sulwyn looked away, keeping her eyes straight ahead but she could sense him watching her. Galahad looked at him as well, stopping the rest, and going to speak with Azhar. Both moved out of ear's reach.

૭-૭

| GALAHAD |

"These people are not from the Empire. They will be punished according-ly," stated Galahad. Azhar paused his sweeping, glancing at the prisoners. "Antac should carry on as it always has. If anything happens again, send word to me directly." He held out his hand for Azhar to take. Azhar considered him for a moment, passing the broom handle from palm to palm. Then grabbed his hand, shaking it.

"You're a little odd for the Empire. You don't seem like you fit in. So I'll tell you something." Azhar lowered his voice, glancing towards Sulwyn subtly. "If you ever need help, you can send word to me. There is always a spare room for someone in need. Not the only time I've done it. Keep her safe." Azhar let go of his hand.

Galahad looked at him carefully, nodding. He bowed politely before walking away, grabbing the end of the rope and pulling the men and women forward.

❦

<h1 style="text-align:center">| SULWYN |</h1>

Shortly after they reached the camp, a small fire and three tents had been set up.

"It's not wise to travel at night when the moon is hidden. We will leave tomorrow morning," said Galahad forcing the men and women to sit near one of the tents. "We take turns watching them, get some rest. I will take first watch."

The other men nodded, retreating to the tents. Caldwell stayed quiet, retreating to the carriage instead and going within it. Sulwyn hung back awkwardly. She didn't trust sleeping. She watched Galahad sit on a patch of grass by the fire. He looked up.

"You should sleep."

"I feel like I've done nothing but sleep recently. I'd rather stay awake." She walked over, taking a spot of grass across from him. Sitting made her feel the dull pain of her wounds, but they had gotten better. The fire crackled merrily between them, a cool breeze flitting by, crickets chirping every so often. Sulwyn brought her knees to her chest. She was burning with questions.

"Caldwell has sharp hearing, as I'm sure you've noticed," said Galahad quietly.

"How?"

"Training, I'd assume?"

"No, how do you always answer my unasked questions?"

He looked at her. Eyes tired and weary, of all people he should have slept first, "I wasn't aware of that..."

Sulwyn looked around. The carriage and tents were silent. The prisoners huddled amongst themselves in despair, not paying attention. She took a fistful of sand, Galahad's eyes on her.

"It might not last long, but bear with me," she smiled slightly. "*Cisza...*" Sulwyn threw the fistful of sand into the air and watched it blow over and around them. Instantly a barely visible dome of translucent blue emitted around their space.

Galahad looked around, watching as it shimmered every so often in the firelight. He looked behind him. The whining voices of the prisoners disappeared.

"We'll have to watch them, but nothing can be heard inside or out." She sat back down, dusting her hands off on each other.

"Are you a Devinal? I'd never heard that." He moved over to sit next to her, keeping his eyes on the prisoners. They were too wrapped up in their fears to notice.

"No...Raghnall taught me the basics of magic. But he wasn't one either, so he wasn't good at it, and neither am I. It also depends on my health and the weather. This might be one of the fancier things I know. And it can fail anytime."

"You didn't think to escape the cells?"

She shrugged, "Wish I could unlock things. I could never get that one to work for me, something about patience..." Her unasked questions were building. But now that she had created this moment, she didn't know where to go with it.

"I'm sorry," he started. "The original plan was to retrieve you from Raghnall and have you under my care. But Caldwell interfered. I only managed to receive you when you first came. I was forced to bring you to the upper dungeons."

"What was he like?"

She watched his jaw clench, "I never had the honour of directly meeting with the Steel Warrior before. But there was nothing during this meeting. I was already angry. Blinded by it. But I felt nothing when I saw him. Nothing at all. He was cold, like a ghost. Our interaction didn't last long. I took you away, and he was taken to Pandora."

Sulwyn rested her head on her knees. That didn't sound like Raghnall, at least not when it came to her. She felt congested and empty all at once. The reflection of fire danced on the silver ring. "So where do I go from here?" she asked, her voice muffled by her knees. Galahad leaned back on his hands, looking up to the sky.

"What do you want to do?"

"I don't know…they know about me now. Even if I escape, I'll just put other people in danger. And it's not in me to run or hide. No one knows who 'Sulwyn' is. All they know is she is their daughter."

"How did you become 'Kintana'?"

Sulwyn laughed, "Raghnall was being funny. He didn't want anyone to know who I was. Not that they would with just the name 'Sulwyn.' He gave me that name, 'blessed sun.' But as he had a title, he wanted to give me one too—to protect me just in case. So, he came up with 'Kintana.' It also means 'the star.' He thought he was clever. We've hidden my face since I was young and carried on as such; the Steel Warrior and Kintana."

"People will realize," said Galahad, "Waves of despair will hit once it's widely known that Raghnall is dead, and so is Kintana. But people in despair always find the strongest source of hope. The timing, the name, and their meaning. Soon they will look to you. And realize you are in the Empire."

Sulwyn smiled, "I thought so too."

"What do you want to do about the Empire?"

Sulwyn didn't speak, watching the blue sheen of the ward ripple in the light "When I was six, a couple of months before I met you, Raghnall reluctantly told me the truth about everything they had done and who they were to me. And then he asked me what I wanted to do. It was all up to me. If I wanted to hide and go far away. If I wanted to observe and try to live normally. Or if I wanted to fight. He said he'd do anything I chose. My answer is the same as it was then." Sulwyn stood, seeing a hole begin to form.

"I will take the Empire from them. And I will set Vartugaul free." Sulwyn stepped right up to the thinning barrier and blew on it. It shattered into a million tiny flecks of blue light before disappearing completely.

VII

A Prince's Truth. A Princess's Tears.

| SULWYN |

SULWYN looked Galahad over, his eyes wide and the skin just below it dark on the edges. "You should sleep, Galahad. I know you've been staying in the upper dungeons while I was there," she smirked. His expression was mildly shocked. "I won't kill them. I won't even talk to them. I'll sit here quietly."

Galahad looked up at her, but she could tell he was fighting fatigue and tiredness. He stood up, the fire between them. "I can protect you in the Empire as long as you say you trust me."

Sulwyn considered him for a moment. "You know I don't need it," she smiled. Despite her congested and confused feelings, he made her feel a little lighter.

"Protection isn't always physical. Rest easy, Sulwyn." He reached forward, gently touching her shoulder before retreating to a tent. Sulwyn walked around the camp for a bit, looking at the stars, looking to the darkness in the distance. She could see small lights from Antac where that hobbled man had lit the streets. The world didn't seem at war when she looked at it like this.

Without her realizing it, hours passed, and the sun began to rise over the horizon. She had stayed awake the entire time. Just sitting, listening to the wind and nature. Birds chirped with first light, alerting the rest.

Galahad was first to rise, opening the tent to find her staring off into space, the fire long burnt out. He stepped out of the tent; the rest had yet to awaken.

Sulwyn hadn't changed shifts with anyone, spending the time silently crying. Even the prisoners had fallen asleep. Galahad walked towards her, crouching down to meet her at eye level. It took a few seconds before she fully registered he was there. She didn't like that. Her defence was low around him.

"I didn't want to sleep…" mumbled Sulwyn. Sound could be heard from within the carriage. Galahad immediately stood up, stepping back, but his eyes never left hers. She looked away, towards Caldwell emerging from the carriage doors, seemingly perfect compared to last night.

"Shouldn't you clean that up?" asked Sulwyn pointing to his bloodied bandages.

"Don't worry your pretty little head, princess," he looked away from her, and instantly she realized he was lying.

"So you let her guard us all night? And we weren't killed? This calls for a celebration. We can definitely stop drugging her, and she can probably leave the dungeons now to learn to be one with the Empire." He smiled brightly. The other men stepped out of the tents, and the prisoners stirred awake at their voices.

Sulwyn turned to one of the women, who started to cry and scream uncontrollably, probably realizing this all hadn't been a dream. Sulwyn got up swiftly, walking past Galahad and Caldwell straight to her. She bent down in front of her, the woman terrified. "You'd do better asleep, love. Your nightmare is just starting." She smiled sweetly and the woman wailed louder. Sulwyn stood, looking at Galahad, his stare a little odd. She looked at the other men and Caldwell, who all shared the same gaze.

"What?"

"I think you fit right in with the Empire, princess," said Caldwell. Sulwyn glared at him.

"I need to take care of something back in the town," said Sulwyn to Galahad, ignoring Caldwell. He nodded immediately.

"Caldwell, help the men take down camp and make room for the prisoners in the carriage." Galahad left before Caldwell could fight back and gestured Sulwyn to follow.

"What are you going to do with them?" asked Galahad while they walked back into town. The sun was barely up, but some people had already started their day, keeping their heads down as they passed. But Sulwyn looked at Galahad a little skeptically.

"You can't read minds or something, can you?"

"No...and that's not common either." A corner of his lips turned up.

"How did you know then?"

"Because you carry regret. I can see that in you, and I heard what you said to Caldwell. I didn't think you'd leave that family without putting them to rest."

Wordlessly, Sulwyn took the crumpled paper from her breast pocket and handed it to Galahad. She watched him read, his expression disgusted by the end of it, returning it to her. "This isn't the first time I've seen something like this."

"I've seen it too...that's why I acted the way I did...but I don't really understand where you fit into this?" asked Sulwyn quietly as they made their way up the slope to the coast.

"I want to help you, Sulwyn."

"But you are *from* the Empire."

He stayed silent as they made their long trek to the houses, until he stopped. No one was around, the only sound the waves crashing against the shore. "I was eight when I first met you," started Galahad, looking down at her. "I was with my parents, we were travelling a bit...for my sake. And from a distance, I saw a child being beaten by the Néosan. But... I didn't know how to help. I was told to stay hidden because of our clan and our background, amongst other reasons.

"And then out of nowhere, I saw this girl, running towards them with nothing! No weapon and clearly no plan. Younger than me, you charged straight at the Néosan that held the child and kicked him as hard as you could. Stealing his blade and stabbing another. I was impressed. I remember it like it was yesterday."

Sulwyn couldn't believe he held on to this memory so clearly. Even she didn't remember all of it. He stepped closer to her. "Then he grabbed you, and I didn't think twice. I pulled my hood up and ran to you."

"You make it sound like I was some talented child. I was reckless and caused trouble. If you could ask Raghnall he'd say that hasn't really changed." She looked off to the side. "You came like the wind, grabbing the knife before the man knew what hit him. You stabbed him without hesitation. But you didn't even say anything. You just looked at me and left."

"I had no choice, but my memory of you at that time helped me during my darkest moments, Sulwyn." Galahad looked around to see the same hobbled man from last night going around and extinguishing the torch lights. He paid them no mind.

"We need to continue," said Galahad gently.

Sulwyn nodded, taking off towards the basement of the house with the deceased. She didn't know what else to do besides burn their bodies to ash.

She bent over them, giving her prayers to the moon and sun before she put all her energy into her words. "Tainted bodies, weak and tired. I pray that you find rest with this fire." Sulwyn used the short blade from Galahad to cut her palm. Squeezing her hand together she let the blood coat her skin before pressing it onto one of the bodies. Instantly it burst into blue flames, leaving a pile of ash in its place. She pressed her hand against each one, watching the fire burn out in turn. Galahad stood behind her, watching silently before he stepped forward with a bundle of cloth.

"This is as advanced as my magic gets. And it's draining,"

"You can create fire strong enough to burn a body, but you can't unlock an iron cell door?" said Galahad a little skeptically. Sulwyn shrugged.

"Raghnall couldn't do it either. We pick locks faster than that instead. He said patience is of the utmost importance for magic and he had none, and I have less. Unlocking is intricate, raw emotion is not." Sulwyn shrugged again, bending down and scooping up the ashes together, wrapping them carefully in the blue cloth, and left the cellar.

She made her way towards the other house, through the threshold and into the kitchen, but stopped. The body of the woman had already been removed. Sulwyn stepped out into the sitting area just as Galahad arrived behind her. She looked around. Nothing else had been moved or touched.

"That woman..."

"A townsperson must have come and collected her." He looked around the house as well, shaking his head. He beckoned Sulwyn to follow. She held the bundle firmly.

The sun had fully risen now, hanging low over the horizon. She went behind the houses to stand on the rocky edges of the coast. Sulwyn looked at the deep blue and green waters, a place that no one could escape to, the current never calm enough to try. Bending down, she unfolded the cloth and scattered the ashes into the sea. The smell of salt and stone filled her lungs, the wind passing through her hair gently as she prayed once more.

Sulwyn breathed in and out slowly, steeling herself. She turned to face Galahad. "What happens when we go back to the Empire?"

He answered instantly, his gaze strong. "Caldwell and I will make a report to Artaxiad about the town. The prisoners will be taken to the lower dungeons to await the bi-monthly trial to decide their punishment. During this report, I will speak of your assistance, and gain permission to guide you in the ways of the Empire."

"And what happens with me? You know how I feel about the Empire. I will not let you get in my way if you hold me back. No matter how long it takes, I will achieve something, anything to make a difference."

"I wish to see the fall of the Empire...of Artaxiad...more than you could ever imagine. Whatever it is you want to do, I will see it through with you." His eyes were fierce, and she almost forgot to breathe. It was the same intensity he had emitted back in Azhar's bar.

"Why are you in the Empire?" she whispered, knowing there was so much more.

Steeling himself, he answered, "When I was eleven, I was coronated and announced as the prince and heir to their Empire. They talked of the troubles I had endured at such a young age, and how they wanted to give love to another unfortunate child after losing you. They asked the people to accept me no matter how difficult I was or how much trouble I may cause or act out on…when I was ten, the king and his army annihilated most of my clan."

Sulwyn's eyes widened, but what else shocked her was that finally, for the first time, she witnessed it. The whites of his eyes became slightly darker around the edges, like a black shadowy something wanted to creep over.

But he continued to speak, the words tumbling out one after the other. "It was chaos that night. Everything was burning, everyone was screaming. And finally, a voice around us said they found me, and before my eyes Artaxiad came and killed my parents. I don't remember much after that. I believe some did escape and are in hiding. But they took me. I was a prisoner at the Solus for a short time until I was moved to the lower dungeons."

"I heard no one really leaves once they've been sentenced to the lower dungeons…"

Galahad smiled, and it was dark and wicked and sent fear through her. "No, they don't."

"I don't know anything about your clan. No one does. But Raghnall said there is a power within it, and I sense it in you. Why didn't you leave? If you hate them so much, why didn't you fight them? Or at least escape?"

"And go where, Sulwyn? Fight with or for what? My family, my clan, everything I knew was destroyed! I barely held on to myself, keeping in mind that my parents died for me, to keep me alive. And then finally that started to change. I became listless; I had given up and cast aside as much emotion as I could because it was easier not to feel anything.

"But then I learned why they took me that night, why they sought an heir. It was because they wanted someone who could challenge and destroy you. They learned about you, knew you were with Raghnall, and heard the rumours. And I vowed to never help them. But more than that, I figured then that if I stayed, one day you'd come, and I'd be able to help you." He breathed roughly, looking away. His hands and jaw clenched. Sulwyn watched the black edges of his eyes grow opaquer but then he froze. And a moment after she heard a yell.

"Sir!" called the Néosan in the far distance. "We should leave now! The winds are picking up; we think a sandstorm is coming!" Sulwyn looked at Galahad, stunned. His face and demeanour, the black in his eyes gone, everything about was him impassive, that wave of intensity and anger nonexistent before he turned to face the Néosan.

"We are done here, we can leave!" Galahad briefly looked back at Sulwyn, turning to go back.

☙❧

They rode faster with the impending sandstorm on its way. The prisoners inside the carriage rioted and yelled, but it fell on deaf ears. Sulwyn and Caldwell rode on their own while Galahad and another Validus steered the carriage. After a few short breaks, they continued in silence until they reached the massive iron doors of the Empire late into the next night. The doors opened upon arrival, and their party slowed to a trot.

Sulwyn followed closely behind but for the first time in her life she saw the inside of the Empire.

Strange round lights atop metal poles lit the roads and paths all along for as far as she could see. The buildings here were taller, denser, with stores and other buildings compared to any other town. The metal roofs were shinier, the structures stronger and more intricate with flourished upholstery and designs. She could only see the Privileged out and about, in their own groups of fun and entertainment, travelling in flocks or shopping alone. It must be after curfew for the Common Ones; not a single person in uniform was out. Fancy carriages led by prestigious horses passed them by, the inhabitants bowing respectfully to Galahad and the others as they went.

She looked ahead as a vast brick and wooden structure came into view: Valens Muros. It was wider than it was high, only six floors up, but it was rich and well built. She noticed a large part of it was built out of the same black stone that surrounded the borders of the Empire. That must be where the tall stained-glass windows used to be. Raghnall had told her that the outside of many things had changed, but it was all still built on the original foundations and inner structures. No one knew the High City better than he.

"Too bad you didn't teach me anything about the inside, Raghnall." She shook her head, slowing as the carriage stopped. Other Néosan came from the black outer walls of Valens Muros to greet them. Galahad stepped down, handing the reigns to one of them.

"Prisoners. Take them to the lower dungeons. Not too far. They're going to be prosecuted."

Sulwyn watched Galahad carefully. The change was amazing, the emotions and expressions he showed her at the coast seemed like a different person. Here, he was stoic, detached, and cold. And no one questioned it. They all listened to him without any hesitation. And she knew now it wasn't just because he was named prince. He would have had to work hard to get this far. Galahad turned to her, surprising her internally. She would never admit he'd caught her off guard, but she felt the heat creep up her neck.

"Let us go see the king, shall we?" Caldwell stepped to her left, holding his arm out for her. Sulwyn regarded him, then turned to Galahad. She understood what it was she was going to have to do here. The plan slowly started to make its way through the fog of her mind. But it was still faint and distorted. She hoped she was going in the right direction.

"I look forward to talking about what I've learned on this trip." She took Caldwell's arm and he smiled, leading her forward. Galahad walked behind them, dismissing the other men.

Sulwyn glanced at the prisoners, watching them comprehend exactly where they were. The women fell to their knees, the men pale as snow. She smiled at their fear and Caldwell's voice resonated in her mind. Sulwyn scowled to herself, frowning. She was not like them.

⤫

Caldwell led her to Artaxiad's large furnished office. A massive dark oak desk stood off to the side across from an ornate mantel over an empty grate. Documents atop documents covered the desk, and bookshelves with heavy books lined the walls. The only thing she found glaringly strange was the sheer number of various clocks that hung along all the walls or sat on top of all the shelves. All ticking loudly; some deep, some higher in sound, some plain, and some very intricate, and of all sizes. It was maddening to her. How and why did he have so many clocks?

"Sulwyn! You look well," said Artaxiad, arms open wide as if to embrace her. Sulwyn bit back a retort, considering that her wounds not only still hurt but showed across her arms even with Galahad minorly healing them.

"As do you, my king," she responded instead, bowing stiffly, unsettled by the ticking. She'd have to slap herself once this meeting was over. She stood straight and counted the clocks instead.

"You look adjusted. Galahad sent word that you gallantly took part during this assignment. I'm glad for it. People like them cannot be tolerated. We cannot have such scum slander what the Empire has worked hard for. People like them, who try to take what isn't their own. It's tyranny."

Sulwyn used all of her will not to roll her eyes at the hypocrisy. "Yes, treason even. As such they should be punished accordingly. I also think they should be investigated. I don't think they are alone in this scheme."

Artaxiad seemed thrilled, but something about the way he stared at her made her uneasy. She shivered involuntarily until a touch of warmth flowed through her. Galahad stepped somewhat in front of her, bowing deeply to Artaxiad with a fist over his chest.

"Yes, Galahad, you have kept your word and Sulwyn, you have proved your worth in the Empire. We will no longer need to keep you at arm's length. You are to see to her training to be part of this Empire." He glanced briefly at Galahad before looking at Sulwyn once more.

"You will be coronated in the next few days and officially announced to all of Vartugaul. Soon after that, a bi-monthly trial is scheduled. You *will* attend and you *will* give feedback. Don't disappoint me. You have already exceeded expectations. Now, please. Get some deserved rest." He smiled at her, his green eyes dull and his lips wet as he licked them.

She had been so blindsided by the events that took place in the Proelium Terra that she hadn't looked at Artaxiad properly the first time.

Their similarity in appearance bothered her. But she noticed something else. A deep, horizontal scar was visible just under his left eye, stretched towards his left ear. Straight through that scar was another, vertical from the end tip of his eyebrow to the end of his nose in length. Someone had managed to injure him. She knew Raghnall never got the chance to fight him directly, so who else could have come that close?

"Lady Princess? Let's be on our way," said Galahad, bowing to Artaxiad again. Caldwell bowed too, leading Sulwyn out.

"I'll see you later, princess. I'll make sure you can come on the next assignment with me." He winked, turning back the way they had come. She watched his retreating back.

Sulwyn was convinced something was wrong with him. He had been quieter since their return, and his arms still seemed like they were bleeding beneath the bandages. But no one else questioned or gave it any attention. Another touch of warmth from her shoulder brought her out of her thoughts. Galahad was now in front of her.

"Let us not linger out here any longer." He gestured for her to walk the opposite way they had come.

The castle was full of deep red carpeted hallways, luxurious furnishings trimmed in golds and silvers, stairs of indigo marble, and paintings of all kinds. She had never seen anything so large and ornamented and quite excessive in her opinion. Galahad stopped walking, but she continued to the end until she looked back. He stood in front of the last door of the hallway.

"This is my room," he said, taking out his large set of keys.

"Seriously, are you the only person with keys?"

He looked at her, humour in his eyes. "I have all the keys necessary. This one is mine and mine alone. No one comes to my room and even if they did, they wouldn't be able to get through easily." He pushed a small, dark green key into the lock. Turning it halfway, it clicked, and the door swung open.

Walking in, her jaw dropped. "Are we outside? No, we can't be. Can we?"

Trees, grass, and small plants lined the vast rectangular space. But on closer inspection, she noticed that they were indeed still inside. His room had an open concept. In the far corner sat a rather large bed, hidden by trees and wispy dark brown fabric hanging from the ceiling. A small desk and chair in another corner with a bookcase, and a sitting area with vibrant blue plush couches sat near the middle facing an unlit fireplace. A door far off to the right led to what she figured was the bathing room. Around the walls were various doors, possibly closets.

"Some in my clan had talent with growing nature almost anywhere. We can earn the assistance of some plants." He smiled, eyes solemn. Sulwyn walked around the entire room. A small river lined the northern walls, going out under another door hidden by thick emerald ivy.

"That door leads outside to the forest. I needed to be near a source of water for this to work. When they let me out and I earned my way, they let me choose whichever room I wanted. I wasn't bothered much, and they let me do as I please because I listened better if I wasn't upset." He turned to her. "I want you to stay here, until your rooms are ready and even then. I can stay elsewhere. But this is safe; no one can get in here without my permission."

"You're leaving me alone?" Her bewilderment fell, replaced by a shaky voice. Why? How could she show such weakness? But now that she was out of the cell and back into the world, the realization of being alone, being in this castle, in the Empire suddenly hit her harder.

Galahad fiddled with the keys in his hands, looking at her solemnly. "Sulwyn..."

"I said I'd trust you. But I won't do it fully. I need you to be here, to show me. I need to be able to see you." Her voice shook again at the end. He looked at her with something she didn't want to acknowledge.

She suddenly felt so tired, both congestion and emptiness welling in her all at once. She knew what she was going to have to do here in the Empire, but to be alone right now...and then it just overflowed.

"Twenty-three years!" she yelled. "I spent twenty-three years with him. He saved my life, raised me like his own! Everything I know and am is because of Raghnall. So how? How did I get here? Like this?" She waved frantically. She was furious with herself for showing tears so openly. She hadn't cried so much in years as she had in these last few days. But the way he looked at her. Why did she feel more pain for him than she felt for herself? Who was he to her?

"You are not alone, Sulwyn. I won't let you go through what I did." He stepped closer to her, hesitant and unsure of what he should do. But Sulwyn already knew. Against her better judgement, Sulwyn trusted more than she should have since she first saw his eyes; she just wanted to fight it. But above all that, she just didn't want to do this alone.

She cried freely, trying her best to hold it all back, but once he reached out and wrapped his arms around her, she couldn't do it anymore. Sulwyn howled out, her tears never-ending as her chest felt like it would collapse just like the world was around her.

VIII

Heart To Ashes

| GALAHAD |

GALAHAD gently wrapped his arms around her, prepared to accept any attacks.

But none came.

He had heard the rumours of the Steel Warrior and Kintana, about their feats and bravery.

But here she was just Sulwyn.

She continued to wail and cry and somehow it brought him even more grief. Gently, he patted her hair and rubbed her back, until suddenly she clung to the back of his tunic, moving them backwards. Galahad slowly led her down to sit on the floor as he leaned against the wooden end of the couch. Without a word she continued to lean into him, her cries becoming softer and her breathing a bit steadier.

❧

| SULWYN |

His heartbeat was strong and calm but had picked up in pace compared to what it was before. Warmth flowed through her as she listened to it, soothing her alongside the sound of the river. Lulling her into calmness. She had never been held or close to anyone like this before. But she felt like it would be okay to stay like this forever.

Her thoughts were quiet, her panic subsided. Over and over she had been telling herself that it was good she was in the Empire, that this was the best plan and the opportune chance to take them down from the inside, just as they did so many years ago.

Over and over she debated whether she could trust Galahad or not, flipping back and forth between her instinct and mind and heart. But she believed in herself, and what she saw in his eyes and in his expressions, she knew. She knew deep down that he was that person all those years ago even if he had lost himself along the way.

"When I knocked your hood off..." Her voice was a whisper, and she felt his chin atop her head. "...the amount of relief I felt when I recognized you...I was terrified. To immediately feel safe when I had been betrayed and in enemy territory, it was wrong. I always travelled with Raghnall. I got used to being with someone, I depended on him. Then when I woke up alone...I had never known such emptiness. But at the same time, I know I'm supposed to fight and what I'm supposed to do. And I can...it just all became so conflicting and confusing. And with it there's this nagging feeling that I can't pinpoint about Raghnall, something I'm missing. I feel like there's a pressure in my chest, holding my heart."

She felt his arms tighten as he spoke in a low whisper. "I woke up in a cell too. Darker than the one you were in, though that's not an issue for me..." He trailed off for a moment as if he had said too much. His chest stiffened, but he continued. "I could hear people, men and women much older, rougher and more experienced, around me, their voices echoing in this unfamiliar place. But I didn't learn where I was until a few days after.

"In the Solus they let everyone go outside for exercise and air in sections. Eventually, I joined this routine but...I blacked out a lot when I was there and was eventually moved into the lower dungeons here."

"They moved you? What did you do?"

"I murdered other prisoners and guards," said Galahad darkly. Sulwyn pulled away to look at him. There was a darkness in him. Something she could never touch or understand.

He looked at her in slight fear and apprehension. What kind of power did he have that a ten-year-old would be considered such a threat? That Artaxiad purposely went to find him and take him?

"I cannot tell you, so please don't ask me."

"Stop that."

He smiled. "I have kept my clan's secrets with me since I was taken. I have power, but I keep it within me. I've displayed enough that they didn't push it. But I cannot let Artaxiad know. Please understand and please be patient. I hope to one day share it with you."

Her curiosity burned at her, but she wouldn't press it. However, she suddenly realized how close they really were and instantly felt the heat creep up her cheeks and neck. Galahad smiled coyly, flustering her further. Swiftly he stood, bringing her up with him.

"You've been awake for almost thirty hours. I think it's time you sleep, on your own this time. There are nightclothes prepared for you in the bathing room. I'm not leaving, so don't look at me like that." He lightly gripped her shoulders, turning her in the direction of the other door in the corner.

Sulwyn looked back once before entering the bathing room. Instantly she ran to the glass mirror and looked herself over. She was dishevelled more than usual. Huffing to herself she turned away. She was Kintana, there was nothing to be embarrassed about.

૎્

It was some time before the water grew cold and her hands and feet were pruney. Getting out of the bath, she went to the small chest of drawers and found nightgowns of various colours, none of which were green. That was another question she would have to ask.

As she searched through the cotton nightgowns, she found a small dagger hidden within the folds. Sulwyn listened carefully as she dressed, taking the blade with her. How strong was he really? It wouldn't be too harmful to test him, would it? And she was aware that there was something about him; she was prepared. Raghnall's nagging voice about curiosity chimed in, but she ignored it.

Cautiously she opened the door, smiling internally at her luck. Galahad had fallen asleep at the edge of the bed, crouched slightly in a ball. He looked peaceful in this state, his face relaxed and his hair falling over his forehead.

She stepped stealthily, any sound she could have made covered by the sounds of gently flowing water. Closer and closer she crept until she was beside him, his breathing deep and tranquil. Slowly, she brought the blade near his neck.

Instantly the dagger was knocked out of her hand, falling to the ground with a muffled clatter. He grabbed her wrist tightly and pulled her arm behind her back, pushing her against one of the tree trunks. She grunted in pain and Galahad let go quickly. Sulwyn turned to look at him; most of the whites of his eyes were black, but his eyes were full of terror and fear. His panicked breathing slowed, making way for anger.

"Why?" was all he could manage, his breathing laboured.

Sulwyn didn't have an answer; she just stared at him instead. He realized why and blinked; the blackness gone. He sighed and she noticed he was shaking. She had done this to Raghnall too, and though he also woke immediately, his reaction had never been this strong or this violent. To her, this seemed like his power or energy or whatever it was surged in a moment to protect.

"I'm sorry. It was stupid of me...I was just curious..."

He sighed deeply. "Sulwyn, I ask you not to do that again. I told you I'd never *willingly* hurt you. But I just need you to understand that I am not always in control of myself, especially in these recent days." His voice was rough and low, and she now realized that the terror and fear he had shown was not for his safety but for hers.

"I apologize...please, go back to sleep..." She looked away awkwardly, but he sighed again, pulling her towards the bed.

"I'll stay this way, okay? Just please, get some sleep."

Despite living with a man her entire life, Sulwyn thought she wouldn't be able to sleep next to him, even if his head was by her feet. But as soon as she climbed into bed, her eyes closed in an instant.

Sulwyn awoke suddenly, her heart racing as she gathered her senses. Waking up in a different location almost constantly had disoriented her. But the sound of flowing water relaxed her. She stared at the ceiling covered in dark green ivy and branches.

All she could say of Galahad's strength was that he was faster than her, had some form of healing ability, and could basically make friends with plants. Besides that and his strange eyes, she had nothing else to go on. Raghnall had told her the first time she saw him that theirs was a unique and secretive clan hidden somewhere in Vartugaul. Only a few ever saw them and all they would ever remember was their eyes. Maybe it was the shrouded mystery that created the rumour of their strength. To kill a clan for the sake of finding someone to beat her...

That meant they knew about her survival from way before. But why did they wait so long to make a move?

Sulwyn looked down suddenly, noticing Galahad wasn't there. She lifted the covers off herself, listening. She didn't hear or sense his presence at all. Not that it meant much. She could barely sense him even in full view. Deliberating, Sulwyn got up suddenly, going to the bathing room. A few moments later and she was walking through the halls of the Empire, a robe wrapped tightly over her nightgown.

The place was a maze. Sulwyn had already forgotten precisely where she had come from the night before and where Galahad's room was, despite just coming from there. But if she was looking for the dungeons, she had no choice but to go down. Judging from the windows she was currently on the first floor. Or so she thought.

As she walked on, she realized she was on an elongated slope going up. Looking out the window again, she was on the fourth or fifth floor. Confused, Sulwyn continued, no sound left in her wake. Every so often she would stop, pressing her ear to a door, then proceed. The last thing she wanted to do was open a door to something unexpected.

But the castle was still and quiet, unsettling her more. Should it be like this? Shouldn't there be mounds of people catering to the whims of their leaders?

This was frustrating.

She would never find where she wanted to go if she didn't find someone to lead her there. Soon she reached what she thought was the other end of the castle but felt as if she were going in a large square. There she saw stone steps without a door descending and ascending in a spiral.

"Well, this seems promising." She quickly walked towards it, wishing she had worn her boots. The stone was cold on her feet, but she was stealthier without them. Sulwyn descended two steps at a time, pausing on the next floor to listen. This floor mirrored the one upstairs, and it was just as silent. She moved on to the next and stopped, leaning against the wall, at the sound of two women.

"I don't want to go..." mumbled the first. She sounded quiet, timid.

"But she asked for ya. I would go, ya know I would. But I don't think she likes my looks. I ain't being punished for tryin'," said a stronger, rougher voice. "You'll be okay, Nori. I won't leave."

Sulwyn heard a slight sniffle followed by a knock on a door. As it opened the other girl sighed. Within minutes she heard the door close again, followed by a whimper.

"See? Quick and easy. Now let's leave before she demands somethin' else," whispered the girl. Sulwyn stiffened, they were coming this way. She ran back up a flight of stairs, looking down. Two girls, one with light brown hair and one with black, walked into the stairway going down. Sulwyn silently followed them at a distance.

The girl with chin-length black hair seemed younger than either herself or the other girl. She was somewhat fair with a slight plumpness to her overall figure, and taller than the other girl with short light brown hair and dark bronze skin. Both wore simple long grey dresses with black aprons tied over them; maid uniforms. Nori's was long-sleeved while the brunette girl wore short sleeves.

They continued to descend the cold stone steps until they reached ground level, turning out into wide hallways. Instead of the plush red carpet, the floor was patterned with violet and black tiles. There were a lot of other maids and menservants moving about their daily business here. A vast difference from the quiet, stifling halls above.

Quite suddenly both girls turned swiftly and into a side door just after the staircase. Sulwyn dashed forward, assuming another hall, but entered a small broom cupboard instead.

"Ya were right, Nori," said the brunette girl. Her eyes were bright blue and striking against her hair and dark skin. Sulwyn was rather impressed that they had detected her even if she wasn't masking her presence. She looked curiously at the girl named Nori. Instantly, Nori looked down, timidly moving behind the other girl.

"Yer...a strange one. Why ya runnin' around the Empire in a robe? That's a little risqué," eyed the brunette girl.

"I got lost...?"

"You one of them mad ones, sweetness? They come 'round sometimes. The ones that our king takes a likin' to. I personally think some of them might be on a little something. Nori was one of them, but I helped her out of it." Nori moved behind the girl completely as if trying to disappear.

"Aren't you being tactless?" asked Sulwyn, but the girl shrugged.

"It is what it is. Just 'cause someone don't say it, don't mean it didn't happen. Besides, most of us have come into something we never wanted to be a part of. Minus those lunatics that follow them all...Oh! goddess of the moon!" gasped the girl suddenly, making a rough curtsy. Nori followed suit though she seemed just as lost as Sulwyn was.

"Why are you...?"

"Yer the Lady Princess! Oh! Please forgive my rudeness...uh tactlessness." She curtsied again and this time Nori curtsied properly, both holding fear in their eyes.

Is this how people would react every time they found out who she was? "I'd appreciate if you didn't do that."

"Yes, ma'am." She bowed instead.

"No, none of that. Please," said Sulwyn, stepping forward, but the girls flinched. Sulwyn stared at them, moving back carefully. "Look, can you direct me to the lower dungeons?"

The fear rose in their eyes. Was there something wrong with her question?

"We can lead ya there if ya need it, ma'am." The brunette girl gestured to exit, moving forward and opening the door. Sulwyn followed, watching both girls straighten their backs and walk on edge.

"What's your name?"

"Eztli, ma'am."

"Call me Sulwyn, please, or even 'sweetness.' I'd much rather that." But Eztli looked petrified as well as embarrassed at even the thought. The others paid them no attention as they passed, something that made Eztli and Nori panic more.

"Oh, they will be in so much trouble for not greeting her," whispered Nori assuming Sulwyn couldn't hear her.

"Just worry about yerself. We won't be punished, we noticed first. We did okay, don't worry about it."

Sulwyn didn't know what to tell them and instead just continued to follow. She hated the looks of revulsion she was receiving, all because she was their child. She never chose to be this. Prickly irritation rose within her but she kept her focus on the task at hand.

They walked for some time, past many busy with their duties, until they reached another hall end. They turned off the path into a desolate stone passageway lit by torches. At the end stood a large iron door that Eztli went towards, pulling the iron bolt back and opening it.

"We aren't supposed to be down here out of schedule. If ya walk down the path you'll see a door," started Eztli, looking around. "That door leads to the staircase that either goes up to the upper dungeon or down to the lower."

"Thank you for your help." Sulwyn smiled, taking Eztli and Nori by surprise.

"Eztli, she has no shoes," whispered Nori.

But Sulwyn was already stepping through and walking quickly towards the other iron door. Fewer torches lit the way here; the air instantly became colder and mustier.

"Ma'am!" hissed Eztli, but her voice was muffled by the shutting door.

Sulwyn was ready for the smell, but she wouldn't be able to hold her breath the entire time. She pulled a piece of fabric, ripped from a night-gown she had prepared earlier, out of the robe pocket. She tied it around her nose and mouth before she descended. At the end of the cold stone stairs was another door. Slowly, she pulled it open.

Even with the cloth she could still smell and taste the pungent reek of death and sickness and rotting. It caused waves of nausea to roll over her, but she needed to concentrate.

The air here was heavy. Cries, wails, and moans surrounded her. Some prisoners just stared, still and silent; others were knocking on the bars, yelling and screaming. And somehow Sulwyn had a feeling it never stopped. There was no sense of time down here. No windows to show if it was night or day. Anyone trapped down here must go insane, their minds destroyed in the constant loop.

Quietly she went, the stone ground wet in spots, some thicker than the rest, some darker than others. She regretted not wearing her boots. But she pressed on.

Her eyes adjusted to the small amounts of torchlight, but from what Sulwyn could see, the cells just went on and on. Hallways led off into other aisles, more screams and moans coming from their depths. Goosebumps rose but she continued, looking.

This was probably impossible. How could she find Raghnall's body amongst all these cells? As she walked, she noticed that some people shared their cells with someone who had already died quite some time ago.

It was sick. The whole situation was sick.

Finally, the people noticed that she was not a Néosan, and they started to call her.

Whispers and yells.

Pleading and begging.

"Save me!" came one hoarse man next to her. His outstretched hand was too far to reach. Another woman tried the same, and then another and another. Each more ghostly than the next.

Suddenly, one person banged violently against the iron bars and she jumped back in reflex. But as she did so something grabbed her ankle, weakly pulling at her.

She looked down to see an old grey woman lying in front of the cell door. Many deceased were behind her, but she was smiling. Sulwyn bent down immediately, grabbing the woman's hand.

"Ma'am?!" hissed Eztli's voice in the distance. "Ya have no shoes! What are ya doing? Why are ya kneeling in this? Are ya mad?" Sulwyn briefly turned to her but brought her attention back to the lady.

"I'm so sorry. I'm so sorry that you are all in here," whispered Sulwyn. She couldn't begin to express how much loathing she had for the Empire more than in this moment. But she stopped speaking as the woman continued to smile brightly amongst the black despair.

"Kintana…" she sighed.

It was almost instant.

Everyone in the surrounding cells who could hear them went silent. Quickly it spread until eventually all she could hear was breathing.

"Kintana, you are alive…we hear rumours, even down here, but the star is not gone." She breathed roughly, her voice weakening. "You would not know, but you and the Steel Warrior saved my children. I thank you with all of my being."

"Please, I don't know what I can do for you. I don't have…no, I can get the keys, I'm sure I can get the keys!" whispered Sulwyn. But the lady chuckled, coughing once she did so. Her rough hands pulled her own slightly. It was there that Sulwyn noticed the worn leather bracelet held together by a tarnished metal symbol. It was a square with a circle wrapped within it: Raghnall's symbol, bequeathed to those who continued to rebel and who had helped Raghnall in the past.

"There is no hope for those of us trapped down here. And if you do that, you will get caught. Keep living, Kintana, continue giving Vartugaul hope…" The old woman gripped her hand tighter, letting out a shuddering deep breath. Her smile never left her face.

"Kintana?" muttered Eztli. Everyone remained quiet, watching Sulwyn stand.

"I shouldn't use it, but I'll do it anyway." Sulwyn recited the same spell from before, slapping her palm across the rough metal bars to reopen the cut. She pressed her hand onto the old woman, watching as she burst into blue flames illuminating the darkness for a moment. A pile of ash was left in her wake. Instantly, Sulwyn felt a sharp pang of pain in her chest and in her head.

Vision swaying, she braced herself against the iron bars, taking deep breaths. She was not meant to use magic. And she had used too much in a short amount of time.

Immediately she felt an intense gaze. She turned to Nori staring at her in confusion before Nori turned away completely, hiding her eyes and looking at the ground. Sulwyn's head continued to throb, but she wouldn't leave until she found Raghnall.

After a few moments, she stood up and continued down the way she was going until, finally, she reached one end where a rather large cell remained.

The ceiling around it was high, easily reaching past the upper dungeons, some unknown light shining through unseen cracks. Whether it was sunlight or from within the castle Sulwyn couldn't tell, but it illuminated piles and piles of old and new bodies. She fought the urge to vomit, scanning the deceased until she hopefully found him.

Finally, her eyes stopped, looking at one body lying in the corner nearby, as if tossed unceremoniously.

Was this Raghnall's body?

It had the same clothes, but the body had become even more decrepit since the last time she saw it less than a week ago, with swelling in various parts of the body, cuts, and dismemberment. They had destroyed him. She could barely make out his face. The only thing noticeable was part of his white hair, most of it covered in blood and dirt. But something about it looked wrong.

"Sulwyn, let's go," said a soft voice next to her. She barely sensed him until he gently gripped her arm, pulling her away. She looked up at his multicoloured eyes. Her sadness reflected in them.

"Let me take his body."

"You know you can't."

"Then let me burn it!"

"I can see it in you. You know you aren't meant to use magic. Look at you!" He placed his hand softly against her neck. She had broken out in cold sweat, the pain in her heart growing.

"Then you do it," said Sulwyn.

"I can't use magic…"

"But you can do something?" Then Sulwyn froze, looking at Galahad as if it was the first time. She hadn't noticed when the wailing screams and mutterings started again. But the sounds of it echoed loudly around them.

"Get out of here," said Sulwyn hurriedly, pushing him and taking his hand, pulling him forward. How could she be so stupid? How could she be so selfish? Sulwyn pushed Eztli forward, making them all hurry out, back through the many iron doors and up the stairs. They stopped just before purple and black tiles started.

"When was the last time you were ever down there?" whispered Sulwyn, looking at him. He was pale, sickly looking. She looked down; one of his fists was clenched, the other held her hand tightly. He wouldn't look at her. "Galahad…"

"Not now, Sulwyn." He stepped past her, letting her hand go. "Eztli, thank you for showing her where to go. I'm glad she ran into you. If it's not too much trouble, I ask that you look out for her when you have the time."

Eztli was flustered, as was Nori. "Of course. It's still rather early. I don't think she's eaten, runnin' around in a robe. Would ya both like breakfast?"

Galahad smiled, but Sulwyn could see he was still shaken. "That would be great. Also, if you could find some slippers…" He shot Sulwyn a glare, but she instantly looked away at a particularly interesting spot of wall.

IX

Past & Present

SULWYN and Galahad walked in silence behind Nori and Eztli down the hall of the first floor. As she looked around at the others working, various smells of foods and baked goods wafted towards her. The path had turned into stone walls and tiled black and red floors before they went through swinging wooden doors.

They entered a rather large kitchen. Many men and women could be seen preparing all types of breakfast foods at various metal-tabled stations around the room. Stoves and ovens lined the walls, and racks of ingredients and spices filled in the spaces. The smell of frying, baking, and boiling all reached Sulwyn. Her stomach growled loudly. After using all that magic, she was starving. She hadn't eaten last night either. She needed to make it up to her stomach for all these missed meals.

"Princess!" called Caldwell, turning to look at them from a small wooden table that Sulwyn hadn't noticed. Caldwell waved, eating breakfast in a corner. She didn't see anyone but servants in the kitchen. Why was he the only one eating there?

"Caldwell doesn't have many people he is acquainted with. He chooses to eat in the main kitchen, if not alone elsewhere," said Galahad.

"Am I really that readable?"

"You aren't any better, Galahad, so don't talk shit about me," retorted Caldwell without looking up from his meal.

"Please take a seat, I'll make something light for you both," said Eztli, gesturing towards Caldwell's table. Sulwyn looked around more and realized that this was the only table for eating. She sighed, shuffling her way over with slippers way too large for her feet.

"That's an interesting outfit you've got going…why are your legs dirty?" asked Caldwell, mildly confused.

"I was praying."

"You don't seem the type."

"I'm not."

Caldwell looked up at her. He was acting like when she had first met him. His bandages were also clean and fresh. They continued to stare at each other for some time until Galahad took a seat next across him.

"Ah, prince. Sitting in the kitchens for once? And you say I'm antisocial. You never eat with anyone."

"There is a time for everything, Caldwell."

Caldwell shrugged, watching Eztli come and set two plates in front of them. A small bowl of cream soup, some eggs, and meat graced the plates. He smirked, standing with his now empty plate. Sulwyn took a seat and watched Caldwell finish the glass of water, handing both to Nori who brought them some bread.

"You're giving her a tour later, yeah? See how much better this is when you aren't resisting. I'm glad you've kept an open mind." He winked at Sulwyn. She glanced over to Galahad, but he kept his eyes on his plate of food.

"I look forward to this tour." She smiled brightly. "Getting to see how far the Empire has grown over these missing years is quite the treat. I hope I can handle the shock of it all. I really am happy for the change of scenery. And the food, of course. It smells much better up here than it does down there."

"Ain't that the truth, the smell of death…well that's not a topic for the kitchens, is it?" He bowed shortly to Sulwyn, taking off out of the kitchens. Sulwyn just scowled after him. Galahad poked her, bringing her attention back to the food.

They ate in silence, Sulwyn listening to the sounds of activity within the kitchen and noticing curious looks that came their way. All the while Nori kept glancing at her. Sulwyn wasn't entirely sure if the stares were negative or simply curious. Galahad followed her gaze.

"I don't know much about Nori," he started quietly. They both watched them bustling around the stoves and counters. "She came a few years ago, I think she was fourteen. For a short time, she stayed in one of the pleasure houses, and Artaxiad favoured her. Then Eztli arrived and was supposed to go to the same pleasure house, but they thought her too boisterous. She took Nori with her when they moved to the Empire for kitchen duties a couple years ago."

Sulwyn stopped eating, watching Nori instead. She was a simple girl, nervous and timid, but she seemed comfortable around Eztli. Nori turned to Sulwyn, catching her stare.

"Eztli seems comfortable with you, though?"

"I stepped in during a collection at her village. They had nothing to offer. It had a lot of elderly. She offered herself. I managed to let that at least pass and spared the rest of her village. It's currently under my protection. After the pleasure house incidents, I managed to get her here in the kitchens. Eztli has great talent as a cook, so I'm able to keep her village safe because they are satisfied with her."

Nori looked away, turning her back on them both as she continued cutting vegetables. "Is that what you've been doing, then? Just helping along while you can?"

"I can't do as much as I'd like. I don't have that much freedom. But they don't challenge me, either, if I don't get in their way. I do as much as I can." He smiled weakly, taking her plate and his to the sinks.

"Did you like it, sweetness? I mean…" Eztli looked up from a large stone pot of some sort of soup she was stirring. Sulwyn briefly wished she could cook even half as well as that.

"Please, 'sweetness' is perfectly fine," smiled Sulwyn. Galahad looked on, drinking milk, a crooked smile playing on his lips. Eztli suddenly pulled

Sulwyn's arm, opened a set of wooden doors, and brought her into a tiny pantry, closing the doors abruptly.

"Are you really Kintana?"

"Please, don't repeat that. I don't know what will happen if that knowledge spreads."

"Then you aren't with the Empire? Right?"

"No. And I never will be," said Sulwyn fiercely. But it was hard to be fierce when another person had squished themself into her, and in a pantry no less.

"I think I can like you," Eztli smiled widely, opening the pantry door. They both stumbled out, earning a laugh from Galahad.

"If you're done conspiring with the spices, our lady needs a tour." Galahad bowed deeply to Eztli and Nori, leading Sulwyn out of the kitchen. Sulwyn waved frantically for a moment, shuffling out loudly as she went.

Galahad did not speak again until they were safely in his room. The door closed behind him and he turned to Sulwyn. A flicker of worry and anger crossed his face. But he only sighed, crossing the room to stand in front of her, his hands resting gently on her shoulders.

"Why would you go out alone?"

"I needed to try and find him," said Sulwyn instantly. She knew he would berate her. But she didn't care.

"This castle is not safe for someone like you."

"I can defend myself, you know that," said Sulwyn indignantly.

"That's the problem, Sulwyn. You cannot make a scene. Listen, we need to be vigilant. They don't expect to control you right away. But I think they really do believe they can. They changed an entire land. To them, one woman wouldn't be a problem. And at this moment you need to maintain the appearance that you are trying, that their story is real. That you were and had been kidnapped and tortured and brainwashed all this time."

"I know. I maintained it with Caldwell, didn't I? I have been showing interest no matter how much it infuriates me."

They were standing closer now. Sulwyn looked up at him, her voice barely a whisper. "I just needed to see him. And I know what you want to say. But regardless of his possible betrayal I still owe my life to him. The least I could do was find him, see him, anything to put my heart to rest."

"Possible?"

"It just doesn't feel right to me...something about his face...and maybe that's just me hoping, but regardless..." she trailed off.

Galahad exhaled, passing a hand over his eyes. "Please, just do not leave on your own next time. Valens Muros is large, larger than anyone could imagine. It's easy to get lost. But I trust your instincts. And I'm happy you ran into Eztli instead of someone else." She felt his thumbs rub her shoulders gently as he looked at her.

They were quiet for a moment, standing in each other's presence, the present task weighing over them. But Sulwyn still had questions. "When was the last time you went down there?"

He held her gaze and she could see it in him. The shadows of all the weeping and screaming and death that he must have faced. "Not since I was let out."

"How long did they keep you there?"

"I don't really know, months? Almost a year? By the time I was let out I had already turned eleven without realizing it."

"I apologize for making you come find me." She placed her hands cautiously over his own. She felt him stiffen as if this kind of interaction was something he feared. She tried to imagine what it must have been like down there. Day after day, with no sense of time, in the dark and cold and screams. It was nothing short of cruel. And she firmly believed he did not get out of there without some sort of damage to his soul and mind. She felt death would have been easier. But Galahad only nodded at her apology, unable to speak.

"I need to give you a tour of the Empire," said Galahad quietly, but neither one moved, the only other sound the soft rushing of water. Instead, they continued to look at each other. "It's where I went this morning.

I had been summoned and given instructions on what you are to see and do before the coronation."

She nodded slightly, but her mind was elsewhere in a conversation she'd had with herself time and time again for the past day. Maybe it was okay to let herself trust him even more than initially. He had seen nothing but pain and hardship. She knew he wasn't an enemy, though she was still unsure if he was a true ally. She could feel something forming between them even though she didn't know what or where it would take her. He continued to look at her with a kindness that seemed hidden deep within himself. What had he seen while living here?

"Let us go, clothes similar to what you are used to having have been prepared for you." He pushed her towards the bathing room.

"Does it look anything like their uniforms? Because I think they're pretty tacky."

Galahad smirked. "No, nothing like that. I chose them. The family that tailors my clothes will tailor yours as well."

"Will that allow me to wear green too?"

"Probably not," he said darkly. She stared at him, waiting for him to explain. "Green had been a prominent colour of my clan since way before the High City was formed and used it as their colour. During my coronation, they gave a pass to let me wear green so that their 'new son may grieve for his clan at the natural disaster that had befallen them.' I would have continued to wear green without their consent. This tailor has permission to keep the dyes of that colour."

Sulwyn smiled widely, "I like that kind of defiance."

"I'm glad you are proud of it. Now get dressed. We have an appearance to maintain."

❧❧

The sky was dark. Pushing through the grey clouds were brown and orange ones. She looked up to the hidden sun, frowning. "It's been a while since acid rain fell."

Galahad looked up as well. "It's not something the Empire really worries about. They've ensured that all their buildings have the best metal roofs and coverage."

"How lucky for them. Have you ever been caught in it before?"

Galahad shook his head. "Where I come from it can't rain like that. And since I've been here, I've never gone outside when it came. You?"

"We got caught in it once. It's only bad if you're in it for longer than an hour or so. But we got rashes after the first half hour. Guess we haven't adapted to it as much as the environment has."

"Then we will keep this tour short. The Empire is fairly easy to navigate, and I only have to show you key points today. Let's go." He held out his arm for her to take and they continued out to the outer walls of Valens to the streets. Sulwyn watched many people scurry about, looking at the sky apprehensively. The Empire seemed like a larger and cleaner version of any city she'd been to.

High-quality brick buildings lined the cobblestone streets; shoppers and workers alike bustled around weaving their way through carriages and horses. They were currently near the outskirts of the Empire, the high mountains of Mortui Gemma in the far distance behind the black-walled borders. Here the castle was buried at the back of the city, the wall of Tranquillum's trees protecting it from behind, and all the Empire defending it from the front.

"How much do you know about the Empire?" He led her along at a brisk pace. People turned to look at them as they passed, whispering and pointing but all still bowing once they laid eyes on Galahad. Sulwyn noticed many Common Ones flitting about their daily work.

"All I know is that everything was updated once the High City fell. The main castle had the most upgrades to reflect their tastes. However, Raghnall said the foundation was something they couldn't change. Proelium Terra was upgraded first with the wooden pole from their first appearance, after displaying the High City king, because Artaxiad and Pandora are extremely dramatic, and other upgrades I'm not too sure about. Something for fighting as opposed to just court." She began to list off as they made their way through the Empire's streets.

"I know the Solus had been there since the High City, but I heard it's worse now. Hmm...there are the Privileged and the Common Ones. Curfew exists for the Common Ones and they all live along the edge within the Empire walls. There are Néosan bases scattered about within and outside the Empire and in other continents. A second castle is around here, and I think that's it..."

"Raghnall taught you this?"

"I read every book he had in his house. He documented everything he could before and after, though vaguely in the off chance that someone discovered them. All real knowledge was in his mind and his mind only."

"He knew a lot."

"He knew everything. No one knew the High City better than he did. I think he knew all the secrets held here...too bad he didn't share them with me."

Galahad looked at her. "I'll share all that I know." He smiled, pulling her to go down a steeper hill. In the distance, she could see another large castle.

"Oh, what are those glowing orb things? Though they aren't glowing now." Sulwyn pointed to one of the many small lighted orbs she had seen when they came back from Antac that night.

"SolarOrbs. Have you heard of them?" Sulwyn gave him a quizzical look. "Have you heard of the Lost World?"

"Vaguely. Raghnall had some books that mentioned it. A friend of ours knew a bit more. But all I know is that it was the world before ours from long ago."

"Artaxiad was or is still obsessed with the Lost World. Any word left about it was that it was a different time, filled with a kind of technology we could never have or achieve again. But a rough timeline states that the world fell into darkness and chaos during something called 'The Shift', where the land of the world became one again. Billions died, but some survived, adapting and evolving. The world we have now is the remaining races after a hundred thousand years. Because of it, various kinds of species of people and animals alike evolved and came about, like my clan or the Velikat. Both of which have been destroyed for the most part by Artaxiad. But there isn't much else written about it. Nothing in real depth or explanation.

"The only thing surviving are these SolarOrbs. Made from a kind of glass that doesn't seem to tarnish or break. Artaxiad tried, but they cannot be recreated. But he scoured the land to find them. I think he still goes out from time to time to try and find more. Of course, he put them on display. There are about three hundred of them and are used in the central part of the Empire."

He pointed to the sky. "They gather energy from the sun, light up at night, and then fade again to absorb energy during the day. Though they probably won't light tonight. He's rather fond of them. I don't think he obsesses over anything more, other than breeding horses."

Galahad pointed ahead of them. "That is the second castle, Eques Muros, where the Uferor reside as well as Captains within the Validus. Training is held here weekly, then the Captains pass it on to the groups they oversee."

"Is this where Caldwell lives too?"

"Sometimes. He lives elsewhere in a small house somewhere near the edge of the Empire. He doesn't like people."

"You both seem similar in that sense."

"Maybe, but I don't like him. We stay out of each other's business for the most part. And he despises me. We have mutual hate."

They stood at the end of the hill, Eques Muros looming in the distance. It was simpler than Valens. Higher but not as wide, plainer, and built with heavy red stone. Sulwyn spotted Validus and Néosan alike come and go across the wide stretch of training grounds, some in groups and some alone.

Galahad led her along another path, away from the castle. As they walked, it became more desolate. The large stores grew fewer, making way for cart stands and handmade shops with small, tented huts standing behind. She preferred this liveliness of people selling their wares as opposed to the more refined, fancier shops near Valens.

"Are we going towards the Common Ones?"

"Shortcut. Proelium Terra and the Solus are outside the Empire walls."

They continued walking, passing many people in the same dark grey uniform, some in short or long pants or dresses. Galahad continued. "The Common Ones are allowed to live within the Empire, taking up jobs to serve the Privileged. The Empire found this a better idea than having people travel in and out all the time or having unsuspected people visit with possible threats. Anyone wishing to live within the Empire walls must register and go through screening. The Triarchy oversees that."

"Triarchy?"

"A council of three. Created with Artaxiad's permission to deal with less important matters. In my opinion, we deal with everything."

"You're a part of it?"

"I along with two other members. A man named Gwydion joined a little over thirteen years ago, before I was added. I've never actually met him properly, only seen his shadow or glimpsed him in the distance, and I don't know much about him, besides the fact that he aided Artaxiad in the killings of the Velikat. I don't trust him. Scholar or something." He waved his hand dismissively then hesitated, looking at her.

"The other member is actually Raghnall's younger brother, who was in charge of creating the Triarchy."

Sulwyn stopped walking, looking at him. But Galahad looked away to a Néosan at the gates. Though it only felt like a few minutes, it had taken them over an hour to reach the north end past Eques. They had reached the edge of the Empire walls near one of the side entrances. Galahad went to speak to a lone Néosan, who saluted, running off to somewhere she couldn't see.

"Horses," said Galahad as the man came back a few minutes later bringing one dark steed.

"Sorry sir, Daijiro had an assignment east of here and took the other horses with Uferor Divi. There is only one." He spoke to Galahad but kept glancing at her. She straightened, keeping her face impassive.

"It's fine, you can return," said Galahad. The Néosan saluted, returning to his post.

Galahad gestured for Sulwyn to mount first before sitting behind her. He reached in front of her, taking the reins. Her back stiffened, but she relaxed soon after from the subtle warmth of his chest. The Néosan pulled open the low gate, letting Galahad take off at a gallop.

As soon as they were out of earshot, Sulwyn spoke, "Raghnall's brother?"

"Did you not know of him?"

"He mentioned he had two but that one died and the other he never spoke to after that."

"His name is Nero. He was part of the High City under Raghnall. I don't know much about their relationship other than that Nero hates him." Sulwyn could feel the tension rising in Galahad. "Nero was there during the attack on my clan. He was the one who tried to beat me into telling them about our secrets after they brought me to the lower dungeons...though I don't remember much of it." Sulwyn tried to look at him, but he kept his arms firmly in place.

"We will go to Proelium Terra first, then the Solus," he said firmly, ending that topic. "I'll cut it short today. The wind is starting to itch, isn't it?"

Sulwyn looked up; the clouds had gotten darker still. Now that he mentioned it, she could feel the slight burn in the wind as it picked up. "What about the Common Ones? Are they allowed to stop working when the acid rain comes?"

"Acid rain, yes. It would cost too much if they or their goods were damaged. For other weather, no. Hold on," said Galahad as he urged the horse from a trot to a gallop.

Soon they hit hard stone, leaving the sand and grass behind. She saw it now, the massive structure of the Proelium Terra. It had been a small mountain, the rock easier to cut here. Once Artaxiad took over he reshaped the land, hollowing it out for a battleground. Galahad turned the horse, leading them up and around the mountain in a curve. The steps became shallow and wide, forcing the horse to slow to accommodate the change. Steadily, they went until a large hole in the wall was visible. Galahad turned to enter a long tunnel. The sound of hooves against hard rock echoed around them, the light getting brighter until Galahad pulled the reins and stopped the horse just at the entrance to the stairs.

Sulwyn looked around her. Benches, carved out, rose from the ground surrounding the entire area in an oval for spectating. In the middle was a large terrain of dirt, sand, grass, and stone. Trees littered the land as obstacles, alongside large boulders.

"Created mainly as a stage to watch battles, though they aren't common anymore. It is also used for the bi-monthly trials and really anything else they want. Like your reveal."

"And to advertise Raghnall's death," said Sulwyn, locating the tremendous precipice of the mountain that rose on the far left corner, creating a stage within a stage, where Artaxiad and Pandora must sit for all events.

"Do you sit up there too, then?"

"No. I stay on the lower level, mainly to make sure the prisoners don't get too wild. The middle level is for the Privileged, the lower and higher levels are for anyone else. The lower levels don't always fill up because some fights have extended towards those seats and caused injury in the past." A sudden burst of wind suddenly stung her eyes. Galahad squinted as well. "Let us hurry."

Galahad turned the horse around, going back the way they had come. Once out and down he veered west, picking up speed.

"Is the Solus located outside of the Empire as well?"

"Yes, to the east of Proelium Terra. But it's still within a good distance in case of an emergency." She felt Galahad look up urging the horse faster. He became silent, concentrating.

With grace, Galahad led the horse along a path of gravel through rough stones and bordering trees, barely grazing branches as they passed. She added leading a horse better than her to her growing list.

"Why are you scowling?" asked Galahad, the trees starting to thin.

"I'm not."

"But...you are?" She could hear the humour in his tone but turned her attention to the building coming into full view.

A massive squared slate building loomed in front of them, surrounded by a solid barrier of iron with barbed wire atop it. Sulwyn could see the heavily guarded entrance and uniforms of blue as well as the standard Néosan colours.

"The blue ones are Protectors. They are on par with the Validus," said Galahad, slowing the horse to a trot. Two men stepped forward, saluting, just as he brought the horse to a full stop. Sulwyn slid off after Galahad.

One bowed to them both before speaking. "We heard you were bringing the princess today. You currently have special permission from King Artaxiad to enter. However, I was told to remind you...you are not to go near the prison holds. Please remain only at the front."

"I know. I won't, and we won't be staying long. The acid rain is upon us. I suggest you change into your metals."

The men bowed again, one knocking hard on the iron door. After a few moments, the door slowly swung open, allowing them entrance.

"Are people normally not allowed in here?" asked Sulwyn, stepping past the thick iron walls and onto a small gravel path ahead. A vast space of trees and tall grass greeted them before they reached the high slate walls. Under a small roof, a single iron door stood before them with two other Protectors standing guard next to it. They bowed to Galahad before opening the doors.

"The Leaders of the Uferor rotate each month, staying and supervising in turns. Artaxiad and Pandora make an appearance once a year. Captains also interchange. Then there are some Common Ones who work under the Protectors as lesser guards; people that we think would have been a waste of strength and skill as shopkeepers or anything else. I'm specifically not allowed here."

Sulwyn glanced at Galahad. That same expression of wicked darkness haunted his gaze. Looking away, she took in the surroundings. The ceilings were low, the lighting dim. They had entered a small, square space fit for no more than about five people. As they continued, the stone walls narrowed further until she was walking in front of Galahad.

On and on they walked, their boots echoing against the stone until finally another door was before them. Sulwyn pulled on it, but it wouldn't open. Galahad reached forward, knocking once, pausing, knocking another three times, then once more. Two knocks were received. Galahad pulled Sulwyn back before the door swung outward.

Stepping in, she saw a few Protectors standing guard alongside Common Ones in grey. Instead of the path continuing forward it went farther underground. Everyone bowed as Galahad and Sulwyn descended.

"This is rather elaborate," said Sulwyn quietly. They kept walking down until the ground began to level out and walked farther still. Sulwyn could see other underground paths that strayed off in various directions. But Galahad continued straight.

"This was built by the Zalman clan with assistance from other clans. Before they managed to control the masses, they had dealt with a lot of chaos. Or so the rumour goes. If there was any place that they put all their effort into it was here."

"Even so, there doesn't seem to be that many guards on the outside."

"During Artaxiad's Ascendancy, Nero and Artaxiad spent time bringing order back to the Solus. When Gwydion came around, he enforced it a bit more. Besides the criminals that were already here before the fall, they had thrown in anyone who was a threat to them or allies to the High City. After all of that, no one tried to escape. It's not worth it nor is it easy."

Sulwyn's questions were silenced when they started to climb up a hill. The fact that this was all underground was a little beyond her. Soon it levelled out again, bringing them outside.

"If you were to look at the very top of the Solus it would look like a maze. The walls continue well past those iron walls and are too high to climb. This is the centre and the only way to get to it is underground."

Sulwyn looked at another wall in front of them. It was high enough to have seven floors of cells upon cells, all next to each other, all atop each other like cages in a giant square. Instantly, many men and women started to yell and jeer.

"I cannot step closer. I ask that you do not as well. Behind us, hidden in the walls, are the barracks for the guards. There are thick, solid walls behind each cell, reinforced with steel. During their daily exercises, sections get released at certain times and are taken down the stairs and through the tunnels to go into the inner garden area behind the cells you see in front of us, in an enclosed space. It looks much like this outside part. Guards don't normally interact with them aside from mealtime." But Sulwyn had stopped listening to Galahad and instead started listening to the voices.

"Get your filth away from here!"

"Murdering scum!"

"Shame to your clan!

"Son of the Empire! Die with them!"

"Galahad..." She looked at him, but he continued to look at the sky until one voice stirred a reaction.

"You killed my brother! Wait 'till I get out of here one day, boy. You will rue the day you ever stepped into the Empire!" Galahad located the one voice immediately. Sulwyn followed his gaze, but the man turned silent. Despite his anger, he couldn't scream at Galahad anymore. And it was then that the rest became silent as well. Galahad gazed around at each of them, bringing silence to everyone.

"You've seen enough. The rain will start soon. Let us leave," said Galahad through clenched teeth.

Sulwyn continued to look at the prisoners, fear evident in most of their eyes. Some looked confused, probably not knowing who they were. And then some started to look at her.

"Kintana?" whispered someone from the bottom far left. Sulwyn barely heard it, spotting the person but unable to recall who he should be. Galahad stepped in front of her, blocking her from view, the ears around them deaf to the call of her name.

"The rain, Sulwyn..." He looked at her with concern, but she could see his unease. Sulwyn reached down, taking his clenched fists in her own, letting him lead her out.

X

You Know Who You Are

| SULWYN |

A few days had passed since her outer tour of the Empire. Sulwyn had been given a full tour inside the castle, forced to go through fittings, taught the history of the Empire as well as various other lessons on etiquette. Though these were things she had never considered, she did have a penchant for learning, excelling more than anyone would have expected.

They also set up a rather lavish room for her on the floor above their own. It was here Sulwyn felt just one, single twinge of envy. The room was extravagant. As soon as she stepped through the double doors, she noted that one day she would have something like this. But not with the sacrifice their rule came with.

It was far larger than Galahad's room, and though she had only seen Artaxiad's study, she knew it must be one of the larger rooms in Valens. The sitting area packed with soft grey rugs and plush couches of burgundy to one side. A large oak dining table to the other was topped with brass decorations of things she'd never seen. The walls were navy, framed by wispy cream curtains against high windows.

A bathing room the size of Artaxiad's study was tucked away into a corner, and vast sliding doors led the way into her room. It was decorated in similar colours of grey, burgundy, and navy. The bed was large enough to fit a small family and the bookcases were piled with what she assumed was their obnoxious history.

But as inviting as it seemed, everything in that room was cold. Cold, soulless, and a reminder of how many people were killed for Artaxiad and Pandora to stand where they did now. She left as quickly as she entered and made her way back to Galahad's room, where they unhappily prepared for the lunch marked by the large, oak doors to the dining room.

"I can just see them tonight, can't I?" asked Sulwyn, turning away from the large wooden doors to face Galahad. He was wearing a light black jacket with a green tunic and velvet black pants. More formal than she had seen yet, his brown hair was combed back with a far part to the side. She turned away again, her neck warm.

"The last time you saw them together was at your reveal. I'm assuming they want to warn you to behave before tonight's events and decided a lunch would be less threatening than coming straight at you."

"Why do I need to wear a dress for lunch?" She looked down at herself. A flowing, light blue (chicken? shifting? something Galahad said) dress was just one of the many dresses provided. This dress was far less formal than the dress she would wear later, but it was still bothersome to her. Galahad reached forward, touching the light blue accented sleeves atop her shoulder. She looked at him.

"Appearance is everything to them. And as much as you dislike it, it is befitting to your image." He smiled lightly, but all she could do was roll her eyes, attempting to keep her heart rate down. A knock on the other side of the door brought her attention back to the front.

"Breathe, Sulwyn," said Galahad, gently placing a hand on the middle of her back, heat seeping through her spine. The doors swung open, showing her a rather large and luxurious dining room.

A long, walnut table was situated in the centre atop a heavy blue carpet. The walls were an earthy deep brown, decorated with various paintings and mirrors in shining gold frames. Tall windows were draped in heavy dark sea-blue fabrics, open to let in the afternoon sun and breeze. Sulwyn looked at the table itself; she had never seen this much cutlery in her life, even during her etiquette lessons. Why were there so many? Was she supposed to use them all?

Sulwyn noted that Artaxiad and Pandora had yet to arrive. She released a deep sigh, letting Galahad guide her to sit at one of the middle seats far from the ends. He pushed in her chair before sitting to her left. Sulwyn could hear the servants working just beyond the other side of another door. She turned slightly to Galahad, who had been watching her carefully.

"Just be yourself," he whispered as a bell chimed somewhere. Immediately his face became impassive once more. He straightened his back, looking to the side. Sulwyn, too, sat straight, following his gaze as two maids opened the door.

Artaxiad led Pandora in with so much grace and poise she almost forgot he was a murdering tyrant. Instantly he looked at her.

Pandora looked so much like her it made her skin crawl. But somehow, she felt this fact irritated Pandora more. She glared at Sulwyn just like she had done the first time she saw her.

Galahad stood swiftly, bowing to them both. But Sulwyn remained seated, observing them.

Artaxiad pushed in Pandora's chair at the right end of the table before taking his seat on the far left. So much space was between them. Sulwyn highly doubted there was anything like love between them. What a stupid thing to be thinking of now. Like they knew what love was.

"I've been told you have been learning well," said Artaxiad conversationally as the servants immediately began to dish out soups. She watched silently as he shook the folds of his napkin, tucking it into the collar of his dark, blood-red shirt. The clothes they wore, with intricate gold patterns and tiny gems of every colour to match, were far more elaborate than anyone else's she had ever seen, even Galahad. She wondered how many people it took to make their clothes.

But Sulwyn didn't answer Artaxiad and instead turned her attention to the young man ladling out her rich cream soup. Galahad coughed. "She's read about a quarter of the books we've given her within the week, as well as taken lessons to better her etiquette."

"Is that so? I don't see any of it right now," said Pandora lightly, dipping a spoon into her bowl, the steam rising gently to her lips.

"I was taught to display said etiquette when faced with people who deserve it," said Sulwyn suddenly, eating her meal with vigour.

"It's good to be so young, isn't it, Sulwyn? When you have little to worry about. Especially now that you are free." said Artaxiad.

"Free, is it? Are you saying that if I were to leave this castle and the Empire, you'd let me go and do what I like in peace?" She put her fork down, looking at Artaxiad. She hated the way he looked at her. It was then that she remembered the scars on his face. "Who did that to your face? It wasn't Raghnall." At this she noticed Galahad stiffen, his face showing even less emotion. She had said something wrong.

"Of course not. Raghnall could never reach your king. Not being the coward he was. But you knew that, didn't you?" said Pandora, smiling at her. Sulwyn had never been so unsettled by a smile more than she was now.

Pandora was the physical embodiment of poison in her eyes. She was beautiful, but there was nothing but hatred and wickedness etched in the shadows of her eyes. Sulwyn understood at this moment more than ever how they had managed to get so far. How they managed to overthrow a thousand-year system and family. She would need to play this game better.

After the soup, silence stretched during the rest of the lavish meal. There were plates of baked meats, cut thinly, their juices sizzling. Deep brown breads with tomatoes and other vegetables baked within and bowls of lightly scented rice topped with tiny leaves and berries were amongst a variety of other foods she'd never seen before. She'd never admit how much she savoured this meal.

But finally, the lunch was at its end and tea was being served.

"He begged, you know," started Pandora conversationally, taking a small amount of pink cake onto her fork.

Sulwyn turned to her. She was smiling, but there was something far more sinister in her eyes. Like how prey watched their food. "He was just, so upset that we didn't uphold our end of the deal. To bring him back into power in the Empire in exchange for, what was it? Setting you free?" She tutted, frowning. Sulwyn clenched her own fork.

"Raghnall would never beg and definitely not to someone like you," spat Sulwyn.

"Wouldn't he? All those months of planning in advance." Sulwyn stilled, her heart hammering in her chest. "Ah, look at you. You know *exactly* what I'm talking about. You knew all along something was happening, but you chose to ignore it. To put trust in what? In the great Steel Warrior?" Pandora sipped her tea. "He was a coward. He lusted after power just like anyone else." Pandora stood up, tossing her napkin to the ground and lifting her cup full of tea. She beckoned one of the maids over.

"What is this?" she asked, never looking the girl in the eyes.

"Strawberry tea, my queen…" murmured the maid.

"I have allergies to strawberries."

"But…you asked for this last week?"

Sulwyn dropped her cup into the saucer sensing danger just as Pandora seethed, whipping the cup against the side of the maid's head.

"Are you talking back to me?" her voice was low and level, but it resonated louder than a scream. A large gash bled on the side of the girl's head, but she didn't dare move, eyes wide. Instead, she bowed and apologized profusely on the spot, her entire body trembling. Pandora turned behind her to look at the table, then picked up the metal teapot. Her dark red hair flowed around her in contrast to the black flowing dress she wore.

Pandora looked Sulwyn in the eyes. Standing before the maid, she opened the pot lid and poured the hot water onto the girl's back. Screams filled the room, but no one dared to move except Sulwyn.

She ran towards the girl now on her knees writhing in pain. Pandora stooped down, ignoring the maid and looking at Sulwyn.

"All it took was a dagger to the heart and the steel was broken," she whispered. Bile rose, burning her throat, but she stayed silent unable to look her in the eyes as Pandora had. The queen gracefully stood, throwing the pot casually to the floor with a thudded clash. Unaffected, Artaxiad walked over, offering his arm to Pandora.

"I look forward to your best behaviour tonight, Sulwyn. It wouldn't do well for anyone if you were to act out at your coronation. We are not unkind. We are giving you freedom amongst us," said Artaxiad nonchalantly. The doors opened as Artaxiad led Pandora out without another glance.

Sulwyn could do nothing but look at their retreating backs in disgust, her eyes burning in rage. She turned to Galahad, still sitting there staring ahead, just as other servants rushed forward with cold towels, pressing them onto the maid's back and head.

"Can you stand?" asked Sulwyn but the girl tried to push Sulwyn away in distress until she bowed in horror, fearing she had been rude. Galahad stood swiftly, bending to take Sulwyn's arm and yanked her up roughly. His expression was empty and emotionless as he dragged her forward and out of the dining room without a word.

"I can help her!" protested Sulwyn, but Galahad never spoke. He continued to rush her along the halls and down the stairs and all the way back until they reached the inside of his room. Closing the door with a snap, he turned to her just as she wrenched her arm out of his grip.

Instantly his face fell. "I'm sorry, Sulwyn. I'm sorry, but we can't. I can't. Those people, did you not see the fear they hold towards us?" Sulwyn felt a sense of foreboding at the sudden change in his emotions. Before he had just as much expression as Artaxiad while watching Pandora. Now he was full of various emotions she couldn't read. She stepped back.

"Eztli and Nori trust you, though?"

"They are a different case; I was involved with their lives. I cannot extend the same thing to everyone. I have to maintain some sort of restraint."

"And does this"—she gestured around her frantically—"does stuff like this happen often?" Her voice was a little higher now.

"Of course it does! Where do you think we are? Who do you think *they* are?"

"You can heal people, can't you?" said Sulwyn incredulously. She had finally made up her mind to trust him a little more, but how did she really know that this, all of this wasn't a lie? He had two faces.

"Only to a certain extent and at a cost. Besides, no one can know about it."

"So you watch? You just…watch while these things happen all around you? While you live protected?"

"I've already explained myself to you. I will not do it again."

"And then when does that end? You are close to them! You could do something! No one else has ever managed to get this close let alone touch them. Save for whoever gave Artaxiad those scars. How long will you continue watching?" exclaimed Sulwyn.

"I gave him half of that scar!" yelled Galahad, a glimmer of madness in his eyes.

Sulwyn froze, her hands falling to her sides.

"He is not untouchable! I was ten when I marked him. And my mother marked the other half just before she died. I am biding my time, Sulwyn. And I will pay for my sins of watching the torture of those around me, when the time is right. But all I can do now is have patience and assist in the shadows when I can. Do not ever believe that I am not ashamed of this!"

Sulwyn had no words to offer and could only continue to stare. A maddening look graced his features as he saw things in his past she could never understand. She flinched at the sudden sound of a loud bell tolling in the distance. One, two, three…it continued to ring, a total of seven times.

"What is that?" she whispered, unable to speak louder.

"The coronation ball is set to start at seven in the evening. We have four hours." He breathed as if he had been running.

And she realized he had been.

Everything he was doing was running towards and away from something they all had been trying to reach for years in their own way.

"Is it essential to make my hair so…elaborate? I mean it's just hair," complained Sulwyn, but Eztli shushed her.

"Galahad said ya'd be a handful, but really, I didn't think it would be this much. Have ya never worn yer hair up?" said Eztli, sticking another pin somewhere in the curls she had set.

Sulwyn scoffed, "No, I haven't. It's pointless. It gives you headaches, and it's pointless." Eztli sniggered as Nori brought out the dress she'd be wearing.

"This is a really nice dress…" said Nori quietly. Sulwyn tried to turn and look at her, but just got smacked for moving.

"Please stay still."

"Sixty-two," said Sulwyn grumpily.

"I don't get it."

"That's how many pins you've got in my hair."

"Well, if ya need to pick a lock, I'm sure I've got ya covered then," said Eztli, placing another pin in her hair. Once her hair and face had been made up, she could finally stand.

Sulwyn moved to bend back and stretch but was slapped on her stomach. Leaning forward, she glared at Eztli.

"Don't make my hard work go to waste!" said Eztli, bringing her forward and pulling the robe off.

"I can dress myself!" said Sulwyn, but to no avail. Sulwyn was now being draped in fancy undergarments before they helped her step into the dress. They made Sulwyn face the mirror as they pulled the ties in the back.

She looked at herself, almost convinced she was seeing someone else. Though her face didn't look much different, her eyes stood out from shades of pinks and black. Half her hair fell gently across her bared shoulders and back, the other half up in ways she could never do herself.

The dress itself was stunning. Even she would admit it. It was rich in quality, thinner to fit the warming weather of soon-to-be-summer but ornate in delicate patterns of gentle red swirls. It was soft, made from fabrics she didn't know the name of. The colour was a deep, night black with the front reaching slightly past her knees. The back trailed out behind her, past her ankles and slightly onto the ground in cascading dark waves. Trimmed around the edges of the top and bottom was crimson lace to match the thick crimson ribbon that they now tied into a medium-sized bow along her mid-back. It trailed down, joining the black folds.

"Taffeta…Galahad has some interesting taste. He should just run away and become a tailor," said Eztli, nodding, walking around Sulwyn and admiring her work.

"Taffeta? Isn't that some sort of sweet?"

"That's taffy…taffeta is the fabric. Taffeta and lace. All the clothes you've been given, I think he's designed most of it," said Eztli, motioning to Nori to get the shoes. Sulwyn was dumbfounded until she was pushed to sit as they grabbed her feet. They weren't too high, leather with one strap around the ankle, red to match the lace.

"Perfect, it's perfect," said Eztli excitedly.

"She looks like Pandora," said Nori darkly. Sulwyn turned to her, but Nori looked away, avoiding her. Sulwyn eyed her suspiciously but put it behind her when the bell tolled again. This time it only rang once.

"What is it now?"

"Time to go. We will escort ya to the entrance yer be goin' through."

"Galahad?"

"He will meet you there, sweetness, relax," she whispered, escorting her out the door.

As Sulwyn walked past the many windows towards the ballroom, she saw hundreds of people entering from the lower entrances. All were dressed in fancy clothes, hats and gloves and capes. She had never seen such a thing. It was only the Empire that could afford to have such pointless parties.

"We need to leave now. See ya inside." Eztli waved, Nori bowing, as they both took off down another path, leaving Sulwyn to face another large wooden door on the second floor.

Silence spread around her as she waited. Looking down, looking ahead. She refused to look behind her, to face the hall in case someone was passing. But no one came. Instead, she listened to the slight murmur of people gathered inside the ballroom.

Suddenly, she heard muffled footsteps behind her. Slowly she turned to see Galahad walking towards her, hands pocketed as he looked outside before turning to her.

Was it because of how he looked?

His brown hair was combed back the same way as before, slightly tousled with a part far to the side. A thin, reddish-gold crown topped his head. His long jacket, the colour of the forest at night with gold-threaded embellishments along the edges, was covered with a modest black shirt and black pants, cotton and fitted.

Was it because of her constant state of confusion and loneliness?

As he walked towards her with poise and purpose, his posture was straight and tall and rather formidable.

Was it because of the night?

The fancy dresses, the party atmosphere and music, were things she had never experienced before, things that a lot of people didn't have the opportunity to indulge in.

Why did her heart beat so fast?

"Are you okay?" he asked gently, stepping next to her. A look of deep concern was clear in his eyes as he looked her over. But she noticed that the edges of his ears and cheeks had a slight pink tinge to them.

"I'm fine. Nervous, I guess? I don't get nervous. But this is new. And all those people…"

"I know you have your doubts about me, so I need you to understand that for tonight I will not be able to help you." He bent down, eyes level with hers, holding her shoulders gently. "I cannot step away from my character. People talk. Now that you are here as the Blood Princess, my title is threatened; I should be furious that I must teach you and aid you. I lose the title of king. I am not next in line anymore, not that that would have happened anyway. But the people don't know that. I will be cold to you. I will have to be impatient, disgruntled, and on edge. Please, do not be dissuaded."

Sulwyn nodded, sobering just a bit.

Who was he, really? His care and his actions, his fire and his ice. How was he able to calm her ever-rising panic but keep her on edge?

"But you need to be strong. Be graceful; show Pandora and Artaxiad all that you've learned this last week. Engage, flirt, and present yourself to the people with poise. Make them love you. Show them that you are their child, that you fit in. That you are finally home from a tragic past. And don't let them get to you. You know who you are." He turned away from her as the crowd cheered, muffled behind the door, the fanfare playing louder at the entrance of Artaxiad and Pandora.

"Normally, Artaxiad and Pandora are last to enter, but because this is for you, they waited until everyone was present. We are next." He straightened, holding his arm out to her.

She took a deep breath.

Even though it was a different setting.

Even though her dress was her current armour.

This was a fight.

A war.

And she was and always would be a fighter.

XI

Curses & Gifts

| SULWYN |

THE doors opened and the sound of trumpets and cheers greeted her ears. She wasn't used to this level of loudness. Most of her days and nights were always spent in a tent or looking out into the wild as they travelled, the loudest environments being the few pubs and inns she and Raghnall had frequented. It made her ears thrum, but soon the assault on her eyes pried her attention away from that.

The room was huge and the most decorative place she had seen thus far. The onyx fan vaulted ceilings were draped in various fabrics of midnight, indigo, and garnet. Tall windows let in the moonlight and stars, while all along the sides and hanging from the ceiling were huge, uniquely crafted brass torches, candelabras, and chandeliers, all shining brightly, casting everyone in a warm orange glow.

Hundreds upon hundreds of pairs of eyes looked at them. Everyone was dressed as lavishly as the room. Wooden tables—long and short, wide and small—littered the black marble floor, all decorated in the same excessive way as the table she'd had lunch on this afternoon.

She looked around, realising she and Galahad stood on a large threshold of sorts, connected to a long set of black marble stairs. She looked at Galahad; his face was expressionless. Gently he pulled her ever so closely, leading her carefully down the stairs. She scanned the area until she found, seated far to the left, Pandora and Artaxiad in large black stone thrones atop a platform. Sulwyn smirked.

She had learned very quickly that Pandora was exceedingly vain, and so they worked to make sure that Sulwyn would outshine her in appearance if nothing else. As gorgeous as Pandora was, her deep violet silk dress with many folds swaying around her, Sulwyn had indeed won this battle. She was impressed with Galahad's taste in design and clothes, something she never thought about or could do. She smiled brightly to Pandora, stepping in front of them. Galahad bowed, but Sulwyn bowed as well.

"A lady does not bow," said Pandora sweetly, but Sulwyn could hear the taunt laced in her voice.

"Forgive me, my queen." Sulwyn curtsied as she had been taught. However, it was in her habit to bow, something she had always done and found harder to shake off. "I had been raised without a mother, without female influence in my life as I was *imprisoned*. Do forgive me." Those that could hear her clapped in approval.

Galahad and Sulwyn took their seats on Artaxiad's left and Sulwyn continued to smile brightly. She would bet everything she owned that Pandora would have liked nothing more than to stab her at that moment.

"Today we celebrate the coronation of our beautiful, long-lost daughter!" cried out Artaxiad, nonplused by the interaction. Many cheered again, raising their fists or glasses in the air. "As you all know, we have finally slain the monster known as the Steel Warrior. A man who stole Sulwyn, imprisoning her and causing her and us great pain and suffering. He did all of this to thwart us. But he knew, deep down, just as the rest know, that we are needed in Vartugaul!" His voice grew in confidence as the rest stared in awe. "No man can bring us down; no man can make our blood suffer!" Artaxiad stood. He beckoned a well-dressed manservant to his side, a thin reddish-gold crown atop the plush burgundy pillow in his hands. The crown matched Galahad's, but instead of a solid thick band, it weaved together lines of vines, red jewels dotting its path. She found it odd, considering neither Artaxiad nor Pandora wore crowns of their own.

Taking the crown, he stood before her and placed it onto her head. "To our daughter Sulwyn, the Lady Princess of Vartugaul!" He picked up his glass to toast, the rest cheering loudly and drinking happily from their glasses. The entire thing felt rather careless, but she wouldn't question the short ceremony. She realised they all just really liked a party.

"Enjoy the night, and if you so please, come and introduce yourselves to Sulwyn." He smiled widely, signalling for the music. The band in the far corner, near the terrace, began their sweet and fluttery music once again. He handed his glass to the manservant before turning and bowing to Pandora, who graciously took his hand to dance, paying no mind to Sulwyn at all.

Couples began to dance; others began to mingle and eat. Galahad rose from his seat, bowing shortly and agitatedly to her before disappearing into the crowd.

Another manservant handed her a glass of wine. Sulwyn took a deep breath, drinking deeply. Sitting for only a moment, she took another long swing before she, too, stood. Sulwyn wasn't sure what to do but slowly walked over to a table that held finger foods and other drinks—something to give her nervous hands to do.

"Psst, sweetness," whispered Eztli, appearing in front of her with a tray of drinks. "Take one. I made these, they're nice." Sulwyn nodded, lifting a glass of some sort of light blue drink and switching it with her glass of wine. Eztli curtsied and winked, taking off again.

Sulwyn observed those dancing and laughing until slowly people came up to her, some in pairs and groups and some alone. But either way, they were all the same to Sulwyn. All of them were like Artaxiad and Pandora. No matter how beautiful they appeared, with their lavish clothes and etiquette, they were all hideous where it counted most.

"You look just like the king and queen. It's amazing that you were hidden all these years," said one lady.

"It's good we have you now," said the lady's friend, "You fit the Empire. We heard about your visit to Antac, with the Validus. You punished some of those traitors, right? Such filth. They should stay underground in the dungeons where they belong. The bi-monthly trials are trivial nonsense that should have been abolished years ago."

"Well, now, our king is a fair man. He needs to give justice to people who deserve it and bring attention to the rotten that don't," countered the lady, laughing all the while as if discussing nice weather.

Another man stepped in. "Well, he should have done that to Raghnall." He spat at the floor. "That man, how he ever got such a title as the 'Steel Warrior.' Weak and cowardly to kidnap a baby. He should have been prostrated before you to beg for forgiveness, fear instilled upon him. I am so sorry for what he must have done to you."

"Lady Princess, we hope that you speak your piece at the trials. The moon only knows we need a firmer hand. Artaxiad and Pandora can only do so much. The prince is soft. He has too much emotion and heart for lesser people, maintaining a passive resolve to conflict. Believes in second chances, but the weak rise when given these kinds of opportunities. They need a firm hand," harped another lady.

Sulwyn gave a high fake laugh of agreement before excusing herself to get another drink, smiling brightly.

This was torture.

She'd rather be facing Caldwell in the dungeon than talking to these mindless people. They were horrible. She had an inkling of what the Empire was like during her journeys with Raghnall, but they only ever really faced Néosan, military men and women forced or chosen to instil the rule of the Empire. She never met the Privileged. Garbage. How could people be so heartless? So cruel? As if they didn't thrive off the sacrifices of those they considered below them. Like they would last a day without them in their privilege.

She found another drink, unable to bring herself to eat. Her tolerance was high, but the event itself was draining. She spotted Galahad sometimes, in the distance interacting with others. He smiled briefly to some, but his stoic face and body were ever-present.

"Princess!" called Caldwell loudly, sliding through the throngs of people. He bowed before her. She would never admit it, but she was happy to see someone relatively familiar. He looked dapper as well, donning a long-sleeved, dark grey jacket with black pants and a purple shirt that ruffled along the chest.

She could see the bandages he wore still underneath, wrapped neatly along his hands. But that didn't matter to her now; she needed a reason for people to stop talking to her. She couldn't hear any more about how they wanted people dead. How they wanted to burn the other towns, eradicate the Common Ones, enslave the prisoners to do even more than they already did. She was starting to feel sick.

"Care to dance?" He held out his hand gracefully and she took it in kind, leaving her glass on a table. The music was light and quick. But she had learned how to dance from Raghnall years ago. So, when they tried to teach her to dance again, she picked it up rather quickly.

"This is nice, isn't it? A different setting to all the violence?" he asked her, but his smile never reached his eyes.

"You are a confusing person, Caldwell," she mumbled as they moved in wide circles. Many looked at them, impressed or in awe, as they cut across the floor. His hand held hers tightly, the other gently on her lower back. He was graceful despite his looks and cruel hand.

"Everyone has their unique traits. I hope you bring some excitement to the Empire, princess. I think it's about time for a good change of pace. If I'm lucky I'll witness it all."

"You dance well."

"As do you. It's not that hard to learn if you think about it. You have to fight with precise movement and emotion. It's almost the same." He smirked, their dance ending, the song changing to a slower one. Sulwyn was unsure if she was meant to continue with Caldwell, but Galahad showed up behind him.

"Finally going to have a dance with the Lady Princess, are we?" said Caldwell, rubbing a finger across his lips. "About time, don't you think? Our lady seemed a little overwhelmed thanks to all the people swarming about her. Take care." He waved them off as Sulwyn stared after him, watching him talk to other guests.

Had he purposely intercepted her conversations?

Sulwyn looked away once Galahad placed his arm around her waist, bringing her closer than she had been with Caldwell. His breath tickled the top of her head, gentle and paced with the music. He took her other hand and led her slowly to the beat.

They didn't speak.

Sulwyn looked up at him a few times; his eyes held unasked questions as her eyes held the answers. When the music ended, he bowed, taking off elsewhere yet again. But she felt warmer now, a little of her unease lessened. After a few moments, a voice called to her.

"Sulwyn, please come to my side," said Artaxiad from somewhere behind, coming towards her and handing her a new drink. Reluctantly, she took it.

She spent most of the night trying to avoid him or Pandora, but it seemed her luck had run out and with perfect timing, she could feel the heat of a fever start to rise within her. Sulwyn laughed a little to herself. It had been a year since her last premonition, and it chose now to show up?

Following behind him, he began to introduce her to a few more important people. Or that's who she figured they were. She had no idea and at this point, they may have well been the same person. She took a sip of the drink and paused.

"Is something wrong?" he asked curiously. She raised her eyes to him, smiling.

He had drugged this.

The bastard.

One sip wouldn't be enough to affect her but mixed with the amount of alcohol she had already consumed; she could not drink any more of this.

"Oh, nothing at all! This is just so much at once, this event." She waved an arm and turned to the faceless men and women in front of her. "As you know I haven't had the opportunity to experience anything like this before. It is a little taxing." She smiled again, and they laughed with her, encouraging her that she was doing well and how much of a delight she was. Eventually, she managed to excuse herself once more and dispose of the drink in a large potted plant unnoticed.

What was he playing at? Why would he want to drug her?

Hours after, late into the night, Artaxiad called for everyone's attention, "I deeply thank you all for coming tonight to meet our Lady Princess. I hope you had the chance to get to know her just as we have. There will be plenty of chances to meet with her again." The crowd, now full of food and drink, cheered louder than before.

"Those of you who join us will see us again at the bi-monthly trials three days from now. We look forward to seeing you there and to seeing Sulwyn there as well. We hope she will be a great new asset in judging the people fairly. I thank you all again and I hope that you leave here with full stomachs and light hearts!" He raised his glass as they all toasted one last time before starting to take their leave. Sulwyn followed suit, seeing the people off in a line alongside Artaxiad, Pandora, and Galahad. The servants cleaned up swiftly behind them.

Just as the last person finally left, Pandora marched straight up to Sulwyn, slapping her hard across the face. "Insolent bitch, aren't you? How dare you embarrass me," she hissed.

Sulwyn stood straight, never touching the stinging in her cheek. She was done with this night. She didn't know how much longer she could hold out before her premonition became more prominent; she just wanted to leave. The fever rising higher in her, cold sweat making the fabric of the dress cling to her back. Artaxiad came to Pandora's side, Galahad watching them. The servants around them paused momentarily but continued to work, straining their ears to listen.

"Now, now Pandora, she is still learning. We have lots to teach her, and she has lots to teach us. I'm sure." He looked at her closely, licking his lips.

"I did what I was taught. I'm sorry if I have offended you in any way." With this Sulwyn curtsied, earning another slap from the queen, her gaze hard, before she turned to exit, storming off without Artaxiad.

"She had a bit to drink, as did we all, right, Sulwyn?" He continued to stare at her, but Sulwyn could barely pay attention now, focusing on Eztli in the background taking empty plates away. "Until our next meeting. Galahad, please take care of our princess." He smirked, following Pandora out the lower side doors.

As soon as he left, Sulwyn rushed off to another exit, unable to go back up the stairs.

She needed to go outside, to get away.

As soon as the fresh night air hit her skin, she moved forward over a hedge and vomited.

"Sulwyn?" exclaimed Galahad, who had followed behind her.

He reached forward, moving her hair away from her face.

She tried to turn away, but he wouldn't have it. As soon as the dry heaves stopped, he gently picked her up, cradling her against his chest, and took off at a brisk pace along a small, narrow path surrounded by delicate plants, stone walls, and windows.

Sulwyn could barely pay attention to where they were going and was vaguely aware of when they went back inside, but knew he had taken her to a spare room on the first floor. He laid her against a small cot with panic in his eyes.

"Why? How? How did you get a fever like this?!" Sulwyn couldn't speak, but a violent shiver ran through her. Galahad noticed and rummaged around the room for a blanket.

He gently covered her, tucking in the edges under her body. "This is dangerous, Sulwyn. I can't heal something like this. Please wait," said Galahad, hurriedly brushing loose strands of hair off her forehead. She wanted to tell him to stay, but her voice would not sound.

Sulwyn was not aware of how much time had passed, or if any time had passed at all, but she knew her fever was going to reach its peak soon. Suddenly, she realized she couldn't move.

"So, you did drink it, didn't you? Though you were trained against poison, luck is in my favour tonight. I picked a slow-acting one just in case," came a rough voice near her head.

Cold fear plummeted through her as she felt the pinch of rough binds of ropes along her wrists and ankles. The smell of alcohol wafted over her as Artaxiad's pale green eyes reflected in the moonlight.

This was dangerous. But she wouldn't move. Not yet. He laughed a giddy sort of sound, kneeling atop the bed, straddling her.

"You're so warm, Sulwyn. So young, so beautiful, so powerful…" he spoke out in his drunken stupor. She watched him pull something from his shoe, still in his evening dress. Saw the moon reflect in the blade, as he used it to tear at her dress by her chest.

Her heart started when a loud bang rattled the door in its frame, a large chest of drawers blocking it. He had managed to set up so much in such a short amount of time. Artaxiad looked over for just a moment.

"Did Galahad really think I'd let him have you, like this? Before me?" He turned away from the banging and continued his work on her dress. She felt as he tore at it, pulling at the undergarments and trying to get it loose.

With force, she pulled at the bindings on her wrist. They rubbed and burned against her skin, but she pulled harder and they snapped. Simultaneously, she lifted her hips with all her strength, flipping Artaxiad onto the floor. A crash came from the door, and Galahad froze in the doorframe, his eyes sweeping the scene and connecting with hers. Quickly, she untied her ankles, light flooding the room.

She gripped Artaxiad's wrist, heaving him to his feet, and watching the confusion flit through his eyes. She squeezed hard and twisted it until finally, a satisfying crack resounded and he roared in pain, dropping the knife onto the floor with a clatter.

"How dare you touch me," said Sulwyn, her voice low and hoarse. With every step forward, he took a step back, his anger thwarted by his drunken stupor and inability to think clearly. "How dare you try and have your way with me. I am your blood whether I like it or not. You disgusting man." Sulwyn moved to kick him, but Galahad grabbed Artaxiad roughly, pushing him out of the room. The king stumbled backwards, faltering as he looked at Sulwyn's eyes.

"You!" he sputtered, his face a mix of shock and disbelief.

"Get out!" yelled Sulwyn and he stepped back.

"You will regret this," he spat, stumbling away, smashing things she couldn't see. But her attention faded as she fell forward.

Galahad wrapped his arms around her, holding her up and bringing her back to the bed. He moved to cover her, but she grabbed his wrist, gaining his attention.

"Sulwyn, you should stay down. This fever—" but he stopped when she tightened her grip. He looked at her and gasped.

"Shhh…" she started, her voice in that same low and dangerous tone. "There is another plan at work within the Empire. Another at work, shaping it. To evolve. To grow. But they are not our friend. They are clever. They are strong and allied with someone far more powerful. They lead an unknown group. Evil and cruel. They are not our friend. They are not our friend. Not our friend." Sulwyn coughed.

⚜

| GALAHAD |

Stunned, Galahad watched her eyes fade from green to their usual grey. He placed his hand against her neck; her fever was dropping rapidly. Galahad blinked in confusion, sitting with her slumped against him, deep in sleep. He looked at the broken door.

Quickly he wrapped Sulwyn in the blanket before fixing the door. With haste, he carried her back to his room.

He was stupid.

How could he have left like that when he knew Artaxiad had been watching her all night? He had seen when Sulwyn dumped out the drink into the plant and should have realized then that he would try this with her as he had done to others. He clenched his fists, watching her sleep. The tinkle of the river did nothing to calm him.

Reaching into his pocket, he pulled out the medicine he had retrieved from Eztli. Sighing, he touched the tattered dress, placing the packet on the side table. Her clothes stuck to her with sweat and a small cut ran across the centre of her collarbone.

Galahad rubbed his face in frustration, getting up to retrieve a nightgown from the bathing room along with a bowl of cold water. Carefully, he placed a soft sheet over her before removing her dress.

Slowly he wiped down her arms and legs before he folded the sheet down to reveal the cut. He placed his hand over it, warmth spreading from his hand to her skin, healing it quickly. She grabbed his hand, eyes opening suddenly, but he was not surprised.

"Why did you leave me?" Her voice was strained with unrest.

"Sulwyn...I was careless. I apologize. I went to find you medicine. Fevers that high can kill. Did he drug you?"

"Did you see that?"

"I didn't see everything..."

"I dumped it before it could have any effect. Did you use your power?" she asked quietly, maintaining her hold on his wrist. But it wasn't as strong as before.

He looked at her, confusion rising. What made her ask such a specific question? "No...I restrained myself as much as I could."

"Did he see?"

"See what?"

"Your eyes..." she whispered. Galahad lifted his other hand to his face, "...your eyes were black, Galahad, all the white was black...did I keep his attention away from you?"

Galahad stifled a cry. "Why? Why would you put yourself further in harm's way to keep him from looking at me—is that why you broke his wrist?"

"Partially." He could see the beginning of a small smirk lift the corner of her lips.

"He will find a way to repay you for that..."

"As long as he didn't see your eyes."

"But he saw yours...I think...they were green."

Sulwyn paused. "He doesn't suspect anything like this from me. I'm hoping that he was drunk enough to just forget all of that, really..."

"Sulwyn..." He pulled his wrist out of her hand and held it instead.

"What did I say, Galahad?" He looked at her incredulously, but she sounded defeated. "I have the gift, or curse, whichever you believe, of premonition. What did I say?"

He looked at her curiously and cautiously all at once. "You said there is someone trying to evolve the Empire but is also our enemy. And that they are working with someone powerful."

Sulwyn nodded, shifting to make space on the bed and pulling him down to lay next to her.

"Sulwyn..." he whispered, fear in his voice, but she tightened her grip on his hand. Without a word, she leaned her head against his shoulder and fell back to sleep.

XII

Blood For Bone

"RAGHNALL, close the tent...the sun is bright," grunted Sulwyn, turning onto her stomach. But the rays of light still streaked through her hair, making her eyelids bright red. She moved her hand along the sheets, stopping over a slightly warmer spot. She turned quickly onto her back, lifting herself forward as the sheet fell off, exposing her skin to the rays of light.

Her breathing began to slow as she looked around Galahad's empty room, the tinkling of the small river bringing her back to reality. She pulled the sheet forward, wrapping herself like a cocoon and turning to stare out the high windows. Though most of it was covered in vines and ivy, the sun flitted through, bathing the whole room in light. She missed camping.

A knock brought her attention to the now-open door. "Good afternoon, sweetness. You been sleepin' for about twelve hours, was the ball too much for ya?" Eztli walked in with a tray of fruits and toast, Nori following behind her with a large jug of water.

"Something like that..."

"Well, ya better get up and ready. The bi-monthly trial was moved up a day. Tomorrow instead. We've brought your robe." She held up a dark blue silk robe with gold trimmings.

"Tomorrow? Do changes like that happen often?"

"Maybe? I mean, everything is at their whim, ain't it?" Eztli came to the foot of the bed, only stopping when Sulwyn jumped out from under the sheets.

"Do you always sleep naked?" called Eztli nonchalantly. Nori looked away while Sulwyn streaked to the bathing room. Quickly, she grabbed a nightgown, only to come back and realize she had knocked a folded one off the bed. An uncomfortable heat rose in her neck.

"You should eat. I watched ya a bit last night. Ya drank all and ate none. Don't ya have a headache? Isn't that why Galahad came for medicine?"

Sulwyn looked to the side table; a small brown packet lay unopened. "Oh, I was feeling a little nauseous after all that. That's all." Sulwyn pulled the soft, black nightgown over her head, sitting back down on the bed to eat the toast. Eztli moved forward, reaching into Sulwyn's mess of hair to  take out all the loose hairpins.

"Understandable…Nori, come here and take the pins out."

"I don't want to," said Nori, her voice a little higher than normal. Sulwyn looked at her under Eztli's arm. She realized Nori had been silent since she arrived. But now her whole demeanour had changed. While Nori usually kept her hands folded in front of her, slouched and hidden behind Eztli, she was now angled, slightly poised, and looking at her fingernails. Sulwyn didn't know what else to do but stare. Eztli straightened her back, tense and alert.

"Nori, you are a maid of this Empire and this is the Lady Princess," said Eztli properly, turning to her slightly.

Sulwyn found her introduction to be strange but continued watching Nori, who smirked.

"That's not my problem. I didn't tell anyone to bring me here. You should have just left me at the pleasure house. At least it wasn't always in the same space as that pig."

Sulwyn's jaw dropped, and Eztli stopped pulling out pins. Sulwyn looked at Eztli, her expression a mix of understanding and fear unusual for her. "Don't get Nori in trouble…you are lucky we are in a safe space right now," mumbled Eztli, facing Nori fully.

"I'm the one that ends up facing the trouble anyway. I should be allowed to act how I like. Besides, Nori doesn't trust her," she sneered, pointing to Sulwyn and looking her straight in the eyes.

And it suddenly dawned on Sulwyn.

"What's your name? I've already met Nori. She seems kind. I have no ill intentions towards her," said Sulwyn. Eztli turned to her in shock.

"You're just as smart as they say, Kintana," said Nori, bowing gracefully. "Duri, not at your service. I don't get to visit often. Please don't sentence me to death." Duri winked but instantly moved back. Eztli stepped towards her, hand raised.

"Go back. Nori doesn't need ya out right now. This be bad timing, it is. The king is furious. Don't make me beat you back in."

"Why is he furious?" asked Sulwyn. The same cold fear from before crawling through her. Galahad had warned her. But she had had no other choice at the time.

"No one knows. The king left to another town early this morning, but other maids found the halls trashed. No one else would dare do that besides him," said Eztli, glaring at Duri.

"I bet I know who the culprit is. Nori watched her all night and he was watching her as well," said Duri, pointing at Sulwyn again.

Sulwyn watched Duri walk forward, raising her leg and stepping up directly onto the bed. The food tray sank, Duri bending forward to take grapes from the bowl. Seeing Nori, with her innocent round face and eyes that rarely made eye contact, stare at her with such defiance and attitude was a little unsettling.

"Why was she watching me?"

" 'Cause you use magic," she whispered dangerously. "She thinks you're a Devinal, but I don't share the same opinion." She bent forward again, this time taking Sulwyn's hand in her own, inspecting her palm.

"No," said Sulwyn quietly.

Duri smirked wider now, pulling Sulwyn's hand closer. In the Devinal tongue, Duri quickly whispered words under her breath. In a slow build,

Sulwyn felt painful tiny pinpricks start from her fingertips and threaten to crawl up her arm.

"Get out!" thundered Galahad suddenly from the doorway, startling Duri. Her eyes rolled back as she fell backwards onto the bed, the grapes falling from her hand as she lay unconscious.

Eztli panicking before she slapped Duri's face a couple of times. Duri began to stir, but Sulwyn noticed her look of dread. Nori had come back. Eztli turned to Sulwyn.

"I'm sorry. Another mind sleeps in her. Please don't punish her." she whispered, beginning to curtsy instinctively.

"Why would I do that?" began Sulwyn, but Galahad was fuming.

"Do not make me repeat myself," he growled. Nori swiftly got to her feet, eyes full of confusion, but she curtsied deeply. Both scurried out of the room, and Galahad closed the door behind them.

"That was uncalled for," said Sulwyn looking at him carefully. He was agitated and clearly on edge.

"Do you remember what we talked about last night? That could mean anyone."

"I don't think it's them," said Sulwyn calmly, then glared at him. His anger defused under it, groaning loudly.

"In all the years, no one wanted to come in here. And now these two requested it of me. They're bold." He walked towards her.

"You don't mean that." Sulwyn shifted over as he took a seat in front of her, the tray dipping once again. She continued to eat the toast and fruit, Galahad pouring her water.

"We have to be careful, Sulwyn...that's all. I never would have guessed that Nori was a Devinal or that she had another personality. Her other self better keep those facts hidden."

"What happened this morning?" She began to pick out the other hairpins between mouthfuls. He wasn't asking her anything about last night, and this made her uneasy.

"Artaxiad left in a rage. We know why, but I don't know where or what he plans to do. The date of the bi-monthly changing doesn't happen often unless there was a good reason for it. He's usually very precise with days and time."

"Is that why he has a million clocks in his room?"

"He's obsessed with time, with youth, and with power. Having him change the date even by one day is out of character. He is going to come at you with something. You need to be prepared."

"There really isn't anything left for me to do but go forward. They want me on their side. He can't do anything that seriously harms me."

"Don't underestimate him, Sulwyn. Pandora seems like the tyrant but she's calculated; Artaxiad is truly mad."

"As I've been told…" said Sulwyn, quietly looking down. She felt Galahad's intense gaze on her.

"Are you alright?"

"You aren't asking me about…about anything…" She looked at him carefully. But he didn't seem fazed by her ability at all. And somehow that didn't surprise her as much as she thought it would.

"It's not…a common ability, premonition. But it's not unheard of. I of all people have no right to judge someone based on an ability they can't control." He smiled at her. "But the fever?"

Sulwyn found herself smiling as well, "Raghnall had me try to suppress it, to hide it in case it was used to spot me. I haven't had one in a long time. There isn't a fixed time to when they come either. But it scares people. I should have realized it wouldn't matter to you.

"We don't know the origin of my ability. But a Devinal we know thinks it might be from Artaxiad's side. The fevers are a defence, a warning. Because I can't remember what I see or say, nor do I have any control over when it happens. My strength, hearing, and overall physical ability are enhanced slightly at the peak of the fever, like an adrenaline rush. If I'm in danger, I can use it. But once the vision starts, I'm knocked out. And, well…sleep to regain the excessive use of energy."

"And you don't remember them?"

"Never. I don't know if I can change that, but unless I'm told about it, I won't know what it was. Only that I've had one. Raghnall told me that on the first morning after he saved me, I had a premonition. But since I couldn't speak, I'll never know what it was. The next one after that was when I was five. It was something trivial; I don't even remember it anymore."

Galahad looked at her thoughtfully. "I'm sure there is a way to find out what that first one was. But I know someone who could tell you about your power. If you can find out, do you want to?"

"Might as well. The visions vary between actual visions or warnings. So it might be useful to see if I can also learn how to control it enough to remember it, or at least not fall unconscious because of it."

He nodded in understanding, taking the pile of hairpins off the bed and putting them onto the side table, "Let us be vigilant; this is a good thing. There are many people here that come and go. At least this gives us a target."

"But do I need to wear the robe...?" asked Sulwyn, suddenly pointing to the dark blue fabric draped across the foot of the bed.

❦❧

The clouds hung over them in a thick overcast. Sulwyn could smell rain in the air. She rode with Galahad again, watching many others on horses, walking, or in carriages go the same way. As they approached the lower grounds of the Proelium Terra, a few Néosan stepped forward, blocking their path to the stairs.

The horse shifted under them as two men bowed, holding out a roll of vellum. Confused, Galahad took it, unrolled it, and read. Sulwyn turned to read as well, but her question was answered immediately.

"What do you mean I cannot enter?" asked Galahad, dismounting the horse. Sulwyn followed, watching hundreds of people in lines to enter on various floors. She looked down at the sheaf of vellum. Not only one, but three signatures were scrawled across the bottom.

"The king has consulted with the other members of the Triarchy to have you sit this one out," said a voice behind them. Caldwell looked over Galahad's shoulder at the signatures. "That was really fast of them, actually. I heard our king only recently proposed this."

"On what grounds?" said Galahad through gritted teeth.

"Doesn't it say?"

"It doesn't say anything besides my banishment from this trial and any other trial henceforth until further notice."

"Ah, does the king not share those things with you? You'd think being prince would give you *some* entitlement."

Galahad crushed the letter in his fist, turning to face Caldwell. "Did you have a say in this too?"

"I think you finally feel a little threatened in your title there. No. I had nothing to do with this, as much as I wish I did. The king felt it necessary to give the Lady Princess a chance to prove herself without your guidance. Now come, princess." He held his arm out to her. Sulwyn hesitated for a moment, looking at Galahad.

"Please, guide me well," said Sulwyn, gracefully taking Caldwell's arm. She could feel the intensity of Galahad's gaze but kept walking forward, the dark blue robe blowing around her legs as the wind picked up. Maybe if it began to pour insane amounts of rain, this whole thing would be cancelled.

"Are we not going up the stairs?"

"No, no. We are part of the panel this time. The others of the Triarchy are not available now, so we have been given the opportunity instead. Aren't you excited?" He smiled at her, but she didn't feel his excitement at all. He fell into silence as he guided her through the tunnel and down along the rows of carved-out seats. Finally, they reached the very edge overlooking the unused terrain. Néosan surrounded the area, but Sulwyn could see no prisoners.

Two elaborate seats had been set up for them facing a lower slab of the mountain, closer to the ground where Artaxiad and Pandora sat waiting. Sulwyn took her place, watching as many others did as well. She recognized many from the ball and remembered their disgusting personalities. They probably looked forward to this more than anything. A chance to feel righteous in their actions.

"Don't glare at the people, Sulwyn. They are *your* people. If you want them to like you, you need to fit in a bit. Don't ruin the reputation you built for yourself at the coronation." Caldwell gave her a meaningful glance, but she still couldn't see his sincerity in the whole thing. Was he hiding his true self as well?

"Oh? What happened to Artaxiad's arm?" said Caldwell, pointing. Sulwyn's heart dropped as she turned to look. Sure enough, she could see his right arm was heavily bandaged and held up by a sling.

A gong resonated in the Proelium Terra, bringing silence down on them all. Sulwyn couldn't deny that Artaxiad was a commanding presence. Everyone around her stood up and looked at him in awe and captivation. She remained sitting as he spoke.

"Thank you for joining us again for our bi-monthly trial. I know many of you think this is something that should be abolished, but I believe in second chances for those who deserve it." He spoke clearly.

Everyone hung onto his words like they were something of a miracle. "I ask you all to please feel free to express your public opinion of those on trial today. The people matter! You all matter! Without this, without your voice, we wouldn't be able to maintain peace and unity. You are what makes the Empire strong! So please, let us go forth in hopes that we can rid ourselves of people who poison Vartugaul." A cheer erupted around them, echoing into the dark and cloudy sky.

"Get ready, Lady Princess," Caldwell smirked.

"First on trial today," echoed a loud elderly voice for all of them to hear. Sulwyn heard the clank of chains before two Néosan dragged a slightly older man forward from somewhere unseen. He looked as if he had been starved and beaten, but she could see the hate and defiance etched in his face as he was unceremoniously tossed into the centre of grass and sand. Boos and jeers surrounded them. How could they behave like this before they even knew what he did and if he did it?

"Reported for stealing food and bringing harm to the Néosan on rotation in his town," called the old voice. Instantly the man began to yell out at them.

"I did nothing! *They* infiltrated *my* store, stealing *my* food!"

"Please explain your reason for harming them," said the old voice.

"I didn't touch 'em! They knocked over my shelving and tripped on their own!"

"Are you insinuating that our men are clumsy? That they are low enough to steal food from their own people?" spoke Pandora suddenly, her voice low and dangerous. And everyone held their breath at her words. "You have brought harm onto men who stand and protect you. I vote that he be sentenced to the lower dungeons," said Pandora uncaringly.

Sulwyn looked up at Pandora, who never once looked at the man in front of them, instead crossing her legs, looking to the sky. Sulwyn was foolish to believe that any sort of justice would remain here.

"All in agreeance with Queen Pandora's sentencing?" asked the old voice. The people around them called "yes" in unison, as did Artaxiad. The man's shriek filled the area, echoing around them in howled injustice.

"You will fall, Artaxiad! You will bring us all down!" screamed the man thrashing in the arms of the Néosan. They whacked him across the chest and head, silencing him, dragging him back the way they had come.

Sulwyn swallowed hard. Did anyone ever get pardoned here? Was that a concept they knew about?

"Second. A possible Devinal charged with the murder of her entire town," called the voice, and the Néosan were back. Sulwyn's eyes widened as they led an incredibly young girl with dark sapphire hair, her arms wrapped across her chest, bound in chains, to the centre. Immediately the sounds of the crowd changed into hisses and fear.

"You know, I personally never had a problem with the idea of Devinal. There was never any real proof that they brought the fall of the Lost World," said Caldwell, crossing his arms, "and if they did, well that's quite the power, isn't it? The power to bring down the world."

Sulwyn glanced at Caldwell before looking at Pandora. She had leaned forward in interest. Her hand up for silence, the hissing stopped.

"This girl? Killed her entire town? How?"

The old voice answered, "A survivor who was away on the day of the incident came home to the result and claims that the town fell into madness at her hand."

Sulwyn held her breath as a quiet but clear voice echoed through her mind: *"Nice to meet you, Sulwyn. Or should I say 'Kintana?'"*

Sulwyn stared at the girl, who was looking down at her own feet. But ever so subtly she looked up through the curtain of hair, one eye bright orange, the other dark green, connecting with Sulwyn's evenly grey ones.

"Are you a Devinal?" thought Sulwyn. She looked around. No one else seemed to hear. Was she imagining this?

"You are not crazy, Sulwyn. And I am not a Devinal. I can read the soul's mind and speak to it like this."

"Did you really kill your town?"

Sulwyn watched the girl's shoulders droop slightly. *"I don't have total control over my powers. I was attacked while my grandfather was away. I can manipulate the way a soul feels. It caused panic and chaos, and everyone killed each other or themselves."*

That was not something Sulwyn expected to hear. Left unchecked, a power like hers could be extremely dangerous. But Sulwyn could see tears streaming down her cheeks.

"Lady Princess?" said Caldwell, nudging gently. She looked at him and then at Pandora and Artaxiad.

"Sulwyn, what is your take on this?" asked Artaxiad calmly.

Sulwyn hesitated for a moment, "I don't think she has any sort of magic in her. Based on the recorded attributes of a Devinal she doesn't fit the profile. If she were, she wouldn't be here right now."

Artaxiad inclined his head to her. "That is a well-made point." The people around her began to whisper at this, slowly agreeing.

"They like your statement. Everyone does."

"Can I trust you?"

"More than them, I think. I don't mean harm onto anyone," said the girl softly in her mind. And somehow Sulwyn knew, could feel, that this was the truth.

"A town running wild isn't unheard of. It happens all the time with the… lower…people of this land. The ones who are uneducated, like us." Every word made her cringe, but she could see she was winning this one.

"Pandora is intrigued by the mystery around me. She's considering positions in Valens Muros."

"I suggest we monitor her. She can be a maid in Valens Muros and I'll take responsibility for her actions and training," said Sulwyn, her lips hiding a smile at Pandora's slightly unsettled expression.

"She dislikes that you seem to have a similar thought process. But the public response is far too great for her to overthrow it without making a scene. And she finds me mysterious."

"Fine. I agree with your suggestion," said Pandora begrudgingly.

The old voice called out again, "All in favour of this decision?" Those in the stadium called in agreed unison. Shortly after, Eztli ran forward, taking the girl with her and shooing the Néosan away.

"What is your name?" concentrated Sulwyn, hoping this was how it worked.

The girl giggled in response. *"That is how it works. Call out for me. If I'm close, I can hear you. My name is Arsinone. Thank you for saving me. I hope to see you again!"* Sulwyn watched the girl follow Eztli closely after being unchained, but she stopped to curtsy to her before continuing.

"You have an eye for distinguishing between fact and baseless rumour," said Artaxiad. Sulwyn raised an eyebrow. Didn't they just sentence a man based on nothing? She was sure the only reason they spared Arsinone was because her past was full of bloodshed.

"I thought as she is still young, we could use her. Especially if there may be something different about her," gritted Sulwyn, but she smiled all the same. Artaxiad smiled as well, waving his hand to continue. More Néosan came forward, bringing with them the imposters from Antac. Sulwyn sat a bit straighter. Her heart was beating quickly.

"These men and women are accused of impersonating Néosan and using the title for their own gain in the Neuore town, Antac." The boos and jeers erupted again, but this time they were far stronger and angrier.

"How dare they mock the Empire!" yelled someone as others agreed.

"Shame! Shame! Shame!" they cried, and Artaxiad stood up, waving his arm for silence.

"Sulwyn, I want you to conduct this case," he spoke, and she stood swiftly, a rise of adrenaline flowing through her.

The boos and jeers melted in the background for her. Artaxiad, Pandora, and Caldwell fell away from her peripheral. All she could see in front of her were the men and women responsible for the deaths of innocent people. And maybe for the deaths of countless others she was not aware of. But she would find out.

"They killed for their own gain. Terrorized an important town while wearing makeshift versions of the Néosan uniform." She thought that these criminals didn't act differently from the official Empire; but in her position, she couldn't go after the Empire yet. However, she could openly do something about them. She could make them pay for what they had done.

"I think it's befitting that they serve time in the Solus like proper criminals. They killed and slandered us," Sulwyn spoke clearly and loudly and realized the crowd was cheering at her words. Instinctively, she held her hand up and was shocked that she commanded the same silence as Pandora and Artaxiad. She frowned at herself and her actions.

"I believe they might be part of something bigger. And I would like the chance to investigate them while they are at the Solus." She looked up to Artaxiad, surprised to see him smiling so widely.

"I agree with this." Artaxiad responded. The unseen voice confirming the agreement of the crowd. The same woman from before began to cry again, but a sense of empowerment and justice rose in Sulwyn.

Swiftly, Sulwyn jumped over the stone barrier of her seat, into the grounds of the Proelium Terra and walked straight up to her.

"I warned you, didn't I?" seethed Sulwyn. "I will find out who else is part of this and I will make this a living hell for all of you."

"Vile! You vile woman! You are scum like your parents! You will die!" screamed the woman hysterically. Néosan dragged them away.

Sulwyn breathed heavily, a sense of confusion and foreboding growing in her. She hated being compared to them. But the woman wasn't exactly wrong either. Was she born with blood as dark as them?

"Our final trial for the day," called the voice as Sulwyn turned. Now that she was down centre, she could see a large iron gate in front of her, a tunnel under the seats. Out came a family of four led by Néosan to the centre. She was rooted to the spot as they walked closer and closer. The old man's voice rang out around the grounds, reverberating in her mind, and yet she only heard it as a faint echo.

"They are charged with injury to the king."

XIII

Freedom In Death

| SULWYN |

OUTRAGE rang throughout the Proelium Terra, but Sulwyn could only turn and look at Artaxiad's standing form, his injured arm in full few. Anger seared through her as she remembered his face hovering over hers in the dark, his lust then replaced by smugness now.

"No one has ever dared to try and harm the king!" called Caldwell.

Sulwyn turned to him, eyes wide at his elated expression. He, too, jumped over the stone ledge down from his seat, walking towards her and the family. Sulwyn looked at them closely. An older man with a limp and an older woman stood together protectively around their young son holding an infant.

"How?" called Sulwyn loudly, turning back to Artaxiad. "How and when?"

"Yesterday, while I was on official business in another town. They took the opportunity when I was unguarded, assisting other townspeople." But despite his claims and the anger erupting around them, he maintained a cocky grin.

"And you couldn't defend yourself–?" goaded Sulwyn, but Caldwell stepped in front of her.

"That's no way to speak to the king, Sulwyn. You are doing well—don't get in trouble." He smiled as well, but Sulwyn grew angrier still.

"Cowardly trash," muttered Sulwyn.

"Caldwell, one of our precious Validus Uferor Leaders, why don't *you* decide the punishment?" said Artaxiad, sitting back down. Sulwyn looked at Caldwell as he smiled even wider, his teeth bared, and his face twisted in ecstasy.

"Please! Please just spare our son and daughter!" pleaded the man, throwing himself at Caldwell's feet, begging and clawing at his ankles. The woman and her son began to cry and plead as well.

"Injury to the king does not give you any right…" began Caldwell, stepping past Sulwyn, quickly grabbing one of the Néosan's daggers and plunging it through the man's exposed neck, "…to beg or plead for forgiveness."

"No!" screamed Sulwyn and before she could stop, she threw herself in front of the woman and her children.

"Princess, are you interrupting my punishment?" His face was wild, just as it had been when they had visited Antac. He bent forward, pulling the dagger out of the man's neck. The sound of ripping flesh and blood gurgling out of his mouth and throat reached her ears. Caldwell kicked the dying man, pushing him forward and onto his back. Blood pooled and dripped down his mouth and cheeks, seeping into the sandy earth beneath them.

Sulwyn looked on in horror. The man's eyes were wide with fear and sadness, the light quickly fading from within them until he was dead. Sulwyn stepped back, closer to the woman and her children.

"It looks like we have a difference of opinion," said Artaxiad, humour in his voice. "I don't think the Lady Princess agrees with this sentence, Caldwell. What should be done?"

"My king, you did ask for my thoughts. I think this entire family needs to be eradicated so that they can no longer threaten us." But at his words, a deep laugh rang out around them.

"Threaten?" chuckled Artaxiad, standing. "Oh no, no. Please, I hope you all don't misunderstand. I did not feel *threatened*. How could I feel fear from my people? How could *I* feel fear at all? What I felt was betrayal! I have taken care of all of you so well, haven't I?" he called to the cheering crowd. "I, who take care of this land, to have my wrist broken when all I wanted…was to become closer to my people. It causes me more pain in my heart than in my hand." He placed his unharmed hand over his chest, his eyes finding hers. Rage and incredulity erupted within her. To calm herself, Sulwyn held his gaze and imagined a sword impaling his heart instead.

Caldwell took a step forward and Sulwyn was thrown into a war of her own thoughts. No one knew she could fight. No one here knew she was Kintana besides Artaxiad, Pandora, and Caldwell. She had earned additional favour during today's events. One wrong move would set her back, but these people were innocent. How dare he make them pay for her actions? It was cowardly. He wasn't mad like Galahad said, he was underhanded and slimy.

"My lady, don't make me move you," warned Caldwell, his face as cocky as Artaxiad's. This was all a game to him in her eyes.

"Try it," she whispered, staring into his ice-cold eyes.

"Try it?" Caldwell huffed, the crowd growing silent. Paying closer attention to her.

"There is no way this feeble family had the power to attack our great king. I do not agree with Caldwell's punishment," announced Sulwyn, looking past him to Artaxiad. She clenched her fists, Caldwell stepping closer still. The man had already stopped moving, his children crying but unable to go to him.

"Step aside, Blood Princess. You know you can't change the minds of everyone here," he said quietly.

"I will not move. You will go through me if you want to get to them. Besides, are you *insinuating* that the likes of this weak family could ever even breathe on our king? That's very rash of you," said Sulwyn, hoping that by mimicking Pandora's previous words, it would maintain her favour.

"I think," started Pandora suddenly, "that we should give our daughter a chance to prove herself."

Sulwyn looked at her skeptically. Artaxiad, too, turned curiously to Pandora as she continued, "I think it has been quite some time since we had an official battle here at the Proelium Terra. Why not give our daughter the chance to fight on behalf of this family? She does make a valid point."

"Hmm, I agree with this idea," said Artaxiad casually, the weight of this family's lives a mere passing thought. He addressed the people, "I hereby call for an official battle between the Lady Princess Sulwyn and the Leader of Validus Uferor En, Caldwell."

The people around them hesitated, whispering wildly before finally breaking out into a raucous cheer. But Sulwyn turned back to Pandora, "I accept this challenge. But you are not to harm this family until the results of the battle are out. I request that they are to be held at least in the upper dungeon with minimal care for their children."

"Request granted," called Pandora. "The match will take place one month from today." Pandora and Artaxiad rose from their seats, the gong sounding, concluding the bi-monthly trial. The crowd stood and cheered before they began to file out of the tunnels, talking wildly of the match to come. And just like that, the lives of three people were in her hands at their whim.

"Well, this is new. To have the honour of fighting the Lady Princess," spoke Caldwell. He moved, sitting atop the dead man, crossing his legs and patting his bloodied face.

"Get off him, Caldwell."

"Why? He's dead, Sulwyn. He's free now, isn't he?" He looked at her with a twisted smile.

Sulwyn clenched her jaw, turning to the woman behind her. "I will win...I promise you," she whispered.

"Why? You are their kin. Why would you even let it go this far?" cried the woman, her son crying, the baby's wailing getting louder and louder. Sulwyn faltered at the woman's despair.

"Silence that child before I do it for you!" roared Pandora suddenly from the top. Sulwyn had thought they left, but they both remained, watching her.

"Just…I'm sorry. Please go quickly and quietly…" pleaded Sulwyn. The woman grabbed her son, taking the baby in her arms, and followed the Néosan back to the iron gates.

"You will regret this, Caldwell," said Sulwyn fiercely, walking towards the stone steps to the first tunnel. Looking back, she saw that Caldwell only shrugged, looking up to the sky as he continued to pat the dead man's face.

❧

The lower tunnels were silent by the time Sulwyn started to exit the Proelium Terra. Her boots echoed loudly as she reached the end. She looked in the distance at the retreating crowd, all buzzing excitingly about what they had seen. No remorse for anyone who suffered today.

Sulwyn turned suddenly, facing a large bush almost up to her waist. Before she could react further, she was pulled over the bush and onto the ground, and hidden by the shadows of the trees and shrubs. Instantly, Sulwyn moved to try and dislocate the arm of her attacker, but she realized that the top of his head belonged to Galahad.

"Are you insane?" growled Galahad.

"Are you?" She spoke to the top of his head before her other arm was pulled forward, forcing her to let go of his arm behind his back. He flipped her onto the ground, his head hovering upside-down over her own as she looked up at his lips. Flustered, she slid forward, sitting up to turn and face him as he sat cross-legged.

"What are you doing?" hissed Sulwyn.

"I snuck into one of the tunnels and listened to everything. Why? How could you possibly get yourself involved in an official battle?"

"He found an innocent family, Galahad. A family that has nothing to do with this. That has nothing at all. He knew I wouldn't be able to say anything. How could I let them all die for something I did?"

"I understand this, Sulwyn. But that's not the point. An official battle…"

"Why? Have you been in one before?"

He looked worried. "When I was training to get into one of the five Uferor groups, they had matches between the top candidates. Whoever won got the title of Leader."

"Okay? So that was the last time they had battles? It's just a battle. If I win, I can save them. I have a month to train. I don't have to fight and give myself away."

"Sulwyn. These battles, unless they see fit to interfere, are to the death."

Sulwyn stared at him. The wind was blowing harder now, a few drops of rain starting to fall gently. "Caldwell is a Leader too, isn't he?" asked Sulwyn slowly.

"He was the first Leader assigned. The concept was new then. There was more competition. After him, there were fewer entries. Daijiro and I were nominated from the Néosan Captains."

"Fewer entries?"

"Caldwell killed a lot of people. Others became wary of the official battles. But they decided to omit them altogether just after I was assigned my position."

"And are all these people trying? Are they all like him? Did they all want to be here?"

"They were. The ones brought here against their free will don't strive to be higher than common Néosan. The ones trying are the ones who live for the Empire."

"How many did Caldwell kill?" asked Sulwyn, dreading the question she knew she was going to ask next.

"At the time, around twenty, I believe."

"How many did you kill?" she whispered, hoping that his murders were against people like Artaxiad.

He studied her carefully. "They didn't omit the official battles because of me, Sulwyn. I killed seven. All were opponents only and all were people who deserved it."

Sulwyn felt a moment of relief. "Then why did they cancel it?"

"I was battling for the Leader position of group San. But on the same day, Daijiro battled for group Divi. Daijiro killed fifteen other candidates." Sulwyn looked at him in confusion, but he continued. "Daijiro...is powerful. But he is controlled by his bloodlust. He killed forty spectators who were sitting in the lower levels and another ten in the middle level. Because those in the middle level were of relative importance to the Empire, he was punished. After that, they decided to omit the battles to keep the peace between those nobles and their families. Make it seem like they cared."

A horse neighed somewhere behind them, pulling Sulwyn from her thoughts. Galahad stood up, taking Sulwyn's hand to stand as well.

"You are right; the battle is in a month. That gives us time to practise fighting." He gestured towards the direction of the horse and she followed.

"I can fight."

"That's the problem. The story is that you had been taken captive. No one knows who you are. You can't fight with unexplained skill." Sulwyn mounted the horse first, Galahad climbing behind her.

"Fear breeds hate. It makes more sense to say that Raghnall kept me hidden from the truth and taught me basic self-defence. We can probably use my blood against them."

"Blood?"

"People think Artaxiad is strong, talented, and unbeatable right? It's possible that I inherited his talent as well, allowing me to learn enough in the next month that I can at least pose a threat. Everyone is so twisted and obsessed with blood and fighting. I'm sure that will be enough to distract them and stop them from looking into my abilities deeper than what is on the surface."

XIV

A Little Of Both

| SULWYN |

SULWYN hadn't seen or heard from Caldwell since the match was announced and no one questioned his disappearance. Her daily lessons on Empire history, etiquette, and all the other trivial things they were putting her through were cut in half, and instead, she spent this time with Galahad.

Galahad was given permission to "train" her without interruption and without witness. He was also allowed leave from any duty involving leaving the Empire.

But she hated it.

No one was watching her practice, no one was questioning her about her thoughts, but she knew that everyone kept their eye on her. And it was stifling. It had been almost two months since she had entered the Empire and it was starting to drive her mad.

"After this…it won't be hard to persuade Artaxiad to let you join me during my Uferor missions," said Galahad a couple of days before the match.

"It doesn't matter where you take me. I just need to be away from here. Every day, sitting there and listening to these people go on and on about the Empire. Knowing full well that their righteous history is based on lies. Forcing me to present myself in a way I couldn't care less about," said Sulwyn, clumsily dodging a kick from Galahad. "We never stayed in one place too long. And maybe that's a bad thing, but right now I'd rather be anywhere than in the Empire." She tucked and rolled out of another kick but stood up quickly.

"This is stupid. We can stop training. I know how to act weaker than I am." Sulwyn stopped abruptly, taking a seat on the compacted dirt. They had been doing last-minute training every night for the last week at the back of Eques Muros where the Captains usually trained. The trees added extra coverage around her, taunting her to escape.

"I know...I just..." started Galahad, sitting across from her and watching her carefully. He didn't continue what he was saying, but the look he gave her made her heart beat quicker.

During this past month, the one thing that gave her a bit of something to her day was that she would spend most of it with Galahad. From the beginning of the day (he insisted on moving a small bed into his room that he could use since she abandoned her own rooms) and into the night they practiced, explored, and ate.

He told her few stories of his past, but she could see the way he looked at the garden in his room, reminiscent of something only he could see. He spoke gingerly of his memories from when he joined the Empire and more about the times spent with his parents. Though she had no idea what his home was like or where it was, she knew part of him wished to be there just one more time.

But she watched as, with the time they spent, he seemed to defrost a little more. As if some of who he used to be was coming back. He was as stoic as ever in the presence of certain people, but she caught a smirk here or a bemused look there. He was showing emotions, something she figured he'd stopped doing years ago. Even though she was trapped here, she had at least achieved this.

"Are you getting some last-minute practice in?" said Caldwell suddenly. Sulwyn turned behind her to see him standing near the stables. He smirked at Galahad, but Galahad looked away, frowning.

"Have you told her about the bets?" asked Caldwell lightly.

"Bets?" asked Sulwyn, looking to Galahad, but he just glared at Caldwell again.

"Have you told her *anything?*" Caldwell smirked wider now, walking over and sitting next to Sulwyn. She continued to look at Galahad, who was as impassive as when she first met him.

"You obviously know, so why don't you share it?" snapped Sulwyn.

"Back when official battles were popular, tons of Privileged and Common Ones alike would bet on who they thought would win."

"That's not surprising," said Sulwyn, but Galahad glanced at her with a look she didn't understand.

"Well, yes, that is common. However, there are rules here." He beamed, and it sent a chill through her. "The Privileged can bet with whomever they choose. If a Privileged and a Privileged bet, it incorporates coins, valuables, typical nonsense. But if a Privileged bets with a Common One and they win, the Common One is either killed or has to choose someone from their family to take their place."

Sulwyn's eyes widened before they narrowed, "Then no Common One should bet."

"They have no choice," said Galahad, suddenly looking away again. "If a Common One is chosen by a Privileged, that is how that wager goes. But not all Common Ones get chosen by a Privileged. Minus the ones that work in the Solus or in the castles, all other Common Ones must place a wager on who they think will win. And if they lose, they are sentenced to one of the four slave towns. They lose either way."

"What happens if a Common One wins?" asked Sulwyn skeptically.

"Nothing. They keep the life they have," said Caldwell, standing.

"Why are you telling me this?" asked Sulwyn, standing as well.

"Because I know you are going to try your hardest to throw the fight. But think of how many Common Ones might be betting for you. If you lose, so do they." Caldwell grabbed her wrist, pulling her closer.

Galahad stood up, but Caldwell just stared at Sulwyn. Despite his monstrous smile, Sulwyn could see nothing in his eyes. They stared right at her, but at that moment she felt like he wasn't seeing her.

"Step down, Caldwell," growled Galahad.

"This is stupid. No one will vote for me over you," said Sulwyn, gripping his wrist back. He winced and she let go in shock, "Caldwell...you..."

He cut her off with a smirk. "If there aren't enough bets for you, they rig them anyway. Either way at least five thousand or so Common Ones will bet for you. But since it's been a long time, I wouldn't put it past them to up that count." Caldwell let go of her wrist, waving them off and disappearing back through the stables.

Sulwyn rounded on Galahad. "How could you not tell me about this?"

Galahad sighed his own breath of frustration. "After all the battles they had with us for the Uferor, by the time it reached the last few matches between Daijiro and my own, they ended that rule because the Empire lost too many Common Ones to the slave towns or death. They couldn't have the work performance rate go down anymore. I didn't know they were bringing it back until this afternoon. I was trying to figure out how to tell you..." He looked at her carefully.

"What am I supposed to do now?" Panic laced her voice. She should have known that they would do something like this. Of course they would. A grand event such as this, she would have been surprised at anything less. "Caldwell isn't going to hold back on me."

"We've gone over his tactics. Caldwell always fights with axes. You are faster than he is. If you fight on the defence and attack in offence using his weight and his movement against him, you will be fine."

"But he needs to die, doesn't he? That's what you said before! That these fights are to the death! With something like this at stake, there is no way they will call this a tie. Not when it could impact me and thousands of innocents."

"This is a test. They hold Caldwell in high regard. I told you that they can also stop a match. And as the last month has passed, I could only think of this. They won't let Caldwell get killed, and they can't have Caldwell kill you. They will *have* to intervene. This is also what I was going to tell you because I knew you would act like this." He stepped closer to her, the setting sun blazing against the blue, purple, and reds of his eyes. "You will need to be a little bit of Sulwyn and a little bit of Kintana," he whispered.

❧

Galahad had been called away on the last night before the match. He advised her to try and relax in lieu of practice and had an elaborate bath drawn for her, requesting Eztli to bring her food. But after the bath, Sulwyn couldn't sit still.

She couldn't bring herself to stay in the room even with the subtle calmness of nature within it. She found herself walking along the quiet halls of Valens Muros, unaware of where she was going. She rounded a corner to the sound of excited, muffled voices from one of the linen closets. Sulwyn stood close to the door, listening.

"What's wrong with your eyes?" said a young, rough voice. "We heard you murdered your whole town, is that true? Why haven't they locked you up?" Sulwyn pressed her ear to the door.

"Maybe they will give her the job of cleaning the lower dungeons," said a higher voice, cackling.

"Don't you speak?" said the other loudly, and Sulwyn heard a thump on the ground.

Without caution, Sulwyn pushed the door open, taking in the scene. A young girl and boy were standing over another young girl with dark sapphire hair. Evidently, she had been pushed.

"Are you lost? Or are you a new maid too?" said the girl with long black hair. But unlike the girl's rough and snarky expression, the boy looked terrified.

"Kestrel, don't be rude!" he whispered suddenly. Before he could say more, the girl on the floor stood up, curtsying politely.

"Lady Princess," she greeted her, her uneven eyes bright.

Kestrel looked at the boy in fear. "Ezhno didn't mean to push her!" But Sulwyn disregarded her.

"You do not have to curtsey to me, Arsinone," smiled Sulwyn, stretching her hand for Arsinone to take it.

"You both should be old enough to know not to pick on those younger than you. This is the Empire. You shouldn't be making a scene amongst yourselves," berated Sulwyn, but Kestrel and Ezhno continued to look at her in fear. "You are lucky it was me that witnessed this and not our king and queen. Heed my warning. Carry on." Sulwyn led Arsinone out of the linen closet, closing the door on their astonished and frightened faces.

"Thank you for helping me," said Arsinone, pulling her hand back, but Sulwyn held it tighter. Surprised, Arsinone turned to her but smiled happily all the same.

"Don't thank me. I hate acting that way. But kids are kids. Probably worse in the Empire." Sulwyn sighed.

"Don't be nervous," said Arsinone, her expression all-knowing though worried.

"I don't want you to come to the match," said Sulwyn suddenly stopping. She knelt, facing Arsinone.

"I've seen bloodshed before," said Arsinone matter-of-factly. Sulwyn continued to look at her carefully. Despite being such a young girl, she gave off the feel of a wise woman.

"I'm sure you have. But it doesn't mean you have to. Besides, for your best interest, I think it's better to stay away. Please do me that favour."

Arsinone stared at her apprehensively, then nodded, "I won't come." Suddenly her stomach growled loudly. Her cream-coloured cheeks tinted pink in embarrassment. Sulwyn laughed.

"I thought Eztli took you with her that day?" said Sulwyn, standing, taking her hand, and walking towards the servant staircase.

"She did. But she didn't know what to do with me. So she gave me the linens. It's not hard. I usually just wash alone. But sometimes those two bother me."

"What about food?" asked Sulwyn as they reached the cold stone stairs. Slowly they made their way to the first floor. Sulwyn had frequented the kitchens so often that she knew where it was by heart despite her general fuzziness of the castle.

"I can't cook at all…"

"I'm sure they can teach you, and if not there are plenty of other jobs in the kitchen besides cooking." They passed other servants running around the castle with nightly duties before reaching the violet and black tiled path to the kitchen doors, opening them.

"Eztli!" called Sulwyn, but she moved back, almost knocked with a metal spoon.

"Why are ya down here?" exclaimed Eztli. Several pots were boiling in the back, using all the stone stoves.

"Are you cooking for the entire Empire?" asked Sulwyn, leading Arsinone to sit on the single table. Nori bowed slightly, keeping her distance. She hadn't said much after the incident with Duri. But she wasn't as afraid of Sulwyn anymore either.

"The after-battle feast. Tons of nobles and other rich bastards will be there. We need to prepare. But forget that, why aren't ya resting?" she snapped, bringing Sulwyn some roasted chicken with buttered vegetables regardless of her complaints.

"Restless?" She smiled weakly but earned a smack with the spoon.

"Are you nervous?" asked Nori quietly, bringing some water.

"Yes." Sulwyn ate slowly, silence falling between them all. Arsinone ate quietly beside her, legs swinging in the chair, watching Eztli lead the other cooks in the kitchen.

"Eztli, can you give Arsinone work here? I'd feel better if you overlooked her. The linens don't seem to have friendly peers," asked Sulwyn after some time.

"I thought it was safest!" she sighed, "Anything ya like, sweetness. I'll mould her to be my successor." Eztli winked, earning a laugh from the young girl.

Sulwyn laughed as well, but she was unable to eat the rest of her food, her stomach hollow and turning with nerves. She had a feeling she wouldn't be sleeping that night.

⤜⤏

"I will be in the crowd…just fight as we discussed," said Galahad quietly.

Sulwyn nodded, unable to speak with the lump in her throat. She had never been nervous to fight anyone before. But this fight was different. She couldn't be herself here. Just like she couldn't be herself in the castle.

She was trapped in an act she never wanted to play. How could Raghnall have gotten her into this mess? Thinking of him brought his battered face into mind, reminding her once again that something just wasn't right, but she put that behind her for now.

She barely registered when Galahad left her side as she climbed down the inner steps towards a large stone hollow. A massive, solid iron gate stood before her, sealing the sounds of the growing crowd outside the Proelium Terra. She could hear nothing but her own slow breathing as she tried to centre herself.

It was easy to kill, but it was harder not to. And she knew she would be on the defence most of the time. Caldwell was talented. She could never deny that. But he was twisted like the rest of the Empire. He fought to kill.

Sulwyn looked up from quickly braiding her hair as a chink of light illuminated her boots. It was then the noise from the gate rising penetrated her fog and grated against her teeth. The warmth of the sun reached her black linen pants before its rays touched her violet short-sleeved tunic. Galahad had given her simple clothes, much to her relief. Chatter, cheers, and screams began to flood the hollow with her, alongside the light. Stomps, calls, and horns sounded in rhythm as if counting the seconds until the gates rose fully.

Her eyes adjusted to the sunlight that shone fully upon her face. In the distance, adjacent to her gate, was Caldwell. Standing poised, his clothes all white as were his fresh bandages.

Sulwyn picked up the black steel spear she had chosen. Her own was lost a long time ago. It wasn't the most ideal of weapons, but she felt comfortable with it. It would at least put space between her and Caldwell as they fought.

A single ring of the gong resonated in the sky, and she and Caldwell stepped forward and out past the gates. The sun was high in the sky, clouds nowhere to be seen. The terrain around her was a mix of stone, sand, grass, and trees.

She breathed in the fresh air around her, her nerves calming instantly as she faced the task at hand. Caldwell walked forward slowly, his smile as wide as ever, axes hanging past his knees. Another gong sounded and they both stopped walking. He was a few feet away from her, staring at her in anticipation.

"Welcome all to this extraordinary event!" started Artaxiad. She never turned away from Caldwell, but she could feel the stares on her. "It has been many years since we've seen a battle. Are you excited?" Cheers erupted for a moment, his smile wide in agreement, before they were silenced at a wave of his hand.

"As you all know, there was a conflict during our bi-monthly trial. As per Sulwyn's request, the family has been in decent care. Please bring them out."

Sulwyn whipped around. She didn't think they would be out to watch the match. Quickly, she spotted them in the lower seats, guarded by a few Néosan. The woman held her baby tightly to her chest, her son standing nervously beside her. Sulwyn looked back to Caldwell, whose smile had lessened, still staring at her every move.

"This match decides the punishment of this family. Whether we decide to intervene depends on how *messy* it gets." Sulwyn could hear the smirk in his voice, her eyes on Caldwell.

"Let me introduce you all again to the Lady Princess, Sulwyn." The crowd cheered loudly. "I have been informed that despite her past captivity, she has taken well to the training. Practising every day. I think the results will be evident. I too have placed my bets on her." Sulwyn finally turned to find Artaxiad; his words bothered her. He looked at her, his smile wide.

"And Caldwell, our very first Uferor Leader, in his charge Validus Uferor En. Many tasks and missions have been carried out by him and his group. I couldn't have asked for a better man."

A strong sense of despair coursed through her. She looked back at Caldwell; he was no longer smiling. He gripped his axes tighter, his eyes never leaving hers.

"But I have talked too long. You didn't come here to hear me prattle on about things you already know. Let us sit back and enjoy, shall we?"

he yelled. Cheers erupted, the gong sounded, ringing in an echo. Instantly she tuned out the sounds around her, her breath the only thing she heard.

All she could see was Caldwell.

The rise and fall of his chest as he breathed heavily, the tightening grip on his axes, and his left foot as it shifted slightly forward. Quickly, he raised his arms, moving the axes outward and away from his legs before he rushed forward.

He was fast. But as always, she compared him to Raghnall, and his speed was one she could fight with. Sulwyn braced herself, holding her spear horizontally to the ground, and waited.

With only a bit of space left, she pushed forward, lashing the spear to the side and connecting with his left wrist. The spear slipped; the impact lessened. She continued moving to the side, rolling out of the way, and putting space between them. But he barely gave her time to breathe.

He turned around, coming closer still as she tried again to disarm him. But she should have known it wouldn't work, not after he had seen through her.

"Are you just going to dance around me, princess?" he called loudly, smirking. Sulwyn kept her distance, pointing the spear at him. She would have to hurt him.

She inched forward quickly, making slight jabs to his shoulders. He dodged as Sulwyn maintained a circled space between them. She kept inching towards his left side, knowing he was righthanded. Finally, she managed to stab his shoulder, but barely. He laughed.

"You know you can't win like this."

"I don't want to kill you, Caldwell," said Sulwyn lowly, but this irritated him.

"You say that with confidence. As if you could. Think of all the things I've done to you! Doesn't it anger you?"

"Maybe I can't and yes it does, but I still do not want to." They continued to circle each other. But Caldwell had yet to try and hurt her in any way. He kept his distance as if flattering her small circle dance.

"You are naïve, Sulwyn. Where did all that talk go about killing those who deserve it and feelings of guilt? Where is your revenge? I tortured you."

"You did what the Empire expected of you. I dislike you, but I have no reason to kill you!" said Sulwyn, aiming another stab, this time to his bicep. She managed a long scratch, but it was shallow. Sulwyn could vaguely hear booing in the background but tuned it out again.

"I am not the only one who has killed in this Empire, Sulwyn. Will you challenge them to battles as well? I'm sure the Empire wouldn't mind. You could become their new source of entertainment. Before they tire of you."

Sulwyn narrowed her eyes. "Tire of me? Do you really think I expect them to hold me in high regard forever, if at all?"

"No, you wouldn't, would you?" He laughed and suddenly charged, kicking her spear up and away from its guarded position in front of her. Sulwyn shuffled back ungracefully, almost losing balance. She stopped before falling, flipping back on one arm, and creating space once again.

"Impressive. You fight very well on the defence." He rushed forward again, stronger this time, and Sulwyn knew she would need to take the hit.

She sidestepped, a stinging burn in her left shoulder erupting, nipped by the axe. Sulwyn took that moment to kick Caldwell in the gut, earning a grunt before kicking his right hand hard. Caldwell's grip on the axe loosened ever so slightly, and Sulwyn used that moment to whack his hand with the end of the spear. He dropped the axe.

Sulwyn pushed him back, kicking the handle of the axe quickly. It slid away along the hard stone ground. But not far enough. She pushed him more, making space between him and the axe, but let go, moving behind him just before he slashed down with the other axe.

"This is no fun," he said suddenly, stopping and tossing the other axe away. She stared at him incredulously. "You can't come at me for fear of being injured. So come, show me what you've got." He smiled wide, but Sulwyn was not fooled. Not this time.

He was crying.

Sulwyn dropped her spear and quickly ran at him, aiming her arm as if to punch, but at the last moment, fell into a slide against the rocky ground, kicking his shins. He lost his balance as she went through the gap between his legs and spun, kicking his thigh hard. He dropped to one knee, laughing more.

"I knew it was a good idea. I knew it had to be you," he said quietly, turning to look at her and getting up slowly. "If we don't fight, they will get bored. So come, let us talk and exchange punches." He held his fists up and Sulwyn followed, aiming punch after punch to his shoulders as he kept his guard. But he spoke to her quietly.

"Sulwyn. I *need* you to kill me..." he pleaded unexpectedly. She faltered, earning a punch to her face. It wasn't a hard punch; her teeth clenched in reflex. But she shook off the pain and returned the blow.

"I will not!" she said forcefully, but he grabbed her arm and pulled it behind her back, holding her. She struggled, only to realize he wasn't really holding her. She continued to fake her struggle instead.

"I can't do this anymore. I hate it here. I am consumed by guilt every day. And when we go on missions, when we have people to kill, it only blinds me for a moment. I hope with each kill that maybe I can be rid of this guilt, but it doesn't go away. It gnaws at me from the *inside*. I hear them in my sleep. I see them when I close my eyes."

He pushed her forward, and she continued their mock fight, letting herself listen to the crowd. They continued to cheer and gasp, no one realizing they were having this conversation. She took a moment to scan the crowd again and found Galahad close by, staring at her in confusion.

He had noticed.

Sulwyn turned back to Caldwell, who moved to grab her again, but she used his weight against him and flipped him onto his stomach, his arm pulled back behind him this time, her hold strong.

Caldwell grunted but continued to speak, his voice muffled by the ground. "I told you that I was given to the Empire. But the real reason I let myself be taken was so that I could find my sister."

Sulwyn looked at him from the side, his eyes full of pain, seeing something she did not. "The Empire came to our small village and took her a long time ago, to sell her to the pleasure houses. When they came back six months after that, I went with them in hopes that maybe I could find her. I searched the Empire every day but could not find her. Eventually, I started to train instead. If they let me join the Néosan, then I would have the means to travel to towns and villages. For years I searched, but at the same time, I was blinded. There is peace here. It may be vile, but for the Privileged it is exceptional! And with each day I stayed here, I began to lose sight of myself."

Caldwell used his other arm to push himself up off the ground and flip, forcing Sulwyn to lose her grip on his arm and topple to the side. He sat atop her, pinning her arms to the ground. She looked up at him, his cerulean eyes still watery with tears. "I became consumed with the life here, Sulwyn. And then with it came the guilt of not finding her. Years passed and that guilt manifested into my urge to kill instead. But each time I killed, I was reminded of when she was taken."

Sulwyn pushed her hips up, forcing him to stumble to the side. She stood quickly, reaching for his arm but instead gripped a piece of the bandage. She tore at it, causing it to unravel from his left arm. The bandage fell into a small pile at his feet. And even Sulwyn could hear everyone watching nearby gasp.

His arm was covered in deep scars, some old and dark but many were fresh and still in the process of healing. Sulwyn counted and realized that the number of new scars matched the amount he had killed in Antac, plus the old man being the freshest of them all. She looked at him, her eyes wide.

"For every kill, I mark myself in atonement."

She'd had a feeling when she gripped his wrist a few nights ago that something wasn't right with the way he acted and his bandaged arms. But she wasn't prepared for this. This self-inflected manifestation of guilt.

To be in enough pain that he had carved his sins into his skin. Sulwyn felt numbness crawl its way out of her stomach, but she wanted to help him, needed to stop this, despite what he had done to her. He was just as much a victim. "Join me, Caldwell," hissed Sulwyn. Both had stopped their farce of fighting, watching each other instead.

"I am not interested in your goal. My guilt came from my inability to save my sister. But I could never deny that I enjoyed the life the Empire had given me here. I don't fight for your cause. I can't." She watched him step back slowly, eyes downcast.

"Then why would you go so far?" she yelled suddenly, all pretense forgotten, "I can help you find her!"

"I already found her, Sulwyn..." He looked up at her, tears streaming down his face as he continued to stumble backwards. He unravelled the bandages of his right arm; a longer, deeper gash wrapped around his fore-arm. Sulwyn couldn't help but gasp, hands to her mouth.

"That woman in the house?" she whispered.

"She asked me to kill her...she had suffered so much, so, so much. I could never save her from what she had seen, what she had been through. She would never be the same again. She begged me, Sulwyn, how could I deny her?" His voice cracked.

"You could have come to me! We could have helped her! I can help you now!" She faltered. He bent down, picking up one of his axes. She watched his smile grow wide, twisted. Every ounce of pain he had just shown gone. He snickered, watching and waiting for her reaction.

"So naive, princess," he crouched.

Sulwyn slowly mimicked him in defence, confusion whirring within her.

But when he took off at a run, it was not towards her.

But to the woman and her children.

XV

You Are Free

| SULWYN |

SULWYN knew she wouldn't make it in time.

But that didn't stop her from running.

The hard stones and gravel pounded through her boots with every step she took. But the fear in the face of the boy, the tears streaming down the woman's face, burned their way through her, making run step faster.

High-pitched screams resounded from the mother as Caldwell ripped the baby out of her arms. He paused only to face Sulwyn. She faltered; his smile was wide, teeth bared, before he dropped the baby on the ground and brought the axe down.

Sulwyn's shriek mingled with the woman's, but Sulwyn watched Caldwell as he quickly turned to the boy, slashing him across the chest, his scream barely out of his throat before he crumpled to the ground at his mother's feet, on top of the infant's body. The woman let out a blood-curdling scream, dropping to her knees. Trying to piece herself back together. Her hands coated in blood.

Sulwyn tackled Caldwell away from the distraught woman, throwing him to the ground, but his grip on his axe never waned. He brought it down onto Sulwyn's back awkwardly and she screamed, unable to move fast enough, the shock of what she just witnessed still coursing through her.

The air touched her tender and wounded skin through the rip of her tunic, burning and tingling and cold all at once. Sulwyn quickly rolled away from him. The ground seemed like it was tipping from the agony in her back. The pull of skin and the sting of dirt from the deep gash on her back sent throbbing pain through her. Luckily she had moved enough that the axe had not embedded. But adrenaline flooded through her, trying to drown out the pain. She turned her ragged breaths into deep ones, forcing the pain back to a dull throb, tried not to vomit. Sulwyn threw herself forward again, wrapping her arms around his waist. But it was too late.

Cackling, Caldwell swung hard, beheading the woman in front of Sulwyn and in front of the joyous crowd around them.

And in her mind, the filter crashed.

Sounds of excited screams and cheers met her ears, roaring through her and clashing with the throbbing beat of her back. She could distinctly hear Pandora and Artaxiad laughing in delight, as everyone around them cheered for Caldwell.

Blood pounded in her ears and seeped from the enflamed wound in her back. But as quickly as it had shattered, her filter had reformed, blocking the sounds of the crowd once again.

Blocking the laughter of Artaxiad and Pandora.

Silencing the echo of the children's screams, of the woman's howling rage and despair.

Cutting off Galahad's warning yell that made its way to her.

Sulwyn let go of Caldwell, pushing him forwards and kicking his back as hard as she could. He fell onto his knees, caught off guard at the force, just as Sulwyn walked to collect her spear. She looked at the terrain around her. They had moved so far from the family at the beginning. She should have seen it coming.

She was naive.

He had led her closer to the family purposely, knowing he would use his lie to his advantage. How foolish she was.

Sulwyn gripped the spear tightly, her hands rubbing painfully against the metal.

She heard nothing now.

Not his breath, not even her own.

All she could feel was rage and the wonderful feeling of revenge.

She charged forward just as he got up on his feet.

He turned to her, smiling, but his smile faltered when she jumped high into the air, bringing her spear down across him. He held the handle of his axe across, catching the spear before it collided with his head.

Sulwyn pushed him backwards, the decapitated head of the woman in her peripheral, the blood of the children on her boots. Sulwyn pulled back suddenly, Caldwell stumbling forward, and whacked his arm. He let go of the axe in one hit.

"That plan again?" He smirked but soon frowned, the tip of the spear plunge its way through his thigh. Sulwyn pulled it out roughly, aiming for his chest instead, but he dodged and she impaled his shoulder, pushing him farther back.

He cried out but had no time to block her. She ripped out the spear and aimed for his throat. Caldwell shifted to his side, her spear colliding with the stone wall now behind him.

"Sulwyn, stop!" called a voice to her.

She glanced up and saw Galahad looking down at her from above. He had run to the edge of the ledge, his eyes wide, but she didn't stop. She turned her gaze back to Caldwell, who had slipped down the wall and moved behind her, running for his axe.

Turning, Sulwyn vaulted the spear and watched as it impaled itself into the side of his lower back. He fell flat on the ground, his hand scraping the handle of his axe, but it disappeared within Sulwyn's grasp instead.

He turned, looking up into her grey eyes, "You resemble Pandora like this," he huffed, reaching behind to pull the spear out. Blood pooled behind him and onto the stones. His white clothes dyed crimson.

Sulwyn looked down at the axe in her hand then whipped it, watching as it embedded into a tree. She charged at him, kicking his back and earning a scream of pain. Blood streamed out of his wound faster. But she kicked harder still.

Finally, she bent down, gripping the neck of his sleeveless tunic, and pulled him upright. Sulwyn roared in his face, forcing him back against another wall as he coughed at the pressure, blood trickling at the sides of his mouth.

Sulwyn looked into his blue eyes and without hesitation, punched him hard in his face, in his stomach, and in his chest. She reached within her boot, pulling out a small dagger, then gripped his neck, choking him and moving her face closer to him. Without breaking eye contact, she plunged the blade into his stomach, dragging it up ever so slightly.

Warm blood coated her hands and drenched her clothes, and still, she didn't think it was enough. He cried weakly, breathing hard, feebly pressing his stomach with his hands. Sulwyn looked down at the long, deep gash on his arm and faltered, her mind rushing out from a daze.

She remembered the young woman in that moment, sitting peacefully in the kitchen. The smile of contentment that graced her face in death, the tears that streamed down her face, and the hollow laugh she had heard before they went into the house.

"You must bring luck, Sulwyn…" coughed Caldwell.

She looked at him, tears streaming down his face again, but his smile had finally reached his eyes. He repeated the same words he had spoken in Antac. Sulwyn let go of his neck, stumbling back. The sounds of the crowd rushed back, disorienting her.

"No!" shrieked Sulwyn suddenly, her screams silencing everyone around her. "No, no, no. Why? Why did you kill them? Everything you said was true. Everything? Why are you so eager to die?" she howled, gripping the dagger tighter. Resentment, dread, anguish, and everything else rushed up within her at her mistake. At her clouded judgement. How easy it was to manipulate her emotions. Guilt crashed through her in waves, but he continued to smile, albeit weakly.

"I have killed many. I have abused myself and even that was not enough to atone. I am sorry, Sulwyn, for staining your hands in my blood…for killing that family in front of you. You know they would have it done regardless of the result of this match. But if there was anyone who could pass judgement on me, I wanted it to be you," Caldwell breathed heavily, each word ragged.

Horror filled her, her hand with the dagger trapped in his palm. He pulled her forward, raising her hand and stabbed himself in the throat with the dagger. She felt the blood pour quickly down her arms, his eyes never leaving hers.

She fell to the ground, Caldwell's limp body dropping with her. His blood flowed freely, pooling at her feet, and through her clothes.

But the tears would not stop despite the hate she felt at what he had done to her and what he had just done now. He was what the Empire had created. No matter what twisted reason he had come up with. He had been a boy who wanted to save his sister. Nothing more.

The cheers of the crowd drowned out her wails of sadness. The gong sounded repeatedly, Pandora's voice calling out over them all.

"The match is done. And with it, no one can question that Sulwyn is our flesh and blood!" The crowd cheered louder still. Néosan came to collect the bodies of the dead family and Caldwell, but Sulwyn glared, stopping them in their tracks.

"Our daughter knows what it is like to experience loss, to feel the pain even of her enemy. She is a true warrior," said Pandora. And with every word she spoke, Sulwyn could feel the bile of hate rise in her. "She respects the dead. And Caldwell, one of our best, has fallen. Please show your appreciation." Pandora began to clap, followed by Artaxiad and the rest in the Proelium Terra.

"Move aside," said a gruff voice somewhere behind her. The Néosan cleared a path for Galahad. The cheers continued as he crouched silently next to Sulwyn, waiting as the crowd eventually exited to go and join the after-battle feast and festival.

"Well done, Sulwyn. I am glad to see that you have the heart of the Empire," said Pandora, gracefully walking towards them, Artaxiad close behind her.

"You will be glad to know that we let everyone choose who they wanted to bet for. In honour of our growing bond with you, no Common One shall see death or punishment today, no matter who they chose," said Artaxiad like it was a gift. But Sulwyn barely heard them.

"Galahad, take care of Caldwell as you see fit. I know you disliked him," said Pandora dismissively, as they took their leave for the festivities. No pause, no remorse or mourning. The Néosan moved as if to go closer, but Galahad stood up, sending them away.

"Sulwyn…" he spoke softly, kneeling down next to her. "We can bury him…we can bury all of them."

"What have I done? I could have helped him! I could have saved him! He played me like a fool, knew that I let my emotions control me. I haven't learned anything. And at the end, even more innocent people are dead." She glanced at the tarnished silver ring on her hand, now covered in blood.

"What graduation, Raghnall? I don't deserve your recognition." She turned to Galahad, the pain and heartache reflected in his eyes.

"I never knew," said Galahad.

"Could you hear us?" she asked, though not surprised.

"Somewhat…if I had known, I might have tried to help him. But I am no better. I hate everything here. I shut everyone out. I never bothered to learn more about anyone. And maybe if I had, we could have come to terms with each other earlier on, before he became so twisted. If I had known that was why he came, I would have assisted his search. However, he was here before me, and he had long been tainted before I got here. I hated him. But he was like me. He tuned everyone out. He kept his relationships shallow and on the surface of the smile he wore. This isn't only on you."

Galahad reached forward, helping Sulwyn lay Caldwell onto the ground properly. Galahad called the Néosan to bring a wheel barrel, sheet, rope, and a shovel while Sulwyn sat in silence, waiting until the Néosan returned. She gently passed her hand over Caldwell's eyes, closing the lids. A smile like his sister's graced his features; she hadn't realized it until now, but they resembled each other.

Swiftly and quietly, Galahad collected the bodies of the family, placing them gently in the wheel barrel. Once he tucked Caldwell's body alongside them, he placed the sheet over them all, covering the bodies and tucking and securing them with rope. Carefully, he lifted the wheel barrel up and began walking. Sulwyn collected Caldwell's axes, carrying the shovel over her shoulder and following Galahad without question.

She was tired.

Everything seemed foggy in the cool evening of the slow-setting sun. She hadn't even realized how long the fight had gone on. Heaviness settled in her limbs, but a lightness drifted through her hands and feet all at once as they walked through the forest in silence, the sound of merriment farther and farther in the distance. The edges of her mind threatened to envelop her in darkness. But she pushed through. They walked for some time. Might as well have been hours or days even. Finally, she stopped, looking up at a large oak tree.

"This. I want them to be buried here," whispered Sulwyn.

They had walked far into the edges of Tranquillum, its trees bordering the Empire, high trunks and grass surrounding them. Without question, Galahad placed Caldwell and the family on the soft grass. Standing, he looked around carefully before approaching Sulwyn. Without a word, he rubbed the sides of her arms gently, taking the shovel from her and leading her to sit down.

Unable to look at what remained of the family, Sulwyn uncovered Caldwell's face, looking at the peace he had finally found despite the carnage. She wasn't sure how long she sat there but felt Galahad reach up to her face, touching her cheek gently. She looked at him, his eyes full of concern. He reached out, taking her hand to help her stand, and looked at her cautiously before attending to the deceased. She watched Galahad lift each body, and jump into the large hole he had dug. Climbing out, he turned to Sulwyn apprehensively as she walked to the edge. Galahad had wrapped the sheet around the family, binding them together as if they didn't share a grave with their murderer. She picked up Caldwell's axes, holding them uncertainly.

"I'll never forgive him for taking the lives of this family. Never. But there is nothing I can say, Galahad. He played me. He knew me well enough to know he could provoke me. Get me to kill him. I am not without fault. He was right, killing is killing and my impulsive behaviour is no excuse...the answers were there. I was just too caught up in the hate and everything around me to notice it."

She looked down at the ground before casting her eyes across the forest. Far in the corner of their small space, she saw wildflowers growing through the bushes and grass. Slowly, she walked forward bending to pick the blue and white flowers. In silence, she brought them over, holding them closely as Galahad refilled the hole.

In no time at all, the bodies were covered by a fresh mound of damp earth, the smell wafting around them. This family. The lives of the children. His body. His life. They were nothing now. Sulwyn crossed his axes over the hill, placing the flowers in between. She wasn't sure if it was disrespectful to mark a new, shared grave with the weapons of death, but she wanted to decorate it somehow.

"You overestimated them," she started, and he turned to look at her in confusion. "They didn't interrupt that battle. They didn't care for him at all. It didn't matter if they praised him, it didn't matter if he had achieved success in his seventy-three missions. In the end, he was nothing. Just like everyone. The people are nothing to Pandora and Artaxiad, not really. He was wrong. They hadn't grown tired of him. They had never thought of him to begin with. This is the Empire. This is what I am up against." She turned to Galahad, and his eyes widened as darkness claimed her once again and she fell to the ground.

She was floating, flying over a gentle cloud.

Sulwyn realized she was being carried.

Her body was weak, her mind foggy and unsettled.

But Galahad's warmth brought her comfort.

She had no sense of time.

She felt as if he had been holding her closely for hours.

But the ride to the Empire wasn't that long.

Where were they?

Where was he standing?

Question upon question began to surface but the constant sound of distorted ticking was confusing her, forcing her thoughts to drift away before she could let them sink in.

Why was there so much ticking?

Two voices now—was he arguing? A shout resonated around her, but before she could fully register it, it faded.

Gentle air passed over her face; she was moving again. The warmth was still strong but Galahad's chest was stiff, uncomfortable—he must be anxious. He must be facing someone difficult. The ticking began to fade into the background and slowly she could hear trickling water. She could smell the green of untouched nature. Her sense of time was still twisted. When did the ticking stop? When did the water begin to flow? Was she in his bedroom again?

Something soft yet slightly wet graced her forehead and then her lips. The thought of it seemed like it would be unpleasant, but it was cool and comforting. It filled her with a new sense of warmth and with it she found herself falling back to sleep, all thoughts melding into nothing.

"Sulwyn!" hissed a voice near her ear. She turned, her body heavy and sore. She didn't want to move. It was warm here, quiet and safe. Another voice harassed her but this time within her mind.

"Sulwyn! You need to get up! You need to go to Artaxiad's study now!" called Arsinone. But her mind was still foggy, the words processing slowly. She had forgotten something. Something important. Someone poked her arm. But she didn't want to stir, why were they bothering her?

Sulwyn sat bolt upright, her breathing hitched and her heart beating quickly, fists clenched. The sense of fear ebbed away as she steadied herself on the bed, eyes wide and ready to defend. She looked up to see Eztli close to her ear, Nori about to poke her arm again, and Arsinone looking at her in concern by her feet.

"Ya need to go, now!" said Eztli. She didn't understand what was happening but listened to them anyway.

Sulwyn threw the sheets off herself; her clothes had been removed and changed into nightwear. Scanning the room, she located her boots that had been cleaned and a robe. Putting both on quickly, she opened the door, stopping.

"I don't remember the way..." said Sulwyn, but Eztli rushed forward, taking her hand and dragging her out the door.

Quickly they sprinted down the hall and up two flights of stairs. A stitch of pain was growing in her side, her back was sore, and her body was protesting at the sudden movement. The growing ache in her back made its way through, but she pushed on. Once they rounded a corner, Sulwyn remembered the rest of the way.

"Eztli, go back," whispered Sulwyn, shooing her away. Eztli nodded, not wanting to stay, and turned back the way they came. Sulwyn ran to the large, redwood doors and pushed her way through them, arms shaking at the effort and reminding her of how weak she was after the fight.

The sound of ticking reached her ears, but she ignored it. Galahad and Artaxiad looked at her; neither seemed too surprised by her arrival. Artaxiad stood quickly, opening his arms upon seeing her. She noticed that the cast had already been removed.

"Sulwyn! The star of the match!" exclaimed Artaxiad.

She went to exchange looks with Galahad at the irony of his sentence, but Galahad looked at her impassively. She narrowed her eyes, looking back at Artaxiad.

"You have won the hearts of the people in the Empire! They could do nothing but talk about your achievement and at your progress over the last two months during the feast last night." He continued, "They were very disappointed that you could not attend, but they knew even you deserve rest. I will have your next assignment ready after a few days' time. You worked hard. You are doing well, so please take this moment to pamper yourself. Take advantage of what the Empire has to offer, especially to you." He smiled widely but then turned his attention back to Galahad. "Our discussion is over. I assume you are ready? I want to see your dedication as prince." he asked.

Galahad turned to face him again, bowing. "I am honoured." Galahad stood straight, nodding slightly to Sulwyn before leaving out the open doors.

Sulwyn looked to Artaxiad in question. "He has been promoted. As for you, I will be sending you to the Solus to gain some experience there. Now you may leave. You have earned your break." Artaxiad dismissed her suddenly with a smile she could not read, nor did she care to.

Where was Galahad going?

She closed the doors on the sounds of a million clocks and ran back down the hallway, ignoring the pain as it flared even more. She wasn't sure where Galahad would go but hoped it would be back to his room. Soon enough she caught up to him in the lower halls, the pain piercing through her as she rounded a corner.

Sulwyn crashed into his back, collapsing to the floor, the carpet silencing her fall. She looked up at Galahad, his face not only impassive but annoyed or angry—she couldn't tell.

"Where are you going?" she asked, still sitting on the floor. He made no move to help her. He always maintained a certain hardbacked posture when they walked the halls, but this time he seemed agitated, and a little on edge. She noticed his fist was clenched, but he tried to pass it off by running his fingers through his hair.

"This is of no concern to you." Sulwyn stared in surprise. He considered her for a moment. "I have been reassigned after finally convincing our king to let you go on your own. You heard what he said. You have earned your place so long as you keep it this way. I do not need to babysit you any longer." He spoke to her in clipped tones. But Sulwyn continued to stare, getting up slowly as panic rose in her chest.

"I don't understand..."

"Of course you don't. Look, my job was to ensure you didn't get killed by Caldwell and that you could prove yourself and hold your own in the Empire. You were given permission to follow us on our mission with the belief that I could complete this goal. But Caldwell was right, in a sense. You are naive." He scoffed, but his words were rushed.

Sulwyn's heart dropped.

What was this?

Everything she feared deep within her resurfaced. Her thoughts of not being able to tell which of Galahad's faces were real. Her inability to trust, her fear of being alone. Everything about him that she had doubted was being confirmed for her. Just like this?

"You're lying."

"Am I? You are easy to read. You made yourself a target. You relied too much on others. I won't lie. You are exceptionally talented, and your company was entertaining. But you are naive, a child unaware of the world around you. Compared to us, who have lived in the Empire, you do not understand. You trust easily. And it is this trust that will get you killed one day. Did you really think that I'd have lasted so long in the Empire if I acted like who you thought I was? Or did you believe that I wouldn't be even the slightest bit annoyed that the Blood Princess is here, threatening all that I have worked for?"

Sulwyn wanted to fight back. This couldn't be what she thought it was, but part of her believed it and part of her didn't, and she would secretly try to hold on to that. She was already acting in this poorly written play on a stage of murder and fear. She would continue to do so with anyone who aligned themselves with the Empire or pretended to do so for whatever reason. Patience was key here, and despite the way she was brought into the Empire, she would hold on to the hope that there would be a moment where she would move her own goals forward. She needed to remember she was alone, clearly. But this was something she always planned to do. And no one would stop her.

Patience.

"I have been rewarded for enduring my time with you. I have persevered and it has finally been recognized, especially now that Caldwell is out of the way. I am now in charge of all Néosan, Validus, and Validus Uferor. And I am moving to Eques."

He stepped closer to her, a strange smirk played across his lips, marring his expression like it didn't belong. "No one can question me now. It is the greatest honour to hold this position. The only person who holds higher command is Artaxiad. Don't you see? I am finally being recognized!" He smiled wider; irritation clawed within her. She took a deep breath, inhaling patience, before making her most impassive face. He stood straight again; a brow raised at her change in attitude.

"As the Blood Princess, I congratulate you on your new position. Since I have arrived, I have learned so much about the Empire, about their ways and the people that reside here. *Of course* you deserve this position. After all the hard work you've done, and *especially* with your past. I'm sure your clan would be proud of this achievement." She looked into his eyes, unable to read anything from them. But he laughed, smirking and betraying nothing.

"I am honoured to receive your praise. I wish you well and hope that you will continue to do as they say."

"I look forward to seeing what you do next, prince." Sulwyn curtsied politely, walking past him.

ᨆᨆ

"He's gone, Sulwyn," mumbled Arsinone once Sulwyn entered the bedroom door. She hadn't gone straight back to the room, instead wandering about, wasting time in hopes that she wouldn't encounter him again. Nori and Arsinone had been sitting on the bed waiting while Eztli went to fetch them lunch.

"We heard about his change in rank this morning. It spread pretty quickly," said Nori quietly. "Apparently, a council was held the night before the battle. The results came out this morning to the public before Galahad was told."

Sulwyn looked at her but didn't take in half of what she was saying. He must have planned this from the beginning. How much of his story was real? How much should she believe? What did she really know about him? Caldwell had been poisoned by the Empire, and it was apparent now that Galahad might have been as well. Was this what happened to people who stayed here over time? Did the luxuries of the Empire shut out their hearts, the fire and love that people once had? Everyone she encountered here was like this; comfortable, overfed, and full of coins and privileges. All given to them in exchange for the lives and happiness of the rest of Vartugaul.

How was she ever going to stop this? Would she escape it? Or would she succumb over time, content with the ease of the Empire life?

"No, Sulwyn. I can see it in your soul." Sulwyn looked up at Arsinone, who stared back at her with fierce uneven coloured eyes. "You are not weak. You are not tempted. You honour and cherish life. Everyone has a past they can't run from. It's only time before it catches up with them, just as Caldwell's did."

"Sweetness?" said Eztli behind her suddenly. She had brought a tray of various sandwiches, and a large pouch on the side of her hip held a sealed jug of lemonade.

"I *am* naive…" whispered Sulwyn. They all stared at her, unsure of what to say.

Sulwyn turned around, past Eztli and straight out the door again. She made her way back to Artaxiad's study, knocking once before entering, pushing the door hard enough to hit the wall.

Artaxiad looked up at her, a smirk gracing his lips. "You are quite the wonder, aren't you? You've got a lot of energy. That fight must have taken a toll on you, even if you are the great Kintana. Caldwell was a strong man."

"You didn't deserve him."

Artaxiad smiled wider. "It doesn't matter what you believe. He played his part. Just as you did, just as Galahad did."

"What did you do to him?" asked Sulwyn, stepping closer to the desk.

"Do? I'm sure you've heard it from Galahad. He earned a position that he always wanted. He had choices to make and did what he needed to, to gain your trust and move on. To have you prove yourself. Caldwell was a sacrifice to this goal. And he would have been honoured if he knew."

"You knew nothing about Caldwell, you were his undoing. Don't speak his name so lightly," growled Sulwyn, but Artaxiad stood up, placing a finger to his lips.

"There is no need for you to be upset. You are doing fine. We approve of the rate that you are going at. We never thought it would be easy.

We are not fools. You loved Raghnall even if he did sell you to us. That is not something we expect you to lose so easily. But Sulwyn, look at what we have created. What we have! Are you not pleased with it? This can be yours, too. Rest. You've been galivanting as Kintana for so long. We just need your cooperation." Artaxiad spread his arms wide, stepping out from behind his desk as if to embrace her, but she stood straighter. "If looks could kill, Sulwyn," he purred, lowering his arms.

"Send me to the Solus tomorrow."

Artaxiad stared at her a little baffled. "You are not in good health."

"Do I need to be to go there? The *great* Kintana and all? I'm sure you aren't worried about my well-being, but about your reputation. How would the others feel if you sent their battle-worn princess straight on to another assignment?"

"I don't care about the opinions of others, Sulwyn. I was doing it for your benefit. If you see fit to go to the Solus tomorrow, then by all means, do so. You will be a Protector for a few weeks. I want you to be part of investigating the impersonators in Antac. And it looks good on you to take an active role somewhere in the Empire, no?"

Sulwyn remained silent for a moment, watching Artaxiad carefully. But his eyes showed nothing, and a smile continued to play across his lips. She looked at the scars near his eye and clenched her jaw. Swiftly she bowed, taking her leave. As the door closed, she could hear quiet laughter amongst the muffled sounds of ticking.

Sulwyn walked along the hay-strewn path of the stables, looking at the horses as she passed. All the horses were cared for and raised by Artaxiad himself with the assistance of a few trusted others. The one thing anyone saw Artaxiad give immense attention to.

She walked farther in, where horses not yet assigned stayed. Most of the horses looked at her for a fraction of a second, mainly because she didn't have any food. But towards the very end, isolated from the rest, there was just one horse that kept its eyes fixated on her.

Sulwyn watched the horse carefully. Tail swishing lazily, his eyes trained on her. Slowly she raised her hand. The horse pawed the ground a few times, then bent forward, letting her pet just above his muzzle. He was warm, his coat smooth and comforting.

Sulwyn took in his appearance. He looked young but strong and a little battle-worn, a few scars along his chest. His coat was shiny black, with a burgundy sheen that reflected the light around them. But there was something different about this horse compared to the rest, not only in size and colour.

Raghnall told her that during the progression of Vartugaul from the Lost World many animals had evolved and grown even more in intelligence. Some might even assist someone in need, if only they had the guts to ask for it. She had done so before, a few times in the past. This horse reminded her of such. As Sulwyn looked into his dark brown eyes, she felt like he could read her mind, touch her soul. Like this horse knew exactly who she was.

Sulwyn smiled. "If you would be so kind as to be my partner during this new journey, I would be honoured." She bowed in a gentlemanly fashion before standing straight and continuing to smile. The horse stomped for just a moment, then he neighed and stepped forward for Sulwyn to rub his head some more.

Satisfied, she called over the servant who had been following her around in the distance to prepare her horse for riding. As she waited, thinking of a name, Eztli came out to meet her with a folded set of the Protector uniform. Sulwyn looked at the dusted-blue clothes, shaking them out. She shoved the pants into Eztli's arms and tied the long sleeves of the thick tunic around her waist. Eztli just stared at her.

"What is a uniform going to do for me? Everyone already knows who I am. And if Galahad and the rest of them don't have to adhere to uniforms, then neither do I," said Sulwyn roughly, looking up to the cloudy sky.

"Ya should still be resting," spoke Eztli softly, refolding the pants.

"What does it matter? Me resting and sitting in this godforsaken castle isn't going to help anyone. The best thing I can do now is to find ways that will benefit us in the future."

"Ya got slashed by an axe and lost quite a bit of blood. That ain't something most people can just stand up and get on with." Eztli moved closer, dropping her voice to a whisper. "Nori was only able to heal ya a little. It costs the user to heal, and she can't be discovered."

"It's more than enough. This is just another scar on top of many. None of which have stopped me before."

"But Sulwyn," started Eztli warily. Sulwyn turned to face her properly just as the horse trotted behind her.

"It's fine, Eztli. This is fine. I have been reminded of what it is I want to do. I'll see you in a week when I get a break." Sulwyn picked up her small sack, placing it in a saddle-side bag before mounting. She waved to Eztli, the gates opening for her to take off.

As she rode through the shops, carts, and houses, she felt a pressure begin to lift. She really did hate it inside Valens.

She galloped past the Common Ones, straight to the gate she had gone through before with Galahad. Unlike the many corridors and rooms of the castle, she could remember the terrain of the land. She knew exactly where the Solus was.

Time felt like seconds to her as she finally passed through the trees, the high walls of the Solus emerging in front of her. This wouldn't be like the lower dungeons. Protectors and Néosan alike greeted her at the front gate as she dismounted. Sulwyn pat the steed's head again, standing close to him.

"How do you like the name 'Ki'?" He swished his tail calmly, rubbing her shoulder with his head. "That's decided then. Be good." Sulwyn patted his side as he neighed loudly while being led to the stables. Someone new came running up to Sulwyn just as she waved Ki away.

The Protector said his name, but she instantly forgot it. In her mind he was just another follower, working in the Empire. He escorted her in.

"We are honoured to have you here, Lady Princess. I watched your match. It was a bit touch and go sometimes, but it looks like Caldwell got what he deserved." Sulwyn glared at the man, his bright yellow eyes unaware of the hostility rising in her. "When it was his turn to patrol it was always so…blah. He never engaged with any of us. Actually, he'd go talk to some of the prisoners. Don't know what about though. He used to do that a lot more in the past. But he stopped in the more recent months."

"What is it you are here to do exactly?" snapped Sulwyn. They stopped just outside the inner doors to the underground slope. He looked at her apprehensively. He was young. Younger than her. And judging from his character and how he carried himself, he was probably related to one of the elitists.

"Sorry, Lady Princess." He bowed hurriedly. "You will have quarters on the upper hill, outside in the fresh air. You will be on the other side of the wall, though, so you may be able to hear the prisoners. Don't let them get to you. It's hard on some, but you are clearly the king and queen's daughter. I'm sure it won't bother you."

"And my responsibilities?" she asked, annoyed. They made their way through the underground tunnel where Sulwyn spotted the varying paths off to the sides. "Where do those go?" she asked suddenly, stopping and pointing.

"Oh, solitary confinement cells, you will end up patrolling there too sometime during your stay. They can't interact with other prisoners." He spoke to her in hushed tones.

"I'm guessing you don't like them?" Humour laced her voice; she was sure these people would have been able to take him out easily.

"Rumour has it that some of them have been in there since before the Empire. Most are enemies to the king." Sulwyn glanced at the torchlit halls as they walked, until they were out of sight.

They continued in silence the rest of the way, the Protector leading her to an empty, modest room and taking his leave. She threw her bag onto the small bed, looking around.

The space was cramped; a bed, a small table and chair, and a tall, skinny mirror stuck to a wall. A small window let in the outside light, but it was higher than she stood. She couldn't see the prisoners from here and they could not see her.

Sulwyn closed the door, removing the uniform wrapped around her waist and lifting her red tunic and undershirt. She turned to look at the reflection of her back. Though the wounds made by the whip had healed into soft scars, a large, long gash travelled from her waist and in between her shoulder blades. Nori had done a fine enough job. Though it itched and pained her, it would heal into another scar. She rolled the layers back down, opened the door, and began to explore.

She would stay away from the prisoner cells for the time being. She wanted to get a feel of the place first. She wasn't sure what it was about Valens Muros, but for the life of her, she struggled to remember its layout without repetition. This place, on the other hand, was very straightforward and simple. All along the whitewashed walls were grey doors to other temporary rooms for those on duty. She located several bathing rooms, all stone and simple in design but good enough to keep hygiene up.

Very subtly Sulwyn heard shoes grinding on gravel. Without warning, a kick came straight near the back of her head, but she bent down quickly, dodging, and aimed a strong kick behind her, hitting something hard.

"Ow!" said a man loudly, and she turned to see a young black man bending over his knee. Sulwyn narrowed her gaze, half confused and half impressed. "I never got that response before!" he said noisily, standing with a little hop. Sulwyn's confusion grew.

"You weren't wearing the uniform, figured you were a recruit. Oh, but you're a woman! We don't get women often. Oh…" he stopped talking, eyes wide. Sulwyn couldn't help herself. She started to laugh and in turn, he smiled a little uncertainly, rubbing the back of his head.

He was a tall man, taller than Caldwell. His smile was bright in contrast to his dark skin. His hair, curly, short, and brown, was combed back into a small nub of a ponytail, the sides of his head shaved cleanly. His jaw looked strong and square, but he still had a baby face.

"Are you a Common One?" asked Sulwyn, looking at his grey uniform. Even though he had tried to attack her, she could feel no malice from him. He didn't seem to have any negativity whatsoever, seeming to radiate a bit of brightness and life.

"Yes, ma'am! They picked me out a few years ago, said I had good muscles." He flexed his arms a bit but stopped when he realized the uniform was too baggy for her to see them. She laughed more. "Buddy passed the job to me to show you the ways. Said you were scary, but I don't think you're that bad." He rubbed his head again, his smile still intact.

"Depends on my mood, I guess. Do you guard every day?"

"Every two days. Me and my sister run a cart shop in the market area, I make jewellery and we sell it." He stopped talking, staring at her closely, "I saw your match by the way. I shouldn't have been surprised at your skill, being related to the king and all. But Caldwell was one of the best. I honestly thought he might win, not that you would be injured or anything. My sister had to partake in the bets. I told her to go with Caldwell, but she said she'd go with you. Glad we did, though I heard they revoked the punishments because they were happy with the results."

Sulwyn felt a chill go through her. So they were that happy she killed him? "Did you ever talk to him?"

He shrugged, "Not really. But he never bothered me, I never bothered him. He always seemed too far to touch, you know? Like in his own world. I guess that's the difference in our status. But I know he worked hard to get where he was. It's a shame. I thought they would actually stop the match for him. But they must have been upset with him."

"Why would they be upset with him?" She watched him look around carefully. But they were the only ones in the hall.

"There have been rumours going around for a while now. Said he'd sneak out of the Empire in search of trouble. Apparently, he was the one who pretended to be a person from Antac and reported the incident."

Sulwyn's jaw dropped. "But isn't that a good thing? He was looking for issues against the Empire!"

"They think he was behind the impersonators. Think he started the group to cause trouble so that he could then report the towns in need and in turn go there and save them. Adding to his high count of missions. That kind of thing."

XVI

Sneaking Past Midnight

| SULWYN |

SULWYN found herself sitting in a corner against the outside walls. It was night now, the darkness hiding her as she sat in plain view of hundreds of prison cells in front of her. Though it was lights out, she could still hear some inmates talking to themselves, or talking to each other. She leaned her head back, looking at the multicoloured stars and the crescent moon that cast them all in a dull white light.

"Kione…" she said out loud.

The man she met earlier seemed like a good man. As he showed her around the outer grounds, she noticed he was smart and despite his baggy uniform, rather fit. He and his sister had come to the Empire some years ago when he was much younger. He always had a talent for making unique glass jewellery, something he had come by while living in the deserts of Uhuru. The Diarchy at the time was impressed with him, letting them set up shop.

She needed someone in the know, outside the castle walls. Someone like him would be a benefit to her fight. But could she trust him?

A hiss drew her attention to her left; her eyes adjusted to the darkness in the far corner. A familiar-looking man stood at the bars, staring at her. Sulwyn looked around her. Other Néosan and Protectors walked the area, but none were close to her. Slowly she stood in the faint moonlight and stepped carefully to the cell, looking in the other cells around him; the inmates were already asleep.

He watched her closely, never moving back, his eyes on her, "Kintana..." he whispered gruffly, and her eyes widened. "I have held my tongue. Do not be alarmed. Do not deny it. I know who you are."

But Sulwyn did not know him at all. She racked her memory for his face and saw nothing. He was much older than her but not nearly as old as Raghnall was. His hair was a light, warm brown and his eyes a darker grey than her own. The shape of his face, touched upon with wrinkles, seemed familiar. He had years of stress and harshness etched into each line on his face. But his eyes were lively.

"Are you the one that called out to me before?" she whispered back, stepping closer. He pressed his face against the bars, nodding. "How do you know me?"

"I have seen you before during my travels. I used to live in the High City. The day of the fall I was away in Guāngcǎi. I stayed away once I learned what happened. A few years ago, one of the towns I was hiding in reached their six-month collection. As luck would have it, they took me as one of their recruits. But I had the emblem of the High City on my person. They threw me in here for treason."

"That's it? Because of an emblem? What about other people here? Are there any similar 'crimes'?"

"Some, yes. Some are thieves, murderers, or committed other acts against the Empire...but a lot are people the Triarchy deemed a waste to go to the lower dungeons. The people sent to the lower dungeons are those they don't think they can eventually use for their gain. Every so often someone from the Triarchy comes to the Solus to try and bribe certain prisoners to their side. I'm sad to say that it has almost always worked. And no one would say no if it meant getting out of here. Even I am in talks of being let out to cook for Eques Muros."

"Then I suggest you take it," Sulwyn moved to step back, but he reached forward, stopping her.

"Please. Remember me. I hope to be able to help you soon," he whispered, stepping back just as firelight came around the far corner. Sulwyn stepped back quickly before the light could find her. She ran back to the inner wall, walking swiftly to her room as a wave of dizziness overcame her. Upon entering, exhaustion surged through her, and she collapsed on the thin bed.

❧

News of her arrival had spread by morning.

When she stepped out to patrol the outer area, many inmates called and jeered at her. She ignored them all. She didn't know who else in here would know about Kintana. Not many had seen her, but some people may have already made the connection. She wasn't sure how much news travelled to the Solus, but if someone in the lower dungeons knew who she was then she wouldn't be surprised if the same applied here.

She guarded the outer walls for most of the morning and was then sent within the inner garden after lunch, with prisoners out for their daily exercise.

She stood stiffly in a corner, watching prisoners in their black uniforms. Men and women of various statures filled the area, falling into the ritualistic patterns of playing ball, stretching, or running about. Some kept to themselves, others in groups.

A worn ball made its way towards her, and the men near her stared. "We heard you're the Blood Princess." said the bald man closest to her.

"She looks like 'em," said another, glaring at her.

"Not all of us have had the *honour* of meeting royalty before. The king and queen come once a year and don't bother with us lesser beings," said a tall man, eying the ball.

"And the prince is a maniac!" sniggered another.

Sulwyn silently watched them. Was she allowed to interact with them? They wouldn't trust her. She wouldn't expect them to either.

"This is boring. She thinks she's better than us." The man in front of her stretched slightly, scratching his round belly.

Sulwyn bent down, picking up the old ball, considering them. "I just want information..." she started, earning their attention. She didn't know if this was the best way to go about it, but she had to try.

"The prisoners that came here a month ago, the impersonators. Where are they?" "She handed over the ball. The bald man took it from her gingerly.

"Ain't seen 'em," he muttered unhelpfully. Sulwyn didn't think they would rat them out. She just nodded and they all walked away, but the bald man stayed behind, eyeing her.

"You seem a little…"

"Different?" she assisted. "I just want to find out if they are part of a bigger problem."

"Why, so the Empire can enslave some more people?" He smirked, tossing the ball back for the others to continue playing.

"No, because if there are more of them, that puts other innocent people at risk," muttered Sulwyn, but she knew it was a lost cause. She waved him off to continue playing before other Protectors became suspicious.

⤲⤳

The setting sun draped the sky in a beautiful array of pinks, dark greens, and yellows. The last turn of inmates had gone back to their cells for the day before dinner. Sulwyn walked back to the inner walls, making her way to the small kitchens. She offered her services to help deliver meals to each cell on the upper level.

She walked with a large cloth bag draped over her shoulder holding small metal tins of porridge, bits of meat, and spinach. She was surprised at the food they made. It wasn't the best, but it was definitely more than the lower or upper dungeons received and even more than most of the population in Vartugaul. She found that strange. But if that mysterious man was right, they kept the inmates happy and comfortable for later use. By doing so, they also ensured riots were kept low. It was better in here than out there for the most part. But no one wants to be locked up forever. She couldn't blame them if they accepted deals with the Empire.

Alongside other Protectors, Sulwyn made her way up the metal, spiral stairs to the fifth level. Men and women banged against the bars excitedly. Whether it was for the food or because she was the one delivering it, she did not know. Either way, she walked by slowly, pulling out tin container after tin container and handing them to hungry hands. Most did thank her; some just stared at her suspiciously. Eventually, she reached the end of the hall, a voice calling to her.

"Hey, princess," said the bald man from earlier. Sulwyn looked around her, but everyone was distracted by the food. Another Common One started giving out water at the other end. She stepped up to his cell, pretending to adjust the bag.

"There's summin' about you, so I'll tell you what I know," he whispered quickly. "The ones you asked for, when they arrived here, the women were killed. They didn' know anything. But the men were each taken to the Pain Cells."

"Pain Cells?" Sulwyn had a fleeting moment of remorse for the women, but only just.

"The single ones, you know 'em?"

"The solitary confinement cells? Why are they the Pain Cells?"

"Depending what yer there for, that's where they interrogate 'em. Not many last long; only the real crazies stay there forever. So, if you want to learn anything, you better get to that part soon." He turned away, yelling excitedly for water and earning a distraction for her to slip away unnoticed.

&c&

Sulwyn's shift was over, and she had yet to be assigned to the Pain Cells. She decided she'd just go there herself. Once midnight passed, the guard count dropped to half.

She opened her bedroom door slowly and quietly. It barely made a sound as she stepped through the crack and closed it.

Quickly she dashed down the hall and back through the iron doors. They squeaked a tad, forcing her to still, straining to listen. Nothing stirred. She closed the door and began her descent down the steep dirt hill. Every so often a torch illuminated her shadow across the dirt walls. She was still impressed with the underground work and layout, but vaguely wondered what would happen if an earthquake, though rare, struck the Empire.

She pushed that thought from her mind and reached the bottom, skidding to a halt. Sulwyn crouched low to the ground, listening again, but no sounds met her ears. She could sense a few guards faintly in the distance and in the other rooms. Sulwyn turned her head left and right. To her understanding, the Pain Cells aligned with the outer iron walls above in one large square. There were only fifty-one cells, though no one seemed to know how many were filled. Sulwyn went right, keeping low as she ran. Her steps barely made a sound as she rounded the first corner.

Instantly she was reminded of the upper dungeon. Lonely and quiet, torch light every so often, keeping most in almost total darkness. But here there were no bars save for a small rectangular space in the middle of each metal door and a locked food door near the bottom. Sulwyn walked forward quietly, listening for any form of movement.

Just like the lower and upper dungeons, there was no sense of time here. No windows to show them the sun or the rain. This was cruel. But she wasn't surprised. Unlike the lower dungeons, each prisoner was alone, completely and indefinitely alone. It would drive anyone mad. But there was nothing here. No screams, no wailing or sobbing. Just silence. Either the people within had already lost their minds, or they were more dangerous than she realized.

Sulwyn walked on slowly, concentrating as she paused by each door, trying to sense life within. She didn't want to peer too closely to the bars. She wasn't supposed to be here, not yet at least.

"This isn't getting me anywhere. I can't even tell if these are empty or not!" she hissed, frustration rising. And with unfortunate timing, Sulwyn could feel the rise of heat within her. To have two visions in the span of a few months was new. She had limited time.

Carefully she walked, but still heard nothing. The men that should be there were only a month in. There was no way they would remain silent, unless they were asleep or knocked out. She would have to keep trying. Walking along, she reached the end and turned the second corner. But as soon as she passed the first door, she stopped.

But not of her own accord.

"Look what I've caught," purred a deep, soft voice behind her. She'd never heard this voice before. But whatever he was doing kept her from looking behind her—she couldn't move at all. Paralyzed in one spot, fear coursed through her. Slowly, she listened to almost inaudible steps walk closer to her. She could sense nothing but malice from him. And her fear grew further still.

"What is a little bird like you, pecking, poking, and sneaking around after midnight, doing here? I didn't hear anything about you being positioned here yet," he whispered coldly. She moved her eyes far to the left and right, waiting to glimpse him, but he stopped short, his shadow cast upon the wall.

He stood close to her, his breath cool on the back of her neck. "The impersonators have been dealt with. You needn't worry, Cailín. You will receive some results soon. But we can't have you down here just yet." She could hear the smirk in him. Her skin crawled in goosebumps at his breath on her skin. But just as suddenly as he had come, he stepped back and the hold on her was gone.

Sulwyn whipped around, holding the back of her neck, the fear creeping away. Undoing the braid to bring warmth back to her skin, she ran forwards, going back around the corner, but the hall was empty. She breathed out, realizing she had been holding it in the whole time. Pure fear wasn't something she was free of, but she did feel it rarely. And at this moment, she had never felt it more.

Sulwyn decided to leave, unable to shake the feeling that she was still being watched. Despite the amount of malice she felt, the voice also sounded truthful. And whether that was correct, she had nothing to go on. Lingering there was dangerous now. She had no idea who was in each cell and what they were there for. She would have to insist on being scheduled sooner. And unlike last time, the vision was creeping through her faster.

She ran back the way she came, maintaining as much stealth as she could manage with the increased fire within her. After what seemed like forever, she was back in her room, quietly closing the door and sitting on the small bed, focusing.

She needed to will herself to remember what she would see or hear. As she breathed deeply, the fever began to seep over her.

Sulwyn concentrated with everything she had. It hurt to breathe, the ache and warmth washing over her; did it always hurt this much? And then suddenly sound fell away, and colours flowed through her mind mixed with the flitting movement of long hair. Fire burning in flashes, mixed with a crowd in a cave. Quickly a gaggle of sounds followed. A distorted voice, woman or man she couldn't tell, egged on the crowd around them, echoing off the walls of the cave. She felt a burning in her stomach, her limbs numb and heavy. Trapped and bound, panic filled her, surrounded by cheers.

But then it all abruptly stopped, the pressure fell away from her, and she could hear the faint sounds of the night around her. Sulwyn opened her eyes, gasping loudly and falling to the floor, shaking uncontrollably.

The stone was cold and comforting as the heat left her. Sulwyn continued to lie there, breathing in the smell of mould and dirt. It reminded her of the upper dungeon. Of the pain she had felt when Raghnall left her, and of Caldwell and what his death really meant. His face flashed before her. His first and only true smile flitted past her mind, his body falling to the darkness along with her.

੯੯

"Heya, princess? Lady Princess? Sulwyn?" said a voice close to her. Her stomach was cold, along with her arms and legs. Though she heard him coming, she didn't want to move. "Fighter chick? Crazy Blood Princess?"

"I am not crazy!" she shouted, lifting herself off the ground and looking around.

Kione stooped in front of her, waving brightly. "You're finally up. One of the other Common Ones came to get me since I'm your tour guide. Said you'd been asleep all morning, missing your shift. Late night?" he asked happily, mildly confused as to why she was on the ground.

"Just having problems adjusting," she mumbled, crawling onto the bed. She stretched, but pulled back suddenly, Kione's hand reaching forward and touching her cheek.

"Did you stay awake crying?" he asked softly. Heat crawled up her neck but pushed his hand away.

"I have leaky eyes. It's dusty here. That's all." She stood quickly, eying him up. He stood straight, bemused.

"Well, you are the princess, so I don't think it matters if you missed a shift or not. Besides, I'm in charge of reporting your actions and well-being. I'll just put you down for extreme allergies to the Solus." Sulwyn looked at him incredulously.

"You're the one doing reports on me? Do you know when I can see the solitary confinement cells?"

"The Pain Cells? Why do you want to see those?" he asked, suspicious.

"I am here for a reason. I need to investigate the impersonators."

"But that's been dealt with already, last night actually." He looked at her darkly. "Only one of them talked, finally, after being tortured for days. He said this all started in a town far east. But no one knows the town he's talking about. Said it's hard to find because of the fog. Before they could get more information from him, he died. But I think they're closing in on it. In time the Uferor will be sent to scope it all out, I'm sure." He shrugged.

She didn't know if it should unsettle her that she was so desensitized to violence but brushed it off. Sulwyn had a feeling the man she met last night and the man who tortured them were one and the same. "What happened to the others then?"

"Lower dungeons. They saw nothing of importance in them..." he trailed off, stepping back out the open door. "I've been given orders. They want to match your schedule to mine and give you a proper tour of the Common One grounds."

"Who? Artaxiad?"

"No. Pandora. Thinks you need to see for yourself how we live and how much we should be thanking them," he said sarcastically. "I came here to get you. You'll spend a few hours with me, then return here." He suddenly looked at her apprehensively. "I mean our queen."

Sulwyn held her hand up. "It's fine. I could do with some normal air." She gestured for him to lead the way.

On horse, they galloped outside the Solus and back towards the walls of the Empire. Sulwyn looked up again; the sky was almost clear, white clouds drifting by.

"Do you close shop when it rains?" She asked while they left their horses with the gatekeeper. He bowed to Sulwyn but eyed Kione with a little discomfort.

"We have a good setup. Our home is right behind it, so even if it rains, we can keep it open without damage. But it shouldn't rain today. I mean, look at the sky!"

Sulwyn shrugged, following him north from the entrance. Little dirt paths wove in and out between small and large carts in the centre, while small stone shops littered the sides atop short blue grass. Sulwyn spotted a few Privileged, but most of the shoppers were other Common Ones. They all stared at her curiously and nodded in acknowledgment to Kione. Not everyone realized who she was, and she liked it this way. She could escape the eyes of fear momentarily. They walked farther still until they reached shops that were more spread out.

"We're just past here," he called, beckoning her to quicken her pace.

"Will I meet your sister?"

Kione looked back at her, a little apologetic. "She...um, doesn't like Empire folk..."

"She hates them, I get it. I don't expect anything less. Give her my regards when you see her, I suppose."

"That might get me hit." He shuffled up to his closed metal and wood shop cart. She spotted his small stone home behind it. Sulwyn assumed it was just one large room and possibly a kitchen. She had spotted other small houses like theirs alongside small bathing houses scattered every so often.

"Well, take a look if you like." He lifted the large metal door back. It pulled away unseen revealing a small but decent setup of various stones, glasses, and colours. Earrings, necklaces, and bracelets lined the front, placed carefully on purple silk. Larger items like paperweights, odd coloured plates, and the like were in the back. It was all rather well made.

"These are beautiful!" She reached forward, lightly touching a necklace of bright transparent yellow. "How do you make them?

"With coloured metals and dyes, heat, sand, and a helluva lot of patience. I don't do much else, besides train and work at the Solus. It's just a joyful hobby."

"Do not underestimate your talent," said a deep, clear voice behind them.

Sulwyn turned, looking up at a rather striking woman. She was slightly shorter than Kione but still taller than Sulwyn. Her dark brown hair was tied into a large bun behind the top of her head, the right side shaved. Sulwyn spotted various kinds of intricate black and white tattoos along her dark brown skin, passing along her neck and down her collarbone unseen. Though her eyes were deep set and her irises brown and orange, she looked just like Kione, but with higher cheekbones. Sulwyn spotted the ends of the tattoos along her right arm, just under the fabric of her long grey uniform dress.

"Nice of you to join us," said Kione a little awkwardly. The woman's eyes had yet to leave Sulwyn's, staring at her intensely.

"The pleasure is mine," stated the woman, bowing but raising her head slightly, looking Sulwyn in the eyes again. "Kintana..." she whispered.

"Wait, what?!" exclaimed Kione, but the woman quickly straightened, smacking Kione on the side of the head. Sulwyn continued to stare at the woman. Should she deny it, or admit to being Kintana? The woman smirked, holding out her hand.

"You should know most of us dislike the Empire. But we also want to live. I would not rat you out." She winked, keeping her hand out. Sulwyn took her hand, shaking it. She could tell Kione was skilled but knew this woman was well practised, older, with aptitude and wisdom.

"I'd prefer if you would refer to me as...well, if it won't get you in trouble, you can call me Sulwyn."

"Diesirae." She held her hand a moment longer before letting go and shoving her brother to the side. "Thank you for tolerating Kione. He is a good kid."

"No wonder you bet for her with such confidence. And I know you're like seventy, but I'm not a kid," he huffed angrily, earning another smack to the head.

"Forty-one is not seventy, where did you learn to count? And at my age, you are all kids." She shrugged apologetically to Sulwyn, but Sulwyn took no offence.

"I didn't expect that...I thought you were only a few years older than me, honestly," said Sulwyn a little shyly. This woman was the embodiment of everything Sulwyn admired. She was tall, extremely fit, yet womanly all the same. Not to mention that she exuded a kind of presence, something that made her *want* to listen to her. But she held her excitement back; this was another person who knew who she really was.

"How do you know me?" asked Sulwyn warily.

"You are worrying about the wrong thing. We both want freedom. When you get to my age, you travel a lot. I have moved from town to town just trying to help others. Much like what you and the Steel Warrior had done. I had the fortune of seeing you both in action briefly. You both were untraceable but left a mark everywhere. It is amazing."

Sulwyn narrowed her eyes. "I ask that you refrain from speaking about this further. This is not a safe place to speak openly," warned Sulwyn, and Diesirae nodded. But this was perfect. She wanted Kione's assistance. They would be able to help her.

Sulwyn turned back to the items of Kione's talent. She looked over them again and stopped, looking at a thin, black leather bracelet. Without realizing it, her eyes watered briefly as she lifted the bracelet off the purple silk. The leather band pushed through one stone, but the colours that created it were blue, purple, and red.

"Take it as a gift," blurted Kione.

Sulwyn looked back to Diesirae, who nodded in agreement. "We all have something in common. Even if we don't put it in words," he finished, taking the bracelet and wrapping it in a black velvet pouch. He placed it carefully in her hands, folding her fingers over it just as light drops of rain began to fall.

❧

The rest of the week passed without incident. She continued to stay close to Kione, finding comfort in the light he gave off and knowing that she had found people like her. She only had two more weeks at the Solus, and though she hated having to go back to Valens Muros for the weekend, there were some perks.

"Sulwyn!" Arsinone's voice yelled through her, much to her discomfort. The sound resonated in her mind, earning a slight throb to her head. *"Oh, I'm sorry…"* she mumbled as Sulwyn led Ki to the stables, petting him. An attendant came to rub him down just as Eztli appeared at the side door of the castle waiting for her.

Sulwyn found herself smiling brightly but faltered. "I have to report to Artaxiad first," she mumbled. Ki neighed after her as she left.

"Don't worry about it, sweetness, just come to your room after." Eztli winked before sashaying away and through the door.

Sulwyn made her way to Artaxiad's study, finally having it memorized. She knocked once but was surprised to find it empty save for one maid tidying the room. Immediately she curtsied, nervously pulling out a letter from her apron.

Sulwyn thanked her, taking it and ripping it open:

> *I am away for the next few weeks. Please make yourself more acquainted with the queen. She expects to hear your reports from the Solus.*

Artaxiad's name was signed at the bottom. Sulwyn wasn't sure if she felt happy or apprehensive. Unlike Artaxiad, Pandora was hard to read.

"Excuse me," muttered Sulwyn, but she stopped, hearing a voice call to her. "Never mind." Sulwyn bowed, hurriedly leaving the room and the maid in confusion.

"Arsinone?" said Sulwyn out loud. In a few moments, tiny arms tackled her midriff in a firm hug. Sulwyn knelt in front of her, wrapping her arms around her.

"I can take you to Pandora's room. I can hear her. She's rather loud today. But I have problems reading her clearly. She has a lot going on in her soul," said Arsinone calmly.

"Who else can't you read well?"

Arsinone pondered, "I can't read complicated people well. Not unless I become closer to them, or if I have direct contact with them. I have yet to really hear anyone properly because there are so many people in the Empire." She looked up at Sulwyn carefully. "I can't read Galahad well, and he's managed to block me somehow. And actually, you're a bit difficult to read too. Maybe it has to do with a person's willpower."

Sulwyn nodded, "Can you hear everyone?" she asked, taking Arsinone's hand in her own as they walked.

"Yes and no. I've gauged my ability to about a fifty-foot radius. I don't know if that's a permanent thing, or if I'll get better at it as I get older. I hear fleeting moments. It's only when I focus on one person can I hear their current thoughts properly. Most people are not interesting. Some are disturbing. I try to keep it shallow. I don't like hearing everything."

"What about when you sleep?"

"I see people's dreams, but I've learned to tune it out, so it doesn't bother me anymore." Sulwyn looked at her sadly.

"I don't mind, I was born like this. I've gotten used to tuning out most of it. And when I'm focused on one person, the rest fades more." she smiled at Sulwyn. She was cutest when she smiled. Sulwyn had taken to Arsinone since they reunited in the closet, wanting to preserve her childlike innocence.

"Do you dream?"

"I can't, maybe because I hear and see everyone else's. But I really don't need it," Arsinone stopped walking and pointed to the door at the end of the hall. "She's in there. She's in a rather good mood. I have to go back now.

I'll see you when you're done." Arsinone smiled again, shuffling down the opposite end of the hall.

Sulwyn walked forward, her hands growing cold at the thought of being alone with Pandora. She knocked loudly twice and waited until Pandora called her in. Pushing the doors open, Sulwyn was greeted by a very stuffy room.

Though it was mid-summer weather outside, Pandora had a fire going, her windows closed, and long, heavy red fabrics draped every inch of her wall. The rest of her study resembled Artaxiad's, if not a bit larger. One thing that stood out most was a small table in the far left corner with twenty or so children's dolls. The other was the fact that Pandora seemed to be journaling. Sulwyn raised a brow but turned her attention to the queen as she cleared her throat.

"The king has informed me that you are here to report to me. So... report."

Sulwyn did not hesitate; anything to get out of here faster. "I was originally sent to interrogate those arrested and charged with impersonation. However, I was told the case was dealt with by someone else."

"Yes, a trusted person was given that task instead. There was no room for error. The results of that interrogation will be in your hands. I suspect we will be sending you on another assignment once we fully...understand the town that we are sending you to. Our king has gone personally to confirm the whereabouts of this place." Pandora barely looked at her. She kept her eyes on the leatherbound journal she was writing in, leaning back in her chair. It seemed she wanted this over with too. But Sulwyn could only think how fascinating it was that someone like Pandora journaled.

"There is nothing else of interest to report. I will continue my next two weeks at the Solus and then report again after that."

Pandora slowly looked up at her, her light grey eyes penetrating Sulwyn's dark grey ones. Did she say something wrong?

Pandora smirked. "Are you not going to ask about the women and why they were killed? Or why we killed the men?"

Sulwyn clenched her jaw. "I thought the men were sent to the lower dungeons?"

"We had already killed most of them, I figured why not all?" She shrugged, "Make an example of this group of traitors and outcasts."

Sulwyn remained impassive and the lack of care within her about that fact surprised her almost as much as her words. "I couldn't agree more."

Pandora stared at her, her smirk becoming a little wickeder with each moment. "As much as I hate to agree with it, the rumours about you are true. You are *strikingly* similar to us not only in appearance but in personality. I should feel honoured. But I'm not."

She stood, putting her journal down. The folds of her dark blue dress caressed her every move. "No matter. I think this works out for both of us. You get to live off our accomplishments, and we get to put you to work. I can't deny your talent. You are an asset to us as long as you stay out of trouble."

She stepped around her desk, "But never forget, that we are watching your every move. Who you talk to, who you connect with…those that hold your hand or embrace you. Everyone. Don't believe for a second we can't take them all away. No matter what you think."

Sulwyn stared in shock and confusion, and this must have reflected on her face because now Pandora was laughing. "It matters not if you understand now or later, or never for all I care. Just heed my warning."

XVII

Eques Muros

| SULWYN |

"**W**ELCOME back, sweetness!" Sulwyn received pink petals to the face, spitting them out as the girls laughed. She looked around the room and noticed three small cots had been moved in.

"You all could have slept on the bed," said Sulwyn, taking her shoes off and sitting on a chair.

"We wanted it to be fresh for you," said Nori quietly. She looked away when Sulwyn looked at her.

"Don't mind her, just thinks yer a bit scary," shrugged Eztli. Nori's face blushed profusely. "What?"

"Tact, Ez," said Arsinone stifling a laugh.

"I'm not...afraid of you. Just a little intimidated. I wish we could be more formidable."

"But you're a Devinal!" exclaimed Sulwyn, earning a pillow to the face.

"Hush, will ya!" said Eztli. Arsinone laughing hysterically.

Sulwyn laughed too but stopped when she noticed the sound of running water was missing. She walked across the room towards the small river. The water was still and already starting to evaporate.

"We didn't do it!" said Eztli waving her arms around.

"No, don't worry about it. I expected it," said Sulwyn quietly. She turned to them, smiling brightly. "Why don't I teach you all some self-defence?"

After about an hour of what turned into play fighting, all four of them lay on the wooden floor, breathing heavily from laughing too much.

Sulwyn was ecstatic. She never had kids to play with growing up and didn't expect to either. She chose her path, and it was hard for kids to play freely anymore anyway. But on top of that, she never got to interact with many other women. And this Sulwyn was thankful for. If there was one thing Raghnall had managed to give her after all this, it was this moment. She glanced at the gifted ring, his sullied face in her mind once again. That nagging feeling she was missing *something* pulling at her.

"We've got to prepare the lunches for the Privileged that live 'ere," said Eztli sadly, sitting up. "Come by later for some food, okay?" Eztli patted her arm getting up. She helped Arsinone stand before they all waved goodbye. Sulwyn stretched on the floor before she too got up and went to take a long-awaited bath.

⤷∘⤶

Sulwyn had fallen asleep in the stone tub, waking once the water grew cold. She understood why people started to fall for the charms of the Empire. Compared to the rest of Vartugaul, the higher the status the more comfortable they became. But she thought about what Arsinone had said and knew that she could never lose herself to this. Not when all of it came at such a high cost.

The rest of her night was a peaceful one. She felt comfortable with the girls around and found herself reluctant to go back to the Solus. But she put it past her for now and instead used this time as a moment of healing.

By morning, Sulwyn bid the girls goodbye. She didn't expect anyone to come and see her off, so when Pandora showed up in the stables, spiked ice dropped into her veins.

Sulwyn stopped petting Ki, watching the queen carefully as she glided towards her, dark red dress flowing around her in the gentle wind, blending with her red hair. Why was she wearing such an elaborate dress so early in the morning?

"I've read the reports from those in the Solus around you. You have been well received," she started, as if she were talking about the weather.

But Sulwyn finally noticed something; unless necessary, Pandora didn't or wouldn't make eye contact with her.

"As you've been told, the Leaders take turns guarding the Solus every so often. You will be meeting another soon; I've left him in charge of the impersonator problem. He will be contacting you since you are so interested." As she turned to leave Sulwyn had a new, reckless idea.

"Wait!" she called, stepping forward slightly. Pandora turned to her mildly surprised, but that soon changed to pure impassiveness.

"How does one become a Leader now?"

"Now?" She faced Sulwyn properly, folding her arms across her stomach. A smirk across her lips.

Sulwyn hesitated. "The prince informed me that at one time, battles took place to name Leaders, but that it was banned for reasons. So how does one become a Leader now?"

"Nomination," she replied, eyes narrowed. "Why? Do you want to be a Leader? With the recent death of Caldwell, there is an opening. However, each Uferor team specializes in a certain skill. Caldwell's was stealth. Either the nominee must match that group's skill, or if we see fit, we can rearrange the Leaders."

Sulwyn's heart beat a bit faster. "Not me. There is a man in the Solus, a Common One—"

Pandora laughed harshly, "A Common One?"

"You said nomination? If he's interested, can't I nominate him?"

"Of course, but that's not the main requirement," Pandora smiled widely now. "The other Leaders have to accept him as well, be it with tests or however they see fit. If they don't all agree, then he won't be appointed Leader."

Sulwyn was taken aback by such an intricate system. That meant she would have to interact with Galahad, but not only him. The other Leaders were people who wanted to be there. How bad were they? This Daijiro person already seemed dangerous enough, what were the rest like? And would Kione even agree? Would Diesirae even let him?

"Looks like you've understood the difficulty of the situation. But I am happy you are showing interest. The Validus Uferor are our top soldiers. If you think you've found someone suitable, then please go ahead. With your title, you can at least prevent him from being killed if he's rejected. Though, you may have to fight for him." Pandora's smile was wicked again; she turned away, laughing.

Sulwyn stared after her until she saw the last folds of her dress disappear into the darkness of the stables to the castle. If she could get Kione into the Validus Uferor it would be an excellent opportunity for them all.

Sulwyn mounted Ki. The steed turned to look at her, wondering why she hadn't signalled him to move. If she could get Kione in that would be good, but if *she* could get in, would that be better?

⇛⇝

Kione spat out his water, forcing Sulwyn to sidestep and almost hit a wall.

"Are you insane?!" He raised his voice, but Sulwyn just hurried to close her bedroom door. As soon as she had gotten to the Solus, she had located him, dragging him into her room.

"It's perfect! I mean if you aren't confident, I can test you first. We will have a mock fight and decide after that. But, Kione, I can tell you are strong, and you fight for the same cause."

"But I'm not insane. The Uferor are a skilled group of people. I, as well as many other people, believe they're responsible for the Empire standing, besides the king and queen. If they didn't have them as enforcement, people would have continued rebelling once Artaxiad stopped raiding everything on his own!" He looked at her with eyes wide and she knew he was afraid.

"When they first created the Uferor, Caldwell was the first Leader. When they were forming the other four groups, his group had already started going out on missions and the rebellion rate dropped to half in no time at all. Caldwell was talented, and that's why his group specialized in stealth. Even if I could make it, I don't have the same skills he does. They wouldn't take me for that group."

"Pandora said they can rearrange the groups if they see fit."

"Do you even know who the other Leaders are?"

"Only in name, but I was told I'm meeting one this week. Just let me spar with you and we can see."

"I'll spar with you, but only if Diesirae agrees. She's my only family, Sulwyn, this isn't a decision I can make on my own." He spoke gravely. Seeing him like this made her fully understand the severity of what she was asking.

"But why don't you just do it? With your skill, it would be easy, and they wouldn't say no to you. You're Kintana, after all!"

"Shh! I'm their daughter who was found after being held captive for years. There's no way I should have the strength to be a Leader yet. It's too early for that, but I plan to pursue it in time. Besides, no matter what anyone believes, I didn't win fairly against Caldwell. He wanted to die; he threw the match. But if this works, we can infiltrate our way into any of the five, no? The only ones capable of defeating a Leader would be another Leader, right?"

Kione breathed out heavily, sitting on her bed, head between his hands.

Sulwyn clenched her fists. What was she doing? She couldn't get someone like him involved in her mess. She shouldn't have asked him at all; her recklessness should stay with her.

"Kione—"

"I've been static for so long that I can't believe this brought fear to me," he said, looking at her. "To show such cowardice in front of Kintana. I should be ashamed."

"No, I shouldn't have asked you something so ridiculous. I take it back, I'm sorry."

A knock brought her attention to the door; she turned to open it, Kione standing up. The man with yellow eyes whose name she'd forgotten was outside. She could see his stubbornness, but at the same time, she could also see his nervousness. He cast a strange glance between her and Kione.

"I'm sorry to disturb you, my lady. I've been told that you are to go to Eques Muros for a briefing on the Pain Cells."

"They can't do that here?" asked Sulwyn, her hands growing cold.

"The prince is also involved and as he is not allowed in the Solus, I'm afraid you must go there instead."

"Fine. I just wish someone told me that before I came here. What a waste of time to go back after I've just arrived. You can go, I'll leave soon." She waved him out as he bowed stiffly and left.

She turned to Kione, who was watching her carefully. She had grown so used to his brightness and light moods that seeing him like this made her feel worse. She really should never have asked him; she needed to get used to being alone.

"Let me talk to Diesirae..."

"No, I'm not going to nominate you. You were right, it's best if I do it myself. I'll just have to wait a bit; maybe do some open training, so it looks like I didn't just gain experience from nowhere."

"No, Sulwyn, *you* were right. If I can get in, we can make a change. And this would let me leave the Empire freely. I've been here since we arrived so many years ago. Diesirae sneaks out of the Empire all the time, but because I work for the Solus, I don't have that kind of freedom. If I did this, I could finally leave. And in turn, use this to help you."

"This isn't your battle."

"This is everyone's battle. No matter how great you are, you can't do it alone."

જ્જ

Sulwyn promised to meet Kione when he got back from talking to Diesirae and when she came back from Eques. If the impersonators had already been dealt with, she didn't have much interest left in the Pain Cells. She wanted to get started on finding out where this fog town was. But she knew she needed to learn about the Pain Cells sooner or later.

She pulled the reigns for Ki to slow down as Eques came into view.

Why was she so nervous? She had no reason to be. Galahad was a mystery from the start. He had changed from the person she first met all those years ago, and it was for mere minutes. For her to even have such expectations of him from that time was foolish from the beginning. Just because he was from some elite clan didn't mean he was a good person.

But she knew she was lying to herself.

No matter what Galahad was, there had to be some truth to what he said about his story. And with that, she would have to be careful and play it by ear. However, right now, she was at full liberty to just hate him for embarrassing her if nothing else.

"We've been expecting you," said a Néosan, greeting her at the doors. He went to take Ki's reigns as Sulwyn dismounted but Ki raised his front legs, neighing loudly. The Néosan let go, stepping back a safe distance.

"Hey! What's wrong?" whispered Sulwyn suddenly, patting him carefully on the neck. He was restless, moving back but closer to her. Sulwyn looked around her, the trees rustling loudly in the wind around them. She felt it too, a sort of foreboding. But she took a deep breath.

"I won't have your reigns tied. Promise to wait here for me and hide if you feel the need to. I will be back, okay?" she whispered. He neighed again, pushing her forward.

"Leave him be," commanded Sulwyn. The Néosan saluted, glad to be away from both of them. He stepped forward quickly, leading her through the doors.

It wasn't just the outside of this castle that was different, but she didn't expect the inside to be so dissimilar as well. It was dull and cold, unlike Valens with its lavish decorations, walls, and floor. Instead, most of it was grey or blue with stone floors and simple side tables. A painting here or there decorated the wall every so often with trivial landscapes.

Her boots echoed loudly against the hard slate tiles, but it did make sense. This was a castle for training and living quarters of people who were in and out every day. It would be a disaster to keep neat and clean if there were so many trinkets and trophies around. Plus, what did they matter compared to the king and queen of Vartugaul?

"The other party has yet to arrive. Please rest in this room while you wait," said the Néosan, taking off before she could say anything else. If there was one thing she didn't mind from being their daughter, it was that Néosan also looked at her in fear. And this was something she had become accustomed to since being Kintana.

But this fear was different.

While she was Kintana, it was fear of a name, fear of Raghnall, and fear of failing to catch them and reporting that to Artaxiad. But here it was fear of torture, fear of being punished on a whim for not being good enough for her, fear she was exactly like her parents.

She looked around the room. This one was a little more lavish, matching the status of the Empire. A clean fireplace sat across from her in wooden panelled walls. Loungers were positioned around for relaxing. A small dining table was set on the other side but looked disused. The windows were covered in thin gold and white curtains, while the walls were the same navy blue as the halls. This seemed like one of the few rooms with carpet, lush and black. What did the other rooms look like?

Sulwyn sat on the couch for about one minute before throwing off her boots and opening the doors. As it was early in the day, she knew that most of the Néosan were out. The Captains didn't train during the week, and the Validus should be out as well. The layout here was simpler to follow. Maybe it was the lavishness of Valens Muros that had been throwing her off.

The floor was cold, but she needed to be quiet. She passed various doors; from some, she could hear servants on the other side. Running to the other end, she hoped this castle followed the same design. And she was right. At the end of the hall, she was met with the same spiral stone steps that went up or down, used by servants of the castle.

What was she hoping to find? Or was it who? The Néosan said the other party wasn't here yet. Did that mean not in the castle or not ready for the meeting? Did it even matter? What was she really looking for?

Sulwyn went up to the second floor. Slowly she walked, listening carefully, passing rooms with murmured conversation. Maybe off-duty Néosan and guests or servants alike.

She stopped at a smaller door, for what reason she wasn't sure. But when she opened it, she was rather happy with her choice.

They never did give her back her original weapons and belt. And after the fight with Caldwell, she still wasn't given anything. When she was at Valens, everything was such a mess for her mentally she hadn't even given it a thought to try and find any. And frankly, it slipped her mind when she was relaxing on her one day off with Eztli and the rest.

But here, she faced a closet full of various weapons and equipment. Smiling devilishly, she picked up a few simple daggers as well as a thigh holster. She really needed to stop her habit of sneaking around without boots. But she managed to stuff smaller knives for her boots into the holster as well. Satisfied, she closed the door and took off. The weight on her leg was comfortable to have again.

How much time had passed since she first left the room? It couldn't be more than a few minutes and she had yet to hear anything. She continued to the third floor. And instantly a wave of foreboding hit her.

This was obviously where the living quarters started for those higher in the Néosan. For one thing, there were nice, thick black carpets on the floors instead of stone. Her feet welcomed the bit of warmth that silenced her steps further. Here the walls were painted a deep plum, with gold patterns running lightly atop it. Larger paintings and mirrors were placed every so often, making the small hallway seem fuller and warmer.

Her heart pounded faster and stronger in her chest with each step. Sulwyn still didn't know what it was she was really looking for or hoping to find. But she had always been too curious, a problem that Raghnall told her to get under control. Her curiosity had always gotten them into interesting situations. She walked slower now, laughing a little. The things they got into because of her...but she had gotten her curiosity from Raghnall. And he had led them into all kinds of trouble too.

"You look rather charming when you smile, Cailín."

Sulwyn froze, and again not of her own accord. She had been expecting to find Galahad, but not this man. He was behind her, stepping quietly closer to her. Once more the unknown terror spread through her at whatever he was doing to her.

"But it looks like this is a habit of yours. Do you enjoy sneaking around?" He purred, and this time Sulwyn felt a different feeling mixed within the fear. A deep sort of pull towards his voice. It was pleasant to hear, sending shivers through her. But this was wrong. Anything that could hold her like this was dangerous.

"Stop hiding behind your power and let me see you," she demanded and could hear his steps falter. What part of that made him hesitate? She heard an exhale of breath—laughing?

"My, the rumours about you are true, Lady Princess, as fierce as they say." Sulwyn held her breath, her legs slowly turning her around without her consent or will. What kind of power was this?

"I like those eyes," he purred quietly, her glare fierce.

The pull she felt from his voice was stronger now, like a kind of allure that was not only caused by his voice but by his body and soul as well. And she felt ashamed. She always found Galahad rather dashing, but this man in front of her was like nothing she had seen before.

He was a tad shorter than Galahad but slimmer and more poised. His eyes were a deep, dark red like blood, fierce and piercing her soul. His hair was long enough to brush his broad shoulders, straight and tied back, a dark golden with streaks white as snow, though some strands had fallen to the side in a mess. It wasn't just his appearance that stood out but also his clothes. It was different than anything she had seen in any part of Vartugaul, though it had a tinge of Guāngcǎi's flowing style. Not to mention it didn't follow any of the Empire's standards.

His pants were a loose-fitting dark brown that tapered at his calves with a thick band. Black slipper-like shoes, with thick black ribbons wrapped up around his ankles. A deep yellow sash swathed around his narrow waist at least twice with a loose sleeveless black tunic. His skin was a golden medium tan. But the more she stared at his narrow face, angular eyes, and sculpted cheekbones, the more she realized that he was different. Much different than anyone; was he mixed with something evolved?

"If you keep staring at me like that I might blush, Cailín," he smirked, and then his expression was instantly feral and teasing. But still she couldn't move.

"Remove your hold on me," said Sulwyn and to her surprise, her voice came out just as strong as it always did. Good, then she wasn't that deeply entranced. There was something at work here, but she didn't know what. He seemed to realize her thoughts because his smile deepened.

"What if I don't?"

"Then I'll have to make you," gritted Sulwyn and she fought. She knew she was struggling, and yet nothing responded to her. Not a single limb. All she could do was stand and stare at him. Breathing, blinking, and speaking seemed the only things she had control over. But she wouldn't give up, not yet.

"That's not a good idea, my lady, you could hurt yourself, and we wouldn't want that."

"Who are you? You are clearly very capable. So, you must be a Leader." She stopped trying. That wouldn't be how she conquered this. Sulwyn took deep breaths, her eyes never leaving his. She could see it in his eyes alone, he was stained in more blood than she could imagine; the malice she had felt before was nothing compared to what she felt now. She had a feeling of who he was, but she wanted him to say it.

He stepped closer, watching her carefully. Instead, he took her in, eyes sweeping over every inch of her. She could feel it as he continued to walk around her before he faced her again.

"You seem to be everything I've heard of. You are quite formidable, Kintana."

"Let me go and I can show you more."

He let out a deep laugh that sent more chills through her. "Are you playing with me, Cailín? That's a very dangerous thing to do." He raised his hand, his fingers reaching to gently stroke her face, but Sulwyn pulled back.

And they both froze before she was paralyzed again.

She had managed to move, and it stunned him just as much. His smile grew crooked, eyes a little darker. "My, my, you are impressive."

But his smile vanished; he raised his hand before her eyes, and then his fingers flicked downwards. She dropped to her knees hard, her teeth gnashing against each other, biting her tongue. Sulwyn forced herself to look up. Her fear was escalating, but her instincts kept her keen. Whatever he was, whatever he was doing, she wouldn't make it easy. She wished she could grab one of her newly acquired daggers but knew that wasn't an option.

He kneeled on one knee, his face so close to hers she could feel his cool breath against her lips. And again, she felt that strong pull; his lips seemed like the only thing that mattered right now.

He chuckled softly, "We're going to go find our All Command." He smiled wider. Suddenly he leaned forward, bracing his shoulder against her stomach.

In one swoop he lifted her with surprising ease given his stature, and she was thrown over his shoulder. Still, she couldn't move. And his touch sent an inferno through her. She shivered, earning another low chuckle.

What the hell was he and where were they going now?

XVIII

A Sickle & Chain
| SULWYN |

EVEN over this man's shoulders, she couldn't move any part of her body. Her legs fell over his chest stiffly, her arms stuck forward. "If you don't put me down, I will scream. It might not do much, but it should still do something," growled Sulwyn. She tasted blood from the cut on her tongue, the sting annoying her.

"I was being nice, Cailín." He had only taken a few steps before he put her down in front of him. He placed her in a standing position, his finger moving up slightly so that she might look up at him. She had lost her small bit of control. "But I think I need to make you understand something."

She looked at his hand held open, fingers pointing to the ceiling, before ever so slightly he twisted it, his fingers bending.

And instantly something like knives ran through her nerves. She screamed louder than she wanted to at the sudden numbing sting, but his hold didn't allow her to fall, to clench her fists, to wrap her arms around herself in some form of protection. As quickly as it ran through her it stopped. Her lungs begged for air as she heaved. She glared at him, involuntary tears forming in her eyes. So she had control of that?

"Hurts, doesn't it?" He bent forward, whispering into her ear. "Are you going to keep challenging me?" His voice was dangerous and slightly unhinged.

This was different than anything she had experienced. Even the torture at Caldwell's hands didn't amount to this.

This man was pure terror.

What the hell was the Empire doing? What was Vartugaul doing, being afraid of Artaxiad, when they had this man living with them in the open? She faded out in her own thoughts, trying desperately not to panic yet again, something she did more frequently since arriving at the Empire. Soon she could hear a warm voice within her.

"Fear only gets stronger if you let it," said Raghnall quietly. They both faced the pitch-black darkness of the mountain they had climbed. She was only nine then, and fear was still something she didn't have control over. But more than anything, she was always afraid of the things she couldn't see.

"Nothing. You can't see anything, right, Sulwyn? And that kind of fear is natural. Being afraid of the things you can't see is okay. But if you can see it, if you can confront it, then you can fight it. Fight it with your heart. Fight it with your soul. Until one day, even the things you can't see will fall away from you."

Sulwyn took another deep breath, the memory of Raghnall fading around her, her enemy in front of her. The shock of the pain subsided, and she knew it would only be the same or worse. But she had felt it. And she could see him. Whoever he was, he too breathed, could bleed, and could see. She would not lose to him.

She could sense his smirk, and shivered as he breathed near her ear, but she wouldn't back down. "Your hold on me is strong. Is it because you are afraid to fight me?"

He stepped back from her quickly, his red eyes flashing. "Afraid?" He laughed, making the same motion again; she screamed louder. And it hurt, just as much as the first time. As if her nerves were being pulled apart one by one. But the tears didn't come. Instead, she glowered and watched his face change. Something worse than it was before, more feral and terrifying. Bloodlust?

"Daijiro, release her. Now," said a voice behind her. She cursed herself at the brief relief that ran through her. Daijiro stepped back, his hands pocketed, and she fell to the carpeted floor. Against her will, she couldn't stop shaking. This is what she got for being too curious.

"Was it her screams? Did you come running to her from wherever you were because of them? I was playing nice."

"She is the Lady Princess, Daijiro, remember that."

"Please, you know Pandora would have liked a front-row seat to even half of this."

Sulwyn could hear Galahad walking behind her, coming closer to where she kneeled. How pathetic, how could she let herself be found in this situation?

She knew the whole time this must be Daijiro. Everything Galahad told her about him, the way anyone looked when they heard his name. She knew immediately after he showed up in front of her again that it had to be this man.

"I'm warning you, Daijiro. I don't have patience for you. Keep yourself under control."

"Or what? You sound just like our Cailín here."

"Cailín?" Sulwyn could hear the incredulous tone in his voice.

"Cailín, the little bird that likes to peck and poke around." mused Daijiro.

Sulwyn gritted her teeth, pushing herself off the ground to face Daijiro. He looked down at her in mild surprise. Fingertips grazed her elbow, but she moved away from Galahad.

"Oh, so it's not only me little Cailín hates. This should be fun—should we start now?" said Daijiro rubbing his hands together and giving her one final look of minor interest before turning back towards the stairs.

Sulwyn stood straight, trying to gather feeling back into her limbs, but Galahad came next to her. "I would have thought you would be smarter after spending this much time in the Empire," he stated, but she refused to look at him.

"Obviously not. I said I would trust you, didn't I? Clearly, I don't make good decisions." She wouldn't show weakness to him, just in case. Where he was concerned, everything just didn't make sense. She stepped forward, the feeling slowly coming back to her, but her knees were sore as hell.

"Sulwyn, I can't look out for you forever. It would be great if you didn't let your guard down so much. I can't watch over you, too." He spoke to her like she was a child. She finally turned to him, deepening her glare.

He looked tired.

There were dark circles under his eyes, his face pale. Sulwyn chuckled as he stared. "What, is your new position too much for you?" she asked. "Not getting sleep? Or is it your guilt? Being a disgrace to your clan and all."

She watched his jaw clench. "You'd do best to stay out of trouble. Listening to Pandora and Artaxiad is your best bet to living a long and healthy life."

"Didn't do that for your clan though, did it? Oh, but I forgot, they were killed as you watched, right? Like you do now. Just watch." She started walking, her strength finally returning. She looked back again and faltered; the whites of his eyes were suddenly black, less than halfway from the irises. But the rate at which the black crawled into the whites was far quicker than she had seen before. As if it was taking every ounce of him to keep it back.

"You're right. I have outlived most of my clan, not knowing where and if anyone else exists. And by doing so have gotten to where I am today. I told you, didn't I? It's the highest position I could achieve."

"This is true. Even when Artaxiad eventually dies, you can never be king. Because I am here."

"As defiant as always. It will get you killed." He walked forwards. The black of his eyes stayed exactly where it was, never going closer to his irises. She wondered vaguely what would happen if it did.

Could she make it happen?

"By whose hand, Galahad, theirs or yours?"

He stayed quiet, looking at her with his impassive face. "It would be best if you followed their way. You know you can't deny it."

"You are the perfect prince, aren't you? Oh, adopted son. Following their rules, doing as they ask. And just like them, you stand atop a pile of the dead to get to where you are. But then I think you might be worse." She started to whisper, watching him. "You said most of your clan was annihilated? If that's true, then you left the rest of them to suffer while you climbed—"

This was the second time he'd slapped her, but she hadn't achieved her goal. Instead, the black was gone, and he was walking away.

"I don't have time to deal with your childishness, Sulwyn. We both have duties to attend to."

⌘

"Well, you both took your time. I had a nap," said Daijiro as they entered the room Sulwyn had left. Daijiro looked from her to Galahad and smiled. "Did you aggravate the prince? That's very bold of you." He leaned back into the chair he occupied at the dining table.

Galahad ignored him, taking a seat at the edge of the table. Sulwyn took her place in front of Daijiro. This seemed to surprise them both, but she wanted to figure him out.

"You were the one I met last time in the Pain Cells," said Sulwyn.

"You went there on your own?" asked Galahad, mildly interested but seemingly not surprised.

"I was trying to do my assigned task. But it looks like you went and tortured them to death."

She understood why now. He must oversee all interrogations. With whatever power he had, she was sure it was rare for anyone to stand against it. Daijiro kept his eyes on her, a smile playing on his lips.

"I couldn't let something like that pass. It's not every day you get a new threat on such a large scale. One or two people occasionally, like you and the Steel Warrior. But a group? It's been a long time."

"And?" she asked, growing impatient. She wanted to clear Caldwell's name. Though it wouldn't free him from everything he had done, she wanted to break his name from the rumours that he caused this. She wouldn't let his death or his sister's years of torture be slandered. His sister was a victim, and by some standards so was Caldwell.

"I need to tell her about the Pain Cells. You both can continue this later," interrupted Galahad, but Daijiro finally turned his attention to him.

"This concerns you too, Galahad." He looked at him pointedly.

Galahad sighed, "How? I was under the impression that Uferor Divi is in charge of this assignment."

"This is much bigger than that. To the scale that it would have been you, Caldwell, and me. Bless that idiot's soul." Daijiro moved back as Sulwyn reached to grab his shirt but missed.

"Don't speak like you knew him," she warned, but Daijiro's surprised expression fell into a darkened one.

"You're lucky we're in front of the All Command. I have to behave, but you shouldn't assume that you are the only one who understood his heart." He sat back more comfortably. The sunlight streamed gently over his golden hair, the white streaks appearing brighter.

Sulwyn was taken aback by his comment but distracted by the name. "'All Command?' That's you? It's a rather…gaudy title," stated Sulwyn, and Daijiro actually laughed out loud. His laugh brought forth that pull again, but she tried to ignore it. However, it didn't seem to work because Galahad just cleared his throat. Sulwyn had been leaning forward without realizing it, and Daijiro had moved closer too, watching her closely.

"Daijiro, tone it down," muttered Galahad, pulling out a sheaf of folded paper from an inner pocket of his tunic.

Daijiro continued to stare at her, moving back again. She felt the heat rise in her neck. Think. What or who did she know to have power like this?

No one.

No one matched what she knew. He didn't seem like a Devinal, but maybe that's what this was? She wished she could ask Raghnall or even Wilkson. What the hell was Wilkson doing now that Raghnall was dead?

"Sulwyn…"

Startled, she turned to Galahad. For just a moment, did concern cross his face? But it was impassive once again and he was sliding the paper towards her, "This is the most updated list of people in the Pain Cells. Most have already passed."

She took the paper, reading four names she had never heard of and much fewer than the rumoured amount, with a brief description of why they were all there.

"They're all murderers…" said Sulwyn. Various murders were listed. But they were violent and gruesome. More than the standard Néosan killing. But killing was killing; what made them different? "Why don't you have them in your army?" asked Sulwyn, giving the sheet of paper back.

"Because they fought and killed for the High City, people who were there during the fall," said Galahad, handing the paper to Daijiro, who only glanced at it. He seemed aware of who was held captive already.

"They've been there for over twenty years?!" she asked incredulously. Twenty-three years in there. Alone, without time, without company. She couldn't imagine what it would be like to be trapped in a small, cold cell for so long. She might not feel the thrill the rest of the Empire does when seated in a lavish room like the one she was in now, but she'd been captive before. The lower dungeons weren't her first time, nor were they the longest. But she knew she would eventually fall into madness if she had been trapped as they were. For so long. So alone.

"They are released once a month. One at a time, for a few hours in the night when all the other prisoners are asleep," said Galahad, standing up.

"And they don't try to escape?" But somehow, she knew who was guarding them when this happened. She glanced over to Daijiro, his eyes staring out the brief slices of outside the curtains created in the gentle wind before he turned to her.

"I can see it in your eyes, Cailín. Yes, I am the one in charge of the Pain Cells. But tomorrow is a release day, and you will be joining me." He too stood, picking up the paper and holding the corner between his fingers before it suddenly erupted in flames, turning to ash. For a moment his eyes narrowed, a tinge of confusion in them, but then the ash slowly disappeared into nothing and his hands were in his pant pockets. "All Command, Lady Princess, I will be in touch soon. They are closing in on the details of the fog town. It will be Divi, San, and you that will go."

"Both our teams?" asked Galahad, now at the door, turning back in surprise.

"Apparently, it's *that* important." He shrugged. "See you tomorrow, Cailín," waved Daijiro, walking towards the door and leaving before Galahad.

The door closed softly but Sulwyn could vaguely sense Galahad still in the room. She continued to sit; facing the windows and watching the trees blow through the cracks of the curtains. It was noon and she needed to get back to the Solus. But he wasn't speaking, so she decided to talk instead.

"Does it bother you?" He stayed silent, so she continued, "That he's in charge of something so delicate, and of the impersonator case?"

"Should it?"

"You're the 'All Command,' but he's obviously more trusted."

"There are reasons for our positions. An outsider like you wouldn't understand."

"Outsider?" She stood up, looking at him briefly before walking to the couch. Sitting, she put her boots back on and placed the two small blades in the hidden inside pockets of each boot before lacing them up.

"You have yet to really understand how it works here."

She stood back up and looked at him again. "I don't think so, Galahad. It doesn't take much to see your desperation. Maybe if you weren't such a maniac, you wouldn't have been banned from the Solus. Or better yet, Artaxiad wouldn't have come for you as a child just to be my competition." She had no idea why she kept trying to egg him on. But somehow, she thought that this would make him crack.

Make him tell her...

Tell her what?

She didn't even know when or if he was lying. What point did she have in making him mad? She needed to remind herself that taking down the Empire was her goal, regardless of if she was alone or not. Regardless of who stood before her.

But as she looked at him, he wasn't getting angry this time. In fact, he wasn't showing anything to her at all. So that's how it was. Maybe she was wrong then. Maybe this really was him.

"My desperation comes from various places, Sulwyn..." he whispered suddenly, and she wasn't entirely sure if she was meant to hear it. "Daijiro is controlled by bloodlust. Be careful around him. As much as you are valued, he holds a lot of sway here."

"I can see why." She walked forward. She needed to see Kione.

"What are you planning?" he asked abruptly. She cursed herself; how was she still this readable? But she would need to convince him soon enough, so she might as well allude him to it.

"I have someone in mind that I may nominate for the vacant Leader position. If he agrees, that is. See you then." She opened the door, leaving without another glance.

☙❧

"She agrees with you," said Kione as they walked together along the inner cells. Sulwyn watched the inmates go about their daily exercise. The one bald man who had given her information nodded to her as she passed. The sun was starting to set and soon it would be time for dinner. What would the people in the Pain Cells be like?

"Sulwyn?"

She turned to Kione, his hand waving in front of her. "What?"

"What, you were serious about not nominating me anymore? Come on, I'm actually pumped for this."

"She agreed?"

"She said if Kintana is in need of our assistance it's the highest honour." Sulwyn wanted to protest, but he held his hand up. "We wouldn't agree because of something as trivial as that. We think it's a good idea. And there aren't many other options. If we can cut off the legs of the Empire, we will have a good start against them."

Sulwyn suddenly looked around. The familiar-looking man who had spoken to her all those nights ago was somewhere nearby. He looked away when he caught her eye, continuing to read his book.

"Do you know him?" asked Sulwyn suddenly.

"Zander? Not really," said Kione, glancing at the man. "I know they have him cook the meals sometimes. He's leaving soon."

"To Eques?" A bell rang around them signalling the prisoners to line up and return to their cells.

"Yeah, I heard he was going to join as a sous chef, but the head chef was killed a couple days ago, so this guy will be the new head chef once he passes clearance."

"Killed?"

"The previous head chef was a different case, a total devotee to Artaxiad brought in when the Empire started killing off various clans. As Artaxiad was heading most of the Néosan at the time, he used to spend time in Eques. He recently sent him to cook for Eques earlier this year since there is a maid in Valens who has more talent."

Sulwyn smiled; Eztli really was an excellent cook. But it faltered when Kione's expression grew dark and she realized what he had said. "Wait, he was killed? Why? Did Artaxiad kill him?"

"I mean, I'm not sorry for the guy. He used to poison some of the newer Néosan who didn't want to be there, who weren't showing enough dedication. But it was the prince who killed him."

Sulwyn stopped, looking at Kione as the other Protectors walked around them. The inner area was empty now, the sun getting even lower in the sky. "*Galahad* killed him? Why?"

"I've heard that ever since he became the All Command, there have been more casualties. Something about losing his temper. I always thought he was too soft for the king and queen, but it looks like I was wrong."

Sulwyn was off duty for the night and promised to meet Kione at the Proelium Terra. It was the best place to have a practise fight without being seen.

Sulwyn whistled and after a moment Ki joined her at the front of the Solus. After her visit to Eques, she was convinced that he was a far more intelligent breed of horse. She didn't need to worry about him running away, so she stopped having his reins tied.

She petted him softly, greeted by a soft nuzzle, before she hopped on, sitting astride. "Let's go meet Kione, okay?" she whispered. He neighed and took off.

It was nice, riding in the night when the Empire was asleep. It was almost midnight now. Most of the animals had already turned in for the night. Sulwyn couldn't see the Empire clearly from where she was riding. The high black walls covered most of the Empire from sight, and at night, from a distance, it was like it fell into a black void.

Sulwyn had sent word about Kione, granting him permission to be exempt from curfew for training purposes. He was in her protection now, and she hoped that Pandora would keep her word. He did have a higher status, being one of the few Common Ones with a Protector title. But she knew that meant nothing to the Empire if they saw fit.

Her thoughts changed when she saw the rising hill of the Proelium Terra in the distance. The moon peeked through the clouds, illuminating her path ahead. After some time, they galloped through the lower tunnels, the sound echoing loudly into the distance. Sprinting past the seats along the stairs, they lunged over the low stone barriers. Soon she was bathed in dim moonlight as she and Ki entered the middle of the stadium.

Sulwyn dismounted, her travel cloak blowing widely around her. Ki continued to run once around the entire terrain before slowing to a trot, stopping in the distance with some trees, nibbling on grass. Sulwyn watched him with a smile.

She learned after she chose him that Ki was passed off as an aggressive horse. They were going to send him back into the wild, but since he had taken to Sulwyn that was no longer necessary.

Sulwyn crouched down, her arms on the ground in front of her, waiting. She told Kione to come when he wanted, and attack however he saw fit. She wanted to see how proficient he was. But also, she was curious about how he fought. She had only had a few encounters with people from Uhuru and knew that they were home to some of the oldest clans and tribes. She was hoping to learn something from this fight.

The wind picked up, but it was calming in the cool night, the edges of her cloak blowing around her, lifting and exposing the short daggers she brought with her.

Sulwyn jumped back quickly, rolling off to the side, a foot resting just where her hands had been. She looked up at Kione, his smile bright but surprised.

"You are really fast." He stepped back, going into a simple stance.

"That's going to be your only element of surprise. You didn't want to try it again?"

"You've already seen me; it would be a waste of time to hide again."

Sulwyn smirked. She liked that kind of cockiness. She ran forward, feinting a punch before bending slightly and kicking at his side. He blocked it quickly with his arm. The strike forced him off balance and she took that chance to aim a punch to his stomach.

But he managed to catch that one, grabbing her arm and swinging her around, using the momentum to push her forward. He aimed the flat edge of his palm to hit between her shoulder blades, but she ducked forward and he missed. Sulwyn stayed bent, watching his legs from behind, and swung her leg back catching one of his own.

Kione lost balance again, tumbling forward and going past her, creating some space between them.

"You're faster than Diesirae." He wiped a few beads of sweat from his brow. But Sulwyn didn't need to test his abilities in hand to hand anymore. She could see that he had strong reflexes and instincts. Knew that if one of his hits connected, it would hurt a lot.

"You've got a weapon?" she asked, though she knew she heard the slight jangle of metal hitting metal when he moved. He threw off his own cloak, dropping it to the ground. Sulwyn followed suit, taking in the clothes he wore. She figured it must be clothes native to whatever tribe he belonged to. They were loose-fitting and light, cotton with dark red pants and a black tunic. Intricate patterns and lines decorated the tunic in fine red thread. She was seeing all kinds of clothes these days.

From a back holster, he unbuckled a rather large crimson sickle and chain. At the end of the chain was a dagger the size of one of her short swords. There were deep lines of delicate engravings embedded on the side of the sickle, and the chain shone bright red in the moonlight.

"That is very different. Not many people fight with a sickle and chain, much less looking like that," said Sulwyn as she pulled out both short swords. A sickle and chain were complicated to fight against, but even more so to defend. And she had no doubt that he knew what he was doing.

Swiftly, he swung the chain with the dagger end around and over his head. It spun faster and faster, creating a slight breeze around them. But he hurtled the sickle instead. With speed and weight, it lunged forward and dipped down at the last second, catching her off guard.

Metal hitting metal vibrated in her ears as she used her left blade to block the sickle. Right then, the chain dropped from the sky, the dagger whistling near her ear. She crossed her arms over her head, blocking the dagger with the side of her blades, her legs steady. It was heavy. Far heavier than she thought it would be.

She looked at him for a moment. His eyes were different in a fight, concentrated but not fearful. This fight reminded her of when she sparred with Raghnall.

He pulled the chain again and the dagger slipped forward from her blades and down to the ground. It embedded itself, but she had no time to look at it as he pulled the chain again and the sickle came at her side. She realized he had less control over the sickle; despite its size, it seemed half the weight of the dagger.

But he pulled the chain once more, bringing the sickle back, and this time began to swing the sickle over his head. The wind was stronger, and she almost felt warier of it. But she wouldn't wait for it to come to her. She would go to him.

Sulwyn took off at a run and jumped, knocking the sickle in midair, disrupting its course. It bounced off to the side, landing flat on the ground. Kione stepped back a little, pulling both the sickle and chain closer towards him.

He took off to her left, running away, and she gave chase. She knew she was giving in to his plan, but she wanted to see where it went. She ran after him, and soon he started to run to her other side. With haste he pulled the chain all the way, catching the dagger in his hand before vaulting it. She was impressed. He calculated where she would run and aimed for that spot, but she paused, running back instead, and instantly ducked.

The sickle had silently made its way behind her. The point caught her cheek, scratching her. The sickle and chain were always meant to be a distraction for each other. But most never paid attention to the dagger as much as the sickle. The odd weight in each and the way they moved made one try and listen for the sickle and forget to look for the dagger. But she was more surprised to find that the cut on her cheek felt like it was on fire.

"Kuvuli?" Sulwyn breathed heavily, taking a moment to catch her breath.

"You've heard of us?" Eyes wide in surprise.

"Raghnall said it's one of the oldest recorded tribes and the reason why they stand out is because of their weapons."

"You know about our weapons too, huh? I'm a bit surprised. The tribe almost died out. Only a few survivors left."

"I heard. They were more battle-oriented as were many tribes and clans back then, but when the Zalman took reign and brought Vartugaul into peace, they hung up their weapons." Sulwyn touched her cheek. Her face burned, and the sting brought tears to her eyes. But it wasn't too bad.

"There are still some very devoted members. My parents were part of it. But I wasn't ever into it. Diesirae was higher in that group and on a different council, but I don't know what they specialized in. We left soon after I received my weapon." he shrugged.

"I think we've battled enough. You are obviously qualified, and having a Sacred Weapon helps."

"Raghnall knew that too?" Kione slumped onto the ground, lying back and looking into the night sky.

"He knew a lot…when a Kuvuli is born, they take their blood and preserve it until the age of ascent," said Sulwyn, walking over, tossing the blades and lying next to him. "And then they make a weapon based off the results of a ritual with the blood from birth. This binds the weapon to that person. And the cuts hurt like hell."

"Encountered one before?"

"Once, I got caught in a fight…"

"How?" He turned to her, his smile curious. She liked his presence. It made her feel warm and content. His smile was extra bright under the moon. She looked back to the multicoloured stars.

"I don't remember much. I was around eight? Someone started a fight with the Néosan, and I got involved."

He raised an eyebrow. "Why?"

"I have a habit…anyway, they fought, I got cut by the woman's spear and it burned for weeks."

"Yeah, the cuts burn and take longer to heal than a regular wound. And if someone other than the blood user uses the weapon, they get burnt."

"Oh? That makes sense." Sulwyn looked at her hand in nostalgia, the light scar across her palm reflecting against the moonlight above them.

"Did you try to hold the weapon too?" He looked at her incredulously, sitting up.

"I thought it was cool! No wonder she yelled at me. Then Raghnall came and took me away." She shrugged, pulling Kione back down next to her. The ground was hard and cold, but it was comforting. The bright stars and moon enveloped her in a velvet blanket. They lay in silence for a while before the night air began to chill a bit more.

"We should go," said Sulwyn, but she was honestly content where she was.

"Hmm…" he mumbled. She turned, seeing his eyes close. Sulwyn sighed, closing her eyes as well. A nap would be okay.

XIX

Number Twenty-Seven

| SULWYN |

SULWYN sat up so quickly that her vision blackened for a moment, the ground tilting under her. She thought someone had touched her forehead, but as she looked around, there was no one but Kione and Ki, who had come to sit next to them. She looked to the sky, a chilly fog hanging over them. Deep greens and blues tinged with a bit of light illuminated the sky; the sun was rising. They had slept all night. She looked at Kione snoring gently.

He was strong; she felt more confident in nominating him to Galahad now, but that was tomorrow. Tonight she needed to spend with Daijiro and the Pain Cells. She leaned back on her arms, looking at the sky. The coloured stars could still be seen, but the moon was already hiding. Time was still right now, silent and peaceful. Sitting in the centre of the Proelium Terra seemed like she was away from the Empire. But that soon faded when she began to recall her battle with Caldwell.

Ki turned to her, neighing softly and nudging her with his head. She wondered vaguely if he could sense her apprehension, but he nudged her again and she felt a calmness wash over her.

Caldwell was at peace. She took a deep breath remembering what he had said about the father of that family. That he was dead now, he was free. Caldwell believed that dying would set them all free. How foolish. She sighed loudly and Kione stirred, opening his eyes and looking up at her.

"Cold…" he mumbled, stifling a yawn and rubbing his arms. Sulwyn laughed.

"How long has it been since you've been out this late?" She stood, giving her hand to help him up.

"A long time. If you left me in the wild, I'd probably stumble around for a few weeks trying to remember how to survive and hope I don't die." He stretched, looking towards the light of the brightening sky. The high walls of the Proelium Terra blocked the sunrise from them. "I need to go back. I'm on shop duty today. And you are off until midnight. You should go sleep."

"I slept plenty here, but I'll go back to Valens," said Sulwyn with a smile; however, she could tell he sensed something was off with her. But he didn't question it and instead mildly saluted, taking off into the distance.

Sulwyn turned to Ki, who got up immediately, shaking his head of sand, waiting. She went to retrieve her cloak and the short swords before they took off back to the Empire.

As they galloped through the thinning fog, she vaguely wondered what they would do if she just continued and left the Empire, left Antiqua altogether and went into hiding elsewhere. Maybe she could go into hiding at Mortui Gemma, but she highly doubted she could make it even with her training in survival. The cold was harshest there, and she heard that no one could navigate it; plus, it was all snow, where would she stay? But she let the thoughts run out of her head and flow behind her with every step they made. She knew she couldn't run; they would hunt her and threaten her with the lives of others. And she couldn't fool herself into thinking it was in her to run anyway.

Before she realized it, the black walls of the Empire loomed in front of her. A Néosan on duty greeted her, opening the gate quickly, surprise in his eyes. She guided Ki towards the forest behind Valens. The journey was quick, the streets asleep, though the Common Ones would rise soon.

As she brushed past the trees, she wished she had been able to bring the family and Caldwell's body out of the Empire and to the edge of the forests of Antiqua. She pulled the reins gently and instantly Ki slowed to a light trot. Soon she was right in front of the large oak tree; the mound of their grave was covered with sprouting grass.

Sulwyn dismounted, slowly approaching the mound of dirt. "No. I won't move you. I'll prove you wrong. Instead, one day I'll show you that I can make the Empire fall and that a different peace will reign over Vartugaul again. A place where everyone will be safe." She stepped closer and sat in front of the mound.

Ki followed suit, taking a seat next to her. The smell of damp soil wafted over her as she leaned against the soft mound. Instantly she fell back to sleep.

捃捃

"Sulwyn…" whispered a voice. She was already awake when the person approached the small clearing, but she knew who it was without having to open her eyes.

"How did you find me?"

"I heard your dreams as I was outside," said Arsinone, kneeling in front of her. Sulwyn opened her eyes to see a small basket in front of her. Arsinone opened it, revealing some bread, meat, cheese, and a small jug of juice.

"Were they interesting?" said Sulwyn taking a small bun and breaking it in half. She gave the other half to Arsinone who tried and failed to refuse.

"Hmm, they were a bit jumbled. And rather…dark. Are you okay?" she asked, eating the bread. "You've been out here for a while, you could get sick. It's not very warm today."

"I know…it's going to rain tonight. And it hasn't been that long, it's only sometime in the afternoon," she shrugged, picking at the meat and cheese. She felt oddly tired despite sleeping so much. Or maybe that was why she was tired.

"How do you know that? The sky is cloudy; you can't see the sun."

"I can feel it. I know vaguely what time it is no matter where I am as long as the sun is up. Inside or out…no, that isn't true…I can't sense it in the lower dungeons." She poured some of the juice into a cup, giving it to Arsinone first.

"Either way. That's fascinating."

"Raghnall could do it too. He taught me how to sense the sun just like he taught me how to sense the rain." Arsinone stared at her intently before Ki nudged her, gaining her attention.

"Oh, I brought fruit for you too!" said Arsinone happily, going into the basket and pulling out a couple of apples.

"How did you know I had him?" asked Sulwyn, leaning back again.

"I can hear him," said Arsinone softly, a nostalgic expression fleeting across her face.

"Does…he speak?"

"No, no…It's not in anything I can put into words, and sometimes it's memories. It's not with all animals. He's like another horse I knew at one point. I can feel their souls more than hear it. He's rather taken with you." She smiled, but it faltered. "He was kidnapped when he was younger. Separated from his herd. I could see his memories hidden in his soul." Arsinone reached over slowly as he watched her. She hesitated for a moment, but he just nudged her again and allowed her to pet him.

Silence spread between them before Sulwyn stood, packing up the basket and giving it back to Arsinone. "Thank you for coming. But you should go back now before they see you are missing."

"It's okay. We haven't been busy because most of the Privileged that live in Valens are out vacationing in a town in Guāngcǎi or something." She made a face and so did Sulwyn. She pulled Arsinone forward, bringing her into a hug.

"Be safe. I'm almost done with the Solus. I'll be back in another week."

"I will be. Don't stress over the Pain Cells. I don't understand exactly what they are, but you are Sulwyn. You will be okay."

Sulwyn couldn't see the moonlight from her room in the Solus. The clouds in the night sky had grown thicker and darker over the evening. It was darker than usual for night, but the rain had held off. She hoped it would hold off while the inmates had their time. Or maybe they would like it? Could they even tell what they felt anymore? Over twenty years was a long time to be held in solitary confinement, no matter what kind of person they used to be. It was unsettling.

All Galahad said was that they had been there during the fall of the High City. There as what? What was their purpose and why did they kill so many? Did they kill Artaxiad's people or their own? Or was it a mixture of both? Being close to the High City was the cost, so maybe they were the last men and women still standing before the fall of the High City king.

"Lady Princess, it's time for your shift. Leader Daijiro has arrived and is waiting outside for you," said the voice of Yellow-Eyes. She really needed to learn his actual name.

Sulwyn stepped out just before he could turn away. She watched a bit of fear and defiance within his eyes and smiled, confusing him more. "Thank you. You can leave now, can't you? You don't normally cover midnight shifts."

"All of the higher Protectors and Validus stay on guard during these nights. Just in case," he shrugged, but gestured for her to leave. He clearly wanted to be free of her. Maybe she'd just keep his name to Yellow-Eyes.

Slightly irritated, she closed the door to her room and made her way down the dim hallway that lightened as a flash illuminated through the windows. One roll of distant thunder sounded, but the rain had yet to fall.

"Princess, you seem rather alert," called Daijiro in the distance. His golden snow hair was tousled in the wind, striking against the torch lights in this darker than normal night. He looked more relaxed than she felt, but she wasn't exactly surprised. He turned his head to her, but his hands stayed pocketed as if this were just an average day.

"As do you..." she murmured, unsure of what to do next. The silence stretched between them. He turned away, looking at the sky just as lightning flashed again. The rumble of thunder seemed closer now.

"Ah, I hoped it wasn't going to rain tonight. It rained last time too. Wanted them to get some moonlight at least." He turned to face her properly, walking towards her.

"You can't move it to tomorrow?"

"It's in the air. It's going to rain tomorrow too, and we do this on the same date every month. I can't change that now."

She vaguely realized he could sense the rain too but was distracted. It was there again, that unmistakable draw or pull that she felt from his eyes and from his voice. Last time it seemed stronger, deeper even. But she was aware of it immediately this time. He smirked, as if he knew what she was thinking, but said nothing of it and instead began to walk down the path towards the Pain Cells.

"I could have just met you down there," said Sulwyn.

"I wanted to see the weather firsthand, and I thought it'd be better if you saw me in person first, given our last meeting." He smiled at her, the pull coming and going like a wave. This was definitely a power and not something that could be learned, something unique to him or where he came from.

They walked in stretched silence until they reached the desolate halls and cell doors. They went farther than she had gone all those nights before, barely making a sound as they walked. Finally, Daijiro stopped at the end of the second bend.

Without a word, he pulled out one key. It was rather large and ornate, but it had way more teeth along the edge than a common key. It wasn't just a straight shape, either, but went down with deep grooves and small holes on the side. And it was old. Probably the original key since the Solus was created.

He signalled for her to move back and she did without question. She watched as he pushed the key through the small hole near the left side and under a small lid. He turned the key left and fully around, then back right up to a certain point, and then left again but only a quarter of the way. With each turn, the key went in farther and farther until all the teeth were covered.

"Don't even bother...the key only responds to my touch, as I have earned its confidence," whispered Daijiro as she looked at him. She hadn't considered stealing it from him, but found the fact that he had a "key's confidence" intriguing.

The door swung inwards with barely any sound. Sulwyn held her breath, waiting. Slowly she heard dragging steps and the haunting face of a woman with past glory entered the light in front of her.

Sulwyn was speechless. Out of horror, despair, sadness…she knew not. However, she could tell that the woman in front of her used to be something mighty. Something Vartugaul hadn't seen since the fall and maybe wouldn't see again. But the woman looked at her with light blue eyes, dead and without awareness.

"Let's move with a bit more haste, shall we, Twenty-Seven?" spoke Daijiro, gesturing for her to come out of the cell.

"Twenty-Seven?"

"Each person in the Pain Cell is assigned a number upon capture. We do not speak their names, or of who they once were. That is Artaxiad's rule in case it may stir lost emotions within them."

"So he still fears them to this day?" asked Sulwyn as the tall woman walked past them both. Nothing bound her arms or legs. Nothing had a physical hold on her now that she was out, but all she did was continue down the hall at a slow pace and without question.

Sulwyn looked back to the cell, now wide open, the key still in the lock. This only confirmed what Daijiro had said. Of course, no one would bother stealing it from him anyway. She watched Daijiro walk along behind the woman, her long blonde hair trailing on the ground behind her. Sulwyn had seen many prisoners in her lifetime, but none like this.

The mind could madden in a short amount of time alone; she couldn't imagine what twenty-some years did. The fact that she could still walk or function was a marvel to her. As if she waited each month just for this day. Possibly standing, sleeping, and sitting in front of the iron door. Just waiting.

They walked back up the dirt hill and towards the back of the cells. Sulwyn hadn't even ventured this far back and was surprised to see another small space. A neat tiny garden was set up away from the cells and eyes of the other prisoners. She figured this was for everyone's benefit.

The clearing was nice, cozy and clean. An elaborate table of food was set up in the centre, trees and flowers surrounding it. Without word or need for assistance, the woman stepped forward and took her seat in front of the food. Small pieces of glazed chicken and other meats were laid out across the table. Alongside were soups varying in colour and thickness. Boiled eggs sprinkled with spices. Green and red vegetables chopped into small pieces swimming in an orange stew. Dark and light breads of many shapes littered the table aside bowls of coloured rice topped with flowers. It was lavish and unexpected.

"Do they receive the same food as other prisoners normally?"

"Yes, but on their day out they get this."

"Isn't this excessive?" asked Sulwyn, anger rising within her.

"Why? Isn't it good to have an occasional treat?"

"I'm not talking about the food. Why not kill them instead of this—this torture?"

"Kill them? Would you really like that? Would you like me to suggest that to the king?" he asked, smiling deeply. It unsettled her, but the pull was less now. She could feel something else instead. Something that bordered on sinister but also understanding.

"This is like insult to injury. She's broken. There is nothing there. I'm surprised she's even lasted this long. Are they all like this?"

"Do *you* want to kill her?" asked Daijiro, stepping closer.

"Why are they keeping them here? It's not necessary."

"Because this is their punishment," he stated seriously. His red eyes gleamed in the torchlight around them. "They, who stood against every-thing the king and queen stood for during the fall of the High City."

"Who is she?" asked Sulwyn in an undertone. She was missing some-thing; they can't have just been murderers. Artaxiad was a cruel being, but this was beyond torture. This was a lesson.

"She, along with the other surviving prisoners in the Pain Cells, were high up in the High City. Higher than anyone, and the personal guard of the former king," he whispered.

Sulwyn gasped, "They were Raghnall's people?"

Daijiro instantly covered her mouth and looked towards Twenty-Seven. Sulwyn looked at him incredulously, but he continued to watch the woman instead. Sulwyn, too, looked, but she just kept eating at a slow, almost frozen pace. She hadn't even acknowledged them yet.

"You don't want to get her in trouble now, do you, Cailín?" He looked at her, his eyes dangerous. Sulwyn pushed his hand away and he stepped back. "She's the tamest one. But at the same time, she's the one I like to deal with least of all." Daijiro warned, "Don't make me regret tonight."

"So they are here because they were the last to try and put a stop to the fall."

"Good, you understand quickly. Yes, they were there during the final moments. I've heard stories, but I honestly don't know how they managed to subdue them. There were originally nine people alongside your beloved. But only four have made it this far. And Artaxiad has seen fit to imprison each one here."

"Bastard…" growled Sulwyn, her anger growing a bit more. Daijiro turned to her again, gripping her shoulder tightly. She felt as if a thousand tiny needles were flowing through her back and arm. They were more uncomfortable than painful.

"I'm warning you, princess. Keep your emotions in check. She's more apt at sensing the things around her, even after all this time. But her instincts are primal. If she senses your anger, she may attack. You wouldn't want me to hurt her, would you?"

"Why did you invite me to this?" asked Sulwyn, trying to ignore the now growing pain. Though the wound on her back was healing, this throbbing sensation was beginning to make the axe injury hurt again.

"Per the king's request, but also to show you the various things the Empire does to those they hate, that is all," he said quietly, his tone strange.

"How long do they get outside?" asked Sulwyn. The needles started to ease away as he lifted his hand off her shoulder.

"Two hours. They can do what they like in this space and enjoy food of their preference."

"How do you know that's what they like?"

"We don't. Or at least I don't. Their preference was established a while ago when they could still request things in sound mind. However, we do change it up from time to time."

Daijiro looked up to the sky again and Sulwyn continued to watch Twenty-Seven. She had almost finished her dinner now and was looking at some flowers beside her. But all too suddenly she looked at Sulwyn, her eyes bright and full of awareness. Sulwyn found herself frozen in the depths of her icy blue eyes. She would take her chance.

"Do they know…that he was killed, Ragh—" Instantly she was brought down to her knees, the bruises from before aching. Daijiro's eyes were maddening, his finger flicked down.

"I warned you," he growled, but Sulwyn forced her eyes to look at the woman. In it, there was a mixture of the light she had just seen along with the deadness before. However, something else was stirring within it and Sulwyn knew at that moment she understood what she had said even if it was fleeting.

"You say they are cruel, Cailín, but to try and take what little hope they had left…why would you do such a thing? Look what you've done…"

The woman stared into nothingness. Her mouth sagged open, eyebrows furrowed and hands slowly gripping at her head and hair. "No, no, no…" the woman muttered, her voice deep and ragged. She must have been silent for so long.

"They have no sense of time anymore. For all we know she believes everything she experienced happened yesterday or a hundred years ago," he said quietly.

"I'm sorry…" said Sulwyn, still on her knees. She looked at Daijiro, whose expression she couldn't read, but to her, he seemed troubled. She should have been aware that that was the worst thing to say even if she was trying to test her. If they were part of his team, then they must have been close to him at one point. To have learned that not even he survived the clutches of the Empire…

"You must promise not to do this again, Cailín, or I won't let you come with me for the others. We have three more people to see to tonight.

Do not make me report you..." He released his hold on her, and she stood slowly. Daijiro returned his gaze to the sky and Sulwyn returned hers to the prisoner. But through her slight wails and moans, she turned her gaze to Sulwyn.

Her eyes seemed brighter than the moment before, fierce even. So she wasn't wrong. Despite how broken Twenty-Seven must be she still had fire buried deep within her heart. Through the cracks of her hands, Sulwyn watched as the woman smiled crookedly before mouthing something.

Sulwyn's heart froze when she realized she mouthed "Kintana."

XX

The Lonely Ones
| SULWYN |

AND that was it.

Twenty-Seven gave no other sign of recognition as to who Kintana was, who was in front of her, or the news about Raghnall. After she had smiled at Sulwyn, Daijiro looked back down and her face was lost and impassive once again. The rest of Twenty-Seven's time was spent stargazing when the clouds moved out of the way intermittently and touching the trees and the grass around her in a slow trancelike state. Sulwyn never took her eyes off her, memorizing her movements and how she reacted to things. And it confused her still.

Twenty-Seven seemed broken, as one would be after that many years in captivity, alone and isolated from everything. But in those few moments, Sulwyn could see the valiant ghost of the women she thought she once was. Was it momentary? Was this all an act? No matter how strong one was, they didn't escape that kind of damage.

"Your time is over for tonight, Twenty-Seven," said Daijiro suddenly. Sulwyn had almost forgotten he was there. He had stopped talking after his brief warning to her and hadn't moved or spoken since. He stepped toward the woman, gesturing for her to move. And for a few seconds, she stared at him, a hint of defiance flashing within her. Sulwyn watched Daijiro, knowing he noticed it too. But he didn't address it and soon they were making their way back to the Pain Cells.

Once they arrived, Twenty-Seven stepped quietly into the cell until she was submerged in darkness once more. Her long blonde hair trailed behind her until she could no longer be seen, and the door closed. Daijiro touched the key gently, and Sulwyn watched as it turned on its own in reverse to the way it had opened. Once halfway out, Daijiro took the key before facing Sulwyn. His eyes were dangerous, but he signalled for her to follow him out of earshot and towards an area that undoubtedly housed no one within its cells.

"I'm not particularly fond of the idea of keeping you around, Cailín. I'm going to give you another chance. Our king is keen on your learning about the different duties of the Solus. But bear in mind they are watching. If you try anything, they will know. And as much as I like a fight, I do not want to have to subdue these particular prisoners." His tone was serious, but somehow Sulwyn felt like he couldn't care less if he had to fight them or not. As if this was a formality. But then all those thoughts vanished when she felt that inexplicable pull of want once again.

He smirked at her.

She kicked him in the shin.

"I don't know what it is that you are, or can do, but I'd appreciate it if you could stop doing that while I'm trying to 'learn the ways of the Solus.' "

His eyes flashed, but he just shook his leg and carried on, his smirk mingled with something else she couldn't really read.

Sulwyn followed a few paces behind him as he walked down to the other hall of cells. Silently she stood back, and soon the cell door was opening. It was another woman, and unlike Twenty-Seven who looked more like a silent leader, this woman was a bit larger, her build heavier, and more than a commander she reminded Sulwyn of someone sent out for tougher missions. Someone who worked better alone than in a group, the last hope. Her curly black hair grew in uneven ways. Sulwyn assumed part of her hair had once been cut short or shaved. Her skin was a faded pale version of a once warm brown with dark yellow eyes, vacant just like Twenty-Seven's, but younger. Though ageing down here didn't seem to go well for any one of them.

"Thirty-Six, it's not raining yet. Maybe this time you will get to enjoy some dry land?" said Daijiro conversationally. But Thirty-Six ignored him and instead turned to walk out of her cell and onwards towards a beaten path.

Once outside, the tall woman automatically went to the dinner table, same as the other, only this time the food was rather different. Unlike Twenty-Seven who had rather typical Empire or High City choices, Thirty-Six had various mini ceramic pots of dark stews and coloured breads. Provisions pressed into disks and fried, lots of smashed green leaves and fleshy purple vegetables. These were not dishes seen often, nor easy to come by.

"She's from Uhuru," she breathed, but Daijiro glared and instead of covering her mouth, he nodded towards her and forced it shut, pain caught in her throat. Sulwyn struggled to gasp and glared at him.

He smirked; satisfied that he'd caught her off guard. "I told you to say nothing. Nothing about who they were or where they come from. Nothing," hissed Daijiro exasperatingly. But their actions got the attention of Thirty-Six, who was watching them rather closely.

"Been there?" She spoke, her voice higher than Sulwyn expected. Her thoughts seemed sound and untangled. Her yellow eyes looked at Sulwyn clearly as she dipped a dark red loaf into her stew. Sulwyn glanced at Daijiro, but his eyes were different now, on edge and curiosity mixed into one. He released his hold on her.

"No, though I know some people who are from there," said Sulwyn softly, unsure of what kind of tone to even use. Thirty-Six's voice was haggard as she expected, but at the same time, it sounded a bit used, more than Twenty-Seven's did during her brief moment of speech. Maybe she liked to talk to herself?

"I don't know what it looks like now, but it's not that special. Lots of sand." she swallowed, drinking water and then sitting still. "This time is

mine, Daijiro. I will speak with this new guest for as long as I am able to."
Sulwyn was shocked, to say the least, but Daijiro seemed dumbfounded.

"This space is yours to use. Just don't try to escape. I don't want to put in the extra hours." Daijiro hid his surprise well, but Sulwyn knew he was unsettled. When was the last time she had spoken? It obviously wasn't a reoccurring event. Sulwyn watched Daijiro walk back to the far wall, sit down and lean against it. He kept his eyes trained on them both, but Sulwyn realized she was at liberty to speak.

But what could she say? This wasn't unheard of, for someone to relapse into their old self. But what could she say without worrying how much was too much? How much did she know? How long did she think it had been? Did she even know exactly who she was?

"Would you like to join me?" she asked, and Sulwyn looked back at Daijiro hesitantly. He tilted his head somewhat, before waving the hand that rested on his lifted knee. Permission granted.

Sulwyn stepped forward, but there was no other chair. Thirty-Six looked at her for a moment, then lifted two pots down and placed them onto the grass. She took a bowl of bread to set next to the pots and patted the bit of grass for Sulwyn to sit across from her. Cautiously, Sulwyn knelt, sitting slowly. She needed to be careful. She knew full well that this moment could slip. That she could be considered a threat or an enemy the moment this woman's clarity left her. Thirty-Six offered her a choice between the thin golden stew or the thicker dark brown one.

"Whichever one you like less I will have," mumbled Sulwyn, and she received the thin gold one.

Sulwyn slowly went for a piece of bread, but it was taken out of her hand with grace. She looked up, body tensed, but Thirty-Six just took the small loaf, broke it in half, and dipped one side in her own stew before giving it to Sulwyn. "In the tribe I grew up in, sharing food on the first meeting was of utmost importance."

Sulwyn took the dipped loaf and ate it, marvelling at its taste. At least they seemed to go all out for these meals when preparing them. She had no idea what the stew was made of, but it somehow tasted rich and subtle at the same time, a strong hint of clover coating her tongue. Sulwyn took a loaf and broke it in half, dipped it in her own stew, and then offered it to Thirty-Six. She nodded her head, taking the bread and eating it.

"It's not quite the same, but they tried. Better than the last time actually." And then she was silent, eating her stew, and Sulwyn eating her own. She hadn't noticed how hungry she had become, and realized her last meal was the one she'd had in the forest with Arsinone. This meal was not only well made, but the company and the surroundings of it all made it an experience she wouldn't quickly forget.

Thirty-Six glanced at Daijiro, but his eyes had never left them. She placed a hand over her stew and muttered something. Soon after, words formed in the reflection of the sparse firelight around them. Sulwyn was amazed at this kind of magic and then froze, looking up at the woman.

She was a Devinal.

Sulwyn read the word; all it said was "Raghnall?" and Sulwyn knew what it meant. She looked up into her dark yellow eyes and shook her head slightly, hoping that Daijiro couldn't tell what they were doing.

"His stance is in you," she muttered, looking at Sulwyn appreciatively. Sulwyn felt a tug pull at the corner of her lips. She knew that. And even after all that had happened recently, she would always find pride in that fact.

"Is that why you still have your mind? Can't you leave?" whispered Sulwyn, using the last piece of her bread to pick up the few dregs of meat and stew left.

"Only for my mind mostly, sometimes a little for the others, and not at all times. There is powerful magic over the Solus that no one seems able to detect. But it's only for sealing. It's not nearly as powerful as the one over the castle, whatever it's called now. I believe it distorts direction as well as other things."

Sulwyn looked at her, eyes wide. No wonder she couldn't navigate the castle. She didn't think it could be magic, had never dreamed of it. But she knew Artaxiad hated Devinal. He would never have allowed it. Unless he wasn't aware of it.

Sulwyn suddenly remembered what Caldwell had mentioned. That Pandora had connections to those with magic. Was it her doing? And behind Artaxiad's back? She didn't expect Pandora to be chained to his rule, but she thought they at least shared the same opinion about magic. Enchanted whips were one thing, but magic over an entire structure was another. What was it that Pandora wanted to keep hidden that they put such magic over the castle?

"Now, I don't expect you to trust me. But to avoid suspicion on both of our parts, I'm going to have to do something a bit…drastic," said Thirty-Six, finishing the rest of her water. "But before that, I want to enjoy at least a bit more of my freedom and food. For now, I'm going to have to shoo you away." She winked, her dark yellow eyes penetrating her own. Thirty-Six reached over, touching Sulwyn's hand lightly.

"I hope I get to meet you again. I look forward to the future, Kintana." Sulwyn glanced over at Daijiro, who had stopped looking at them and was now looking up to the even darker sky. It was going to rain very soon.

"Wait, can…I ask your name?" whispered Sulwyn. A cold fear went through her, fear that she might make this woman crack. But she was sure that her mind was sound at least for right now.

"Ildri…who else have you met so far?"

"Twenty-Seven?"

"Ah, Eleri…my poor, poor Eleri. She was his second in command." Ildri looked down solemnly at her hands. Sulwyn noticed many scars that crossed her brown skin where the black sleeves did not hide. Her yellow eyes found her grey ones once again, and Sulwyn knew she was being dismissed. Slowly, Sulwyn got up, but Ildri held her gaze. "Remember in some time I'm going to have to be a bit…reckless."

Sulwyn nodded, standing straight, and walking back to the wall where Daijiro stayed. He did not look at her but continued to look at the sky just as a few drops began to fall.

"Will you keep her out here if it rains?" asked Sulwyn quietly. She didn't know if they treated them when they were sick, but anything to limit it would be great.

"There is a room we bring them to. It's almost the same thing as the cell but with windows. She likes the rain. She won't mind as long as it's light."

And just like that Daijiro fell silent again. They both watched Ildri finish her meal then lie on the grass, staring at the sky. The raindrops were a bit more consistent now, but still not heavy enough to worry. The night was still warm, and a look of relief passed over Ildri's face. Sulwyn too looked up, the rain gently hitting her skin, cool and welcoming on her still aching body. It was calming, peaceful even.

Time passed quickly; Ildri's time was almost over just as the rain began to really pick up. She was pulled out of her reverie when Daijiro stirred next to her, standing quickly and cautiously. Sulwyn looked ahead, watching as Ildri slumped over on her side. Immediately, Sulwyn stood and dashed over.

"Wait!" called Daijiro, but Sulwyn had already reached her.

Ildri was lying still on the grass, and then all too suddenly she rolled over and grabbed Sulwyn's ankle. Her grip was tight over her boots, surprising her. But she did not move. What was Ildri doing?

With unexpected force, Ildri pulled Sulwyn's leg, forcing her to lose balance for a moment. In that time Ildri stood up, grabbing a small ceramic pot and swinging.

Sulwyn dodged it, knocking it out of her hand. "What are you doing?" hissed Sulwyn, but she realized what was happening. Ildri wanted to throw any suspicion off them both. But doing something like this…

Ildri released the pot and lunged; her hands wrapped around Sulwyn's neck and squeezed tightly. Plan or not, she didn't expect Ildri to have this much strength. Pain rose in her throat; she was trying to breathe in and failing. Should she fight back?

Suddenly Ildri let go as if burned. Sulwyn bent over, coughing, looking up at Daijiro. His eyes flashed in not only anger but something like excitement. He held his hand out, paralyzing Ildri where she stood. Her hands and legs stuck to her sides, fighting against bonds she couldn't see. But he didn't stop there, his palm became a fist and Sulwyn could hear Ildri gasp for breath.

"Daijiro, stop!" yelled Sulwyn, but he smiled instead, opening his fist and pointing his fingers to Ildri. He flicked them down, bringing her to her knees.

"Let me start with those hands of yours," he growled, and Ildri screamed just as Sulwyn heard several cracks in her fingers; was he breaking her finger bones?

Sulwyn moved forward, standing in front of Daijiro. "Release her. She has had years of punishment. She doesn't need more."

"Lady Princess, your actions can count as treason. Are you okay with that?" He smiled at her, never releasing his hold on Ildri.

"Then I will tell them I provoked her with my naivety. Is that better?" she hissed, stepping closer. Ildri screamed again, and Sulwyn threw a punch. Daijiro caught it in his other hand, squeezing her fist and pulling her close.

"Beg me for it," he growled, "or I'll move to her toes. It's the small bones that hurt more than most think."

Sulwyn glared at him, turning back to Ildri who at that moment looked as if she were slipping in and out of consciousness. Even if she were a Devinal, being subjected to pain like this so suddenly wasn't something she would be able to cope with. Not in this state.

Sulwyn stood her ground and pushed her fist forward, his hand nearing his face. "Beg for it? Do you think I've never done that before?" Sulwyn dropped to her knees, her glare like steel, his hold over her fist never loosening. But her actions made his eyes waver and that was good enough for her.

"Well, if the Lady Princess is demanding it." He let go of her fist and dropped both hands.

Sulwyn could hear Ildri's faint whimpers as she curled into a ball. Sulwyn knew she would be able to heal herself, but that wasn't the point.

"You're pathetic," spat Sulwyn, standing straight again.

"I am not only here to oversee their hours, but to protect you if you are attacked." But Sulwyn was sure that was a lie. He couldn't care less if she were stabbed in front of him. He just wanted to have a go at her, or at anyone for that matter.

"Thirty-Six, your time is up. It looks like you've decided to waste your peaceful time by acting up. I had no choice but to do what I did." He spoke to her as if he were reprimanding a child. "I didn't break your toes, so you can stand on your own. I know you won't give me any more trouble, right? Since you seem rather clear of mind today, or at least you were." He stepped closer, but Sulwyn pulled him back.

"I will help her," said Sulwyn shortly, not giving him another glance.

She stepped past him, bending forward to help Ildri up. But Ildri smiled at her, and within the sleeves of her shirt, she secretly flexed her fingers; healed. Sulwyn breathed a sigh of relief just as Daijiro smirked, turning around and leading the way.

怇怇

"Are you tired yet? The night is young. We still have two more," said Daijiro causally as the door closed on Ildri. Sulwyn stayed silent for a moment.

"I will not indulge in your madness. It was my mistake for influencing her. I was careless. I will not allow you to hurt someone in front of me like that again. She was undeserving."

"They may be prisoners, but it doesn't stop them from once being killers. She could have done worse."

"I do not need your concern." And she was done. She would not speak to him again for the rest of this night if she could help it. She was tired; he was an effort to deal with. His pressure, his allure, whatever it was about him, she hated it. It was confusing; she didn't feel like herself. And she knew it was all a game to him. She would never want to fight him if she could avoid it.

"Lady Princess!" called a voice behind them just as they reached the next door. Daijiro and Sulwyn turned in surprise to see the yellow-eyed Protector come running forward.

"You are being summoned..." he huffed, catching his breath and saluting them both.

She narrowed her eyes. "Who would send a summons at this time?"

"The king, princess..." he hesitated, before looking her in the eyes and flinching.

Sulwyn clenched her jaw. "What time is it?"

"It should be around three in the morning," said Daijiro quietly.

"Isn't he the one who wanted me to be here to learn all of this?" asked Sulwyn a little haphazardly. "Does it have to be immediately? Wasn't he away?"

"He has just arrived. I believe he's come back from investigating the fog town."

"That seems important," said Daijiro, dismissing them both and turning back to the cell door. He was about to turn the key but stopped, looking back up. Sulwyn had turned her back on the Protector and instead stood behind Daijiro, waiting for him to open the cell door.

"Lady Princess…" said the Protector, a little uncertainly and a bit annoyed.

"I'm not going now. Tell him you tried everything, but I could not be budged. I will fulfill the task at hand before I go to him," said Sulwyn, her teeth clenched. Daijiro just chuckled.

"He may be killed for defiance on your part; will you still say no?" said Daijiro calmly, turning the key left and right.

Sulwyn looked directly at the man. "Then you will stay here until we are done," she demanded, and the Protector looked at her like she was crazy.

Daijiro laughed, pulling the door open. "By all means, do stay with us. Just do not speak, it could get you killed." He smirked at the man as they all stepped back.

৵৽৻

Forty-Two was a tall man with brown skin and dark orange eyes. She couldn't be sure, but he seemed related to Ildri, their features similar. He had a scruffy white beard and dirty grey and black curly hair to his shoulders. But she had never seen anyone with as many scars as he. Sulwyn had many scars, as did Raghnall, but this man seemed to be made of scars. Small, thin ones to long, thick ones. What this man had seen in his lifetime she might never know.

His time was like Twenty-Seven's; he was silent and ate his all-vegetable foods in peace. The rain had let up after Ildri had been sent back and held off for the rest of the night.

She caught Forty-Two staring at her a few times, either out of curiosity for the new face, or out of recognition; she was not sure. However, when it was finally his time to go back, just before he stepped into his cell, he aimed a sharp kick to the yellow-eyed Protector's shin before running into his cell and closing the door himself. Sulwyn tried to hold back her laughter and realized Daijiro was trying to do the same. The Protector looked at them angrily but knew better than to pick a fight with either of them.

The last prisoner of the Pain Cells, Thirty, stepped out and looked directly at them. His eyes were angled, like Nori's or Daijiro's, but they were a light hazel and deep set. He was taller than all the other prisoners of that night and walked like he had nothing better to do at the time, as if this were a pleasant stroll. His skin, formerly light golden, was pale from the darkness of the cell. His hair, a short dark brown, was self-cut by the looks of how it grew in odd lengths. Sulwyn thought he would have been the fastest and quietest out of the four of them, and probably once specialized in stealth. He also looked like the youngest one there. How old had he been when he was captured?

His food choice was similar to Twenty-Seven's, with more meat and vegetables and less fruit. Unlike the others, he had a book and finished it within his time. It seemed like they supplied him with a different book each month, and he never complained of the choice. She wasn't sure what books they would pick but didn't think they would be anything radical. They needed to keep him subdued.

"Thirty, your time is over," said Daijiro quietly. Thirty looked up at them both, just as he closed the book. But his stare lingered on Sulwyn before he followed.

Somehow or another, she had the feeling they all knew who she was. Whether they could process this besides Ildri, she was not sure. But at the same time, when they realized who she was, they also realized that

Raghnall was no longer living. And in those moments when they stared at her, despair crossed their eyes.

Thirty's eyes never left hers as the cell doors closed, and at that moment, Sulwyn felt her heart break. All four of them, trapped in a cell for over twenty years, waiting for something…anything…to happen. But what had happened was probably something out of their worst fears. Raghnall would have been their only hope. But he had stayed in hiding as she grew and dedicated his time to her.

Had he forgotten about them? Had he given up on finding them when he had given her up to the Empire? Or long before that? Did he even know they were alive, or did he think they all died that night?

"Lady Princess…your duty for the night is done. Please let us go," said the Protector hastily. Daijiro pulled the key out, placing it within an inner pocket in his indigo tunic. As he pulled the shirt away from his neck, Sulwyn glanced at a thin, bright silver necklace. He caught her stare just as the shirt fell back.

"Princess…" whined the man.

"You can leave now; I will give my report on your assistance later. It's best not to keep the king waiting any longer." He smiled lightly, raising an eyebrow. Question upon question built up in her mind, but she was too tired to fully register them. She looked back at him once more before turning to leave.

XXI

You Should Control Your Anger

| SULWYN |

"HOW brazen of you. I shouldn't have expected less," said Artaxiad once Sulwyn had knocked and entered his infernal ticking hell. "I was able to rest anyway. You may go," he addressed the Protector, who looked as if he just escaped death.

"I was told that you are back from your journey to the fog town," said Sulwyn, taking a seat across from him.

"You will get the full details later today after you have had rest. It is now just past dawn. I am glad that I returned to news of you taking your assignment seriously. Even if you made me wait. For that, I will forgive it and the Protector who failed to bring you to me." He seemed tired as well. If he was going to half-ass his explanation, why did he even bother to summon her?

"I did not summon you here for that alone. I thought I should give you a proper warning. I am ending your assignment at the Solus early. You will be joining Uferor Divi and San on this new assignment. I know you asked to be part of this investigation. I take pride in the fact that you seem to see yourself as part of our Empire."

"Maybe," said Sulwyn, hating to agree even in a lie, "but mostly, I don't think the lives of the innocent should be put at risk at the whim of some group. They already go through enough." Because of the Empire, they went through hell.

"I agree, we must protect our people." Sulwyn clenched her fists at his words, digging her nails into her skin. She wanted to stab the hypocrisy out of his face. "I also wanted to discuss your nomination. Pandora has relayed the message, but he will have a hard time. You have dealt with both Daijiro and Galahad. Galahad's opinion is most important now. As the All Command, he can overrule the rest. But if they are unhappy, your nomination will end up dead." He smiled widely at the thought. Sulwyn stayed silent; nodding was all she trusted herself with.

"There is one other thing. I am giving you freedom within the Empire. You have proven yourself worthy on many occasions thus far in these last few months. But you have duties to attend to as the princess of this Empire. Starting tonight, and on every other night, you will have dinners with marriage prospects."

"What?!" said Sulwyn loudly, standing and knocking back the wooden chair. It fell to the carpeted floor in a hard *thump*.

"You must eventually bear a suitable heir." He licked his lips slightly, and Sulwyn knew full well that if he had the chance to be part of creating that heir he would. Waves of disgust rolled through her, nauseating and dizzying.

"Why? I don't see you relinquishing your seats anytime soon. Whether I have a child or not in the future is not of your concern. I am still learning the Empire, and at this point in time I don't think I should be trusted with that much more." She grit her teeth, glaring.

"These are dinners to meet with potential candidates. I don't expect anything anytime soon. And we wouldn't need an heir for an awfully long time. But to get you integrated and trusted in the Empire as one of us, this is a necessity. And you must do it to make sure that those around you don't suffer the consequences of your choices. Or lack thereof." He too stood to face her, smiling in a way that made her urge to stab his face that much stronger.

"Are you threatening the people around me?" she growled.

"Aren't we always? You should know well enough. You are not trusted *that* much." Artaxiad gestured to the door. The conversation was over. "Six in the evening, Sulwyn. I will not tolerate lateness again."

What utter bullshit.

It wasn't the fact of having marriage dinners that bothered her; it was who she would be meeting. Anyone they chose or anyone that would come wouldn't be any different from them. She would have to somehow sit through dinners, forcing her food down while trying not to throw it up from their nonsense. Sulwyn growled angrily, startling a few servants as she passed.

Unlike the first time when she travelled these halls with Nori and Eztli, all the servants she passed made sure to bow or curtsy elaborately. And this just fueled her anger more. She needed to fight someone. Anyone. To release some of her pent-up rage. Weariness of the night wore on her, but the newfound adrenaline pushed it to the side.

Screw this castle with its magic and its walls and its people. She made her way down to the front of the castle, but within seconds of being outside, she was soaked. The rain that had held off all night was in full swing and though she usually enjoyed the rain, it just infuriated her more.

"*Sulwyn!*" Pain shot through her knees as she crashed to the ground, Arsinone's scream resonating through her mind, sending throbbing waves through her head. But it wasn't just her scream that brought on pain. Rushed images of the kitchen reached her mind, distracting her from the pounding in her head and in her knees. She realized the view was from Arsinone's eyes under a table. She watched Nori clutching a cooking knife in fear as they both watched Eztli being dragged away.

After a few minutes, Sulwyn stood up. Willing the dizziness to fade, she wobbled her way back into Valens Muros to get to the kitchen. Arsinone's voice and cries keep ringing through her mind. Sulwyn couldn't counter it and instead just listened, trying to focus on getting to her.

"You weren't here. I didn't know what to do. I couldn't leave the kitchens! But I heard your voice when you came and then it disappeared when you went to Artaxiad because it's too far away."

"I'm sorry, I'm sorry," thought Sulwyn, her mind clearing faster. *"How much time has passed since this happened?"*

"About half an hour or so..." she could hear her soul crying.

"Nori? Arsinone?" called Sulwyn crashing through the kitchen doors, dripping water all over the floors. The other maids and menservants kept their distance, trying to continue their work, but Sulwyn could see them shaking. Arsinone ran to her, crying.

"Where is Nori?" asked Sulwyn, wiping tears from Arsinone's cheeks. She managed to point to the counter. Sulwyn picked up Arsinone, walking to the other side. Nori had fainted but was beginning to stir. Instantly Sulwyn realized it was Duri.

"Duri, look at me," whispered Sulwyn. "I don't care if you like me. Take Arsinone back to the room and lock the door. Understand?" Duri glared with Nori's soft eyes but nodded. Sulwyn put Arsinone down. Duri took her hand and ran off.

This was Artaxiad's doing. She knew it; it was a warning to her and punishment for not coming at his summons despite what he said. Sulwyn took off out of the kitchen hesitating over where to go.

"Arsinone? Do you know where they went?"

"I caught their thoughts. Sulwyn, they want to hurt her. They were told to do whatever they like to her! I think they went to Eques."

Sulwyn turned, running towards the side doors and through the stables. The quickest route she had discovered to Eques Muros was directly through parts of Tranquillum that bordered the Empire. They had a head start. And she couldn't bring herself to think about what they had done or could have done in the time she wasn't here. Artaxiad was cheating, and she shouldn't have been surprised. What kind of game had she gotten herself into? She whistled loudly, and within seconds Ki arrived by her side.

After several anxious minutes of galloping through the trees, the rain was but a light drizzle. She could see the tall structure of Eques loom before her, mocking her. Well, now she had somewhere to take her anger out. Sulwyn jumped off Ki, and without a word, he stood guard near the gates.

Sulwyn reached the back doors of the second castle, but it was locked. She banged hard against the wooden doors, the iron handles rattling in her wake. Looking up to the windows above, she saw a few Néosan high up looking curiously down.

"Open this door!" she yelled in command, startling a Néosan who took his head away from the window. Sulwyn continued to bang harder until the door swung inwards. She faltered only slightly, stepping back quickly as four men came out. She saw their smirks. They were distractions.

Then that's all they would be.

Sulwyn lunged at them, trying to get past, but they pushed her back. "The king said that you need some training. We have permission to play with you for a bit." Sulwyn growled in frustration. They were underestimating her, assuming Caldwell was weak, unaware that she was Kintana.

She rushed at them again, but the pain in her knees made her misstep. At that moment, two of the Néosan grabbed her under the arms, forcing her back and outside. Trees surrounded them, blocking from view the city behind her. No one would see how the Empire treated their "long-lost daughter."

She dug her boots in the ground, stopping them from pushing her back farther. Shock flitted through their eyes, but the other two Néosan took their chance to punch her in the gut and in the back. Sulwyn groaned. There was one area on her back where the axe had cut deeply. That had yet to heal fully. And all these hits against her would reopen the wound.

"Heard that maid's been around for a while. She was at the pleasure houses before, didn't last long. But I heard she was talented, if you know what I mean," leered one of the men.

Sulwyn roared, lifting herself up. Quickly, she pushed against him, gaining a little bit of air between his feet and the ground. She dug her heels into his shin, forcing his leg higher until she threw herself at him, knocking him over and releasing his hold on her.

Swiftly she rolled away as another Néosan came to kick her down. She turned, dragging her feet into the sand and kicking small wet chunks into the air. She used that moment to steal the short sword from the fallen Néosan and charge at the one man blinded by silt. Without hesitation, she stabbed him in the stomach.

"Looks like you lost, princess," said another one, staring at his two fallen comrades. Sulwyn stopped, looking up just as three other men exited the castle, dragging Eztli behind them. They threw her unconscious body to the ground and just like before, sound fell away from her.

They had beaten her until her eyes were closed. Cuts covered her face, her maid uniform ripped. Sulwyn howled as the new men came forward. She took the short blade out of the other man's stomach and spun, bringing it around her and connecting with someone she couldn't see.

She turned, looking at the other Néosan, and the short sword cut deep across his throat. She didn't give him a second glance, turning to the remaining four, ripping the sword out. More blood coated her; this time a mix of her own dripped down her back, the cut stinging. The chill of her rain-soaked tunic cooling the wound helped her to ignore the dull, growing pain.

Sulwyn moved forward again but was blocked mid-swing. The Néosan held her arm, forcing her to bend the sword back, trying to push it closer to her neck.

"Are you sure you're allowed to kill me?" she spat.

In his moment of hesitation, Sulwyn head-butted him as hard as she could. He hollered in pain, letting go of her arm. Sulwyn stumbled for a moment, ignoring the stars in her eyes; without giving him time to recover she jabbed forward, missing her intended target but stabbing his leg all the same. He fell to the ground in agony. Two men stood in front of her. But she had messed up. There were three left.

Sulwyn looked behind her; one of the men had snuck up, grabbing her arms behind her and lifting her up. He was strong, but she continued to struggle.

"What's this?" called a voice from the door. All the men froze, staring ahead as Sulwyn tensed. Daijiro had come out from the castle doors and was walking towards them. Shouldn't he be sleeping? His night was just as long as hers. She watched him glance down at Eztli, eyes full of nothing at her battered form. He looked to Sulwyn and saw the blood around them, and she knew what was coming.

"I'm assuming the king planned this? It is very like him. Should I take over?" he purred, stretching and looking to the cloudy sky. The men released their hold on her, dropping her to the ground. She stood up quickly, watching the Néosan bow and run back into the castle in haste. So they all feared him.

He looked down, smirking. Sulwyn knew he was revelling in this fact. That he held terror over so many. He looked back at her, eyes full of that same excitement she had seen in the Solus. She stood firm. Her stance set. Waiting.

"You should have gone to sleep, Cailín. This is an old trick from our king. Was this punishment for not going to him when he called? A warning?"

"All of the above, I'd assume. He's forcing me to say yes."

"Yes?"

"You don't need to know about it." Sulwyn ran forward, but Daijiro didn't hold himself in any sort of stance. He kept his hands in his pockets, watching her before he moved to the side with grace. She was too tired for this. He could take her easily at this point. But he was playing with her. If that's how he wanted it, then fine, she would bring out all she could; there was no one to witness her here.

Sulwyn went past him as he dodged, picking up another short sword and turning behind her. He was already facing her, ready for her next move, hands still in his pockets. He wasn't even taking her seriously. Sulwyn paused, taking a deep breath. The cuts were burning, her back bleeding, but she would land at least one hit. She had to.

"Is this all you're good for? You seemed to have lost some of your talent in the months at the Empire. Are you becoming content with their hospitality? You wouldn't be the first." He spoke smoothly, calmingly. But there was a strange edge to his voice, something underlying that she couldn't read.

"Why don't you fight me seriously so I can respond in kind? I don't like fighting people who can't or won't defend themselves," ground Sulwyn.

"Are you sure you want that?"

"Fight me without your strange power. Or is it that you can't? That you never managed to learn to do so because you relied on that cheating gift of yours."

"Gift? Cheating gift?" He scoffed in an insane sort of way. "These were the cards I was dealt. I can't help it if it's a power you can't comprehend."

"So it's luck? Is it luck that brought you into the Empire? Did you get complacent and comfortable? And forget how to fight?" She was edging her way closer. She didn't know what got him ticking but could see the bloodlust and the madness grow in his eyes. Whatever he was, he let his emotions rule him as well. "Why aren't you higher? Why aren't *you* the 'All Command'? It looks like you deserve the title more, no?"

He took his hands out of his pocket, flexing them slightly. But he wasn't using his power on her. He just stared at her, his smirk ever-present on his lips. "I can't deny your command, princess."

He dashed forward, lithely closing the space between them, trying to disarm and punch her at the same time. This was all she wanted. She raised her arms in defence and aimed a kick to his thigh, intending to strike. But she missed, the strength lessened. She still managed to make him stumble. And at that moment, she brought the short blade forward and slashed his arm.

And that was her mistake.

Upon seeing his own blood, his eyes flashed, and he viciously tackled her to the ground. If he was playing before, it was all gone in the savagery that flooded his mind and sense. She coughed out blood, her back landing on protruding rocks. She looked to the side, Eztli stirring for a moment.

Sulwyn needed to get this over with. But Daijiro was like an animal, primal and instinctive in this moment. And he aimed for her face.

She blocked his fists with her forearms, taking the hits. He paused for just a moment, and she used that to grab his collar between her fists, pulling him towards her. With all her energy she head-butted him, forcing him to stagger back. The second head-butt didn't go over as well as the first. Her mind was reeling, the edges blacking as she stood. Blood dripped past her eyebrows, tickling her mouth; the same mirrored on Daijiro. He licked the corner of his lips, tasting the blood that ran down.

But Sulwyn faltered, not from the hit but from the sudden rise in heat.

Again? She was having one now?

Daijiro's eyes locked on hers; he was beyond her control and faster than ever. Distracted, she could feel the fever rising quicker than the last time. She was too tired to hold this one back, let alone remember it.

He ran towards her before she could fully stand and gripped her arms, turning her and pulling them behind her back. Wincing, she looked up at him in distress and instantly he let go. His bloodlust was replaced with shock as he looked from his hands to her eyes. Her eyes must have changed to green at this point. Daijiro stepped back abruptly, and Galahad was in between them both with speed none of them saw.

"Look at me, Sulwyn," he whispered quietly, moving her away from Daijiro and onto the ground in one swift movement. She didn't want to tell him. She didn't want to say it. Against her will, she gripped his wrists, watching him wince at the burn of her skin.

And the vision pulsed its way through her.

She clenched her jaw, refusing to say anything. It was like her last vision. Colours, cheering, and a cave. But this time was different. At the end she gasped, opening her eyes and focusing on his that were black around the whites.

"In the cave…your eyes…" was all she could mutter before everything was dark.

She wasn't out for long, that was promising. Tiny rocks poked into her back, stirring her awake alongside Galahad's yelling voice. She opened her eyes; Eztli was staring at her with blurry ones. Sulwyn looked to the other side, the Néosan were back outside, all kneeling in front of Galahad, and Daijiro was off to the side still staring at his hand. Even though her body was tight and stiff with pain, the memory of why she was here rushed forward. Slowly and carefully she stood, masking the unsteadiness of her feet.

Daijiro looked up at her, and Galahad turned, following his gaze. She picked up the short sword and ran at Galahad.

"Look what they've done to her!" she yelled, and he made no move to stop her even as she pointed the blade at his neck. Sulwyn snarled but could not bring herself to stab him. He glanced past her, looking down at Eztli with barely any emotion.

"Your weakness created that. Just like your weakness stopped you from stabbing me," Galahad moved his arms comfortably behind his back. "Who ordered this?" he asked nonchalantly.

The Néosan looked stunned at his sudden change in tone; she had no idea what he had been saying before, but that didn't seem to matter. "The king, our lord," said the Néosan.

"You've killed two of my men and injured two more." He sounded mildly impressed.

"You should have trained them better," she growled, but she never moved the blade from the crook of his neck; instead, she pressed it further, drawing thin, shallow beads of blood. Somewhere near where she first cut him all those months ago in the lower dungeon. But he made no acknowledgment of this.

"Anger can only carry you so far. If you are to live in that castle with a clear mind, you'd do best to be rid of it," he spoke smugly, and this made Sulwyn press the blade closer still.

"And turn into you? I don't think so," she hissed, earning a smirk. She felt the rage burning in her and she couldn't remember what happened once her vision started. She couldn't even remember the vision despite her progress last time. So she spat in his face.

He looked at her nonplused, lifting his hand to wipe the spit away. "You should be on your way. She doesn't seem in life-threatening danger, but I don't think she should stay that way either." Sulwyn dropped the short sword at his feet, stepping back and glaring at the Néosan.

She walked back to Eztli, bending down. Grunting from the pain in her back she hefted Eztli up. In quick strides Galahad was behind Sulwyn, his hand reaching to touch between her shoulder blades. She looked at him, his eyes unreadable for a moment, but she stepped back.

"I don't think you have permission to touch me so freely. Unless you think you are like the king now?" said Sulwyn, but he wasn't looking at her. He was looking at the Néosan, and Sulwyn could feel a sort of pressure emanating from him, like at the bar in Antac. "Though if you have that kind of interest, they're going to be holding dinners for me and marriage prospects. Not that I would say yes to any one of them," she spat at him.

She looked at Galahad, all trace of emotion gone as he stepped back. Daijiro too looked at her oddly, but he slipped back into the castle before them all, leaving them to stare at each other.

"Keep an eye on your maids, Sulwyn," said Galahad with a note of finality.

"Keep an eye on your men. I have no qualms with stabbing the rest of them. I've remembered their faces," she barked, carrying Eztli and walking to the gates where Ki awaited her return.

৵৽

Sulwyn made her way back through the forest at a much slower pace walking alongside Ki. He carried Eztli gently across his back, trying hard not to jostle her. She had lost consciousness along the way.

Arsinone's voice greeted her mind once she entered the castle, and she carried Eztli back into her room. Arsinone shuffled over, quickly closing the door. Sulwyn glanced at Nori but then stared at her apprehensively.

"Just lay her down, please," said Duri hurriedly and panicked, Nori still asleep in her mind. Sulwyn bent her knees, trying carefully to place Eztli down on the carpeted spot of floor.

"Did they have their way with her?" hissed Duri, removing the ripped clothes off her. Sulwyn went to grab a bowl of water and a nightgown, while Arsinone pulled down a stack of towels from a shelf.

"Do you know the same spells as Nori?" asked Sulwyn quietly, as she quickly and gently wiped the blood off Eztli's bare skin. Cuts and bruises left traces all over her arms and legs, with some minor bruising by her stomach. Sulwyn tried her best to keep the anger at bay, sleep and exhaustion tugging at her, making her even more vulnerable.

"Unfortunately, yes. Her training was cut short. And after she came here, she had to hide her magic. I know as much as she does, and it's not at the level she should be at." Sulwyn looked at her as she began to speak the Devinal tongue. A faint purple glow coated her palms. She hovered them over the larger cuts before moving on to the smaller ones. "It's good that there are some trees in here. I can borrow their energy," said Duri, concentrating. Arsinone and Sulwyn stayed quiet, only able to watch as Duri slowly but surely healed the worst wounds.

"Duri, you can't heal all of them. It will expose you both," said Sulwyn but Duri glared at her, tears in her eyes.

"Don't tell me what to do, princess. She wouldn't be going through this if it weren't for you. You don't know what Eztli has done for us, for me!" She spoke loudly and realization hit Sulwyn.

"Are you…Do you love her?" she whispered, but Duri just started to cry, stopping her healing process.

"You've done a lot…Sulwyn is right, it will get you caught if you fully heal her," said Arsinone softly. Sulwyn handed Duri the nightgown, helping her hold Eztli up and put it over her head. Sulwyn bent down again, hefting her up and placing her onto the large bed.

"Come here, you freak," said Duri, pulling Sulwyn towards her. Before she could protest, Duri lifted the back of her tunic and pulled it off her. She tossed it to the floor, gently rolling up the undershirt to reveal the now open cut.

"You look like garbage," said Duri, and Sulwyn felt warmth hover over her back. She turned to look at the bloodstained tunic on the floor. "Did you at least get some payback?"

"Killed two Néosan, injured two more." Sulwyn smiled at Duri's huff of approval.

"You met Galahad," stated Arsinone. Sulwyn turned to face her, but Duri pushed her back in annoyance.

"Was he in on it?" asked Duri. The heat left her back, the fabric cold with wet blood.

"I don't know," said Sulwyn blankly. They all stopped speaking, turning to face Eztli who grunted momentarily.

"We should get her some water, and maybe some soup?" suggested Arsinone. Sulwyn nodded in agreement.

"Arsinone, you stay with Eztli, we'll get it."

"Why both of us?" asked Duri in annoyance.

"Because I said so. Just let me follow you, okay?" Disgruntled, she followed Duri out of the room.

"The kitchen is that way, and really, you should change first." Duri crossed her arms, but her remarks fell silent at the expression on Sulwyn's face.

❧

"There is only so much insolence I can tolerate, Sulwyn," said Artaxiad sternly.

Sulwyn had burst through the wooden doors without so much as a knock. Duri decided to wait in a hall away from sight. Sulwyn walked forward, grabbing the dagger out of her boot and pointing it directly at him. But Artaxiad just smiled.

"You know you can't kill me."

"We can test that," said Sulwyn, glaring at him.

"I'm assuming you received my gift."

"Don't insult me, Artaxiad. Whether it was out loud or not, I have agreed to play your games. Maybe even settle here one day, who knows?

But you're making it awfully difficult for me to forsake my previous life and join yours."

"You are something new and entertaining, Sulwyn. I thought we could play a bit. And you did disobey my summons. This was to help persuade you to see things my way."

"I have no intention of playing with you. I will partake in your dinners, but swear to me that you won't harm them ever again. They are maids. They have nothing to do with this battle. And it's unfair."

"I'll agree to your terms if it will keep peace with you. But you cannot blame me for showing you your place. This is the Empire. I will not play with you like Raghnall had, feeding you the idea that you have control over anything around you. I will not tolerate these actions again." He stood up, escorting her out the door. "The time does not change. Six this evening. It's up to you if you want to sleep or not until then. Dress finely."

∾

Once they had gotten food for themselves and the others, they went back to the bedroom. Sulwyn was silent for the rest of the morning, finally sleeping until the afternoon. Eventually, Duri fell asleep at Eztli's side, waking up as Nori.

Eztli was still asleep by the time Sulwyn needed to get ready for dinner. Nori and Arsinone took it upon themselves to help her dress. They weren't as extravagant as Eztli and Sulwyn was a little thankful for it. She didn't feel like prostrating herself to some nameless man. They left her hair down, curling it a bit for neatness, and dressed her in a light silk grey dress with capped shoulders, similar to the blue one she had worn for the lunch all those months ago.

Nori's style of makeup was different, subtle and more suited to Sulwyn's taste. But when Eztli woke up, she would let her dress her however she desired.

When it was quarter to six, Sulwyn made her way to the large dining room from before with Arsinone as her guide. Arsinone had no qualms with the layout of the castle as she could get guidance from other people's souls. But she forgot to ask Nori about the magic that was supposedly cast over the castle.

Sulwyn knocked on the door once before entering. No one else had arrived, which suited her just fine. She took the seat she had sat in last time and waited while the servants flitted around her, adding the final touches to the already elegant table. At precisely six, the wooden doors opened and in entered Artaxiad with Pandora. Sulwyn realized they wore the same style of clothes each time just in various colours. Today Artaxiad was coated in blacks and blues, and Pandora was in dark plum. Why did she have to look so similar to them?

Artaxiad greeted her, but Pandora stayed silent, looking at anything but Sulwyn. Within a few minutes, a heavy knock pounded against the door. Sulwyn refused to turn around or stand. This was her meeting after all, why should she put effort where she didn't want to be? Pandora shot her a glare, but it fell once she smiled at their guest.

XXII

The Roar Of A Star

SHE expected it from Artaxiad; knew this dress was cut too low for the type of company she would be around. But she didn't expect the man whose name she had already forgotten to be so brazen as to keep his eyes lower than her face the entire time.

He was exactly what she expected; older than her, clean cut, wavy slick ash hair and the mind of anyone else in this Empire. He was a Privileged residing on residence at the other side of Valens. He did something along the lines of architecture or whatnot. He could have had the most exciting job in the world, but she couldn't care less. She focused on her dinner, only speaking when necessary. By the time dessert rolled around, her patience had snapped.

"If you had any sense, I'd expect you to hold your conversation with my eyes, not my breasts," spat Sulwyn. The man looked startled and instantly embarrassed, but instead covered it with anger.

"Your attitude reflects that of your parents; you should hold your tongue if you don't want their respect to fall. If you can't keep yourself in line, you are not worth my time." But the man realized his words as soon as he said them, horror in his eyes.

Sulwyn just rolled her eyes; he was doomed anyway. He had just insulted the king and queen at their table. "I have no interest in anyone who cannot go one second without undressing me with their eyes," she addressed Artaxiad with forced calm. And whether they had a deal or not, he knew she could at least cause enough of a scene to make the people talk for days. If they wanted her to comply, they would have to step up their choice in men.

"I do not mean to upset you, my good sir, nor does my daughter. You must excuse her behaviour; she is as sharp with her tongue as she is with a sword." Tension filled the air at Artaxiad's change in tone. "She is the Lady Princess of this Empire, after all. If she does not approve of your behaviour, then you are of no use to her or me." He cleared his throat returning to his blueberry pie.

The man went pale, fully understanding his position, "I am deeply sorry, my king, I am honoured to have even been considered for this opportunity. I should have minded my tongue."

"Minding your tongue does not excuse you for the thoughts you obviously hold," said Pandora quietly. Sulwyn stared at her, surprised at her comment. But she continued to drink her tea without looking at either of them.

"I think I am right when I state that you are no longer welcome in this castle. I know your dedication to the Empire, but I cannot have you reside here any longer." Artaxiad smiled lightly, but Sulwyn knew what that meant. This man had just lost all his job opportunities with the king.

Guilt rolled through her, but then she forced it away. This man was the Empire. He was part of what made it the way it was. What problem was it of hers if he was now cut from them?

"I...understand, my king. Thank you for this dinner and this opportunity. I will take my leave. If you will excuse me." The man bowed, his dark brown eyes sweeping the room once, lingering on Sulwyn's eyes. She could see the hate in them.

"That was a bit harsh, wasn't it?" said Sulwyn conversationally once the man had left.

She hated this.

"Not at all. Thank you for weeding out someone who was obviously so ungrateful." Artaxiad pushed his plate away, taking his napkin out of the folds of his shirt. "I'm happy you have decided to attend. Do not forget we will have one every other night, at least for now, until you are on your assignment and we are elsewhere. When we have the time, we will hold a dinner."

They stood together, Artaxiad escorting Pandora out. He stopped shy of the door, turning back to Sulwyn, who was quietly finishing her tea. "This is mostly practice for you and your standing in society. I do not expect you to desire anyone, but if I find someone that is well suited, I will make it happen."

"You never asked if I was interested in men. What if I desire a woman?" asked Sulwyn. The idea wasn't beyond her. Though she was more inclined to men she was equally attracted to women. It mattered more to her the type of person they were. Not that she would ever explain that to him.

"I'd still expect a child in time. Whether you have someone on the side regardless of their gender or status, that is not my concern. It's who you marry that matters, social standing and all."

Sulwyn returned to the room with Eztli sleeping quietly. Nori and Arsinone could not stay in there without being noticed missing from their post, but if there was anything that Galahad said that was true, it was that no one came to this room, nor had he revoked their permission. She wondered vaguely if it had its own enchantment set against it. Sulwyn walked across the room, kicking off the heels she was forced to wear and slumping onto the couch in front of the cold fireplace.

Some time had passed and Sulwyn didn't realize she had fallen asleep until a yelp behind her woke her up. Eztli suddenly sat up, looking around her wildly, spotting Sulwyn. It was dark, only the last rays of the setting sun lit the room in an eerie fire of light. Sulwyn stretched, then started lighting each torch just as Arsinone and Nori came into the room.

"Eztli!" exclaimed Nori, rushing forward to help her prop herself up on piles of pillows. Eztli smiled gingerly.

"How are you feeling?" asked Sulwyn a little wearily, walking to her.

"I've been better...thank ya, sweetness." She lifted her arms weakly, bringing Sulwyn into a hug.

"You shouldn't thank me. It's because of me this happened. If you continue to associate yourself with me, I can't promise they won't try this again. I don't understand what it is they want from me," stated Sulwyn, frustrated. "They announce me to the world as their daughter, speaking about how they want me on their side. But they continue to do things like this."

"You can't say you are surprised," said Arsinone quietly, looking at her.

"I'm not. I just wish they would be a bit consistent." Confusion was rising in her. She turned away from Arsinone's knowing look and looked back at Eztli. "Do you...want to talk about what happened?" she asked softly, sitting next to Eztli. Arsinone joined them on the bed as well.

"Why are ya...in a dress?" said Eztli, a little stunned. "Ya look nice though."

Sulwyn almost forgot she was wearing the thing; it was so light and not at all uncomfortable. "I'm having marriage dinners, but that's not what we're talking about. Don't change the subject!"

"Marriage dinners?" Her expression reflected what Sulwyn felt.

"Another time. It's your turn," said Sulwyn, waving her hand.

Eztli looked at them in surprise, but smiled. "Ya don't need to look at me like that. It wasn't as bad. And I've been through worse."

"That doesn't make it okay," said Sulwyn loudly.

"No one said that, sweetness, but...something like this wouldn't break me. This is what it's like for all the Common Ones, one way or another. We've all experienced something terrible since the High City fell. Most of us were born into it, not knowing any other time."

Sulwyn clenched her jaw, her hands balled into fists, but Eztli placed a hand over hers. "I have faith in ya. And I know this is going to take time, so don't dare tell us to stay away from ya. It doesn't matter if ya were here or not. One way or another, something would have happened in time anyway. It always does." Eztli looked at her closely, and Sulwyn closed her eyes in defeat.

"I don't remember much of what happened, honestly, but I know it was stopped before they got too far. I escaped with only beatings," started Eztli.

"They came into the kitchen and I knew if I didn't speak up, someone else would be targeted. Once I challenged them, they dragged me away and knocked me out. When I came to, I was in a dark room. I don't know if they drugged me or not, but I couldn't concentrate on anythin'. I couldn't move or yell."

Sulwyn held Eztli's hands, feeling them shake, "I was beaten, but before they could go any further someone yelled from somewhere. The voice was strong, but I couldn't understand them or recognize it. The Néosan fell back immediately and dragged me out. I passed out just as they threw me outside."

"Arsinone, can you hear the voice that she heard?" asked Sulwyn suddenly.

Arsinone shrugged. "If she wasn't in a proper state, I'll only hear it back the same way. Though I read the soul, it's still like the mind, just purer. But I can try." Arsinone moved forward, crawling over their legs to Eztli.

She placed her hand on Eztli's forehead, concentrating. Soon after, she beckoned Sulwyn closer. She placed her other hand on Sulwyn's forehead and immediately she was taken out of the room and into a dark, round sort of training room. Eztli's vision was blurry, men hovering around her. Just as they ripped her clothes, a yell could be heard. It was gravelly, deeper but vaguely familiar. Neither could understand anything that was said. The scene quickly faded, melting away into the edges of her mind as the bedroom came back into view.

"See? I couldn't get anything…sorry," shrugged Eztli before she winced in pain. Arsinone flicked Eztli, turning to look at Sulwyn's frowned expression.

❧❦

Sulwyn was facing Eques once again; she was coming here more often than she wished. They had rescheduled their briefing of the mission to the next day given the events of the day before. How thoughtful.

Sulwyn stepped forward, opening the door with force, not bothering to wait for anyone to escort her in. Now that she was aware of it, she could feel the light prickle of magic that covered Valens. Nori was already aware of it from the first time she entered but had no idea why it was put in place and there was never a reason to investigate it. Eques, however, did not have it.

She walked in, going back to the lavish room from before. As always, she arrived before everyone else. And unlike last time, she didn't feel like exploring, so she took a seat on the couch and waited.

A few minutes later Galahad and Daijiro entered together. Galahad looked rather grim, the dark circles a bit more pronounced under his eyes than even yesterday. But Daijiro looked like he had no concerns. He glanced at Sulwyn, smirking and taking a seat at the wooden table. Galahad seemed unsure of where to place himself, opting in the end to remain standing away from both, going near the window to look at the cloudy sky.

"You look better than you did yesterday, Cailín," commented Daijiro as if she were the weather. "Heard you had your first dinner yesterday. His family has been escorted out of the Empire altogether. What did he do?"

How had he already heard about it? She wasn't even impressed anymore. She glanced at Galahad, whose face showed that he knew too. "He violated me with his eyes."

"Fair enough," Daijiro's smile was crooked. He seemed to like her response. She had no other thought for him other than that he was definitely twisted but beguiling.

Before any of them could speak further, the doors opened again. And instead of Pandora as she was told it would be, it was Artaxiad. A look she couldn't decipher passed between Daijiro and him. And instantly Sulwyn felt wary. Nothing good could come from the two of them.

"There has been a change in some things. I felt it best to address the contents of the mission to you all myself." He walked in fully and took a seat at the head of the large wooden table. He gestured for them to join Daijiro and himself.

Reluctantly, Sulwyn got to her feet, sitting at the farthest chair from them all. Daijiro turned his attention to her for just a moment before giving Artaxiad all of it. A sort of glint crossed his eyes, and Artaxiad sighed, lacing his fingers together, taking them in.

"As you know, Galahad, Caldwell, and Sulwyn were responsible for catching a group that had been impersonating our Néosan. A crime of treason and embarrassment. We have a name to uphold!" he started. Sulwyn watched him carefully; no hint of remorse at Caldwell's name or the death of the prisoners.

"With careful *persuasion*, we were able to learn about this place known as the fog town. It's been a while since I needed to track down a location; most places are already in our watch. But this one has eluded us for quite some time. After finding it, I know the town well enough. It consists of people who kept travelling, escaping our rule. I applaud their efforts, and as a reward, have decided to leave them be for now. However, this town has been experiencing mysterious deaths.

"I do not know if they are related to those of this radical group, but I do know they did hold a lot of their meetings at this location. And I would like you three to investigate and eradicate our threat."

"Eradicate? What happened to your fair trials?" asked Sulwyn.

"We know the group is in the wrong. There is no need for justice. As for the other deaths, they seem to be monthly. One woman and one man are taken from near by towns. We don't know how or why or where they go. But I do not want this reaching the Empire. We must stop them now before they get too powerful."

"What, like you and your radical group all those years ago?" huffed Sulwyn. Artaxiad looked at her sharply but smiled a little wickedly all the same. "Regardless of what you think you know, what we did was for the people, Sulwyn, never forget that." He leaned back, but somehow the tension had risen. "We have another issue to attend to, but it does not involve you, Sulwyn. You may take your leave."

"Nope. I'm going to stay *right* here. You're sending me on a mission with them. I want to know what they know." She spoke defiantly and mimicked his actions, leaning back into her chair.

Artaxiad's eyes were dangerous, but he complied. "Galahad. Your actions cannot go unpunished after last night's incidents," he stated, and Sulwyn was instantly confused. "Rage is a dangerous thing. And I cannot have you injuring or killing any more of our people. The Néosan are one thing, but good Captains are hard to find. I will be denouncing you back to second in command. It seemed this was too much for you to handle." Sulwyn looked at Galahad, his jaw set but his blue, purple, and red eyes clear of any blackness or any emotion at all.

"Instead, I have agreed to let Daijiro attempt the position of All Command." Galahad stood up now, his fists on the table as he looked at Daijiro and Artaxiad like he'd never seen them before. Sulwyn turned to Daijiro who had also leaned back, his face smug. How had he managed that? Wasn't it his bloodlust that kept him back all these years from becoming a proper Leader and from anything higher? Was what Galahad had done worse?

"We have an accordance between us." He gestured between himself and Daijiro. "And he feels that you are now a threat to the rest of our army," said Artaxiad, standing with Galahad. They glared at each other for just a moment, but Galahad backed down first, sitting down again and taking a deep breath.

"And what of *our* accordance?" growled Galahad, keeping his eyes low.

"You will see soon enough that I have rewarded you in kind. I have not gone back on my word," said Artaxiad calmly, but somehow Sulwyn knew there was something unspoken flowing between them. And by the sounds of it, it wasn't in Galahad's favour.

"I have fulfilled my part of this assignment; I expect you to sort out your plans for the rest yourself. However, pick the best five from the other teams. This mission should have been one in stealth. Feel free to pick Validus from Uferor En. They are currently without a Leader, though I know this matter will be addressed soon. Isn't that right, Sulwyn?"

"After this assignment is over, I plan to go forward with the nomination," said Sulwyn stiffly, aware of all the eyes watching her. "However, with this change in leadership..." started Sulwyn, but Artaxiad followed.

"Daijiro *and* Galahad will have final say. However, if they don't agree, then that is between them and how they want to solve it." Artaxiad smiled widely, turning and taking his leave without another word.

Sulwyn turned her attention to Galahad, who was having a stare-off with Daijiro. "Anger can only carry you so far, *Galahad*," she said, throwing his words back at him. "You'd do best to be rid of it."

But his eyes found hers with scorn as well as fear. His expression surprised her, her unspoken words fading from her tongue. What had he gotten himself into that he would look like that?

Daijiro cleared his throat and rapped on the table to get their attention. "I feel a little left out here. As you have little background in assignments, Cailín, we will make most of the decisions without you. I hope you don't mind." He smiled, either unaware or uncaring of whatever it was that was transpiring before him.

Sulwyn crossed her arms. If that's how Galahad wanted to continue playing, fine. Whatever he was hiding would come out sooner or later. For now, she needed to focus on the tasks at hand, even if she was burning to ask what "last night's incident" was.

"I will listen. I know not the names or faces of the Validus, nor do I really care. As long as they don't get in my way."

"Then maybe Galahad should be the one to rule on who we bring? They seem terrified of both of us, but I think you have a little more honour holding you up in their eyes." said Daijiro complacently. Galahad just closed his eyes, rubbing his tired face.

"We haven't been given the location—" he started, but Daijiro cut in.

"I have already been given the map for the approximate location. The fog seems to be a bit mystical. Covers the town as an illusion. But Artaxiad and his men found it all the same. To my understanding, he's spoken to the head of the town in private, but never entered the town itself. Leaving us with all the dirty work." Daijiro stood, stretched obnoxiously, and turned to Sulwyn.

"You should introduce us to your friend, princess. We need to go talk to the other Leaders anyway if we are to borrow their men and make substitutions for them. We can inform them of what's to come."

"That's fine with me. I'm sure I'll be seeing you more than I want to until then. When are we setting off?" She stood as well, Galahad still sitting.

"End of the week, should be enough time to choose the right people for this assignment as well as reassign the others," said Galahad without any debate.

Daijiro shrugged, taking his leave with a wink. "Come soon, prince, you are my second in command now. I'll need your assistance." As the door closed, Galahad stood up, aiming his fist at the table. Sulwyn instantly guarded herself, watching as the wood splintered slightly beneath his knuckles.

"Your position was short-lived," said Sulwyn, watching him carefully. "What did you do to make Artaxiad worry for his men?"

He kept his head down, eyes closed. "It's none of your concern."

"No, it's not," said Sulwyn shortly. "I'll bring my nomination sometime before the end of the week. Try not to destroy the table further than that." She turned to leave, faltering for a moment before the door closed behind her.

She could have sworn he whispered her name.

๑๑

There wasn't much for her to do until the assignment. As much as it bothered her, Daijiro was right. She didn't know enough about how these missions were carried out and had to leave it up to them. She spent the rest of that day wandering Valens Muros. Now that everyone was aware she was the princess, she needn't hide. And instead, she forced herself to memorize the layout of this castle. She knew magic liked this worked less once you were aware of it. But soon she realized that spending months, let alone a day, wouldn't solve this so quickly. If she had learned the layout from Raghnall before she had come here, she wouldn't have had to go through all this trouble.

On the next day, she had her second marriage dinner. Eztli was up and about, but she still could not attend to her maid duties—something Sulwyn made sure everyone was aware of in the kitchens. She wouldn't tolerate rumours.

"Please, you really don't need to go through the effort. Just make me presentable," said Sulwyn, but it fell on deaf ears. Eztli was excited to be doing something. "Seriously though, these aren't people I want to appeal to," muttered Sulwyn, and Eztli looked at her through the mirror's reflection.

"I'm sorry, I just really like this. But ya right. Let's keep it simple, ya? That dress ya wore the other day, it looks like ya got it in about seven different colours. Why don't we jus' make it ya dinner uniform? Wear a different one each time and start back from the beginning."

Sulwyn smiled. "That's a great idea. And that dress is rather comfortable. Alright, pick a colour."

৯৵৶

By the time the dinner ended, Sulwyn had almost stabbed the man with her fork. Though this time she didn't get him banned from the castle, she did make sure that he would never interact with her again.

"You seem to be settling well with all of this," said Pandora once the man left, his cheek bleeding thanks to Sulwyn.

"What, instilling fear into the people around me? I am born from you. It must be in there somewhere," said Sulwyn, finishing her tea. She wasn't sure what scared her more: the fact that she could have conversations like this with Pandora and Artaxiad over tea, or that she acted just like they did at dinner. With every bite of food she took, her thoughts were brought back to the fear within her, falling into the temptation of the simplicity of life in the Empire.

"You will have one more dinner before you head out for your assignment. The journey will be a bit long, but you will not be leaving Antiqua. We will pick up your dinners when you are back and rested," said Artaxiad, but a dark smile played across his lips. Was it because of who she would be meeting next? Or because of the town she would be going to?

Sulwyn took her leave shortly after the man, leaving Pandora and Artaxiad alone. But she couldn't breathe; suffocating, she panicked once again. She noticed this becoming a new pattern for her. Without warning, without consent, unknown fear and panic would rise in her chest, in her heart, and choke her. Sulwyn had experienced it before all of this, a long time ago. When Raghnall first told her about why Vartugaul was in the state it was. When she learned about Pandora and Artaxiad and understood fully what they had caused. Since then, it rarely happened until she woke up in that cell.

Now she wanted to rip her heart out.

But instead, she ran, the folds and trails of her deep red dress flowing behind her as she exited the main doors of the castle. It was late, the Common Ones inside for curfew. Only the Privileged walked about and around her. Though given the weather in the last few days, even they were home before the storms came.

Nevertheless, she kept running.

People glanced at her, not recognizing her face in the darkness. The SolarOrbs had been dark for the last few weeks, not collecting enough sun, so torches were lit instead. But they weren't as bright and cast the streets in dark, crawling shadows. She could have called Ki, but she needed this movement, though she wished she had swapped out the heels for her boots.

Sulwyn continued running against the cobblestone until it turned to grass and sand. Stumbling, her heels sank into the ground. Annoyed, she bent down and took them off, running with her bare feet instead, enjoying the cool tickle between her toes. It must have been over forty minutes of running before she finally stopped, breathing heavily at her knees and finding exactly what she was looking for.

Far behind Eques Muros, a large pond graced the edges of the forest. The water splashed around her, as cold as it was dark, even in the summer wind. The moon was not out tonight, and instead thousands of multicoloured stars reflected beneath her, blurring the line between sky and water.

In frustration she flung the shoes out into the water knowing full well it was a wasteful thing to do, but she could not help it. The burn of loathing, fury, and fear erupted in her all at once and she yanked at the dress. But the threads were strong and would not yield to her hands alone.

She lifted her skirts up, the water already soaking through the hem to her knees. Pulling the dagger out of the holster on her calf, she cut the dress. The sounds of tearing and ripping brought satisfaction to her. Sulwyn pulled at the frays until she shook out of the fabric, flinging that too into the pond. She watched as the water ate the red threads, soaking it deeper like blood as it sank.

Sulwyn looked up into the night sky and suddenly she could breathe. A shiver rolled through her; the only thing she had left on her was the black silk chemise that reached mid-thigh and barely covered her upper body, the thin straps hanging loosely on her shoulders. This might not have been the best idea, since she'd eventually have to go back to the castle. But she didn't care.

Again, the frustration filled her and this time she bellowed.

One clear, high-pitched roar of rage cut across the silence of the sky, vibrating the water around her ever so slightly. And then she ran in farther, unaware of how deep the pond was, and dove.

The cold water lapped over her, making her colder still yet clearer. She continued to swim deeper and deeper under the water. The light of the stars faded and only darkness wrapped its way around her. Thoughts floated out of her mind as she went deeper still, her chest burning to breathe in, but she pushed herself down more until she could no longer take it.

She flipped in the water, kicking hard to push herself back up the way she had come. She had travelled farther down than she had expected, and her lungs protested for air or for anything as bright lights erupted behind her eyes.

Sulwyn kept kicking, but her lungs betrayed her, and she inhaled water just as she broke through to the sky. She choked and coughed, trying to breathe deeply. But this only made her cough more and her head spin.

Haphazardly, she swam back until her feet could touch the sand and rocks. Sulwyn stumbled closer to the shore until she could sit, the water reaching up to her thighs. She pulled her knees close to her chest, breathing deeply to calm her lungs and the dry heaves of her stomach. She didn't feel as cold as she had before, though the light drips from her hair did send a shiver through her every now and then.

"That wasn't the safest thing to do," spoke a hushed voice behind her.

Startled, Sulwyn turned around quickly, her legs ready to stand if need be, but she did not move.

Daijiro was standing at the edge of the shore; he too wore no shoes, lounging in sleepwear of loose white cotton, a blue robe hung over his shoulders.

"How long have you been there?" asked Sulwyn warily.

"Since the beginning. I was sitting just over there when an ungraceful bird decided to disrupt my thoughts." He pointed somewhere behind a set of trees that lined the pond. His eyes wandered over her briefly but came back to hers quickly.

Sulwyn turned her back to him; what a pathetic thing to show to the enemy. "Do you normally walk around at night in your nightwear with no shoes?"

"Do you normally scream like a madwoman and strip in the middle of a pond attempting to drown yourself?" He stepped closer, his feet splashing gently against the water until he was level with her.

"You've seen a terrible side of me. Please remove it from your mind," she muttered, wishing he would just leave or stay or do something besides watch her silently.

"I could, but I don't think many people see this side of Kintana. I'd like to cherish it." He sat down next to her cross-legged and she eyed him in surprise. Somehow, she took him to be too high and mighty to sit in the water of a pond.

However, she regretted looking at him instantly.

His crimson eyes captured hers and she could do nothing but stare. But the strange allure or pull was not around. Whatever that was, he was not using it now. Like this, he seemed calmer, vulnerable even, compared to the person she had originally feared. And here Sulwyn hated the night.

It had a way of making her sensitive and weak, wanting to spill all emotions into the pond like blood from a deep wound.

She moved to turn away, but he carefully caught her chin between his fingers. "Even like this, you are lovely. More so in my opinion. Your guard is down, you are not Kintana here. Just Sulwyn."

Sulwyn's eyes widened. His smile was coy, but she forced herself to turn away. "You are a strange one, Daijiro." She stood up, the water dripping heavily beneath her from her slip and her hair. She didn't feel exposed with him the way she had with those Néosan guards from the dungeons all that time ago. He too stood but turned away, looking up to the sky.

"I don't know why you are in turmoil. But I suggest you snap out of it before we go on our assignment. This one seems dangerous, and I don't want to be held accountable for the Blood Princess's death. Artaxiad is only human. Don't think beyond you. It's unbecoming." He smirked, taking off his lush blue robe and draping it around her instead.

Daijiro stood silently in front of her for a moment, his eyes on hers. His white pants dripped in the water, his white shirt hung loosely over his frame, and his golden tanned skin was somehow bright even in the lack of light. She watched him leave gently through the water, leaving almost no sound or trace until he was back at the shore and walking through the grass.

XXIII

Reckless & Jagged

| SULWYN |

EZTLI and Arsinone berated her for coming back way past midnight with no dress, no shoes, and someone else's robe.

"Do ya crave danger? Do ya like fighting that much?" hissed Eztli, smacking Sulwyn in the head. Nori quickly drew Sulwyn a bath and they all threw her in to warm her up.

"I just needed to do that…" muttered Sulwyn as they all took seats in the bathing room with her. It was one of the weirdest things she had experienced yet, bathing while three other girls watched.

"Whose robe is that?" asked Arsinone, but Sulwyn turned her head away.

"Why aren't you answering that?" asked Nori. They all stared at her suspiciously.

"Is it that Kione guy? Are you…" said Arsinone, more frustrated than the rest.

"Shouldn't ya of all people know?" asked Eztli, looking at Arsinone. But she just stood up, annoyed, and stomped her feet.

"No! I can't read your soul at all! Ever since you've come back from the Solus I can't get anything from you!" she huffed. They all turned to look at her, including Sulwyn.

She never intentionally tried to block Arsinone. She couldn't deny that she tried to keep more things to herself but didn't realize she could actually keep Arsinone out.

"Does that happen often?" asked Sulwyn, her hands pruning. She stood to reach the towel, drying off.

"No! It doesn't! There are very few people I can't read, and now you're one of them!" whined Arsinone, leaving the bathing room in a tantrum.

Sulwyn pulled a nightgown over her head in haste and ran out to tackle Arsinone. She picked her up and placed her on the small desk. "Don't be like that, we've talked about this briefly. Who else can't you read? I thought you could read me but with a little difficultly."

Arsinone was silent for about ten seconds, unable to stay mad at Sulwyn. "Out of the people I've met, you apparently…someone in my family from long ago, Pandora, and Galahad. I know I said that before, but somehow, you've become harder. Same with Galahad." Sulwyn nodded, not entirely surprised by this list of people. But she wanted to test something.

"Would you like to come with me tomorrow?"

ø←§

For once in the last few weeks, the sun finally made its appearance, casting the clouds in bright yellows and greens that reflected off the sky. Arsinone and Sulwyn trotted with Ki through the Empire until she made her way to where Kione lived.

"You don't need to say anything. Just stay close to me and encroach on all the thoughts from the people I'm talking to today." Sulwyn smiled widely.

"Isn't that a little intrusive? Aren't some of them people you trust? "

"You can't be too sure anymore. Just stay close to me, we're almost at our first destination."

After some time, they trotted up a hill until she saw Kione in the distance, setting up new items in his shop. Sulwyn dismounted, moving to help Arsinone off. Ki lowered himself to assist, rubbing the side of his head against them both. Sulwyn took Arsinone's hand in her own and led the way.

"I'm almost ready!" He called, looking up at the sounds of their feet. "Diesirae is taking over for me while I'm gone. Do I need a weapon? Who is this shrimp?" He looked down, realizing that Sulwyn was not alone.

"Her name is Arsinone," said Sulwyn, and a hint of recognition flitted through his eyes. "She's assisting me a bit today." Kione stepped out from behind his shop and knelt next to her, sticking out his hand.

"Nice to meet you, Arsinone. As a token of my friendship, feel free to choose something from my shop!" He smiled brightly, earning a smile from Arsinone as well. Sulwyn picked her up, letting her see all Kione's unique creations.

"What did you do with that bracelet?" asked Kione, who continued to wipe down the larger plates in the back.

"I wear it, just not as a bracelet," said Sulwyn shortly. Arsinone turned to look at her, but Sulwyn just smiled.

"Can I have this one?" asked Arsinone after a few minutes. She pointed to a necklace that had a rectangular stone of mixed grey and light brown. Kione picked it up and wrapped it in a small, purple pouch of leather.

"Are you allowed to make anything green?" asked Sulwyn suddenly, but Kione shook his head.

"I did that once. I didn't realize the rule spread to pretty much everything. They only gave me a warning, surprisingly. But they did take anything that was green and destroy it." He shrugged just as Diesirae arrived from the back.

"Good morning, Sulwyn, Sulwyn's friend." She stuck out her hand for Arsinone to take. She looked at her a little apprehensively but shook it all the same.

"My name is Arsinone. Thank you for letting me have something of this shop for free," Sulwyn put her down and Arsinone curtsied lightly.

"You will go out of business if you keep doing that, Kione." But Diesirae smiled, slapping her brother across the back. "Go. Make a good impression of yourself. You are not being tested today, but you want them to remember you."

☙❧

Kione had taken their single white horse and they all galloped away to Eques Muros. By the time they finally arrived, it was almost noon and Sulwyn just wanted to get this over with so she could return to Valens for lunch. She would invite Kione back with her and introduce him to Eztli and Nori. He was under her care now, and she was at full liberty to invite him into the castle as she saw fit, though she would still stay in the kitchens.

But her plan was foiled when she brought them into the fancy room she had dubbed the "meeting hole"—the table was being prepared for lunch. Maybe they had moved the meeting place? Sulwyn went to lead them back out, but one of the maids addressed her.

"Lady Princess, you are to stay here. We only expected you and your guest, but we can set up another plate for the young one?" said the blonde girl, her cheeks flushed at having to address her.

"Yes, please, that would be great. However, I feel like there are a lot of plates being set?"

"Ah, yes...are you not aware...?" the maid trailed off, afraid she had done something wrong. At that moment, Galahad entered, glancing at her before turning to Arsinone. He stayed silent for a moment, staring at Arsinone for several long seconds before he turned to Kione.

"I assume you are who our lady is nominating?" Galahad put his hand out for Kione to take, but Kione just glared at him, bowing instead.

Sulwyn nudged Kione hard, her eyes wide. "This is Kione, a Common One and a Protector in the Solus."

"It is my honour to meet with you personally," said Kione, deeply bowing again. If he was stressed or panicked, he didn't show it. But he did stand up to his full height, his shoulders squared.

"This isn't the setting I was expecting," said Sulwyn, looking at Galahad for some hint of exactly what this was all about. But he disregarded her, turning away and taking a seat in front of one of the plates.

"I have just as much idea as you. All I know is Daijiro set this up," said Galahad stiffly. Sulwyn took a seat across from him, Kione and Arsinone on either side of her. She noted that the table had been repaired.

"Why have you brought her along?" asked Galahad, looking at Arsinone again. Arsinone did not look away and instead continued to stare at him in interest.

"Experience in the Empire?" shrugged Sulwyn.

As the four of them sat, she noticed that there were three extra plates. One was for Daijiro, but who were the other two for? Arsinone poked her side suddenly, looking at her in worry, but she needn't say why. The doors opened and in walked not only Daijiro but Artaxiad and Pandora as well.

"What is this?" asked Sulwyn, suddenly standing.

Kione and Arsinone looked at each other, but Galahad motioned for them to rise as well. Pandora eyed Kione carefully, then glanced at Arsinone. Though Sulwyn wasn't sure what she thought of her, she was convinced that Pandora must hold some sort of respect for Arsinone given the rumours that followed her.

"I didn't expect this type of event either, but as you are leaving in the next two days, I figured Daijiro's proposal was a good one," said Artaxiad, pushing Pandora's chair in. Sulwyn sat immediately, still refusing to fol-low the etiquette of standing and sitting when they did. The rest sat when Artaxiad was seated. Pandora was at one end, Artaxiad at the other.

"It's been a long time since I've had lunch in this castle," reminisced Artaxiad. "I heard we have received a new head chef as well. I look forward to this meal."

So that mysterious man named Zander from the Solus finally got out? But Sulwyn could barely focus on that fact. What was with this set of peo-ple? If Kione was nervous before, he must be a wreck now.

"How is Kione holding up?" asked Sulwyn in her mind.

"He seems alright. He's on guard though, very tense. I'd suggest you do most of the talking and just let him eat. He's never met Artaxiad or Pandora in person and only seen Daijiro and Galahad from afar."

"And how are you?"

"I'm okay. Pandora still has enough curiosity in me not to ask why I'm here or dismiss me. Artaxiad doesn't care if Pandora doesn't."

"Sulwyn?" said Artaxiad, raising a brow. She had missed something.

"I apologize, this sudden lunch date has taken me by surprise." She mentally hit herself. Caught off guard, her tone was all wrong. Artaxiad looked at her in astonishment at the kindness in her voice. Whatever; it worked in her favour anyway.

"Please introduce us to your nomination," he asked again, drinking water while a maid began serving them soup.

"This is Kione. He is a Common One, but also a Protector at the Solus."

"Not a lot of Common Ones ever get so far as gaining the title of Protector," stated Pandora, her tone mildly impressed. "What do you do here otherwise?"

"I make coloured glass," he said a little uncertainly. "I use it to make a variety of things from jewellery to household items to decorations."

"Ah, I know of your store. The Diarchy favoured you," said Artaxiad, dipping into his soup. He made no comment, but his face showed how much he enjoyed the taste. "The Diarchy, Gwydion in particular, spoke highly of you. Yes, I remember you now. You would make a decent candidate. I hope you can tough it out for Sulwyn's sake. She's taking a huge step in nominating you. Your life is in her hands." He smirked, and Sulwyn's stomach fell. He was indirectly threatening not only her but Kione as well.

"Galahad, Daijiro, what are your thoughts on this young man?" asked Pandora as she too tasted the soup. Sulwyn watched her falter, a strange look crossing her face, but then it was gone before anyone else could notice it.

"He looks physically capable," said Daijiro and now they all began eating.

"We won't know how he fairs until we come back. But I warn you that there is dedication to this title," said Galahad, looking at Kione and Sulwyn seriously. "The other Leaders must accept you even if we do. If not, they will find a way to kill you and it will be on your hands." He looked at Sulwyn with eyes she couldn't read.

"He won't need to worry, and I won't let anyone past me," said Sulwyn fiercely. She could feel Kione tense, but she placed her hand on his arm, looking at him with confidence.

Artaxiad watched her actions carefully, beckoning the blonde maid to take his empty soup bowl away. "That brings us to the next topic on our agenda. Sulwyn, you will have your marriage dinner tomorrow."

"I'm aware of that, thank you." She didn't look up and proceeded to eat the soup in front of her. No wonder that man got out—his skill was incredible, the rich tomato and basil coating her tongue. She had never tasted soup so smooth and flavourful in her life. She mentally apologized to Eztli. She was good, but this man was clearly a genius.

"It will be your last marriage dinner for a prospect. Any scheduled dinner after will be with the same person," continued Artaxiad, and Sulwyn dropped her spoon into the bowl with a loud splash.

"I don't understand. I only met two terrible people. I will not accept either of them or I'll be forced to be rid of them, if this is what you've decided," said Sulwyn angrily.

"Not them, no," said Artaxiad, his smile wide. Sulwyn looked at his eyes; he seemed a little more out of it than usual. Did he have a few drinks before this lunch?

"Daijiro will be your suitor," said Pandora, her bowl removed as well.

Sulwyn just stared at them both before turning to Daijiro who had just finished his soup as well. Arsinone stopped eating, looking at all of them and trying to shrink her presence away at the rising tension.

"When was this decided?" She seethed. Kione looked at her silently, eating his soup, also taking a page from Arsinone and trying to pretend he wasn't there.

"Daijiro proposed the idea when we discussed his promotion. He has worked hard for where he has gotten. Holds a strong reputation in the Empire. He is the most suitable. And you are already acquainted with him." Artaxiad's voice held a note of finality. The servants brought out the main meal of chicken stew with carrots and potatoes in small individual bowls crusted with cheese. Bread and rice were placed in the centre to choose from, along with a bowl of spinach, squash, and a medley of other vegetables she couldn't recognize.

"Don't get upset, princess, I think we're rather suited." He smiled at her and his allure was at its max. But she wouldn't fall for it. Even if the rest of the room did. She knew it now, knew what it felt like, what it smelt like. Whether it was in her mind or not, when he used his power it smelt like sweet rain with a hint of burnt wood. Did this work on Pandora? She looked at her, but surprisingly she seemed unaffected. Sulwyn now wondered if this was why Artaxiad appeared a little drunk. Did this affect him too? Maybe in a different way? Did he persuade this decision? And if so, why?

Daijiro smirked, but she turned her eyes to Galahad, who had been silent the entire time. He focused on his food, taking rice to eat with his stew. He was ignoring them all. But Sulwyn saw the slight tremor in his hand. Be it out of anger or out of the effects of Daijiro, she wasn't sure. But she knew one way or another, she wasn't winning this. She sighed.

"Fine. Daijiro is someone I am acquainted with. He's cunning, snarky, sarcastic, and blood-lusted. I don't see anything good about him. But I have fought him. If anything, I am confident I can kill him if I have to. Bring it on," said Sulwyn, toasting her water in his direction. Galahad looked up at her.

Artaxiad gave a hearty laugh, something she didn't even know he was capable of doing. "You'll have *fun* with her, Daijiro. Please don't get killed. I don't think I could stop her."

"I don't doubt it." Daijiro's tone was oddly jagged.

Sulwyn clenched her jaw until her teeth hurt. She was being mocked, undermined, and ridiculed. How dare they pull this on her? But she wouldn't lose here.

The lunch continued. Few words passed after that about the assignment, about their future dinners, and about when they could announce this next step to the Empire and the people. Sulwyn promised she'd kill Daijiro if they did any sort of announcement without her consent again. As soon as the lunch was over Artaxiad and Pandora took their leave, needing to attend to other matters.

Silence spread between them all until Kione stood up slowly. "I need to get back to my shop...my sister needs to get back to her own duties. Thank you for meeting with me. I look forward to whatever tests you give me, and I thank you for the opportunity." He bowed deeply, looking lastly to Sulwyn who nodded, smiling tightly. She wanted him out of the room before anything got too intense.

The door closed behind him and the silence stretched on. Daijiro drank his tea peacefully, but Galahad continued to look down at his interlaced hands. Sulwyn couldn't take it anymore, so she took the butter knife and threw it at Daijiro. He deflected it easily with his own.

"Don't be so childish, Cailín. For lack of a better word, we are in some ways betrothed. That's not a nice way to treat your prospect."

Sulwyn was lying when she said she was confident in killing him, especially after their brief fight. And based on his reflexes alone, she knew full well that he didn't just rely on his strange powers.

"Daijiro..." started Galahad heavily, standing stiffly. They both looked up to him, his eyes devoid of anything. "I'd appreciate it if you'd warn me in advance the next time you plan to do something like this. And let me remind you, you may be the All Command, but I still hold a title over you. Whether we like it or not."

"Warn you? I didn't think this was something I needed to tell you about in advance. Why? Don't trust yourself not to go on another rampage? Careful! You're almost like me." Daijiro gave a wry smile; there was something between them she did not know. What did he mean, rampage? Everyone kept hinting at Galahad's recent rage and actions. What had he done that warranted this response? Didn't everyone think Galahad was passive, wasn't that the image he worked to achieve?

"But I just need you to understand that I am not always in control of myself, especially in these recent days." Galahad's words rang out from the time she tried to attack him in his sleep. She watched him, and she knew concern crossed her face just as he'd looked down at her. Sulwyn didn't understand the correlation with his eyes to his anger, but at this moment they were free from any blackness. Maybe she was getting this all wrong?

"I'll see you at tomorrow's dinner, Cailín." Daijiro downed the rest of his tea. "I have a few things left to take care of before we leave in two days. I should tell you. We are leaving early in the morning before sunrise." He stood up, winking at her before sweeping out of the room. Silence settled like dust around them at Daijiro's departure. She didn't know what to do, but Galahad made the decision for her.

"It's about time you leave, Sulwyn. Take Arsinone with you and go back to Valens," he said tightly. He refused to look at her, and for once Sulwyn had nothing to say. She took Arsinone's hand and led her out the door. Sulwyn turned back, looking at Galahad, who remained standing exactly as he was, his eyes hidden as he stared at the ground.

❧◦❦

"There is nothing for me to really tell you other than what you saw," said Arsinone as soon as they had reached the safety of the bedroom. "I can't read Galahad much. We already know this. Artaxiad is an open book. He doesn't think of anything other than power and looking for ways to torment you and those around him for entertainment. Though there is something he is excited about." Arsinone ran across the room and jumped, flopping onto the bed.

Sulwyn followed her, lying next to her. "What about the rest?"

Arsinone sighed, turning to look at Sulwyn, "Kione was terrified. He's never been more scared than he was then. But he left safely. And his drive to help you is strong. Diesirae…was strange." Sulwyn propped her head on her hand, looking at Arsinone more closely.

"There wasn't much. She was empty. I felt like I was being fed what I wanted to see. It's not like Galahad or Pandora…it was like a set picture. She was unusual."

"She seems experienced…maybe she keeps her soul and her mind clear?"

"It's not like that. It's not like magic, where people can intrude on thoughts on a surface level. The soul cannot lie, but I think it can be hidden. I think you should keep an eye on her," said Arsinone seriously.

"You've avoided Daijiro," said Sulwyn after silence spread between them.

"I couldn't read his soul either."

"It's not like mine or like Galahad's, is it?"

"No…it's not. I've never heard anything like it. It's jagged and scratched and screaming. Sulwyn, his soul is broken."

৯৩

Artaxiad sent word with one of his personal maids to Sulwyn. She was to be dressed in a more formal outfit than she had worn the last two dinners. As this was now a dinner between an engaged couple, it became that much more important. And as much as Sulwyn wanted to protest, she knew it would only endanger Eztli, Nori, and Arsinone if she failed to follow his instructions. So, when six o'clock rolled around, Sulwyn was outside of the dark wooden doors in a rather elaborate black and blue dress.

Like the one she had worn for the coronation, it stopped just before her knees in the front but trailed down to her ankles at the back. Dark blue patterns of swirls and intricate designs wove across the black fabric. The sleeveless bodice was dotted in silver moon-like stones coating the surface like tears. The back of blue ribbon tied snugly in fabrics she knew nothing of. But it was soft, and maybe silk.

Unlike those from the last two dinners, this dress was designed by Galahad. Somehow this fact brought her courage and a sense of fear all at the same time. But she wouldn't dwell on that now. Sulwyn knocked once and entered.

Daijiro was already there, stirring a spoon into his water absentmindedly until she came in. He looked up, dark red eyes widening as she walked in. With grace, he stood and pulled out the chair next to him. Sulwyn had a slight urge to just go with the flow and sit in the chair. Instead, she looked at him defiantly and with her own grace, pulled out the chair across from his, sitting in it instead. He laughed.

"I shouldn't have expected less." He combed a hand through his hair. Daijiro did look much more presentable than usual. His golden blonde and white hair was fixed back, parted to the left with a slight tousle. It exposed the silver earrings he wore on each ear; the right with three different studs, the left with one long dagger.

Had he always worn those?

He too wore black, his clothes similar to what Galahad and all the other men leaned towards for fancy occasions, with a long black jacket and pants and a deep burgundy shirt that matched his eyes, though he still wrapped a black sash around his waist. Heat crawled up her neck but he wasn't even doing anything.

He sat down, chuckling lightly. "If you keep looking at me like that, I might blush."

"Why is your hair like that?" asked Sulwyn suddenly, drinking water to clear her throat.

The sudden question threw him off guard, but he collected himself quickly. "Like what, like hair?"

"Two colours."

"That isn't uncommon," he smirked, taking his spoon out of his water.

"No…but I've just never seen it like that," she mumbled.

He studied her carefully, his eyes hidden by various emotions. Sulwyn just stared. Here he looked calm for once. Usually, there was a sort of chaos in his eyes, whether to act or not to act. To spill blood or not. But here, with just a dinner at hand, he seemed composed. And that was when she noticed the necklace again.

Normally his tunics were casual fabrics with high collars and slight V cut outs by the neck. But this was a dress shirt and he had left the top two buttons undone, the bright silver necklace glittering in the light around them. It was subtle with small intricate leaves that went around the whole thing. Somehow it matched him and then somehow it didn't. Someone so destructive couldn't wear something so delicate.

But she realized something. That was a special type of metal. The kind that reflected a soft rainbow glow when the light hit it directly. Sulwyn looked into his eyes, her brows knitted. And he was looking at her with a sort of caution. But before either could address it, a knock sounded, and the doors opened.

Artaxiad kept to the dress code as well in dark browns and blacks, Pandora in dark flowing pinks. To see all four of them being as fancy as one would require for a party made Sulwyn feel a little silly. She was convinced they just wanted reasons to dress up. Not that they really needed it, being the rulers and all.

"I'm glad you did what you were told for once," started Artaxiad, looking at Sulwyn's dress. Instantly she felt exposed and uncomfortable. The dress that was meant to feel like protection seemed like an enemy once faced with Artaxiad's eyes, but she wouldn't ever show that.

Daijiro looked from her to Artaxiad, a glint in his eye. "It's rather becoming on her, but I think the clothes she battles in are much more suitable for our Lady Princess."

Pandora looked at Daijiro, her eyes narrowed, but she said nothing. After they settled, Sulwyn experienced a rather normal dinner. Unlike all the others she had attended, the pace of this one was not too long and not too short as to be awkward. Despite whatever she thought of Daijiro, he held good conversation to the point that even Pandora was taken and joining in rather joyously, all without a hint of that strange power he wielded.

As the teas and coffees rolled out near the end, Artaxiad finally gave Sulwyn all his attention. "This fog town will prove to be difficult. I've had your original weapons and gear cleaned and repaired. I think it best if you are comfortable with the weapons you bring."

Sulwyn eyed him, taken aback. That was a generous thing to do...and she didn't trust it. Something must be severely wrong with this town. "It's in all of our best interests if you would come back alive," he finished.

"You should be on your guard," stated Pandora, looking at her as well. "There may be more than one threat. Keep your mind open to all possibilities. It's been a while since you've been on a true hunt. Being in the Empire mustn't dull your abilities."

They were warning her? Out of regards for her safety? Normally a person would be happy with this, but they were the farthest thing from normal and they cared less about death than anyone she had met. A dreadful heaviness settled in her chest about this mission. But then Artaxiad clapped his hands and stood up.

"After this dinner, I think our decision was a sound one. You both are rather compatible. I look forward to hearing about the results of your assignment." And with that Artaxiad and Pandora were gone, leaving Daijiro and Sulwyn alone to their tea.

He looked at her, his head cocked to one side. "Are you worried? You seem less calm than when you first came in."

"That's the effect they have on people," sighed Sulwyn, running a hand through her hair. She had been trying to ignore it before, but as the days crept closer to the departure something had been gnawing at her from the inside. And with their recent behaviour, this proved double.

Raghnall always trusted her instincts. She was almost as good as he at it, but her curiosity usually brought that back down to half. So, she would listen to what her heart was saying. She felt it more than ever now. Something was coming.

"It's rude for me to leave before you...but if you want time alone..." said Daijiro, though she couldn't tell if he was as concerned as he sounded. He was a mystery to her, and then a bit of rainbow caught her eye.

"That necklace," she said suddenly, "it's made of Velikat metal, isn't it?" She said it like a question, but they both knew it was a statement. And for the first time since she met him, his guard diminished completely in surprise.

"It is. I'm surprised you know this, but then again you did travel with the Steel Warrior and his knowledge was almost next to none." His tone was soft, nostalgic even.

"You aren't a Velikat..." she started, though she wasn't entirely sure. She had never met one, and she didn't know if they had any physical traits that made them stand out like Galahad's clan. But she knew no one had seen one in a long time, since even before Artaxiad's army annihilated them.

He interlaced his fingers, leaning his head against them and looking at her with serious eyes. "The technical term would be Velika, as I am male." Sulwyn looked at him in confusion, and he chuckled.

"Velikat is what they are called collectively, as a race of elite humans that evolved sometime after the Lost World. Velika is the term for men, and Velikai is the term for women." He paused and she realized he was debating on whether he should go further or not. His eyes darted around them slightly. The servants had gone into the back rooms, waiting until they left to clean, but she knew he was wary of speaking openly in the middle of Valens.

So, she did something reckless.

Sulwyn looked at him as she slowly stood, hefting a handful of sugar in her hand and tossing it into the air, *"Cisza..."*

The almost transparent blue dome settled around them and Daijiro stood up carefully, looking around in genuine awe. But Sulwyn felt it. Her magic nudged the magic in the castle. And she knew it wouldn't hold for nearly as long as it had when she did this with Galahad.

She looked at Daijiro in urgency and he sat back down. "I didn't know you knew magic."

"I know some."

"That was a risky move on your part, to do so here and in front of me. You're not a Devinal. You shouldn't use a spell that you have limited control over."

"I have limited control over any spell I use, I suck at magic, even worse than a non-Devinal." But she narrowed her gaze. "You know what spell this is..."

He smirked. "I'm not a Devinal either, but I learned quite a bit of magic a long time ago. This isn't bad for someone who used sugar instead of earth and is fighting against magic stronger than her own."

"You know about the barrier?"

"Of course I do. It's rather annoying. I hate this castle for it." He was silent again, looking at the light blue swirls that reflected in the light and watching it shiver a bit. It would break soon.

"This isn't something I share. Not many are even aware we exist. Probably because we are so sparse, I've never met another one. For all I know I am the only one." He looked at her, his eyes genuinely vulnerable for just that moment. The blue shimmer reflected in his red eyes, making a strange purple flash across it.

"I am a Velyūn. A half-breed of a human man and a Velikai."

The barrier shattered just as the maids came in uncertainly to clean the table.

XXIV

Its In The Eyes

SULWYN opened her eyes slowly to the darkness around her. She couldn't feel the sun yet; it must still be too early. But she felt unease begin to creep its way through, making sleep ebb away quickly.

She breathed out slowly, listening to the sounds of Eztli, Arsinone, and Nori breathing around her, all three deeply asleep.

Sulwyn continued to look above her; in the dark, she could see the faint outline of the vines and the trees. Though the water source had stopped its flow, the trees and plants still survived. The warmth of the sheets made her want to stay, but the tension rising in her would soon become unbearable.

She needed to move.

Sulwyn sat up carefully; Eztli was sleeping next to her though she had refused to sleep on the bed at first. However, the other girls forced her so she could heal quicker, and she let them have their way. Sulwyn lifted the sheets off her legs, feeling the cool air touch her bare skin. How she just wanted to go back to sleep! To sleep and curl into a ball and hope all of this was just some long nightmare. She rubbed her face and sighed.

Quietly, she got ready in the bathing room. The water was cold against her face and neck, but she'd had a bath before bed, so she wouldn't make noise with another one. A torch light flickered lowly against the rough walls, aiding her to find the things she had packed earlier. Sulwyn put on a pair of loose black cotton pants and a navy tunic with sleeves down to her elbows. Artaxiad was not lying when he said he had her things fixed and cleaned. She had touched each one of her unique blades once she got them back.

She wrapped the worn brown leather belt around her waist twice. It was purposely longer so she could carry more weapons alongside a small canteen and medical packs off the sides. She hated too many pockets; the bulk always irritated her legs.

Sulwyn double-checked her packs, canteen, and knives, making sure they were in proper order. Finally, she stood in front of the mirror, her reflection looking double her age in the flickering light. The dark shadows of her face extended, making her look even more exhausted than she felt. She looked around the small room for something to tie her hair back with but quickly gave up, giving it a light brush with a wet comb and braiding it loosely.

Sulwyn reached the bedroom door and donned her heavy black boots, wrapping the long laces around and around until they felt secure. She looked up to see Arsinone standing in front of her with sleepy eyes and a ribbon for her hair.

"Did I wake you?" whispered Sulwyn, kneeling to face her properly and taking the black strip from her. She quickly tied the end of her braid.

"I heard your thoughts for a bit, the fleeting ones. Don't be nervous, Sulwyn." She squeezed her unevenly coloured eyes, trying to rub the sleep out of them. But Sulwyn just stood up and hugged her.

"I'll be fine. I am Kintana after all." She winked, patting Arsinone's messy indigo hair and shooing her off to sleep. She nodded, stumbling into bed with Eztli.

☙❧

The castle was quiet.

Only a handful of servants bustled around the first floor going about their nightly duties. A few Néosan passed her way, guarding Valens at night more so than in the day. But regardless of what time it was, no one would dare attack Valens when either Pandora or Artaxiad were in the castle. And at this point it didn't matter if both were gone; no one had the nerve to even try.

She reached the stables, walking over to the end space where Ki was kept away from the other horses. He was sleeping when she came, but it only took a few seconds to rouse him awake with an apple. He looked at her, pawing the ground. Was he nervous too?

Sulwyn opened the gate and they walked out slowly until they reached the clearing. She rubbed the side of his head a few times, giving him another apple before lifting herself onto the saddle. Once ready, they took off at a brisk pace. She was still early and didn't feel like waiting in the Eques. But too soon they were trotting their way up the slight hill and towards the back stables. Galahad was already there, readying not only his horse but the other horses the Validus would be using.

As she neared, he glanced at her briefly before continuing. Figuring they would be travelling for quite a while, Sulwyn hopped down and let Ki roam around the space freely. She could feel her nerves getting to her but squashed them down and took her steps towards Galahad.

"We leave in about half hour. Everyone woke up earlier, so we might as well," he said, feeding the horses. Sulwyn saw a few large bags in the corner packed full with what she assumed was food and camping gear. All she knew was that halfway through the journey a carriage would be impossible to guide so they would go without one. Without a word she went forward and began strapping a bag to each horse. Sulwyn beckoned Ki over—he was frolicking somewhere on the side—and tied a bag to him as well.

"How many people are we going with?" asked Sulwyn, trying to fill the silence in the still twilight, torchlight flickering around them. She then realized this was a stupid question. She counted the horses and there were nine.

"Not including the three of us, we ended up choosing six other people," he answered quietly. Whether he realized what she had really asked or not, he didn't show it. "I think you know one of them."

"I do? I don't know anyone…" But she looked up when a few men came out, all dressed in uniform, all wearing various weapons and gear. She instantly recognized the man with yellow eyes.

He was a Validus? She always assumed he was only a Protector. Before she could stop herself, she laughed out loud, quickly turning it into a cough just as Daijiro followed behind them. The yellow-eyed man glared at her, annoyed, but tried to force an aloof expression.

"I saw that," whispered Daijiro, passing her and calmly going forward to a brown and black steed. The horse seemed a little apprehensive to take him at first, but Daijiro patted his neck gently and the horse was calm. Did his allure work on animals too?

Yellow-Eyes still looked annoyed yet fearful, but suddenly walked straight up to Sulwyn. "Did you laugh at me?"

Sulwyn stared a little impressed, humour in her smile. "I just...wasn't expecting you is all."

"What does that mean?"

"I didn't realize you were a Validus."

The man frowned, swallowed, and decided to speak his mind. "I am part of Uferor En." He stated hotly, "I understand you are the Lady Princess, but I don't think you should be looking down on the army of this Empire. They brought you here with good intentions." She noticed Galahad and Daijiro turn to look at them as they moved around, silence spreading between them.

But Sulwyn raised a brow, her hands on her hips, and stared at him. "What is your name?"

His yellow eyes widened. "What do you mean?"

Now somewhere behind her, she heard Daijiro and Galahad, as well as the other men, stifle a laugh. "I just...you said your name way back when we first met at the Solus and I just never remembered it and figured we were too far gone at this point. But now that we are sharing an assignment..." She trailed off awkwardly.

But he just looked affronted. And then she saw the conflicted emotions dart through his eyes. Should he call her out? Should he say something? His struggle made her try hard to hold back her laugh as well. "Just tell me your name." She smiled.

"Demir," he grunted, face flushed.

"Demir, thank you for all those times in the Solus. I hope our assignment goes well." She held out her hand, not really meaning to be any sort of friendly to him. But they were going to spend several days together so she might as well.

"You should stop doing that," said Daijiro, now beside her. "Looks like his heart will explode." Demir glared at him in embarrassment. He hastily took her hand, shook it briefly then chose a horse.

"It looks like we are all ready. Let us be on our way," said Galahad, mounting his grey horse. Sulwyn noticed Galahad carried a sword strapped to his side. She eyed it momentarily, only able to see the hilt. It was ruby engraved with plum vines, embedded in the corners with navy stones. She looked up at him. His eyes and his sword matched—what did the blade look like?

He caught her stare but soon looked forward as Daijiro mounted his horse and went in front of them. "Daijiro is the one who has the map. Please keep formation while following him. As it is still dark, let us travel at a slower pace until first light."

And then they were off, trotting lightly through the city, passing buildings, castles, small Néosan bases, and then finally through the massive black walls. It felt like ages ago since she'd left the Empire on the first assignment, and unlike last time she was going through the front of her own accord. She wasn't nervous anymore, but excited. Excited to be out of the Empire and away from the poison it spread around her.

As the sun hit the horizon, they picked up the pace and headed south. Sulwyn was not familiar with Antiqua as much as she was Guāngcǎi. They had mostly travelled the edges of the border, visiting small villages around there. Raghnall never wanted her too close to the Empire. How times had changed.

A few hours passed through the grass and the sand that kicked up behind them as they galloped farther and farther south. Eventually, Daijiro led them a bit off course to a small collection of trees and a small pond.

They all dismounted, letting the horses find a spot of pond to drink, eat, and rest. Sulwyn followed Ki, who purposely avoided all the other horses and went the long way around to the other side before stopping, bending his long neck down and drinking deeply.

Sulwyn sat beside him watching the Validus stretch or feed their horses. She figured she should stretch too and wandered off in the small thicket of trees. As she walked, breathing in the fresh open air around her, a twig cracked behind her and she turned to see Daijiro a few paces away.

"I'll get straight to the point," he started, his voice low. Unlike the dinner night, he was guarded and a little on edge. She doubted she'd ever catch him like that again. She looked at him fully, fiddling with a leaf in her hand.

"You asked me a lot of questions the night before. I think I have a right to ask you one," he continued, stepping closer until he was just a few steps away. So he did always wear those earrings and now that she looked closely, the necklace was tucked under his loose yellow tunic.

"When we fought, something happened to you. Something I've never seen at all let alone in a fight; and just like you, I have been in many."

Sulwyn's hand tightened over the leaf, watching both of his eyes stare her down. She could barely remember that moment. She didn't know how much he saw, if he heard anything, or if anyone heard it at all. She tried and tried after that to remember what she had seen but came up blank. The last thing she did remember was that Galahad came between them.

"That was a while ago, you'll have to be a bit more specific." She replied but he stepped closer, and that strange madness was in his eyes again. He grabbed her wrist tightly, a sharp pain going through her arm as the leaf fluttered away.

"Your skin was hot. Fevers like that can kill. But you didn't seem at all affected."

"So I had a fever. I'm not sure if you realized, but I had recently been injured and was fighting again. I'm under a lot of stress. Not that it matters to you. This isn't anything to be interrogated about." She pulled her arm out of his grip, but he still stepped closer, forcing her to step back.

"Your eyes changed."

"Your eyes are obviously not well if you are seeing things." But he pushed her against the tree, his hand now gripping her shoulder.

"Do not underestimate me..." he growled, but soon let go and took a step back. "Then I will ask Galahad. He seemed well aware of what was happening."

"Feel free to do as you wish. But you won't find answers to anything if they don't exist. What does it matter to you if I have fevers or my eyes change? That doesn't concern you," said Sulwyn harshly, rubbing her shoulder.

"I have told you things," said Daijiro, his eyes flashing, his voice wavering for just a moment. Why was this bothering him so much and why now? He could have asked her during dinner. What possessed him to want to know after time had passed?

"I didn't ask you to. You chose to, and I created a space for you to do that. But in no way does that mean I am required to do the same. Especially when you act like this," said Sulwyn loudly, but they both stopped. Galahad had entered the thicket of trees.

"I didn't think you were one to get angry when someone didn't share stories with you," said Galahad, leaning against the tree. Sulwyn realized he had been there for a while and yet she didn't notice him.

"Curiosity gets the best of even me sometimes," said Daijiro.

"Well, it's wasted on her, there isn't anything special other than what you see in front of you," said Galahad coldly, standing straight. "We've been here for too long. There is something in the forests behind us. It would be best if we continued away from here." He looked at Sulwyn briefly then turned, leaving them both behind.

҉

After five days of straight terrain, they turned directly into the trees of Tranquillum. According to Artaxiad, there was a specific path they needed to travel and if they strayed off that path, they wouldn't find the town.

Once the sun set, they set up camp for the last night. On the first night, they tried to get Sulwyn to sleep in a tent of her own, but she insisted on staying out and sleeping next to Ki. By now they were used to taking turns to watch through the night and at first light were off again.

The trek was slower now. Not only were there trees and brambles, but the path was uneven and littered with large rocks, forcing them to adjust their stride every so often. As they continued through the forest, it grew darker as if it were going to rain. But Sulwyn knew this was not the case. She could not smell it in the air, and when she glanced over at Daijiro, she knew he couldn't either. She could still sense the sun; it was a bit past noon when they finally decided to take another break. But unlike last time, they didn't wander to find a river and made do with what they had.

Jugs of water were filled during last night's camp, and Sulwyn poured them out into two collapsible buckets. In turns, the horses drank and rested before they took off shortly once again.

As they travelled deeper in, a chill touched the air, the temperature dropped, and the sky grew darker still. "Keep your guard up. We should be close," called Daijiro as they pressed on. An hour or so later the fog hit them all at once. They were forced to dismount, tying the horses together in a line.

"I've never seen anything like this," said Demir, tying his horse to another. Sulwyn was placed behind Daijiro while Galahad was placed at the back. He made sure everyone was safely mounted before walking back to his horse. He called out to Daijiro, and they cautiously started again through the fog, looking down every so often to ensure they were still on the path.

This was not natural. No matter what Artaxiad tried to fool himself into believing, this was one hundred percent caused by magic. And powerful magic at that. Something that wasn't seen often anymore. Who would guard their town so well that Artaxiad could not find them? And then, who would they be that Artaxiad decided to let them stay and continue and not follow the Empire's rotation rule? Was it because it would not be worth the travel? This was the part that would have men lost and wandering in a second.

They continued their slow trudge, but Sulwyn couldn't shake the feeling of being watched. She could barely see Daijiro's horse in front of her let alone the trees beside them. No, she was working herself up, that was all. The horses were uneasy; being unable to see their surroundings had them whining. But Sulwyn noticed Ki remained the same, tense and alert but calm. She patted his neck.

Suddenly she couldn't see Daijiro, and then she could only see white when finally, the bright rays of setting sun blinded her as they stepped out of the fog. A league in the distance she could see the outline of a small town amongst a few trees. It did not have any low walls to mark its official perimeter like other towns and villages. And there was no flag of their symbol. If Sulwyn didn't know better, she would have marked it as abandoned.

They galloped on until they reached a few yards away from the edge of the town. A shallow river wrapped around it, breaking just where the entrance was. A wooden path had been buried into the sand for easy travel across.

"The sun is setting. Let's set up camp. Tomorrow we will announce our presence," said Galahad, moving to dismount, but stopped.

"We should go today before the sun sets," stated Daijiro, and Galahad turned to look at him, wariness all over his face. "You know I'm right. We don't know anything about what we are facing here. It could take us longer than a few days to solve it. The way this is being treated it's obviously much larger than anything we've had in a long while."

"Fine," agreed Galahad, as Daijiro smirked.

As they trotted closer, a hooded person spoke to Daijiro fleetingly before granting entrance. Daijiro spurred his horse into motion and galloped into the streets.

Unlike Antac, this town was rather quiet. There were quite a few buildings and stores untouched by Néosan the way others were. But there was a lack of people. Sulwyn remembered that some sort of monthly disappearance was happening with people from towns in the surrounding area. She assumed the inhabitants were indoors, trying to stay safe and hidden from whatever it was that was happening. But as they rode past, many faces hidden in the shadows of buildings began to peer out of the windows.

Daijiro rode to the centre of town, a giant area with a large depiction of the sun decorating the ground in various coloured bricks. He turned his horse around just as a crowd started to gather. Everyone was hidden by cloaks and hoods but Sulwyn could still sense fear. Even if they had managed to evade the Empire, they all knew deep down it wouldn't last forever.

Daijiro hopped off his steed alongside Galahad and the other Validus. Sulwyn followed suit as Daijiro walked to the very centre. The Validus flanked him on either side in threes. Galahad stepped forward, standing somewhere behind Daijiro and off to the side. Slowly, Sulwyn joined them, standing on the other side of Daijiro in line with Galahad, and stared.

Whatever Galahad said or did, she knew he was a leader, but seeing Daijiro give off a similar if not more sinister kind of presence made her shiver. His heart was darker, and she was afraid of exactly how he dealt with missions.

"We are from the Empire, but I'm sure you already knew that," started Daijiro with a smirk. Sulwyn glanced to Galahad; his head was looking down at his feet. She looked back to the front and noticed a man coming forward from behind the crowd, his mustard cloak blowing gently around him.

"We've been sent to assist as well as investigate some ongoing incidents regarding your hidden town, but let's start with the investigations, shall we?" Daijiro called, his eyes carefully following the man as he slowly made his way through the civilians.

"Some time ago, the Empire discovered a group of people travelling Vartugaul, slandering the name of our king and queen. They dressed as our men, stole from our people, and killed others. But finally, after some… poking around, we managed to trace their origins back here." He opened his arms in front of him, gesturing to the town.

"It is a crime to impersonate or insult our Empire. And before we assist you with your mysterious deaths and kidnappings, I'd like you all to assist us in capturing these treacherous fools."

"Why should we help you?" spoke the man, finally stepping in front. His voice was a bit gravelly, hoarse even, but as soon as he spoke the people who were slouched in fear and uncertainty straightened their backs and stood stronger together.

"I assume you lead the town?" asked Daijiro, looking at his nails.

"There is no leader in our town, only companionship. I am just the representative."

"If you say so. Will you speak for the rest of them as I ask questions? Or will you discuss it openly? Honestly, either one is fine. As long as I get answers."

Sulwyn could only see half of the man's face, but he gritted his teeth and balled his fists. "We do not and will not submit to the Empire."

Sulwyn looked at Daijiro and then at Galahad and paused. Galahad was still staring at his feet, but a strange expression had passed over him. His eyebrows were knitted, and he stood rigidly as if afraid to move.

"I did try to negotiate, remember that," warned Daijiro, and Sulwyn moved a step closer to him. He wouldn't do anything to these people, would he? "You have until tomorrow at noon. I will come back here, and you will give me answers. As it is late, we will leave you. We had a long journey through your fog, and I'd like our men to get some proper rest. But do tell me, what is your name? Just so I have someone to call to on my way here tomorrow."

The man stepped forward, lowering his hood, and at his movement, everyone else lowered their hoods as well.

"Well look at that..." muttered Daijiro, chuckling, but Sulwyn could only stare at Galahad, who finally looked up.

"My name is Tiergan. If you have any questions, come to me first."

The last rays of the setting sun illuminated Tiergan's eyes, bringing a sense of foreboding to Sulwyn. His eyes were multicoloured with bright red, light brown, and dark orange, separated in rings of three colours in his irises just like Galahad's. But if that was shocking, it was nothing compared to the fact that scattered in the large crowd were people who had tricoloured eyes as well. Tiergan's eyes looked at each one of the Validus and at Daijiro. He found her own, lingering for just a moment. And finally, he turned his attention to Galahad.

Sulwyn looked between them both, but if Galahad was thinking or feeling anything, his face betrayed nothing. Tiergan turned away suddenly, his mustard cloak swishing around him as he nodded gently to the people, ushering them back home.

XXV

A Grand Sacrifice
| SULWYN |

GALAHAD was barely off his horse before he stomped straight to Daijiro just as he dismounted, landing on the ground. Swiftly, Galahad grabbed the neck of Daijiro's clothes and pulled him close. Sulwyn arrived just after, jumping down and running towards them, pausing a few feet away.

"Explain. Now," growled Galahad, and Sulwyn realized it took a lot of effort to even say those two words. His arms were shaking as they gripped Daijiro's clothes even tighter. But Daijiro was calm, his hands at his sides, a smirk playing across his lips.

"I know as much as you do, prince. I never expected to see anyone with the same kind of eyes as yours for as long as we all lived. Last I heard they were all annihilated."

"Daijiro," warned Sulwyn, stepping closer to them both. She placed her hands over Galahad's fists and looked at him firmly. But Galahad didn't pay her any attention and only tightened his grip.

"I'd be happy if you didn't ruffle my clothes. I didn't bring too many with me on this trip, and I'd like to look a bit presentable tomorrow when I go interrogate them all."

"Answer me, Daijiro," seethed Galahad just as Sulwyn removed her hands. But this time Daijiro stood straight and lifted his own hands. Instead of pushing Galahad's arms off, he held a palm out in front of Galahad's stomach and pushed. Galahad huffed, clenching his jaw, but only loosened his grip slightly.

Surprise flitted across Daijiro's face. "Shouldn't have expected anything less, but need I remind you that you are part of the Empire, Galahad? Whether those people have the same eyes as you means nothing." He held his ground, his eyes flashing. "We are here to investigate treason and possibly solve another issue at the same time. If you can't handle it, go back to the Empire. I'm sure they would love that." Daijiro lifted his arms in between Galahad's and pushed out, forcing Galahad to let go. But Galahad moved forward, grabbing Daijiro's neck and squeezing.

No matter how defiant Daijiro was, being choked was not something he could pass off with a calm look. Sulwyn came between them again, and this time pulled out two knives. She pointed one at Galahad's neck, the other to Daijiro's stomach.

"We are all from the Empire—what good will it do us if you both kill each other here? Plus, the only one who knows how to get us back through that damn fog is Daijiro," she yelled, and only then realized the rest of the Validus had been watching them the entire time. She lowered her voice. "You both aren't showing a very good example..."

Galahad finally looked down at her, and even though the sun had almost set, she could see the black creeping its way along the edges of his eyes. She pushed the blades closer to each of them and Galahad finally let go. Daijiro breathed out roughly, rubbing his neck.

"I will not join this assignment," said Galahad quietly so only they could hear. "Why haven't you all started setting up camp?" he snapped, looking at the rest of the Validus. Instantly they dispersed, unloading the bags and making fires. Demir went to tie the horses to nearby trees. As he came closer to Ki, he was almost kicked down by his hooves.

"Leave him!" called Sulwyn, Demir stepping back in fear and embarrassment. She walked to Ki, petting him gently, but continued to watch Galahad and Daijiro. Both had retreated to opposite ends to do different tasks and soon Galahad had retreated into a tent. No one else wanted to go in with him, so Sulwyn just offered her tent to the rest of them.

"Looks like he's upset," said Daijiro next to her as the fire finally burned. They began preparing pots for food and drink.

"I don't know how you deal with people on your missions, but if it's anything like how you interrogate people, I will not allow it," said Sulwyn, gathering the bread.

He turned to her, his brow raised. "What if they don't cooperate?"

"It doesn't matter. I won't kill these people. You heard Tiergan—they probably don't know anything. And according to Artaxiad, their people have gone missing too."

He turned to her, a glint in his eyes, and walked closer. "We'll have to see, won't we, Cailín? Honestly, I couldn't care less about the people in this town, about who the impersonators are, about the kidnappings and murder. To me it matters not if the entire town were to die. No one will miss them. These people who have defiance in their eyes and in their hearts... how far do you think it will get them? Running and hiding. How far do you think it will get you?" He was in front of her now, his hands gently on either side of her neck. "There is no such thing as a happy life, Sulwyn. You should know that. This land is evil. There is no importance. Nothing matters."

It was different this time. Whatever he was doing muddled her mind and her senses. What he was saying made sense. What was the point in defying everything? All of her worries and troubles would go away if she accepted the Empire for what it was. The place trying to unite Vartugaul once again.

As if in a daze, Sulwyn lifted her hands, bringing them up to Daijiro's arms. The fire glinted off silver, and Sulwyn looked at the worn ring on her index finger.

"Are you speaking from experience? If nothing matters to you, then you've already lost this war," said Sulwyn firmly, pushing his arms away. He gave up without a fight and watched her step back. A curious smile pulled at the corner of his lips.

"You are very interesting, Cailín." She looked at him oddly; he had said something similar before. Always stating the facts that made up the Empire, but somehow not meaning them from his own heart.

"The food is ready!" announced Demir from the roaring fire, distracting her from her thoughts.

❧

Galahad never came out of the tent to eat, but Sulwyn placed a metal plate of food in front of the entrance. "Eat it hot or cold or however..." she started, unsure if he was paying attention or even awake for that matter. "But you should still eat." Silence met her words and she just walked away.

The night settled fast and after all that travel the Validus turned in early. No one wanted to share a tent with Daijiro, either, that night, so it would be three men to the two leftover tents.

"Lady Princess, are you sure you don't want a tent?" asked Demir, but she knew it was out of obligation more than anything.

"I'm fine with just this blanket and Ki," she said shortly and watched as he didn't bother to insist, walking away into one of the tents. Another Validus had first watch, and as she was the first to watch last time, she would be last this time.

She waited until the Validus turned in and the watch looked away before she sat up quickly. Ki watched her soundlessly as she crouched forward, cloaked herself, then streaked hurriedly into the town.

Sulwyn pulled her cloak tightly around her, the hood up, hiding her face in the shadows as the torchlight bounced off her head. As she walked farther in, she spotted a few people out to finish any last-minute business. Hooded and huddled together, whispering here or there, they seemed more afraid now than they would have been before. Mysterious disappearances and deaths aside, the Empire had come knocking on their door.

Sulwyn skulked the street corners using the shadows to her advantage. She eavesdropped on conversations here or there.

"Is it true?" whispered one man.

"I wasn't close enough to really see, but I think so," said a lady.

"He is the prince of the Empire, isn't he?"

"Wasn't there a woman with them? I've never heard of a woman in the Uferor."

"That doesn't matter. She's probably a consort..." said another man. Sulwyn went out of her way to step on his foot but moved farther into the shadows before he could spot her.

This group was full of people from Galahad's clan. Or so she assumed. She never got him to confirm or deny anything.

"It's Galahad, isn't it?" they continued.

"Dante's son? I thought he died...he can't be the same one."

"No one else was named Galahad."

"But why is he in the Empire? Why did he betray the clan?"

"Do you think *that* rumour is true?" asked another lady, and now all of them became even more hushed. But she never learned what the rumour was. They all suddenly walked forward and away from her hiding spot.

She cursed internally and continued ahead. She managed to reach the other side of the desolate town after some time, spotting the dark forest encroaching at the end. Somehow it looked a little ominous to her, but she had no desire to go that far tonight. Sulwyn decided to turn back, annoyed at the lack of anything learned.

Suddenly a larger group walking briskly to their destination came towards her and she instinctively ducked into a dark alley. She turned, a strange draft blowing behind her. Sulwyn strained trying to see down a very narrow and shadowy path.

Without a second thought, she followed it, and then after a good twenty minutes or so regretted her decision.

Where the hell was she going? The dark path only got darker and more cramped with hard stone as she continued. At some point, the ground sloped upwards and now she just wanted to reach the end. But as she kept walking, feeling a familiar sensation, she realized that the magic that guarded Valens was terribly similar to the sudden magic she felt now. Was this the same magic responsible for the fog as well?

She persisted, walking and walking, until finally after what felt like an hour she hesitated, her heart in her mouth. She had stopped just a few inches shy from the edge of a cliff. And then like the lower dungeons, a putrid smell mixed with the outside air smacked up her nose and in her mouth. There was no light here and the moon was not near full to cast over her. She looked down, straining her eyes to see something, but all she could distinguish were mounds of darkness in a dug-out hole. Whatever she had found she would have to come back during daylight to see. It would be reckless even for her to try and scout it out now. She turned around, going back the way she came and trying hard to ignore the prickle of hairs raised along her neck.

❦

Sulwyn had a few hours of restless sleep and when it was her turn for guard duty, she almost castrated the man when he woke her up. Unfortunately for both, it was Demir, who probably disliked her even more. Not that it really mattered to her. Stretching, she gave him a half-assed apology, tucking her dagger back into her leather belt.

She sat along one of the rocks in front of the remnants of last night's fire. The sky in the distance started to lighten with blues and greens. Soon they would ride back into town, without Galahad. Was that a good idea?

Less than an hour passed before Galahad finally stepped out of the tent. He glanced at her for only a moment before turning to face the sun as it rose over the horizon. They both watched the clouds turn from dark indigo and emerald to vivid yellows, reds, and greens. A cool wind passed over them and Sulwyn found herself standing.

Just as she was about to walk towards Galahad, Daijiro came out of his tent, his face unreadable, calling to all the Validus. He seemed more than eager to go. Sulwyn gave Galahad's back a fleeting glance but turned and walked over to Ki, waking him instead.

❦

One of the Validus blew sharply into a black horn, alerting the town of their arrival. In an instant people were looking out their windows, watching as they galloped by. Sulwyn could see the town clearer now. The wooden buildings and small huts were old but well kept. The town itself was a fraction of the size of the Empire and could probably fit twice into Antac. But it was quaint, set in its ways and most importantly, away from the Empire's eyes.

But that's when it struck her.

The reason Artaxiad and Pandora had been so elusive and so encouraging. They did this knowing full well who resided in this town. Sulwyn clenched the reins in her hands. Why? What was the point in all of this?

Daijiro reached the circle first; the Validus and Sulwyn followed. They aligned themselves the same way as yesterday minus Galahad. With poise, Tiergan came forward, the same cloak hanging off him making him stand out amongst the growing crowd.

"I'll cut to the chase," started Daijiro smugly. "I want information, and you will give it to me. If you want us out of your hair sooner than later, I suggest you cooperate." He finished loudly, smiling widely, and the people looked at him in discomfort, edging back slightly. But Tiergan held his ground and walked forward.

"We don't know anything about these impersonators. This is the first we have heard of it. You can search my home—all our homes—and you won't find a single point of evidence."

"Isn't that something you should discuss with the rest of the town? I thought you weren't the head. Surely you can't decide something so bold on your own?" He smirked and Sulwyn knew he was playing with them. But Tiergan suddenly looked at Sulwyn.

"It looks like you've added some talent to your group." He gestured to her and Sulwyn looked at him in surprise. But Daijiro turned to her and suddenly pulled her his way, placing his arm around her waist.

"This is the Blood Princess. You should feel honoured to be in her presence." The rest of the town seemed a little confused and astonished. She didn't expect them to have heard the news of everything thus far, especially since the town was so isolated from the rest of Vartugaul. But Tiergan's eyes were wide.

"Why would the Blood Princess come to us? Surely, we aren't worth that kind of time," he said, but his tone was odd; somehow it was worried and sarcastic all at the same time.

"It's the Blood Princess who caught the impersonators in the first place. Without her, they'd have been running wild doing as they liked."

"We don't need your filthy princess in our city! She carries their dirty blood within her!" shouted one person with normal brown eyes. Daijiro tightened his grip around her waist and instantly she sensed danger.

"I said you should all feel honoured. In fact, you should all bow." He held out his other hand and one after the other, the people in the crowd dropped to their knees, fear wide in their eyes.

"Daijiro, stop," hissed Sulwyn, but his eyes were wide with excitement.

"You think you can bring fear into our people with your tricks?" hollered Tiergan.

"Since you're so outspoken and like to speak for the people, you're going to come with me," growled Daijiro and Sulwyn knew it was too late. Before Tiergan could move, Daijiro released his hold on her waist and brought both hands in front of him. Slowly he closed his left into a fist and kept his right palm open. Everyone watched as Tiergan stood rigid, unable to move, his expression one of surprise and slight fear. Daijiro nudged his head and one of the Validus moved forward, binding Tiergan in rope.

"I will take your leader and wring him out for all he is worth. Remember that if he dies, it was all for you. How honourable." He sneered at the horror on the peoples' faces.

Sulwyn swore to herself. She could not act, not without betraying her intentions or killing all the Validus here. And both options were unexplainable and out of the question. So as much as it annoyed her, she got back on Ki and followed behind Daijiro and the rest with Tiergan bound to another Validus.

◈◈◈

Galahad stood up at their arrival, watching them carefully until his eyes widened at the sight of Tiergan bound in ropes. When the Validus came to a stop, they pulled him down and he landed hard onto the ground.

"You like to talk, so we're going to have a nice long conversation," said Daijiro, grabbing Tiergan's arm and forcing him to stand.

Tiergan shook his arm free of Daijiro's hold and glared at Galahad. Sulwyn watched them with bated breath, but Daijiro only smiled. "I feel like I'm going to learn a lot here." He pulled Tiergan forward, then kicked him towards one of the tents.

"But first we must investigate, so for now, we will just keep you here. This is your final warning. If I have to walk into this tent to get you to talk...well, let's just hope it doesn't get that far," warned Daijiro dangerously, pushing him into the tent and closing it. The Validus saluted him without question and three went to stand guard in front.

"Cailín, you should scope out the town with us," said Daijiro calmly, looking at Galahad fleetingly but waving the other three Validus to follow him.

"Fine...but I'm taking the forest," said Sulwyn stiffly. She went back to Ki and took off around the borders of the town without another word.

Sulwyn was not thinking of the impersonators or the mysterious deaths. All she could see as she rode around the edges of the town was the look that had passed between Galahad and Tiergan.

They knew each other.

And she had no idea why neither was acknowledging the other. Or why the people were cold to his existence. Was it because he was part of the Empire? But if they were part of his clan, then they should know about the night Artaxiad attacked; they must be the survivors. So why were they afraid? Unless everything Galahad told her was a lie. But his anger had to stem from somewhere...

Deeply lost in thought, she hadn't realized when they rode into the forest. Ki slowed his pace to a gentle walk, unable to go faster for the number of wild plants and thick tree roots. This part of Tranquillum was much denser than the woods that lined the inner area of Antiqua. They must be close to the bordering forest that passed between the edges of Antiqua and

Uhuru. Sulwyn paid close attention to the sounds around her but found that there were none. And this worried her more.

There was no sound at all.

Not the wind, or bugs and animals. Nothing passed over this forest. It was dead quiet. She remembered Galahad saying something about the forest on the way here. Was it connected? But soon she heard a stream and decided she would have to follow that.

As they walked closer and closer to the trickling sound of water, a smell wafted up her nose. Instantly she gagged, remembering the lower dungeons and remembering last night. But that was impossible. That walk took her almost an hour, how could she be anywhere near that strange pit of rot?

She pulled the reigns, dismounting, Ki halting just in front of the thin stream. But she pushed him back and away from it. The water was deep blue with an orange tinge that shimmered atop the river like an extra layer. It was toxic; one of the few bodies of water that held poison from the Lost World unable to escape anywhere.

She had come across a large lake once, back in the farther parts of Guāngcǎi. Raghnall told her that this water was impure, toxic to all, and trapped, unable to leave the earth or evaporate. But as long as it stayed exactly where it was, no harm would come to Vartugaul. Most animals avoided it, and people learned to stay away from it. But why would anyone locate their town so close to this? It meant another larger body of the water was somewhere within or near the forest.

Sulwyn bent down, grabbing a stick and swirled the sluggish water. It wasn't as thick as it looked, but something about it coated the stick in dark blue and brown. She frowned, throwing the stick in. A crack of a twig reached her, and she whipped around to face it, but before she could react, a masked person smacked a heavy metal rod across her face.

She had been drugged so many times in the last few months that she knew instantly it had happened again. But that was it. That was all she could comprehend. Sulwyn tried with all her might to move, to do something, but her body just wouldn't respond. Heaviness pressed over her.

As she lay there with her eyes unable to open, she became more aware of her other senses. A slight ringing was in her left ear, the kind that might just be in your head and not around. It was cold but drafty, unlike the upper dungeons that were just cold. She could vaguely sense the sun; she wasn't underground but somewhere damp. Still unable to move, she tried to feel what her hand could in the spot it was stuck in. Hard. It was rough and cold. Stone.

She was in a cave.

That must be it, it had to be. But if this was a cave, then this was the place where her vision in the Solus took place. Sulwyn's heart beat faster. She urged her mind to think faster too. But everything was just so slow and so cloudy it made her feel itchy and panicked. A few more minutes passed like this, trapped in a nightmare. She didn't even know if it was minutes or hours, but with each breath, she felt a pinch in her chest.

"Don't panic..." She thought this over and over in her head. She forced the words to go through her and carve a path through her muddy mind. Either with sheer willpower or whatever she was drugged with had started to wear off; it didn't matter. Her thoughts came in just a bit quicker now, but she still couldn't move.

"Princess..." The voice flowed over her. Her hearing was muffled too. The voice was low and echoed around her but distorted like her thoughts. Ice chilled her veins. Whoever had her knew she was the princess. All the way out here it was either a townsperson or one of the Empire's people.

Or the ones responsible for the murders.

Sulwyn's eyes opened slowly. It was dim. She could see metal bars above her and stone past that. So, it was a cave, and she was in a cage this time. But her eyes wouldn't stay open. It burned just to keep them even half up. She closed them again, fighting the sting and forcing them open again. But with each slow blink, the next one came even slower until her mind fell back into darkness.

⁂

The ringing was getting louder. But she just wanted to sleep. Why wouldn't it go away? Who was causing it? What was even ringing?

Sulwyn tried to move her hand to the side. It managed to lift slightly before crashing onto hard metal. But her mind was awake again, and she could think faster than she could the last time.

It took her a moment to realize she was moving, but not on her own. Slowly she opened her burning eyes, managing to keep them open this time. Four people in cloaks carried the cage she was in through the rocky path. Where was she?

Torch light after torch light scorched her eyes as they passed, her vision blurred and swaying. But with every footstep that echoed onto the rocks and the walls, the thoughts in her mind cleared. And with it, pain came.

Sulwyn gasped out loud, grunting and gritting her teeth. Startled, the people carrying her hurriedly put the cage down. But she could barely focus on them for the bone-deep ache that was flaring up around her.

They had beaten her. Probably by the same metal rod that had knocked her out. She could do nothing but lie on the bars of the cage in a pitiful curled-up ball, the bars burying into the bruises on her back.

"She's awake," said a male voice.

"Go get Ubusuku," said a woman in hushed tones.

One of the cloaked people left, and silence passed between them all. The three left behind stood stiffly, not even looking her way. But that was fine with her. She was trying to ignore the agony but only felt it more. She concentrated on moving any part of her body, and though it was quite the task, she managed to move enough to figure out what state she was in.

A rib or two seemed fractured. Her head and one of her eyes felt tight; it must be swollen. She bent her fingers slowly, a sharp pain passing through them all but nothing worse than that. She curled her toes and felt that her boots were still on, but the weight of her leather belt and weapons had been removed. She was possibly unarmed but hoped beyond hope they didn't take her boots off at any point. There she had two small daggers hidden inside and though it might not do much, it was still something.

She breathed in slowly, her ribs and chest aching each time, but she could breathe. She pulled her shoulders back, uncurling her limbs. Nothing else seemed fractured or broken, but everything was bruised.

"Princess, I should have known you would somehow defy even my drug," said the voice she'd heard earlier. But then she noticed it still sounded filtered—how were they hiding it? She could not distinguish if this person was male or female or something else entirely. She slowly looked over, not surprised that they too were hooded, hidden by shadows and cloth.

"You are our *extraordinary* guest. Who would have thought you would come to us?" said the voice. They were most likely the ones responsible for the disappearances and deaths. How would she escape this?

"Who…?" Sulwyn managed to croak but stopped. Pain grated against her throat, raw and torn.

"Hush now. After all that screaming you do not want to damage your throat any further, do you?"

Screaming? She screamed and she didn't remember? What had they done to her? A stinging suddenly made its way through the ringing and the throbbing, and she felt it along her thighs and arms and back.

They had whipped her. Tortured while unconscious. This was new even for her. Whoever they were, they loathed her enough to be able to do this.

"Leave us," commanded the voice and the four cloaked people bowed without question, dispersing. Sulwyn listened to their footsteps fade farther and farther away.

She clenched her jaw, breathing slowly, but tried again. "Who are…?"

"I like this defiance you have. Against people, against drugs and weapons. I will not lie; it is surprising and refreshing. Raghnall raised you well."

Her heart dropped; if they knew about Raghnall, then they knew she was Kintana as well. Were they with the Empire? But why would the Empire try to get rid of her here? With the type of pride that Artaxiad and Pandora had, they would never eliminate her in silence like this.

"Normally, I like to give my sacrifices a few moments to themselves so that they can make peace with their minds before they go. But you are much too special and too clever for that. You see, I do not like to use drugs on them. I think it lessens the impact of my sacrifice. But I know that if I were to let you wake whole and in proper mind, we would all be in trouble."

Footsteps echoed around them again and soon a male voice whispered, "Ubusuku...it is time."

"Ah, time it is!" said Ubusuku.

Time for what? Time for the sacrifice? Was this who they were? Some sort of cult that sacrificed the innocent?

The cage opened and two pairs of arms dragged her forward. Everything in her body protested at the movement, but she couldn't stop them. She couldn't even stand. They put her arms around their shoulders and hoisted her up, dragging her down the path they were on.

How could she have let herself get into this situation? Was this how it ended for her? She hadn't achieved anything. She hadn't even found out why Raghnall betrayed her. No matter how quickly her thoughts were coming now, they wouldn't make their way to her legs. All she could feel was the vibration of her boots as they dragged against the rough rock. She couldn't even feel fear properly. Instead, there was guilt and shame at bringing herself to this moment in time not having managed to take anyone down.

How could she leave Vartugaul like that?

They carried her over carved stairs, her boots bumping up with every step, causing the bruises and the cuts to hurt more and more. But she could move her arms. Sulwyn focused all her attention on her legs instead. If she could just get the strength back in her limbs, she might have a chance.

Whispers and flickering fire reached her ears and a light draft crawled over her skin. This was the cave from her vision, the crowd close below them full of hooded people all hovering close to the precipice, Sulwyn and her captors raised above. Candles had been placed everywhere, in every crease or corner of the cave. At the front edge of the elevated slate of rock stood an elegant and slightly stained crystal bowl on a podium of stone. It sparkled like tiny diamonds in the flames around them, a large ornate knife with a strange curve rested over the opening.

The body of a small but beautiful black and gold wildcat lay at the side of the podium, and as they got closer, she could see its blood had been drained into the bowl, coating the crystal in fresh dark red. So, she *was* going to be sacrificed. But for what purpose? They had to believe they were doing this for something.

The arms under her were gone, pushing her to the edge of the precipice, her knees hitting the stone hard. She could move her body at a snail's pace but moved her hand stealthily to reach the inside of her boots. However, her hands came up empty. They had taken the knives.

"Now, princess, what do you take me for?" said Ubusuku, but the voice was no longer distorted. It was deep and female. And awfully familiar. The four cloaked people stepped back and knelt on one knee, their arms across it and their heads bent forward.

"My family!" bellowed the woman's voice. All the hoods below looked forward. But the shadows cast by the firelight kept their faces hidden. Sulwyn looked around her, for anything she could do or use. The only thing she could see was the knife that sat atop the bowl.

"With this sacrifice, we shall gain more than we ever have," she started, and they looked at her while raising their palms to the sky in unison. "This is the Blood Princess, and in her lies strength and will that have not been seen for decades. Her blood carries power and unyielding faith. And it will be ours."

"You sacrifice people for power?" croaked Sulwyn, turning her head to look behind her.

"See?" said the woman, completely disregarding her. "Her strength managed to fight off even our spells."

"Spells? There is no magic here, only drugs and chemicals," challenged Sulwyn. Was this person leading them all with some sort of false idealism? Sacrificing humans to give them bodily strength? Such an archaic and far-fetched thing from the depths of the Lost World's worst times. But Sulwyn looked closely at the bowl and saw the stained blood from previous use and the marks around the edges. Realised these people *drank* the blood.

"This is beyond magic, stupid girl. This is something the Empire can never achieve or touch. The power is given to us by those who still have the power to fight. We will take their offerings, allowing us to become elite in body and mind, and use it to renew the Empire."

"You're actually crazy," scoffed Sulwyn, but the woman grabbed the knife and brought it to Sulwyn's neck.

"It does not matter what you think. The results will not be seen by you once we have ingested your blood. But do not worry. We will make sure to elevate Vartugaul." The woman pulled Sulwyn to her feet and pushed her to lean over the bowl. She pressed the knife against Sulwyn's neck, speaking in a tongue she didn't know. A faint burn stemmed from her neck where the knife had dug into her skin, and suddenly Sulwyn knew.

Yelling, she forced herself back, to the woman's surprise. Sulwyn brought her hand up and pushed the knife away, earning a burning cut along her fingers. But she managed to use her other arm and reach behind her, grabbing the cloak on the woman and pulling it off.

"Why hide your face amongst your followers if you planned to kill me anyway, Diesirae?" said Sulwyn, throwing the cloak into the pit of people.

But Diesirae's smile was wicked. Most of her hair was down now and to the left, the shaved side reflected the light of the flames against her dark, hairless skin. She dressed like one from her tribe, with blowing oranges and reds woven softly from her waist down in loose pants, and a long tight-sleeved purple tunic. Many bracelets were stacked along her wrists and earrings covered her left ear. Her white and black tattoos shone menacingly alongside the flames in the cave. Her appearance was vastly different from her modest Common One look.

"Does Kione know about this?" asked Sulwyn thinking of his bright smile. But she knew the answer; he knew nothing.

"What he does not know cannot hurt him. He would not bode well among us."

"For good reason. You're filled with cracked idealism and followed by fools."

"It does not matter how strong you are, Sulwyn. You cannot fight me here." Diesirae moved forward quickly and redirected the dagger to Sulwyn's throat. She could only guard herself with her weak arms, each cut burning.

The people below began to protest, but Diesirae called to them, "Stand down, this just proves how much worth she has. We will have her blood, and we will gain the strength to protect our people!"

No matter how much Sulwyn struggled, Diesirae was right. She was not in any state to fight back no matter how much movement she gained in the last few minutes. But she couldn't give up. Sulwyn tried to kick behind her but slipped, moving her body closer and against Diesirae's, and in the end gave the woman a stronger hold against her.

"Leave Vartugaul in our hands," she hissed, moving the blade back. Sulwyn's heart rose in her chest even as she tried and failed to push Diesirae's arms away from her.

"Release her!" bellowed a voice from below, at the back of the cave.

Diesirae froze as all the hidden people looked behind them to another cloaked figure. Sulwyn breathed heavily, only then remembering her other vision.

The person lifted the hood down from their head, and Galahad's eyes found hers.

XXVI

The True Prince

S ULWYN looked down. There were definitely more than a hundred people in this cave. Even with the arrival of Galahad, there was no way they could escape this without some serious harm. But Sulwyn lost track of these thoughts when she realized Galahad had yet to move.

"Ah, the adopted prince!" called Diesirae. Her grip on the knife slackened, but Sulwyn would not make her move yet. "I wondered vaguely what our reward would have been had we been able to capture you as well…but it looks like I will not have to wonder anymore."

"I said to release her," said Galahad quietly. Somehow his voice carried to every corner of the cave, and that same heaviness she was used to feeling descended upon them all. But it was stronger now, intimidating and thick.

"We cannot do that…you see, she has been chosen for a good cause. She shall aid us in our goal to right Vartugaul into what it should be. The Empire now has faded into a pastel version of itself. It is our goal to bring back its vividness." Diesirae looked at the guards behind Sulwyn. Quickly they came forward, grabbing Sulwyn tightly around her arms. Diesirae stepped forward to the edge, jumping down into the pit.

The people scattered away, creating a large berth of space between her and Galahad, but soon most of them moved slowly behind her, waiting to fight.

"Is it not better this way?" said Diesirae, her smile crooked. "By the princess taking it upon herself to help us evolve the Empire, you can finally get the seat you were always meant to have."

But Galahad continued to stare at Diesirae, his arm moving under his cloak. Sulwyn was suddenly pushed to her knees, a cry escaping her. Her nerves shook with the movement, and all her pain flared up.

Galahad faltered, looking at her in alarm, and at that moment Diesirae launched forward. She swung the knife, aiming for his face, but Galahad sidestepped and whacked the back of her elbow and wrist simultaneously. She dropped the knife but swung her leg to the side.

Galahad moved out of the way and back towards the group of people as Diesirae did the same, creating a berth of space. Sulwyn watched them. Each expected the other to move. But this Diesirae was nothing like what she thought she was. The cool, mature woman she had met all those times before seemed like a shadow or a persona of some sort. Here she seemed wild and a little desperate, trying to hold her plan together.

"Attack him! He dares to disrupt our ritual! It will be tainted!" she yelled, her deep voice echoing around them. And though some of the people began to circle him, quite a few of them stayed perfectly still. This made the other members pause as well. Unsure of what they were witnessing. Galahad looked at the few around him, crouching and waiting. But still, the others closest to him did not move.

Diesirae picked up her knife, looking at them. "Are you defying me? Everything we have worked for?" she whispered. But one person spoke up.

"We cannot attack him..." said a man.

"We believe he is the true prince..." said a woman, and Diesirae looked outraged.

"The prince? And?! She is their Blood Princess!" she bellowed, but the man shook his head and lowered his hood. The few in the front who had refused to fight started to drop their hoods, one by one. And Sulwyn saw that all of them had tricoloured eyes.

Even if some seemed similar to another, all the eyes were different and unique in their own way. But they all looked towards Galahad, fear buried in their eyes. He looked at the ones around him, his expression unreadable.

"What is the purpose of this group? Why are some of you here while the rest are in town?" he asked in barely a whisper.

Another man with purple, green, and white eyes answered, "We sacrifice strong women, men, and animals once a month. We drink their blood, mixed with our own, to gain their strength, in hopes that we can change the Empire. A ritual found from the Lost World. As for the others...we live away from them, this is our choice. They do not know of us here, assuming us to have disappeared."

"How dare you betray me...right before my eyes," said Diesirae gravely, looking at the man in disappointment.

The man fell to his knees, bowing and begging for her forgiveness. "He is the prince!"

Sulwyn looked at Galahad. She didn't expect these people to be so adamant about him being the prince; he wasn't even related by blood and they should have known that he never really had a chance to take over the Empire. Why were they so insistent?

Diesirae rushed towards the man, lifting him by the neck of his cloak. "You have no problem drinking the blood of the princess, but you have a problem with the prince? What has he ever done for you?!"

"We don't have a choice," stated the man, his voice strangled. "We think...we are sure...he is *our* prince, the prince of our clan. By law, we cannot harm him." Diesirae looked at the man in disbelief and then slowly turned to Galahad, but the man kept talking. "By a spiritual force far stronger than anything I could ever explain. It has been told that we cannot harm him without some form of consequence to ourselves. He is a direct descendant..."

"What does that even mean?" fumed Diesirae, her voice full of anger but her eyes full of panic.

"If we are right...he has inherited the power of our clan far stronger and far greater than anyone else since the First Children." Suddenly all the members of the clan knelt and bowed deeply to the floor, keeping their heads down.

Weariness crossed Galahad's face and he passed his hand over it, rubbing his eyes. "I wish you weren't correct but…you are all aware of the actions that you have taken while being part of this group?" he asked, looking at them and studying their faces. "You have disgraced us. You have brought shame upon this clan by using the lives of the innocent in your goal to further pursue your own selfish needs. Considering our clan's history and strength, resorting to something like this when the founding parents spent their lives saving others…"

Sulwyn couldn't explain it. The cold that dropped into the cave. The pressure. The fear. The menacing. It was stifling, distressing, and heartbreaking. She could see that with every word he spoke. It tore at him. The sting of tears crept behind her eyes, but she hung on to every word he spoke, feeling shame at herself for calling him the very same. A disgrace to his clan.

"These are people that belonged to families, to friends, to other people who are struggling to live in this world the Empire created. You have stolen their time. Their past, present, and future. If we ever come to find peace again, they will never see it because of your actions and your decisions."

He stopped, looking down at his clenched fists, "I know in theory, the effects of what I am about to do will cause. But I don't know what will happen in the long run and I only hope that you can forgive me."

They all raised their heads with eyes of shame and fear, and in unison they gasped as Galahad lifted his head as well. Sulwyn found her gasp joining theirs as she looked at his eyes. Not only were the whites now black, but she watched as it crept past the blue, purple, and red of his irises until both eyes were solid black. He frowned, eyes finding hers for just a moment, and continued.

"Those of you who are part of the Kurome clan…you are hereby dismissed."

Instantly all the men and women on their knees started to scream out in agony. The guards behind Sulwyn ran down the slope to aid Diesirae as she turned around, bewildered. The other hooded people of her group stepped away from the fallen members of Galahad's clan as if they might catch whatever was happening.

Sulwyn looked at the people nearest her and watched in disbelief as the tricoloured eyes soon became one solid colour. Whatever the colour of the outermost ring was now defined what their new eye colour would be. But what else did that mean? Galahad didn't know the long-term effects. What would the consequences be? And how powerful was he really? With just one phrase he had the ability to strip them of clan traits.

Soon the screams turned into weak cries and whimpers. However, Galahad only had eyes for her. He stepped forward, but as soon as he moved, unaffected members of the group barred his way. Diesirae turned around and ran back up the slope to the top where Sulwyn was.

"He has forsaken you! Fight with me! We shall gain strength with her blood!" roared Diesirae. Before Sulwyn could stand steadily, Diesirae advanced on her, bringing the curved blade up and slashing. Sulwyn fell backwards, the knife missing its mark and instead hooking her in the shoulder. She cried out, the burn of the knife tearing at her, but grabbed onto the hilt and Diesirae's wrist, trapping her.

"I'm surprised that you partake in something so baseless," huffed Sulwyn smirking at her surprise before Diesirae's face hardened.

Sulwyn looked past her to see Galahad walking towards Diesirae from behind, pulling his sword out of the sheath at his waist. The blade was pure black just like his eyes and light seemed to avoid it. There was no glint of metal, no reflection of the flames. But soon he brought it down in front of him and stabbed Diesirae somewhere in her back.

Diesirae roared in agony, bending forward. Sulwyn let go of her wrist and crawled back, trying to make space between them. The rest of the people started to rush up the slope as well, tumbling over those who had fallen. But Galahad wasted no time and swiftly pulled his blade out of Diesirae, sheathing it and dashing forward. Without much of a struggle, he bent down and picked Sulwyn up, carrying her across his arms.

Yells sounded behind them, but Galahad took off back down the stairs she had been dragged up and into the hollow paths of the cave.

"I'm sorry, I'm so sorry," repeated Galahad over and over as he ran down the path.

Sulwyn looked up at him, looking into his black eyes and his anguished expression. She had known it all along, or maybe she just hoped she was right. Either way, she knew he hadn't truly betrayed her. Not this time. Sulwyn moved her arms around his neck and held on tighter despite the burning in her shoulder. She felt his shoulders tense for only a moment until he picked up the pace and ran faster.

"Artaxiad made a deal with you? Leave me to them, or the remnants of your clan would suffer? Something like that I'd think…" whispered Sulwyn, her throat still raw. He looked down at her, guilt across his face. "No matter how fast you are, they will catch up Galahad. Put me down."

"No." He clenched his jaw and held her tighter against him. Sulwyn looked past him and saw the crowd growing in the distance. She looked to the front and saw a bright light from an opening shine closer and closer. Just as the sun hit them, so did the smell.

Sulwyn squinted at the sudden flare of light, looking around her. They were in a deep pit, dense trees surrounding the area, and in the centre was a small pond of dark blue and brown water. So, this was where the source was. Looking into the water carefully, she realized bodies were floating within it. Bile rose up burning her throat. Disgusted, Galahad looked around. They needed to find a way out of the pit.

"Galahad. Put me down," she said quietly, her tone final.

Reluctantly, Galahad knelt and braced Sulwyn to stand. Pain ripped through her. Like when she had been tortured in the upper dungeons but far worse. The bruises from that metal rod would take longer to heal.

"How did you find me?" asked Sulwyn but her answer came in the form of a loud neigh. Just above them, within the trees she saw Ki peep his head forward, stomping the ground restlessly. "Oh, how I love him!" said Sulwyn happily.

Galahad remained quiet, looking back to the cave opening and standing ready to fight. He stepped in front of her, pulling out his sword again. "I missed. I tried to stab her heart, but at the last moment, she shifted. I stabbed her side. But I think she's protected by magic. She will heal soon," said Galahad, looking back at her.

"Whoever is helping her is in the Empire too. The magic is the same. I realized it when we came out here. I found this pit last night by mistake, but the way I felt while walking reminded me of how I feel in Valens and the Solus. There's some sort of distortion to the senses regarding direction and time."

"I found this last night too," said Galahad, but turned to the sound of yells.

"You can't fight them alone. You've shown Diesirae a bit of your power, you can't reveal any more."

"Worry about yourself, will you?" he pleaded, but she smirked.

"I haven't had this much excitement in a while, let me be." But she couldn't stop the tremors of pain no matter how much she tried to ignore it.

Finally, the group emerged, running towards them. Sulwyn bent forward and reached beneath Galahad's cloak. His eyes widened in surprise, but she pulled out a short blade from his waist, smirking wider still. "Eyes in front, Galahad."

Sulwyn ran forth, pain screaming with every movement, but she would not stop. All those bodies in the pond. What Galahad said about their past, present, and future all being taken for the selfish goal of these people, for blood sacrifices of all things? Whether it worked or not didn't matter to her.

She wanted vengeance.

Men and women attacked them. Sulwyn, not aiming to kill, made her path by slashing at their knees and ankles. Most dropped to the ground instantly, but some managed to trap her in a fight. She forced her arms up, to grip the hilt tightly, but strength was leaving her.

Warmth seeped into her back, Galahad's bracing against her. "Don't push yourself, Sulwyn, these people will have been sworn to silence. Diesirae is our enemy, but she is the Empire's enemy as well. She won't talk about my powers lightly to them."

"You trust easily," she huffed, catching her breath as he followed suit, attacking the legs. She stood up again and pushed forward. But her vision was becoming blurry. Galahad's arms wrapped around her and soon he was carrying her again.

"I don't care what you say. We can't fight them as you are now. We have to leave." Galahad ran past the murky and rotting waters and towards the other side of the pit. "Start climbing. I can hold them off until you get up."

"And what about you?"

"I'm not injured, worry about yourself!" he replied, with no room for argument. She watched him run back, heading them off and keeping them at bay.

Sulwyn looked up to see Ki pacing back and forth. She looked at the hard dirt and rock in front of her, searching for open holes or roots until she found both. Placing a foot on a protruding rock she steadied herself. Her muscles screamed as she gripped at roots and pulled her weight up. The wound in her left shoulder made her hold even weaker and her skin stretched heavily along her fractured ribs. Sulwyn bit her lower lip, concentrating all her energy on going up. She didn't look back at Galahad, putting faith in the sounds of yelling and thudding.

One foot up.

Another.

Grabbing a root.

Pulling.

Breathing.

Sulwyn didn't have the luxury of trying to pace herself, she had no idea when her arms would give out, but she was halfway up now. Sulwyn looked up to the sound of rustling and realized Ki had disappeared. She clenched her teeth, pushing herself up and trying to go faster. Sulwyn looked down, finding the next rock. She yelped, losing her grip on the root in her left hand as her stomach lurched uncomfortably, the rock falling loose.

With all her might, she willed herself not to let go of the other root while she looked down. Galahad's alarmed stare earned him a jab to his arm. Sulwyn slammed into the wall of dirt and mud, forcing herself to dig into the earth with her boots. She grabbed another root and pulled. Soon, a thick branch was shakily lowered in front of her. Sulwyn looked up and saw Ki, turned slightly, the branch firmly in his mouth.

Sulwyn smiled widely, carefully gripping the branch with one hand and then with the other. Ki pulled, slowly walking backwards as she dug the toes of her boots into the dirt and finally made her way up. With one last pull, she tumbled onto the grass, breathing heavily. "Galahad!"

She heard a sort of strangled yell and a clash of metal. Sulwyn rolled over, forcing herself up by the arms, and looked down. Galahad sheathed his sword and pushed many people back. Some toppled over the others, before sprinting towards the wall. He jumped and made it halfway up, quickly grabbing the roots and pulling. Ki offered the branch again and Galahad gripped onto it. Soon he too tumbled over onto the grass, but he didn't stop there. He threw the branch back into the trees and pulled Sulwyn up, helping her onto Ki. Galahad jumped up behind her, and without waiting for any instruction, Ki turned and trotted towards the forest.

Galahad steered Ki along paths he saw quicker than either her or her horse. Sulwyn knew then and there that Galahad didn't have to do anything to earn Ki's trust. He'd already had it.

They jogged quickly through the thinner areas of the forest until soon they were back out and on the outskirts of the town, opposite where she had entered earlier. In the far distance, she could see their camp and then realized that the sun was close to setting.

"Galahad…" Worry laced her voice, but he just kept riding. He continued back around the forest. Sulwyn couldn't see any of the Validus but couldn't be sure they wouldn't look behind them and see them galloping in the distance. But still he kept going, until soon they hit the fog.

"This isn't safe." She turned back to look at him and realized his eyes were still black.

"I can see through the fog perfectly fine. I found this spot last night," he muttered. Ki paused only for a moment, but blindly trusted Galahad's lead and continued at a light trot.

Sulwyn couldn't tell where they were going but felt it as they turned slightly left and right and then, without warning, the fog fell away and they were entering a beautiful clearing of lush trees and a small pond of clear water. The sunlight riffled through the spaces of the green and blue foliage above, creating light and dark patterns on the sand and grass below.

Galahad pulled Ki to a stop, hopping down and turning for Sulwyn, but the horse had already bent down. Galahad smiled, helping her off. "You've found yourself a brilliant horse."

"He's perfect," whispered Sulwyn.

Her adrenaline had finally run out. The pain and aches across her body were almost numbing, her thoughts were muddled, as her body still sweat and shook from the assault. Exhaustion and nausea rolled through her. Galahad bent down, picking her up again, and carried her to lean against one of the larger trees near the water.

She watched him remove her boots, putting them to the side before walking back to Ki, who was now drinking water. Galahad rummaged through her bags on Ki's saddle. Most of the contents were back at their camp, but they both knew she had another medical pack in there.

Galahad sat cross-legged next to her and emptied the pack of its contents onto the grass. Sulwyn leaned forward and looked at her reflection in the water. The left side of her face and eye were swollen, with dried blood stuck onto her skin and in her hair. Her clothes were ripped, bruises and cuts showing through on her arms and on her legs. She sighed, leaning back against the tree.

Galahad reached into the water, dipping a cloth and soaking it thoroughly before squeezing the excess out. He reached for her face, slowly dabbing the dried blood off. Soon the light yellow cloth was stained red even after he rinsed it. Over and over, he dipped the cloth, squeezed it, then wiped the blood from her skin—from her face, from her neck, shoulder, arms, and legs.

The cool water brought a pleasant relief over the open wounds and the swollen spots of skin. Soon Galahad reached forward, eyes unsure, but lifted her tunic. Sulwyn sat forward, pulling the blue tunic off completely and rolling the black undershirt up to reveal her stomach, stopping just before her breasts.

"Pretty sure some of them are fractured," she huffed, sitting a bit straighter and pointing to her ribs. Galahad looked at her in concern but dabbed the blood from there too.

"I'm not well versed in healing. And it's not the same as Devinal magic," stated Galahad. He got onto his knees, pulling Sulwyn forward gently and turning her back towards him.

"What makes yours different?" Sulwyn wasn't asking what she really wanted to but had a feeling she would learn soon enough. She was content with whatever he was telling her now.

"Devinal are born with the gift to hold magic in their bodies. They gain assistance with nature and with the position of the moon and the sun. If they aren't born with that gift, then it's just like you, who likes to try to use magic when your body can't hold onto it, suffering the consequences." She knew he was giving her a stern look, but she looked around as if she had no idea what he was talking about. He laughed.

Gently, he pulled the fabric strap from her shoulder and placed his hand over the stab wound. It had turned a dark purple, mixed with dried and fresh blood. Soon, a cold tingling entered the wound, eliciting a shiver. But it wasn't uncomfortable. The wound felt warm, stinging lightly along with the tingling. Sulwyn reached up, touching the wound, straining to see it. It was still dark purple, but the skin had healed over.

Galahad sighed heavily.

"My clan…" Her back stiffened at his touch on her lower back, but she stayed silent. He pressed lightly against the spine and onto the sides until she winced. "My clan has a long history. The All-Mother was able to take in negativity and turn it into positive energy for the people and the earth around her. From this, she was able to push her own energy into the ill and the broken and fix them. Though I have inherited power, I didn't get that much from the All-Mother. All I got in that aspect was gaining a sort of partnership with nature and using small amounts of my own energy to heal."

"How is that any different than a Devinal? It all sounded the same," shrugged Sulwyn. She was extremely aware of the fact that he had started lightly caressing her back, almost absentmindedly.

"I can't hold magic within me. I can't replenish it with the elements around me. My communion with nature is only for the peace and gardening aspect. And it's not strong enough to farm. Whatever energy I use to heal, I must remake from within with rest. Depending on what it is, it can weaken me too. Just like you, or really anyone who isn't a Devinal. But I've never really healed anything large enough to do so." Sulwyn felt a light sting where her fractured ribs were. He pressed his hand against them, using the other hand to straighten her back.

"So you are using magic?"

He sighed. "No, I'm using my own energy. You use spells that your body can't hold. The spells call on the energy outside and Devinal store it within. For non-Devinal the energy can only hold for that moment during small uses. *I* just use my *own* energy. It's quite different."

"If you say so." She felt him lean against her back and turned to see his face over her shoulder. He looked at her in mild irritation, and she snickered.

Grumbling, he placed his hand back over her ribs. Soon the odd sticking pain began to lift, and her breathing felt unhindered. She took a deep breath, everything else aching instead.

"I can't heal anything else right now. I've already used a lot of energy from earlier, but the rest of your wounds aren't too deep, and nothing is bleeding anymore."

Sulwyn stretched her shoulder and arms, the pull against her ribs sensitive but bearable. "Your healing...power, whatever it is, it's cold and tingly and rough. Different from the Devinal magic."

"What does Nori's feel like?" he asked quietly.

Sulwyn put her arms back down, thinking. "Warm? Warm and smooth... but not mature."

"Mature?"

"We're...or I guess, *I'm* close to another Devinal. His magic feels warm and comforting. Real healing. But he's a genius, so..." Sulwyn smiled at the thought and wondered if word had reached Wilkson about what was happening.

Silence continued between them, neither moving, but she was conscious of the fact that Galahad was just behind her, almost a few inches away. She looked back at him in wonder but was caught in his stare. He had been looking at her the whole time. She turned to face him properly, sitting in front of him.

His eyes had returned to their tricoloured glory, no hint of black anywhere in the edges. Startled, he moved back when she suddenly lifted a hand to the side of his face, resting it there. "I don't expect you to explain anything more. Whatever it is you have gone through and what your power is and what happened recently, it is yours. I trust you. I trusted you even when you tried to push me away."

Galahad frowned. His hand reached up to hold her own. Then he pulled her forward into a gentle embrace. Again, he apologized over and over, and Sulwyn could hear all the emotions that had built up in him through every word. She looked up through the trees noting that the sun had almost set, the evening getting darker by the minute.

"We need to go back...I'm sure they realize I'm missing by now," whispered Sulwyn. She was reluctant to let go. She felt him nod, but he didn't loosen his hold either and instead ran his hands softly through her hair, down her back, patting her gently.

Neither spoke while Ki trotted calmly back to camp through the fog and forest, but Galahad had pulled Sulwyn closer. The heat of his chest seeped through to her back, keeping her warm through the cold haze. His arms rested gently along her thighs, holding the reins loosely. Sulwyn felt relaxed, sleep trying to call her, but she knew she needed to stay awake for when they arrived.

By the time they reached camp the sun had fully set. Only deep indigo illuminated the sky where the sun was now hiding. But only Demir stepped forward to greet them as they dismounted. He looked at them in confusion, shock, and fear all at once.

"What's wrong?" said Galahad suddenly, and Sulwyn looked to the lit tent that held Tiergan. Muffled sounds reached their ears. She looked past the guarding Validus to see a dark colour splash against the inside fabric of the tent.

Sulwyn rushed forward, the effort tiring, the stings of the whip burning when the air touched it. The Validus looked at each other nervously but soon stepped aside. Sulwyn untied the ropes binding the tent flap and ripped it open. Daijiro looked up and an expression she couldn't decipher crossed his face, but then she turned to Tiergan who was bleeding from almost everywhere onto the floor of the tent.

"Daijiro...what? Why are you doing this?" yelled Sulwyn. Galahad slinked into the darkness, listening, she was sure. She stepped in and was instantly paralyzed.

"Cailín. Glad of you to join us...where did you get those injuries? You look like hell." His eyes flashed, and a smirk graced his lips. One palm was up before her, the other swinging around a piece of wood with tiny tacks embedded into it, most of it covered with blood.

Tiergan hacked up, hefting himself to his knees. Sulwyn took him in. Cuts from his head bled into his eyes and pasted his hair. Blood dripped with every movement he made, his arms bound behind him and legs tied by the ankles.

"What are you doing?" she growled, trying and failing to fight against Daijiro's hold on her.

"Interrogating, of course. He didn't keep his part of the bargain so I made this fun thing to hit him with. And you've been missing for quite a while. I thought he might know where you went."

"He has nothing to do with the murders," stated Sulwyn and Tiergan turned to her, spitting out blood.

"Oh? Do you have proof?" He leaned against the spiked wood casually.

"I AM the proof! Those murders and disappearances were not caused..." she hesitated and knew he noticed, "...they were not caused by people of this town. There is a cult. Holding radical ceremonies. Sacrificing the innocent for their own beliefs."

"And what of the impersonators?"

"I haven't figured that out yet," she muttered angrily.

WHACK.

Tiergan's shoulder was assaulted by spikes, shoving him to the side. But he was resilient. "Well then, I guess I'll find out about that instead." Daijiro smiled, but she saw the savagery in his eyes.

"Is this what you like, then? Feeling high from the torture of people who can't defend themselves?" she spat, fighting against the invisible bonds. "Why even tie him up? You can hold him there on your own, can't you? Or better yet, do whatever you did to me in Eques on him?"

"I could, but he's not worth the effort. And this is easier for me. Gives me space to concentrate on this." Daijiro brought the wood down over the side of Tiergan's leg. A loud smack vibrated around them.

"I'm warning you. You can do this another way. What good is it if you beat him like this? He won't tell you anything! He has a town to protect! He has *something* to protect!"

Daijiro glared at her, bending his fingers slightly. Sulwyn caught her breath as the ghost feeling of tightening rope wrapped across her body. "Do not interfere with me, princess, I am here to solve a mystery. You did not bring me evidence. And many things need to be answered."

Daijiro raised the spiked wood again, aiming for Tiergan's head, but it never hit.

XXVII

A Hidden Past
| SULWYN |

SULWYN managed to break Daijiro's hold on her for just a moment. Each step she took to get in front of Tiergan was like running through a thick swamp, but she managed to kneel in front of him, taking the hit to the side of her head instead. Luckily, it didn't have tacks.

"How?" Daijiro struggled to speak, or do anything for that matter, staring at her with wide eyes. She watched as he dropped the weapon to the ground slowly. It thudded softly against the fabric and dirt underneath. Sulwyn glared at him, her knees in more pain than before and her vision swaying.

Sulwyn reached up; just when the blood from before had stopped, she'd gotten herself another wound. "Still on the left side of my head…" she wheezed.

"WHAT HAVE YOU DONE?" Daijiro bellowed, and Sulwyn was disturbed by his reaction. He looked at his hands, and then at her and then the weapon. Unable to figure out what to do next, he advanced on her, grabbing her collar and pushing her down to the side.

"I told you! You have no evidence! We cannot return without it! What are you going to say if we go back empty-handed?!" he hollered. He looked truly mad, but something more like dread had ebbed its way through his eyes. She couldn't believe he of all people was afraid of the Empire. What did he truly fear?

Sulwyn reached up and grabbed the fabric of his tunic, pulling him down closer to her, and smirked. "Are you afraid of the king? And what he'll do because you've injured me?" She whispered, but she could barely see his face even at this proximity. The edges of her vision were fading. She blinked quickly.

That hit was hard—even with just one hand, Daijiro was strong. Sulwyn felt his shoulders stiffen, moving his arms on either side of her. His expression changed into pure shock as if seeing her for the first time. She watched him lift a shaking hand towards her head, but before he could touch her, he was violently yanked back.

Sulwyn looked past him to see Galahad's blurred face full of fury, the black at the edges of his eyes. She watched him blink quickly as if willing it away before he turned Daijiro around and punched him square in the jaw.

"Get out of this tent," he seethed, shoving Daijiro out of the flaps without a fight. Galahad knelt next to Sulwyn, lifting her carefully.

"I should have intervened. I never thought he would attack you," he said quietly, but Sulwyn sniggered.

"He didn't attack me. He actually hesitated! Last second but too late! I got in the way...I do that, get in the way..." Sulwyn slurred, snickering again, his face out of focus.

"She might have a concussion," she heard Tiergan whisper, and felt Galahad tense. "There is a doctor in the town..."

"Shut up, Tiergan," snapped Galahad.

Sulwyn felt him move behind her head, pulling her up gently to rest against his thighs. She opened her eyes again, finding Galahad's in full concentration. No black to be seen. Who was Tiergan to him that he would speak like that?

"What are you doing, boy?" hissed Tiergan.

"I told you to shut up. I have no qualms with letting Daijiro continue his assault on you. She should have never bothered to protect you."

"Galahad..." Sulwyn was surprised by his tone; how could he say that? Galahad took a deep breath, placing his hand around her head.

"That is a dangerous thing for you to be doing without the right power," coughed Tiergan, but Galahad did not respond.

"Assist me then. Bring that bucket of water to me."

Sulwyn found his request obscure but soon the ropes on Tiergan's hands fell away and he was shuffling over to the bucket.

"You should let me do it," Tiergan reached forward, but Galahad grabbed his wrist and pushed his hand away.

"Don't you dare touch her. Just wet the cloth for me," demanded Galahad. Tiergan searched around, finding a stack of towels amongst the Validus' belongings. Sulwyn watched his back, water sloshing. Soon he handed Galahad a cloth, and cool water was on her skin once again.

"I've never really healed something like this…" he said, but Sulwyn smiled.

"Don't overexert yourself." She lifted her hand up, searching for his face, but found his neck instead. She touched him gently, the sleep finally making its way through.

࠸

Her back was stiff and sore, her skull weighted. Sulwyn reached up and touched the bandage wrapped around her forehead. The other injuries took a back seat to the throbbing in her mind, but she felt better rested than she had in a while.

Sulwyn kept her eyes closed, sensing the near rise of the sun. She had slept the entire night. Breathing deeply, she passed her hand around the tent floor but brushed something warm. She opened her eyes slowly and spotted Galahad curled up next to her. Her hand bumped his arm. Sulwyn looked at him, his eyes shifting lightly and his disheveled brown hair falling to the side. It had gotten longer in these past months, almost down to his neck.

As she stared at him sleeping, she suddenly remembered the sound of ticking. Tons and tons of ticking surrounded her, enveloping her in the noise. She frowned, thinking harder. Sulwyn looked at his closed eyes, his nose, and then his lips. And slowly she touched her own.

After the battle with Caldwell, and after they buried him, Galahad had taken her back to the castle. Carrying her the same way he had done yesterday, holding her closely. Was it then? He had been called to see Artaxiad, and once the ticking left and they were back in his room…

Galahad's eyes opened suddenly, just as Sulwyn touched his lips with her fingers. He grabbed her wrist in reflex but quickly relaxed, bringing her hand down interlaced with his. Awkwardly Sulwyn turned onto her side.

Galahad watched her apprehensively, but as she settled, he looked into her eyes instead. Sulwyn looked at him, her heart beating hard against her chest, paining her bruised body. Heat crept into her legs and arms and neck. But she never broke eye contact.

"How are you feeling?" he whispered softly, looking down for a moment and back up to her eyes.

"Better than I thought…though I feel like there's a rock in my head."

"I think you have a concussion." But Sulwyn only nodded, unable to speak. Her mind was too busy trying to put together a fragmented memory from the thoughts of someone who was in and out of consciousness. Maybe she had just imagined things.

He looked at her in concern, moving slightly closer to her. His breath tickling her nose, making her want to sneeze. But soon her sneeze disappeared along with the space between them.

Galahad moved forward, his eyes closing slowly, until his lips pressed softly against hers. In shock, amongst other emotions, she kept her eyes open.

Sulwyn was talented in many things. She was a fighter, a warrior of kinds. Someone who didn't back down. Reckless. Threw her body in harm's way more than she could count, and was way too curious for her own good. She was relatively smart and skilled in various weapons and combat. She was much more than those things too, but something she was not, was this.

In all her years travelling, Sulwyn never really had time to consider a relationship with someone else. Nor did she understand it. It wasn't like she wasn't attracted to anyone. There had been men and women she mildly daydreamed what a life could be like with them. And she had witnessed it many times. Like Wilkson and his wife—they seemed happy. And just like them, she had seen various families or couples in her travels getting by and doing it together.

She also wasn't ignorant, nor a stranger to self pleasure. She had even witnessed the act of sex a few times. Places with alcohol were the best to look for information, but also where people did what they wanted.

Galahad opened his eyes, looking at her timidly, but she stayed still and looked at him. The heat from before had flared more into fire and decided it wanted to spread out around her completely alongside her nerves.

"I know what sex is," she blurted.

Galahad's eyes widened, "I...what?"

"I don't know what to do though."

"Wh-what? I'm not...that's not...I wasn't going to try and have sex with you?"

"Why not?" she asked incredulously, but the back of her neck prickled. Goosebumps had spread out across her.

Galahad was stunned, and then he just started laughing.

Sulwyn had never seen him laugh so much since meeting him. As if he were making up for all the laughing he didn't do. Her heartbeat quickened and she cursed Raghnall wherever he had ended up. He was just as bad as she was when it came to relationships or anything of the like and had not taught her how to deal with it. How he was once married she never understood.

Galahad reached out and pulled her against him, his laugh still deep within his chest, turning into small chuckles. But she really wanted an answer now. "Why not?"

He looked down at her and gently pushed her onto her back, hovering over her. Bracing his arms on either side of her, all laughter gone, replaced with a gentle glint of desire in his eyes. Sulwyn forgot how to breathe, never breaking eye contact. The sun was rising now lightening the tent around them. Galahad bent forward carefully, keeping his weight off her. His nose touched hers, his lips a breath away from her own and a hand gently caressing the side of her cheek.

What kind of torture was this?

Sulwyn lifted her arms and pulled him closer, bringing his lips back onto hers. The weight of him pressed against her, tugging at her bruises, but the distraction of his lips on hers kept the pain at bay. She closed her eyes and decided to go with what she felt.

Galahad was gentle, his lips hot, his breath a little musty but also warm. And as with anything she tried, she caught on quickly. Understanding the flow of a kiss. Until his tongue passed over her bottom lip and she froze. She opened her eyes and found his opening slowly as well. He looked at her carefully, kissed her briefly once more, then pushed himself off her.

With his weight and his warmth gone, she was very aware of the pains that coursed through her body. Wincing, she forced herself to stretch. Her back was begging to get off the ground. Galahad knelt next to her, holding her hand and bracing her lower back, helping her sit.

"No more, Sulwyn..." he whispered. Heat still thrummed through her despite the pain and she wanted to protest, but he looked at her sternly. "I think I gave you my answer." His breath tickled her forehead just as he placed a light kiss above the bandage. "Let's get you food, you need to recover."

Sulwyn begrudgingly agreed, her hunger now ploughing through all other emotions. He helped her stand and the covers fell away. She had been changed into one of Galahad's nightclothes of loose green pants and a black long-sleeved tunic.

"We aren't near the Empire or the Néosan, it won't matter much if you wear it," he answered her unasked question and she found herself smiling. He turned to her, picking up something from next to her boots.

"I found this on you. The band is a bit damaged though. It fell off in your boot." Galahad lifted the black rope bracelet with the stone that matched his eyes. Heat trailed along her neck. "Thank you for having faith in me even when I didn't." He hugged her closely.

Galahad and another Validus prepared breakfast until soon everyone, except Daijiro, was in attendance and eating around the small fire keeping an eye on the tent. They all observed Sulwyn with worried and confused eyes. No one knew where she had gone or what had happened to her.

"Is Tiergan causing any problems?" Galahad asked Demir.

"He's quiet in that tent. He was re-bound more complexly as you requested."

"Daijiro?"

Demir was quiet, fear in his eyes. "He hasn't come back since. We don't know where he went."

"That's fine. When you are done, take two others and carefully guard Tiergan. He isn't to be trusted."

Demir saluted him, confusion all over his face. As soon as they finished, three Validus went to stand closer to the tent and Galahad beckoned Sulwyn back to his.

Once they were inside, Galahad gestured for her to sit back onto the sheets. She watched him leave the tent then return with a small metal bowl of water, a cloth, and clean bandages.

"I couldn't heal it well after healing you before, the wound is still open. I don't think I can heal for the next couple of weeks."

"It takes you that long to rebuild the energy?"

"I'm not practised in it. I'm sure I could learn to sustain it longer, but as I've been trying to just repress all of my power...well..." He knelt down, carefully undressing the wound on her head.

Sulwyn looked up at him, question upon question building. He sighed, sitting down and dipping the cloth in water. "*Kurome*...it's the name of our clan. I don't know where the name originated, but it literally means 'black eyes.' Though I've heard it can mean 'turn wrong to right.'" He spoke quietly.

"The lore of our clan is the All-Mother, someone who was cherished on this land once the Lost World had diminished, helped bring life and peace back to what is now known as Vartugaul. After The Shift that reconstructed pretty much everything on Earth, many kinds of people and creatures erupted and evolved around the land, causing war and panic. She aided in defeating these threats. Amongst the things that terrorized the struggling population were creatures that awoke from under the earth. Demon-like things that could appear human and wrecked havoc.

"Amongst thousands of these land demons, there was just one that was born with a heart. He broke away from the rest, ashamed of what he was, and travelled alone until he met the All-Mother. They fell in love and eventually had the First Son. He had never-before-seen powers, surpassing both parents. They had three more children and they became known as the First Children. After their parents, the four of them spent their lives helping others."

Sulwyn had never heard this before. She knew something of what he called the "All-Mother," though under different names. And the land demons were far in the past. But she had never heard about one with a heart.

"Unlike other races, the blood of the Demon doesn't weaken. But the power doesn't always pass on. A definite trait is our eyes, each different and unique. Some have enhanced strength physically or mentally, and all live rather long lives." He dried off her now clean wound, adding a salve, before he rewrapped the bandage slowly around her head.

"There are about thirteen generations of branch families and six generations of head families. Those in the branch are children and descendants of the other three siblings, and those in the head are descendants of the First Son. My father was from the fifth-generation branch family. My mother, a fifth-generation head." Galahad paused at the mention of his parents, his voice softer. He finished dressing the wound, sitting a little uncertainly. Sulwyn just took his hands in hers and urged him to continue. He breathed in deeply.

"Dante, my father, was powerful. It had been a long time since someone like him had shown up. When the time came to choose the next Head of all the clan families, he was nominated over anyone else. But he was the younger brother. And the older brother did not agree." Ice slid into her stomach. He nodded. "Tiergan is my uncle, my father's older brother." He squeezed her hand.

"The people had chosen. Dante was the Head and there was no going back. The issue was dropped until I was conceived. Tiergan had a son about five years older than me, but his awakening was slow. He showed above-average power, but it wasn't noted to be special. Once I was born, I was marked as having more power than anyone since the First Children. But my parents didn't want many to know this fact and so they hid it for a time until I got older.

"Tiergan's son, Aden, and I got along really well. But Tiergan is twisted. He was born with an unstable mind and…" Galahad stopped speaking; his gaze furrowed and concentrated on Sulwyn's hands. "Eventually, something happened and though my father was patient, Tiergan challenged him for the title of Head. My father wanted to back down, but then…it escalated. My father was furious and finally, Aden stepped forward to defend me. Tiergan, in blind anger, killed his son and fled in anguish. I hadn't seen or heard from him until now."

Sulwyn was stunned beyond words. There was nothing she could say, and she knew there was more to his story than he was telling. But before she could digest it further, a yell was heard.

Galahad stood up quickly. "Don't even ask me to stay," said Sulwyn seriously.

Reluctantly he helped her up and they both stepped out of the tent. Daijiro had returned, his eyes glinting in the morning sun. Sulwyn noticed his clothes were dirty and his hands had small cuts on them, but he marched straight up to Galahad and punched him in the face.

"That is payback," he growled. He turned to Sulwyn, the anger in his eyes wavering for just a moment before he rounded on Demir. "Bring him out."

Another Validus went forward, undoing the ropes to the entrance. But he soon stepped out, looking like he wanted nothing better than to evaporate right then and there.

"We just checked on him about fifteen minutes ago. No one left the post," said the man, his voice shaking. Daijiro was furious, but Galahad rushed forward, ripping back the tent flap. Sulwyn came behind him; the tent was empty, a pile of ropes in the centre.

"The rest of you, prepare to leave back to the Empire, replenish anything we need. Demir, the funds are in my tent," commanded Galahad.

Sulwyn whistled and Ki came running forward from the trees where he had been strolling. With haste, she forced herself up, Galahad jumping on behind her, before they took off back into town.

Sulwyn glanced around—the streets were unusually quiet. But as she strained her ears for sound, shouts could be heard in the distance. She turned to look behind Galahad, where Daijiro closely followed on another horse.

👁️‍🗨️

"Look at me! Look at what the Empire has finally done! We are in danger! I tried, we tried to hide from them, but now look at this!" yelled Tiergan frantically to a growing mass of people. She could see him in the distance, hear his shrill yells, riling the people up. They all gathered at the far end of the town near the forest.

"The man with our eyes, he is a disgrace! A fraud! An Empire man through and through!" He addressed members of their clan. The people looked at him in disbelief, but that quickly turned into anger and yells, even from those not part of his clan. Sulwyn and Galahad dismounted, Daijiro following suit. But uncharacteristically, he hung back.

"Sulwyn..." whispered Galahad. He looked back at Daijiro, and she nodded.

"Why are you turning your anger onto him? He is one of your own!" stated Sulwyn, walking towards the throng of people. Tiergan turned to her in surprise and then to Galahad and Daijiro. "It is he who kidnapped and tortured this man!" continued Sulwyn, dramatically pointing at Daijiro.

Daijiro stared at her incredulously, before looking back at all the glares. Without warning a bunch of the men ran forward and grabbed Daijiro's arms and legs. Suddenly another man brought forth a large rock and swung, whacking Daijiro in the head and knocking him out. They let his body fall limply to the ground, moving back to their places and admiring their work.

Sulwyn looked at Daijiro suspiciously. That was far too easy. But her attention was called before her as more men came and grabbed her. They pulled her towards the centre, restraining her and pushing her down on her already sore knees in front of Tiergan. She glared up at him, but they forced her head back down.

"Don't look at him, filthy blood of the Empire," barked one of the men holding her.

"Tiergan, stop this!" demanded Galahad, clenching his fist. He moved towards Sulwyn, but one of the men held a blade to her throat. She looked up. The men holding her were not part of his clan.

"Seriously? This is getting old," huffed Sulwyn nonchalantly, eying the blade. She looked at Galahad reassuringly, catching his lip twitch in a slight smirk before he turned his full attention to Tiergan.

"You are putting these people in danger. You've brought the Empire's attention to this small town. No one here is safe once we leave!"

"Did you hear him? Hear how he threatens us?!" yelled Tiergan, and Sulwyn thought he now looked much madder than before. Even when he was being beaten by Daijiro, he had seemed more composed.

"Tiergan, please listen to me. Stop this, and let the Lady Princess go," said Galahad, but Tiergan looked at him in defiance.

"Why should I leave? Why should we leave our home? What right do you have, you are a fraud!" bellowed Tiergan, taking a step towards Sulwyn.

"If you do not stop your actions, I will have to force you," warned Galahad. The people were silent. Sulwyn raised her head a bit, looking around her. People of the Kurome clan walked closer, looking on between the two clan members, as non clan members began to step back sensing the growing tension. But Tiergan whipped around and looked at Galahad like he had never seen him before.

"How dare you?! How dare you utter threats to me? Who are you? Thinking you can back up such threats! You are no one. You have no power. You betrayed your clan and fled to the Empire!" he hissed. Sulwyn could see a slight tremor pass through Galahad.

"How dare you come before the fallen members of this clan with the Empire behind your back? You do not deserve your eyes, or to wear green, or to speak of us!"

"Don't you dare talk to me about betrayal!" shouted Galahad. Sulwyn watched the black start to creep into his eyes, wavering and waiting. But she wasn't the only one. The other members of the fallen clan saw it too and whispers began to fly around them like a hiss.

"You are just like your father. Full of lies and dreams. Deceiving those around you, speaking of things you claim to be able to do," spat Tiergan.

"Lies? What lies have I told? Has he told? What exactly have you told these people?" asked Galahad.

"Who are you, Empire filth, to come to our town and spew nonsense?" interjected one of the men holding Sulwyn down. "He helped our town! Kept us hidden from the Empire for years!"

"He is not the one that kept you hidden!" said Sulwyn loudly. She avoided the blade and carefully placed strength into her legs, hoping to keep her balance, and forced herself up. The men were shocked, but she continued, "There is dark magic that hides you. You sit on the border of a cult leader who have taken clan and non-clan members as their own. You think the Empire will leave you alone now that this town is associated with a Devinal?" threatened Sulwyn.

She struggled to break free of their arms, but her body was still sore. She grunted; someone pulled at her hair. Galahad turned towards her but was almost hit by a thin metal rod. Galahad dodged it, redirecting it to his arm instead of his head. Tiergan had grabbed it from one of the men, holding it like a sword and pointing it at Galahad.

But Tiergan suddenly rushed in front of Galahad, trying to whip the metal rod towards his head again. Galahad caught the metal between his hands, but that was merely a distraction. Tiergan used that moment to place his hand over Galahad's forehead and instantly Galahad dropped to his knees.

Silence fell around them before a scream of pure fear erupted from Galahad's throat, his eyes closed and his body stiff. His cry echoed around them, bouncing off the skies. Tiergan looked at him with a sort of hunger.

"How long I have waited to do this to you again," he whispered.

Sulwyn threw caution to the wind and slammed her head back and into the chin of the man holding her. Her concussed head was screaming, her mind blackening for just a moment. The man grunted, dropping the knife, and swore in pain, letting her go.

Sulwyn scurried away, going to grab the metal rod but stopped. Another man grabbed her legs and pulled her back, sliding her across the rough stone. She turned to kick, but he kicked her stomach and then slapped her. "Do not interrupt while our saviour deals with the Empire's guard dog!"

"Saviour? What do you even know about him? You aren't even part of their clan!" she argued.

"He was abandoned, just like most of us, by our towns and our families!" yelled a woman.

"Abandoned?" asked Sulwyn, but she looked back to Galahad, his yelling now turned into pained laughter.

"Abandoned, you say?" whispered Galahad.

"You've gotten stronger, boy," said Tiergan. "Even against this you can keep your mind, unlike when you were younger. Maybe I should bring forth other memories? There should be more in here since the last time I did this." he whispered just low enough for Galahad and Sulwyn to hear. And too soon, Galahad's eyes tightened and instead of screaming, he froze, shaking in fear and hopelessness. Sulwyn watched his body stiffen, tears falling from his closed eyes.

Sulwyn turned onto her stomach seeing the other clan members watch in apprehension and confusion. Even the regular townspeople were afraid. This Tiergan was different from the calm leader they were used to.

"You may have gotten taller, but you are still that sad excuse of a boy who was revered too much by his parents," hissed Tiergan. He smirked, but it faltered. Galahad unexpectedly straightened up. Hands clenched.

"You left us. You left our family's clan, our village, to die," growled Galahad.

Tiergan scoffed, "Left you?" He pushed his hand further against Galahad's head, yanking his hair. "You were supposed to be smart, weren't you? I didn't leave you to die. I told the Empire how to go through Mortui Gemma just to find you."

Sulwyn gawked feeling the stares of everyone around her. Tiergan hadn't whispered it this time. He didn't even seem aware of the fact that everyone had heard him.

"You...told them? You brought them to our home?"

"No one can find their way through those mountains without the assistance of a clan member. Didn't you ever wonder how they managed to find you all? Dante and his might! I wanted to test him. Show him he wasn't fit." He laughed maniacally now.

"Dante?" gasped one of the men in the background. Sulwyn looked behind her to see the clan members step forward, enclosing them all. The other townspeople stepped back, noting that this was not their place or battle.

"Dante, the one who was Head of all families?" said a woman, her hand to her mouth.

"So he really is his son?" said another man, looking at Galahad's kneeling form.

"The prince?"

"He is not a prince!" shrieked Tiergan, finally losing all composure, "He is not the prince! His family lied to all of us and in turn, all of you! He is nothing, he lacks power! His father lacked power! All he had was heart and compassion. The people fell for such cheap words!" he spat out again, gripping Galahad's hair harder. But Galahad reached up and grabbed Tiergan's wrist, squeezing it.

Galahad braced himself with a hand to the ground, breathing deeply before he stood shakily, crushing Tiergan's wrist until it cracked, earning a strangled yell. Sulwyn looked at the tears still streaming down his face, until she bit her lip, watching his eyes fully open. The blue, purple, and reds of his eyes had been replaced with full black.

XXVIII

My Enemy's Enemy Is My Friend?

| SULWYN |

GALAHAD laughed a pitiful, mournful laugh as he looked into Tiergan's eyes, "I watched them, one after the other, get slaughtered before my eyes. Hundreds of Néosan and other men, even Artaxiad himself, ripped apart our homes. Only a small group managed to escape...the fires, their cries...everything is burned in me. I watched our entire village burn!

"After you left that night as the coward you are. Even after you killed your son...even after everything you had done to me. Dante, my father—your brother—told me not to harbour hate for you."

All the clan's people got to their knees and bowed deeply. But they were unable to keep their eyes away, all raising their heads to watch. The regular townspeople remained behind them, watching with bated breath. And just like them, Sulwyn couldn't stop herself from looking between the two. Even her assailants had left her on the ground. And as she sat up slowly, she never took her eyes off them.

"He had faith that you would come home. He believed that you would be okay even after all you did and that if I ever saw you before you came back, I was to tell you that he loved you. As a brother and as a friend, no matter what happened between you...and you gave us away?" He whispered the last words. As if saying it finally set it in stone. The disbelief that crossed his face showed how sincerely he had believed that maybe one day,

Tiergan would have come back to save him all those years ago when he was trapped in the Empire.

Galahad stood slowly, and stepped forward, a power of menace and cold anger falling around them all. "You led the Empire, the plague of Vartugaul, into our home? And you let them kill almost all of us?"

"You can't see them, these memories you pulled forward!" bellowed Galahad, the tears gone as if the anger had evaporated them. "It wasn't enough for you to break our family's hearts. When they found out what torture you had put me through? It wasn't enough to kill your son in anger. How…?" Galahad choked, unable to finish what he was saying. His voice trembled and Sulwyn could see that he was barely breathing.

"They were at fault!" roared Tiergan, never backing down. "Since your father was chosen as Head no one could see that he lacked what we needed! And when Mina was pregnant, they came up with cock-and-bull stories of how you were the prince, the one with the First Son's power. How insulting, insulting to the Demon father of our clan! What twisted lies!"

"They didn't even announce that! It was a hidden fact that only a few people knew!"

But Tiergan wasn't listening and continued to talk over Galahad. "They let it get to their heads! I was more than enough! And had I been there, the Empire would never have learned about you! I would have protected all of us!"

"You led the Empire there!" thundered Galahad. "How could you even say that? How far do your delusions go?!"

"THEN THEY DESERVED THEIR DEATH!" shrieked Tiergan, eyes bulging. "If they could not even keep the Empire off their backs, then it furthered what I had always said!"

"You…for some feeble reasoning?" muttered Galahad.

"How could you?!" yelled other members of the clan.

"We lost our families that night!" they continued.

"They came for Galahad. It was his fault!" hissed Tiergan.

"I have no choice, Tiergan…" said Galahad, his voice hollow, "…you leave me no choice. Your sin is far greater than those that had partaken in…" Galahad's voice fell away, and he frowned. "Did you lead us here?" Tiergan started to laugh hysterically now, his eyes wide, but Galahad continued, "Did you give Diesirae some of our people? And the impersonators?"

"How else could I bring them here? The Empire doesn't act unless it is something of worth. I used Antac, their weapon source. Which, by the way, that fool of a man made it so easy. I found the Leader. Learned he was looking for his sister. Found her too and put her there. I knew he would come. And that let them have leverage over you. Artaxiad was pleased to hear from me again."

Sulwyn stood up now. "You orchestrated that? You put Caldwell's sister in that house? Innocent people died because of you!"

"They weren't strong enough, that is all," he shrugged, not a shred of remorse in his eyes or in his face. Galahad walked forward and grabbed Tiergan by the neck, squeezing it tightly. Choking him. Tiergan tried to look around wildly, but no one was cheering for him or assisting him. They wouldn't even look at him.

"Galahad…" said Sulwyn, moving forward. Galahad looked at her, staring at her with his unwavering eyes of blackness. A tinge of fear shivered through her but she moved closer still, reaching out to him.

He clenched his jaw, releasing Tiergan. "As weak as ever, Galahad…just like your father."

"Death is not enough for you. Someone whose sin is far greater than those you placed in Diesirae's group. The blood of our people is on your hands, stained in your heart, and bringing you down into your own hell of corruption. There was never anyone for you to beat. You challenged your brother because of jealousy. You corrupted yourself by torturing me. You killed your son because of madness. You led the Empire to the innocent then, and now."

"What can you possibly do to me?" goaded Tiergan. "So you have full black eyes? That doesn't give you any right. That doesn't make you the prince!" Tiergan's eyes turned black as well, but only up to the irises.

Galahad just closed his eyes for a moment. "I don't pass judgement, Tiergan. The First Children do. Just remember that."

Tiergan stepped forward but stopped, unable to move. Sulwyn turned behind her, Galahad following her gaze, to see Daijiro sitting up on the cobblestone, hands resting on his knees and no wound on his head.

"I think I've heard enough of this to count it as evidence. Even faked a hit for that. But I would like to say, I *was* right in some respect." His palm was out, holding Tiergan still. Daijiro curled his index finger, forcing Tiergan to his knees.

"Daijiro…" said Galahad, and Sulwyn could hear the waver of fear in his voice, his expression void of anything but worry. He had spent more than half his life hiding this all from the Empire.

"I know what it's like to lose a clan…" said Daijiro quietly. "Besides, I was hit with a rock. I have selective hearing now. Carry on." Daijiro lowered his hand, stood up, and dusted the dirt off his loose black pants. He bent down and picked up a small rock, throwing it towards one of the unlit torch lamps in the distance, hitting the thin pole perfectly. Daijiro bent down again and picked up the large rock he had almost been hit with and whipped it at the man who had tried. Sulwyn watched it whiz by his head, startling the man instead.

"I have perfect aim, remember that." Daijiro rubbed his nonexistent wound and turned around, walking back towards the horses.

Sulwyn looked at his retreating back in confusion but turned to Galahad. He too seemed a little dazed but looked back down at Tiergan, his anger fully present.

"No matter what you do to me, it won't bring any of them back. Their deaths are on you," hissed Tiergan.

"Tiergan…those deaths are on *you*." Galahad hesitated, holding back the words she knew were coming. "You are hereby dismissed from the Kurome clan."

Tiergan looked at him in horror, face drained of colour until it was now his blood-curdling scream that echoed across the early afternoon sky. Birds erupted in fear out of the trees and into the bright yellow and green skies.

It was a beautiful day, but the weather did not reflect the scene in front of them.

Tiergan curled into a ball, his fists rubbing into his eyes. Sulwyn noticed tears of blood streaming down, his cries even louder. Everyone stood around them, unable to look away from the man who had held some part of their heart only minutes ago. Soon only the echoes of his voice rang against their ears. But everyone continued staring, some in shock and some in uneasy triumph. These people had been betrayed too.

"What will happen to him?" asked Sulwyn. Galahad walked over to her, his eyes were still black, checking her face and arms and body. The bandage around her head had come loose, exposing the deep gash. He glared at the men who had grabbed her but shook his head and turned back to Tiergan.

Tiergan finally stopped moving altogether, breathing heavily and sweating, his arms and legs splayed out. Slowly, he opened his blood-soaked eyes, and everyone who could see him gasped.

His eyes had become a translucent grey.

"They've decided to make him blind," said Galahad quietly.

&s&

As they made it back to camp, the other Validus had just returned from purchasing food. With all the commotion that happened, most places were left unmanned, forcing them to wait. But as soon as Sulwyn and Galahad slid off the saddle, Galahad collapsed.

"I'm fine…just too much…" he muttered, getting to his legs shakily. He shrugged off Demir and another Validus and looked at Sulwyn. "Let me bandage your head…" but he grabbed Sulwyn's arm for support. Her knees buckled, but she gathered her strength and just led him back to his tent.

"I've bandaged myself before. Just rest. It's too late for us to depart now anyway, it wouldn't be safe. We can leave at first sun tomorrow." She smiled gently. They went through the tent flaps and he crawled along the sheets, immediately falling asleep. Sulwyn carefully removed his boots and weapons before closing the tent and tying the flaps shut.

Sulwyn glanced around until she made her way into Daijiro's tent. She scoffed at his sleeping form huddled under the sheet, nudging him with the toe of her boot.

"You can't be sleeping in the middle of the afternoon," snapped Sulwyn. She prodded his leg, but he still didn't budge. Maybe if it had been night, and if that incident had not just happened, she would have let him get away with it.

"I will hurt you," said Sulwyn seriously.

"I am trying to rest. I was hit with a rock. Galahad can sleep, and I can't?"

"I want your word," said Sulwyn, ignoring him.

"My word?" He opened his eyes, crimson irises dark.

"Yes, your word." She stooped down next to him. He placed his arms behind his head, looking up at her curiously.

"I could lie, even if I give you my word."

"You won't," said Sulwyn confidently.

"My, Cailín, aren't we trusting." But she caught it again, the look that passed his eyes every so often. Ever since he had hit her by accident, he looked at her this way. A faltering, almost terrified look that she only noticed because it stood out against his otherwise confident gaze, even if it was just for a second.

"Daijiro…please."

He studied her, eyes wavering for just a moment. Passing his tongue over his lips, pursing them. "About what?"

"I don't want any more innocent people to die. They will have to leave this town."

Daijiro sat up quickly, his face suddenly much closer to her than before. She stared at him perplexed. "I told you, I have seen the proof. Tiergan was the one who set the entire thing up. And I found that cave. But what Pandora and Artaxiad choose to do with that information is all up to you. You and Galahad were injured. They will use that as an excuse to hunt down anyone in this town. It's clearly no mistake that they sent Galahad here; they've been in contact with Tiergan before. I feel a little used.

I'm the All Command now, but they did this to keep Galahad in line." Sulwyn looked down at his bruised and cut knuckles. He clenched his hands, moving them under the sheets.

Silence passed between them, then he looked at her carefully. "You have my word, Sulwyn." He stared a moment longer but soon turned away, lying back down. "You should rest too, Cailín…you've been through a lot." He didn't look at her again, and Sulwyn knew it was time to take her leave.

☙◦❧

Once night had fallen, Galahad came out of the tent. Sulwyn stood up slowly from her duty of peeling onions on the ground, one in hand.

"Daijiro?" he asked wearily.

Sulwyn shrugged, thinking back on the cuts on his hands. "He left again. I think he's trying to find physical evidence." But Sulwyn could only stare at Galahad. He looked worse than he had before he went to sleep. He only nodded and walked behind the tents into the open land. Sulwyn sat back down, knowing full well that he needed his space. She wasn't entirely sure what Tiergan had done to him but knew that the encounter had brought back his past. Galahad had the same expression as when they had come out from the lower dungeons those months ago.

By the time dinner was ready, Sulwyn got up to go find him. But as she walked behind the tents looking into the distance, she couldn't see anything. Night cast them into a dark dome, the only light from their fires. She had no idea if he was somewhere too far for the firelight to reach or not. Without hesitation, she walked forward. She would use the campfire as her guide and wouldn't stray farther than that. Sulwyn wasn't walking for long when the sound of sand beneath boots reached her ears.

"Did anyone ever tell you that you're a bit too…" started Galahad, but she smiled.

"A bit too curious? Yes."

"It's dangerous to walk in this dark. Look how far you've strayed." Sulwyn watched his eyes change back to their tricolours before she turned to where he pointed. The campfire was just a speck of light in the distance.

"Are you okay?" asked Sulwyn quietly. Was this a subject she could push? She wrapped her arms around herself, looking everywhere but straight. But he stepped closer to her.

"Take a walk with me?"

Sulwyn followed him, his eyes changing back to black. He kept pace with her, walking slowly east. The sand and grass quieted their footsteps. They walked closer to the fire, but still too far for anyone to see or hear them.

"I owe you a better apology..." he started, and she looked up at him. "You never asked me anything. All of your concern was focused on escaping, or about my past, and you didn't ask about my behaviour and attitude towards you in the Empire." He stopped and turned to face her, the blacks of his eyes receding again.

"I thought my assumption was correct. After the fight with Caldwell, Artaxiad threatened you."

"But that isn't an excuse!" He looked at her intensely. She could see the faint light of the campfire reflect in his eyes and illuminate the side of his face. He was tense and something like fear or dread etched itself on the edges of his expression.

"Sulwyn, I said terrible things. I was rude and angry, and I just wanted to keep you away."

"Galahad..."

"Listen to me, please. Artaxiad told me that my clan was alive. And in that instant, I didn't care about anything or anyone around me. I just wanted to find them. But he wouldn't tell me where they were. I couldn't be sure if he was lying but in the chance that he wasn't...I couldn't ruin this opportunity. I couldn't have more of their blood on my hands.

"He mentioned the fog town, but at the time they hadn't pinpointed it yet. His source, which now I know was Tiergan, had confirmed that people of my clan existed in this town. But if I wanted anything to do with it, I had to stay away from you." Galahad raised one of his hands, touching her cheek.

"I pushed you because I knew you could survive the Empire even if I was not there to guide you. I believed in that much. But I didn't want to hurt you..." He rubbed his thumb alongside her cheek. She knew he was keeping something about this from her. He hadn't mentioned the true reason why he was demoted from All Command, or about the deaths that had happened in Eques since he started living there. But she would wait.

"If you were referring to when you slapped me, don't apologize for that," said Sulwyn, taking his hand in hers. "I was out of line, I talked about things I knew nothing of to purposely try and provoke you. I wanted to know what happened when the black touched your irises."

She looked at him steadily. "I doubted it. Half of me believed you were lying. But in the end, just like with Raghnall, I chose to believe in the part that I thought was right. I think there was more to his betrayal, just like I thought there was more to yours."

"That's reckless of you."

"I was told I have great instincts. Let's go with that," smiled Sulwyn. Galahad smiled as well, but she could still see the pain his eyes carried until he gave her a scrutinizing gaze.

"Why did you sneak around the Solus?" he berated her, and she just laughed.

"Have you been dying to ask me that?"

"Sulwyn..."

"I wanted to do my job and investigate. And now that I've found my answer, I'll clear the rumours of Caldwell and then we can both move on." They continued to walk again, this time hand in hand. She felt the heat rise in her neck but focused her attention on their conversation.

"Fine, but you need to be careful. All kinds of people run around the Empire..."

"I know, I met Daijiro the night I went to the Pain Cells. Are you going to reprimand me for exploring Eques as well? That run-in was also Daijiro's fault. Are they sure he should be the All Command? Let alone my fiancé?

I'll end up killing him." Sulwyn looked down as Galahad clenched her hand a little tighter.

"Tell me more about your nomination?" He changed the topic unabashedly.

Sulwyn turned to him. "Kione…" but she stopped. "Galahad…his sister is that woman, Diesirae. She was the person in my visions."

"But she's not a Devinal?"

"No, whoever that is, it's someone else. And they are in the Empire too. But how am I supposed to tell Kione about his sister?" she fretted, but he looked at her skeptically.

"Are you sure he isn't part of it?"

"He isn't part of it," said Sulwyn defiantly. He looked at her oddly. "Kione is a good person."

"You've met Diesirae before?"

"Yes." She knew where he was going with this conversation, and she knew he was right. She hadn't sensed anything sinister from her. "But I was a bit wary of her. That day when I brought Arsinone, she met her too. Arsinone couldn't read her soul and warned me of her. But she had no issues with Kione."

He considered her for a moment. "If Arsinone gave her approval of Kione, then I guess I'll accept it. But Sulwyn, it's not easy to be accepted as a Leader. The times when we had battles were straightforward. Now everyone must approve, and he has to demonstrate not only skills in fighting but also in tactics and espionage and leadership."

"I will help him," said Sulwyn.

"You already have my vote. If you believe in him this much, then I'm sure he's worthy." He smiled lightly and Sulwyn soon realized they had walked back even closer to the camp. But she held him back, holding onto his elbow.

"What did he do to you?" She could see he knew what she was talking about. But just witnessing the fear that flashed through his eyes again made her want to forget about asking entirely.

He hesitated, breathing deeply, "I mentioned that my father had become enraged the day that Tiergan confronted him? Much like today, he lost his composure and told my parents and everyone around us that he had been punishing me. And as you heard from one of the men in the cave, it's against our laws to harm me. I often feel like that is what drove him madder still. He lost his sanity by harming me."

"Harming? Punishing? For what? How?"

"There are black spaces in my memory from when I was about five up until that same day. I was physically and mentally tormented for being a 'creation based on lies.' But I could never tell my parents. And most of it I had forgotten. I don't know where he learned it. He can bring forth a person's worst memories as well as erase them, but he never removed them all, only some. I don't know what made the ones he removed different from the others.... He also knew how to heal rather well, ensuring there was no physical proof."

"But they didn't notice you were missing?"

"I was best friends with his son, on those days I did go to play with him. And on a lot of those days, he left me alone. But sometimes he would send Aden on an errand and use that time. I think he was convinced he could beat the power out of me or get me to retaliate. If I was as powerful as my parents claimed, that should work, right?"

Even though Tiergan was no longer a threat, she knew those memories would haunt him forever. She didn't blame him for being as reserved and as nervous as he was. So she did the only thing she could think of and embraced him. Without hesitation Galahad wrapped his arms around her, holding her tightly.

"I'm sorry for all of this, Sulwyn," he whispered, but she just shook her head.

"You have no one to apologize to," muttered Sulwyn. "You aren't alone, Galahad, please remember that."

☙❧

It was late in the morning.

Most of them had decided to sleep in, while Galahad kept watch for much of the night in turn with Daijiro. While the Validus prepared to leave, Galahad excused them both and wordlessly led her back into town. They were currently in the forest behind the town facing a large mound of wood and grass on the woodland floor.

"What is this?" asked Sulwyn, but he just smiled enthusiastically. She watched him, unsure. She knew that Galahad's mind was still a battlefield of emotions. But to see him smile in such an innocent way…

"I didn't realize he was here. Sometime after you guys left to investigate the area, before Ki found me, I had gone into town. I came upon a rumour of a strange old man that lived in the forest. They wondered if he was responsible for the disappearances, because he would talk to objects." Galahad led her towards what she now realized was a tiny house.

The house was almost completely buried in ivy, leaves, and actual earth. She wasn't sure if the house was sinking or if it had always been like that. Flecks of purple paint, flaking off the aged door, littered the grass. But Galahad didn't knock. Instead, he stared at it. Until finally they heard a mysterious yelp and then the sound of a hundred bolt locks sliding back. Finally, the door opened a crack and Sulwyn could only see a tuft of purple-tinged white hair.

"Galahad! Long time no see. Okay, bye," His voice was younger-sounding than she expected, slightly high but rather energetic. He went to shut the door, but Galahad placed his boot in the doorjamb.

"It's been years since you've seen me. I'm lucky you were even here. And you know I've brought a guest along," said Galahad, humour in his voice.

"I don't want to be cursed," he replied. "Not you, no. You won't be cursed. You aren't part of his clan," he continued. Sulwyn was now beyond confused; who was he referring to?

"Neither are you, Taru, now let us in." Galahad pushed on the door and Taru huffed in annoyance. They stepped in, lowering their heads under the low door frame.

"Fine, but don't touch anything. I don't want to hear them complaining." Sulwyn looked at the small old man. He seemed to be made of nothing but olive skin and tufts of thin, light lilac messy hair. He turned to look at them both, and instantly Sulwyn was reminded of Arsinone. Taru had two different coloured eyes. One was grey and the other a light brown. She looked at Galahad, as he realized the same thing.

"Stop that!" He scuttled towards a corner of his small home.

Sulwyn took in the place, full of rickety shelves and tables. All of them were stacked with tons of various objects from pots to scarves and shoes to boxes of nails and more. Nothing matched anything. She had no idea what or why he collected any of these things.

"I told you, you can't eat it," he barked.

Sulwyn noticed the potted plant in his arms. She looked at Galahad a little uneasily, but he laughed. "This is the person I mentioned before, who would be able to look into your ability of visions. Taru can read the history of a soul."

"What?"

"Everything has a soul, even things we deem as objects, which is why he is now talking to that plant."

"Are you sure he isn't just crazy...?" whispered Sulwyn.

"Taru, I want to give Sulwyn a reading," asked Galahad politely.

"Yes but, pie is for humans," said Taru still talking to the plant.

"Taru..."

"Yes? Oh, yes! Galahad, oh, you are so much taller than when I last saw you. I stayed once I knew your clan was here in hopes of meeting you again. Your clothes don't like you." He waved him off, turning to Sulwyn with adoring eyes. Galahad just looked at his clothes.

"Princess?" asked Taru knowingly, holding out his hands. He offered her both, was she supposed to shake it?

"Give him your finger," said Galahad, moving to look at a collection of books.

Sulwyn held out her finger, and Taru pulled out a small pin, pricking it. She flinched in surprise, but he gripped her hand with strength she didn't think he was capable of.

"Listen to him carefully," said Galahad, stepping back next to her. Sulwyn looked at him, then at Taru, just as a drop of blood collected from her fingertip and fell into the palm of his hand.

Instantly his palm closed and his eyes shut, lids moving rapidly. It continued like this for what seemed like minutes. She looked back and forth between them, but Galahad didn't seem too alarmed. Suddenly, Taru gripped her hand tighter, his eyes still shut.

"The gift of premonition…" he started, his voice raspy. "During the times of the Lost World there was a group of prominent Seers who prophesized The Shift, but once they fell, the power became dormant, only passing on to those worthy from the Great Seers. You were chosen after a long sleep. Their power burns through you once a vision is collecting in your mind. Your body is given defences to stop anyone from approaching you before it unfolds, for it leaves you extremely vulnerable. If you are ever severely injured during a vision…" he trailed off, and his face wore an expression of confusion, his thin eyebrows furrowed. Sulwyn found herself holding her breath, but soon he spoke again.

"A trained Seer can keep her mind during the visions and not fall prey to this weakness. The more you open yourself to them, the more frequent they will become. Especially if you come near danger. The power derives from Artaxiad's lineage, his brother the last one before."

Sulwyn had suspected most of what he said, though she didn't know Artaxiad had a brother. But to have it confirmed in detail like this made it seem that much more real. A foreboding chill crept through her from what she had just learned. Exactly what would happen if she were defenceless during a vision? Now that she thought of it, she had never been near danger when they happened. Raghnall always made sure that she was safely away from anyone or anything when they came.

"Artaxiad has no other family left. Pandora…your will comes from Pandora. She is alarmingly strong of mind and soul, passed on to you. She has a brother still alive."

"What?"

"Pandora has no other history I can read from you."

Instantly, Taru opened his palm and dropped to the floor. Sulwyn was startled, but Galahad just bent down to slide him over to one of the many pillows that decorated the surface.

"After every reading, he falls asleep. The length varies on how large the history. He will probably wake up very soon. He slept an entire week when he read my power."

"He read yours? When?" whispered Sulwyn.

"When we were travelling, the same year I met you. We met Taru while he was on his travels as well. My parents heard about him and wanted a clear understanding of my power. It's how I learned about all these things I could do. He talked for hours on end. It was a lot to take in." He shrugged. Taru stirred, sitting up quickly.

"You can't eat pie either!" he hissed towards a small shoe. "Oh, do you want tea?"

Neither Galahad nor Sulwyn answered, but then he just pointed to them both. "Why aren't you answering?!"

"Sure! I love tea!" said Sulwyn quickly, snickering.

Once the pot boiled, he made strong honey and grass tea for himself, Galahad, Sulwyn…and the shoe.

"Ask away, girlie!" he said happily, all three of them sitting on the floor.

"That's a shoe," said Sulwyn.

"That it is," he sipped his tea.

"Can…shoes drink tea?" she asked a little uncertainly.

Taru looked at her sternly. "Of course not, girlie. He just likes the smell. He doesn't have the chance to smell a lot of good things, you know, being a shoe."

"Yes, of course, what a strange question to ask," said Sulwyn enthusiastically.

Galahad just stifled a laugh. Sulwyn pinched him. Taru looked at them closely.

"I'm glad you are safe, Galahad. Let me remind you…don't let it consume you." Taru warned, sipping his tea. Galahad nodded stiffly, not looking at either of them.

"Taru…do you know a girl named Arsinone?" asked Sulwyn hesitantly. Taru almost dropped his mug.

He smiled bittersweetly, "I did, yes…"

"Is she related to you?"

"She's my granddaughter…but I've lost her," he said sadly. Sulwyn wanted to give him every hug in existence at that moment.

"She's in the Empire," said Sulwyn. He looked up in horror. "But she is under my care and another maid that I trust." His face fell in surprise, before a wide and rather toothy grin spread across his face.

"Oh, that is wonderful! I'm so happy! When I came back to the town, there was no one there. Everything was burnt to the ground, the people were dead, and traces of Néosan littered the earth. A cat told me what happened. I was so afraid she had been killed." He cried a little, tears of happiness trickling down his crinkly chin and into his tea. Soon a comfortable silence spread between them all while they enjoyed their tea.

No sunlight could make its way into the house, but Sulwyn could sense that it was now around noon. "Galahad, should we go now?"

He nodded. "We have one more place to go to." He stood, taking her mug as well as Taru's.

Taru pushed them out of his small house, smiling widely and throwing glances and glares at two different rocks. He patted Sulwyn on the back, nodding. "You've grown up well. You have a nice soul."

"Thank you for reading my history. This was a nice experience. I hope to meet you again," said Sulwyn, bending forward and hugging him.

"Oh, my pleasure, be sure I will see you again. I think I need to leave anyway. That rock there is rather rude. I don't want to share my space with him anymore. Please take care of Arsinone for me."

"Besides that, you should leave anyway, Taru. The Empire knows the location now," warned Galahad and Taru nodded with a smile.

"Artaxiad could never touch me. Don't you worry about it. Unlike you, I am close to the All-Mother." Galahad's eyes widened, but Taru was already turning back to his house and facing the door. "How many times have I told you, you are not allowed to be purple anymore?"

XXIX

Bitter Sun & Sweet Rain
| SULWYN |

A person from Galahad's clan led them to Tiergan's house on the east side of town. It was a small, two-floored home, with wooden everything. A little run-down with a look of past luxury. Old navy paint chipping off the sides, the stone path to the front door cracking and uneven. The front door, rickety and worn.

"Why are we here?" asked Sulwyn.

"I need to see…" said Galahad, knocking on the door.

A few moments later a young woman with dark reddish-brown and white hair answered the door. She looked at Sulwyn oddly, her orange eyes judging her with a sort of disdain, before addressing Galahad instead.

"Zalika, pleasure. You are the talk of the town, yeah?" Her voice was high and rough. She opened the door wider now. She was shorter than Sulwyn, her skin a light bronze. But Sulwyn couldn't stop staring at her hair. It was long, and down to her waist in thick waves. But it had white streaks…

Galahad seemed unaware of what this could mean and just walked into the house. Sulwyn followed closely behind, even though Zalika was already closing the door. She cast a glance at Sulwyn, but only spoke to Galahad.

Sulwyn smelt something slightly bitter, if you could smell a taste. It wafted around her, the smell of bitterness and sun. Looking around for the scent as they walked, she found nothing that made sense.

The house itself was rather plain. The walls were painted in dark greys and browns with little decoration. For someone who had pretty much sold out a massive clan to the Empire, she thought he'd be living better. But then again, he was also living a lie.

"He was expecting you. I'll leave you to it." Zalika lightly brushed Galahad's arm, staring into his eyes briefly before she turned to leave. He glanced at her as she sauntered back up the stairs. Galahad frowned but turned his attention towards the open door.

The room was dark. Tiergan had been carried back to his house after yesterday's events. Sulwyn heard the civilians agree this would be suitable. They would all be leaving shortly without him.

"Galahad..." he moaned. Sulwyn could see faint spots of dried blood that hadn't come off his face. "Dante raised a good son. I am ashamed to face you." Galahad walked in farther, listening.

Sulwyn stood close behind him, looking at Tiergan in the large bed. Somehow, he aged, as if years had passed in one day. His eyes were white against the darkness of the room, staring aimlessly to the ceiling.

"I have nothing but guilt as my friend. You took my ability, the traits of our clan. I am just...human before you. Maybe I can repent for the rest of my life, for however long that is now."

Galahad remained silent, staring at Tiergan in resentment and melancholy. His hands clenched the wooden bed frame, but soon he turned and walked out of the room.

Sulwyn went to follow him, but Tiergan called out to her, "Please, princess...bring Zalika with you. She has nothing here. I managed to help her by giving her work. She doesn't deserve to wait on a punished man like me. I will find my way. Keep true to your heart, Sulwyn."

She didn't particularly want to do any favours for him but didn't want to leave someone behind when the Empire would be arriving soon. It would be safer for her if she came with them, not found by the Empire. Sulwyn stepped out of the room, closing the door behind her. "Galahad..."

"I heard." He looked towards the sound of feet against the wooden floor. Zalika was coming down the stairs. "Zalika, Tiergan has dismissed you. If you would like, you can come to the Empire with us."

Zalika's face lit up, her plump lips turning into a wide smile. "Yeah? That would be wonderful! I'll get my things." She turned and ran back up the stairs.

Galahad stared after her, but soon turned to Sulwyn. "She seems interesting?"

Sulwyn shrugged. "She clearly lacks loyalty and only glares at me. She seems to like you though. Didn't think she could keep her eyes in her head." Galahad raised a brow, and Sulwyn furrowed her own. Irritation crawled through her, why?

"Are you jealous?" he smiled at her a little slyly.

"Jealousy is not in my vocabulary," she huffed, looking away and leaning against the wall. Galahad stepped closer to her, looking down into her eyes. Carefully he placed a hand on either side of her, bracing himself against the wall.

"Are you sure?" he asked, and something about him seemed different. Sulwyn didn't like it, and this only raised her irritation. What was wrong with her? But her thoughts just trickled in when Galahad lowered his face closer to hers, his head tilted.

Sulwyn refused to face him, confusion swirling. She never felt like this before. But from the heat of his face near hers she turned to look up at him. Just as he started to move closer, he suddenly jumped back at the sound of footsteps. Sulwyn looked at him, slightly offended. Why did he want to hide his actions from Zalika?

Zalika placed her bag on the ground, going into the room to say her goodbyes and thanks to Tiergan. If she felt so indebted to him, she should have just stayed here. Finally, Galahad picked up Zalika's bag, further irritating Sulwyn.

They stood in silence until Zalika came out. "Let's go, Galahad!"

Zalika led the way out of the small house and onto the cobblestone road before linking her arms with Galahad. People passed and nodded in acknowledgement, while clan members bowed to Galahad. Suddenly Zalika pulled the bag from Galahad. "Why would you carry this?" she said and tossed it to Sulwyn. "Isn't that what the help is for?"

Sulwyn dropped the bag to the ground without a moment's hesitation and stormed off.

"Hey! What if there was something fragile in there?" called Zalika, but Sulwyn just kept walking. She regretted wanting to walk instead of riding into town since they would be travelling back to the Empire. She heard Zalika babbling in the distance; why did she have so much to talk about? She had just met Galahad!

Sulwyn could see the entrance to the town in the distance. Soon she could just ignore her while they travelled. But her thoughts were disrupted when Zalika called out to her again.

"Hey!" Zalika ran forward and yanked Sulwyn's shoulder, a dull throb flaring. Though Galahad had healed the outside of the stab wound, it was still bruised deep inside, the Kuvuli sting harder to heal. She saw Galahad just behind Zalika. A moment of worry crossed his expression but was soon replaced with a shrug.

"What?" snapped Sulwyn, taking her shoulder out of her grip.

"What is your problem with me? You aren't very nice," said Zalika, her hands on her hips.

"Do I need to be nice to you?"

"Sulwyn, why are you so riled up?" asked Galahad.

"I'm not 'riled up.' I don't know her. Why do I need to be nice to her?"

"She's going to travel with us for a while, so we might as well get along." He patted the very same shoulder. For a moment he hesitated at his actions, uncertainty crossing his face, but then his hand fell and Zalika and Galahad were walking away.

Sulwyn's heart was racing, her blood boiling, but she didn't understand why. She trudged past them both and soon arrived at the now-packed camp before them. Ki came towards her, stomping at her anger and stepping back.

Daijiro was tying his bags to his horse when Sulwyn arrived. He looked at Ki, who was pacing uneasily, and then to her.

"My, my Cailín, what's got you all riled up?" But he immediately stepped back.

"I am NOT riled up!" huffed Sulwyn. The other Validus stared just as Galahad and Zalika came forward. Daijiro narrowed his gaze at them, then looked at Sulwyn a little more carefully.

"Ah, who is the new guest?" asked Daijiro, but his tone was dangerous.

"We're bringing her back to the Empire," said Galahad nonchalantly.

"Interesting." He looked at Zalika closely, his lips turned up into a smirk.

"Hello, name's Zalika," she muttered, her tone more reserved with Daijiro. Sulwyn looked between them, her annoyance growing. So, he was interested in her too? Was she that fascinating to look at that even *Daijiro* would pay her attention?

"Why are you glaring at *me*, Cailín?" asked Daijiro, but Sulwyn grabbed her belongings and put them in Ki's saddlebags.

"I'm not glaring at you, or anyone. Feel free to look around all you like," she grumbled. Sulwyn could feel his stare lingering. She turned back to him and realized that all malice and teasing had dropped from his expression. He was staring at her in true wonder. But then the malice was back, and he directed it towards Zalika. Somehow this satisfied Sulwyn.

"I think you may be a bit mistaken here. Zalika, was it?" he said, and she glared at him. "Who will you ride with?"

"She can't even breathe near Ki, thank you," called Sulwyn, waiting to leave. Daijiro smiled.

"You heard the Lady Princess, so who else would you like to ride with?"

Zalika frowned. "Galahad, o' course...Lady Princess?"

Daijiro raised an eyebrow, looking down at her smugly. "Did you not know? I'd hold your tongue if I were you," he whispered lowly, a wicked smile gracing his lips. "Now, why don't you bow to the princess, Zalika?" His eyes flashed in the sun, but Sulwyn noticed his hand behind his back, index finger curled slightly.

Zalika hesitated, a shiver passing through her, eyes wide, until she bowed. "You're something after all, my lady."

"Good, glad we sorted that out," purred Daijiro. Sulwyn watched as he walked to his horse but stopped in front of Galahad. "Has using all that power weakened your mind?"

Galahad turned to Daijiro, surprised and confused by his words. Daijiro stared at him, his eyes boring into Galahad's, but soon he turned and got onto his horse.

"Let us leave. That group ran off so we should be fine, but we want to pass the fog and get out into the open before the sun fully sets."

The fog was now a thin, pitiful version of itself from when they arrived a few nights ago. With Diesirae and her cult gone to who knows where, it seemed like the Devinal followed. If it were Sulwyn, she would have left an ambush in the fog. But at the same time, that was a typical move. However, she would report them to the Empire and gain permission to hunt them down. Sulwyn couldn't care less about the Empire but needed to stop them from harming any more people for their selfish cause.

Her stomach squirmed in discomfort. How would she tell Kione about his sister?

As they rode, all irritation and anger flowed behind her. Whatever it was that bothered her before disappeared. Without the fog, they were able to make it through Tranquillum slowly but at a good pace. By the time they reached the edges of the forest, it was already sunset. Daijiro led them off in another direction to the west, by a stream just within the thinning trees.

"We will stay here for the night. We should be able to make it to the Empire sooner at this pace," said Daijiro, dismounting. The rest followed suit, Sulwyn watching Galahad help Zalika off his horse.

"This is new! I've never done this before!" exclaimed Zalika. The other Validus looked at her doubtfully but continued with their duties. Even Demir was a little wary of her. So why was Galahad paying her attention?

"Cailín?" said Daijiro, suddenly in front of her, holding out one of the empty water buckets.

"Why does it smell bitter again?" spat Sulwyn, annoyed. She went to grab the bucket, but Daijiro pulled it away, giving her an odd look.

"You don't seem up to the task, princess...I can ask our new member to come and gather water with me instead?" Daijiro tilted his head to the side at Sulwyn's glare.

"Go ahead, why don't you and Galahad both just go with her and sight-see in the dark forest. I'm sure that's new too," she seethed. She hated this; what the hell was wrong with her?

"On second thought, you're far more capable," he said, smirk gone. "Come with me, Sulwyn," he whispered, taking her hand and leading her towards the stream. Sulwyn didn't resist, letting him lead her to the calming sounds of clean rushing water.

"I'm not exactly surprised you're acting like this because of Galahad... but for me as well?" muttered Daijiro, but she barely heard it. She was focusing on filling the bucket, happy that the bitter smell lessened here.

"What are you talking about?" snapped Sulwyn, but Daijiro stooped next to her.

"What do you smell now?" he spoke low, softly. She stared at him for a moment. Atop her irritation, a sort of calming lull fell over her.

"Rain...but sweet and burnt wood..." said Sulwyn breathlessly.

"Then, for now, make do with that," he smiled, taking the now full water bucket from her. Daijiro turned and walked back to the camp alone as she stared after him, all her thoughts a bundle of confusion.

By the time Sulwyn decided to join them, the tents had been set up and the Validus were preparing a simple meal of bread, mead, and cheese. Sulwyn glanced at Zalika, who was sitting in a far corner of the space, leaning quietly against the tree, observing. Galahad prepared the fire while the rest of them prepared the plates.

Wordlessly Galahad handed Sulwyn a small dish of cheese and bread, smiling a little uncertainly. Sulwyn felt the rise of irritation but fought it down with the lull of sweetness that had overcome her at the river. She just needed to make it back to the Empire and have time alone. She never thought she would say that to herself.

"Do you all sleep in the tents?" asked Zalika, but Demir shook his head.

"We usually share, and someone is always on watch. We didn't bring that many tents this time as it is still warm weather."

"Why? Are they not up to your standards?" spat Sulwyn. Zalika glared but turned to Daijiro instead as he got up and sat next to Sulwyn against her tree.

"Entertain me instead, Cailín. Do you want to know where I got all these cuts from?" He teased, showing her his arms and hands while taking a sip of mead. His skin glowed in the firelight, the small red cuts dancing along his forearm. He finished his bread and cheese, placing his plate to the side. Daijiro shifted closer to her, nudging her with his shoulder.

"I assumed you were looking for evidence?" said Sulwyn shortly. He was being oddly talkative recently, that fleeting, guilty look still in his eyes from time to time.

"Close. Are you done?" He nodded to her empty plate and stood up. Daijiro held his hand out, helping her up. She turned and stared, listening closely, hearing Zalika's mumble across from her.

"Well, aren't they close?" said Zalika slyly. Galahad looked up from his own plate, his eyes narrowed.

"They are engaged," said Demir through a mouthful of bread.

"Really?" said Zalika in shock, but she only looked at Galahad, confusion in her eyes.

But Sulwyn stopped paying attention to them. She followed Daijiro back to his horse, wondering what kind of proof he could have found. He opened the bag flap, searching around until he pulled out a long leather something.

"My belt!" she gasped, taking it from him. Some of the daggers were missing, but those had been from the Empire. Her unique collection of blades were still in their holsters. She had no words for him. Though the belt was old, it was the one Raghnall had made her when she was finally able to handle each one of these blades.

Sulwyn looked up at him curiously. "Why?"

He made no sense to her. Daijiro had terrified her, but during their meetings and during this trip she had learned that he was far more complicated than he seemed. Just like Galahad and just like Caldwell, he was a by-product of the Empire. But unlike those two, she had no idea what his motive was and where he really stood.

"It doesn't take a genius to know it has sentimental value. It's not nice when you lose the things closest to you," shrugged Daijiro, absentmindedly touching the necklace she knew was hidden under his shirt, "I came across it in the caves amongst other things that I'll be reporting to the Empire once we get back."

Sulwyn looked at him—that same curious stare was in his eyes. No malice, no anger, nothing. Just complete wonder and a bit of confusion. "Thank you," she muttered, wrapping the belt around her waist.

"We'll need to fill the rest in with more weapons, but you can make do with those," he smirked, gesturing to go back to the fire.

એન્જી

A few days passed in strained silence and awkward encounters. Sulwyn rose with the sun and the distant sound of birds and animals scurrying unseen. This would be the last time she awoke outside before they got back to the Empire.

The other Validus switched out during their turn to watch and Zalika made a scene about getting a tent to herself. The Validus found this rather disrespectful to the Lady Princess but could not argue on her behalf, since they knew she didn't want a tent anyway.

"Lady Princess?" said Demir, crouching near her, "you always rise first. You rise earlier than the prince," he pointed out, walking away to wake the others. Sulwyn sat up, a little disgruntled but well-rested.

Within less than an hour, they quickly ate, refilled the bottles, and dismantled their camp. It was still dark as they took off at a light jog out of the forest and through the open terrain of sand and grass. A cool mist hung low over them in the early morning, the sun yet to rise. Sulwyn didn't really like mornings, but she enjoyed it when the weather outside was like this, the air fresh and crisp. She smiled, inhaling deeply, until her moment of peace was shattered by Zalika's voice.

"Geez, my back hurts. How do you all do this for so long? Galahad, doesn't your back hurt? You don't even sleep in a tent!" Her voice was loud and grating to Sulwyn so early in the morning.

"Zalika, it would be best if you kept your voice low," called Sulwyn.

Zalika turned to look around Galahad. "You aren't that quiet yourself, though?" But Zalika caught Daijiro's eye, faltering. "I apologize, you're right...I'll keep my voice low."

Sulwyn stared at Daijiro his eyes boring into Zalika's with a sort of warning. Maybe it was the morning or the fact that she had gotten some sleep, but the thoughts that were gnawing and jumbled in her mind before were making their way through clearly.

Zalika had white in her hair just like Daijiro. What made it stand out to her the first time she saw Daijiro was that it didn't just look like fashionably added streaks. It was intricately weaved in between his dark golden blonds in a way that no one could create unless natural. Zalika's hair did the same thing. It wasn't rare for people to have odd colours or more than one, like Arsinone who had indigo hair or even herself with a violet tint to hers. But what if white was a Velyūn trait?

ॐ

It was late in the afternoon, the sun low in the sky, but they were almost near the Empire. Sulwyn could faintly see the high black walls that encased it in the far distance. As much as she hated it, this place was somewhat home, and she was looking forward to seeing the girls and Kione.

"We should slow down a bit, we're losing light and we're only a couple hours away at this pace," started Demir, but Sulwyn only heard him in the background of her mind. Far quicker than she had ever experienced, the heat grew within her again. Opening herself up to visions made her more susceptible, but did letting Taru read her soul, open her to vulnerabilities? This was not the place to fall victim to her own ability. She needed to stay focused.

"Cailín?" said Daijiro from her left. He had fallen back to ride in stride with her, Galahad taking the front alongside Demir and another Validus. She turned to look at him. This wasn't good. How could she have a vision and stay on her horse? Ki neighed restlessly at her unease.

One breath at a time.

Eyes narrowed, Daijiro moved closer to her, reaching out for her hand, his awareness alarming. Sulwyn automatically pulled away, but he was too fast and caught her wrist. Alarm crossed his face, and he turned to look at Galahad as if to say something. But Sulwyn cut him off.

"I'm fine, Daijiro," said Sulwyn quietly, taking her hand back. She would have to force herself to stay conscious like she did in the Solus, no matter how hard it was or how painful it was. Taru said one could be trained, she'd just have to hope she could do it now. But the heat was rising rapidly. She looked at Daijiro again. "If...if I happen to pass out, just keep Ki straight."

"What—" but Daijiro was cut short when an arrow flew past them both and landed in the grass behind them. Sulwyn and Daijiro looked forward at a giant haze of dark purple rising in haste and encompassing them in a vast circle. They could no longer see the Empire, the fog blocking out the setting sun and the rest of the terrain around them.

Daijiro galloped forward, and instantly the Validus went into a protective formation covering each other's backs and front.

"What's this? What's happening?" Panicked, Zalika was turning this way and that. Sulwyn narrowed her gaze to Galahad, who for the first time seemed caught in a daze.

"Galahad?" whimpered Zalika, clinging to Galahad's thighs. Sulwyn's irritation rose along with her fever. How could Galahad be hesitant in a moment like this?

"Shut up, newcomer!" demanded Daijiro, looking around wildly. Before any of them could react, a rain of arrows shot through the sky, some with fire, some without. Their formation broke apart, swords out trying to knock the arrows away. Sulwyn's longest weapon was a short blade, but she still managed to hit an arrow astray.

"It's them, it has to be!" called Sulwyn. Daijiro turned to her, but with them caught in the haze they only had two options. "We either sit and wait, or we ride them out," said Sulwyn loudly, and she knew the rest of them agreed with her.

"We ride it out then," decided Daijiro, moving to the front.

"Are you people insane?!" squealed Zalika, squirming on the horse. She turned around and clutched onto Galahad, who looked down at her in surprise.

"Galahad, you need to go to the back," demanded Daijiro, but Zalika was distracting him and making their horse unsteady.

"You go to the back. We don't have time for this!" ordered Sulwyn, just as another rain of arrows launched into the sky. He cast Sulwyn a worried glance, but without warning, she rode forward.

"Sulwyn!" yelled Daijiro impatiently, but Ki picked up the pace.

If she could end Diesirae now, then she could deal with the others later. The onslaught of arrows came down upon them. The Validus rode forward, moving past or knocking them back, and continued. Sulwyn heard laughter just before more arrows fell. The circle of purple haze encroached further, bringing the hidden attackers closer. Suddenly, at that moment, several things happened all at once.

A pain shot through her already injured shoulder, the burning pull of an enflamed arrow ripping through her. Yells from not only in the distance but in her head erupted. The heat from the arrow and the heat from within her rose to their peak and she found herself lost between consciousness and her vision as they both flashed before her.

Sulwyn grunted out, biting her tongue to keep herself in the present. Needing to stay in the moment and not black out. She had done it once before and she would do it again now. But the effort was straining on her already injured body.

Like a strange sort of layered dream, Diesirae and about twenty or so of her people emerged from the mist in front of her, while colours and a scene that had yet to happen played through her mind. But she couldn't decipher it.

Red passed over her, as fabric or as blood she didn't know. Green eyes bore into her own, a grin of evil before her and pain searing through her skin until all she could feel in the end was the heaviness of her own body.

Sulwyn collapsed forward slumping onto Ki. He slowed his pace and turned back around towards the Validus. But even as he turned slowly, Sulwyn slipped off the saddle with her boot caught in the stirrup.

She managed to hold onto her consciousness, but the pain from both the arrow and her mind was unbearable and hot. She hung limply on the side of Ki, her hair dragging onto the grass. Quickly she lifted herself up, her stomach burning with the effort to hold herself upright through the agony. She freed her boot and dropped, rolling, onto the ground. Ki jumped over her and away, circling her carefully.

The Validus flanked her just as Diesirae put her hand up. The people paused their assault, the bows nocked and aimed, ready for her call.

"Galahad! What the hell are you doing?" she heard Daijiro yell, and turned to see him jumping off his horse, running towards her.

Sulwyn couldn't move. An uncomfortable tingle had spread throughout her body, and it was only then she realized the arrow was still in her shoulder. Daijiro knelt next to her, and for once his face was pale and void of any emotion. She looked down at him and noticed he had been scratched by an arrow on the side of his chest. Blood seeped through his yellow tunic. But for once he wasn't affected by his bloodlust.

"You're bleeding," mumbled Sulwyn, each time she blinked, her vision blacked out, taking longer to focus.

"So are you," he grunted, bringing his hands to her shoulder and looking at her wound. "You have two-coloured eyes, by the way..."

"What?"

"One is grey, the other is green," said Daijiro, turning around. The Validus stood in front of them, waiting, but Diesirae remained still. Sulwyn looked past Daijiro to see Zalika still latched onto Galahad. He had yet to come off his horse, his face impassive. But her annoyance wouldn't rise any further and instead turned to anger.

"Hey!" said Daijiro holding his arms out for her to grab. She forced herself to sit, the numbness spreading, and a new sound was growing in her. A quiet, soothing, distorted kind of voice.

YOU LOOK LIKE YOU'RE IN PAIN.

This was different than Arsinone. She had no direct link to this new voice. They projected their voice into her mind. It made her head spin, a kind of buzz wrapped around it.

COME WITH US, WE CAN EASE IT FOR YOU.

WE CAN HELP YOU, TOO.

ARTAXIAD IS A FOOL.

HE IS DRUNK WITH POWER, WITH GREED.

HE IS NO LONGER ENOUGH.

THEY ARE NOT ENOUGH.

BUT YOU.

YOU ARE FRESH.

YOU HAVE BLOOD STRONGER THAN HIS.

"Face me!" shrieked Sulwyn, startling Daijiro. She grabbed onto his arm, sitting up properly now.

"Told you she was impatient," called Diesirae. So that was the Devinal behind her then, this voice that whispered sweetness into her mind: *"Let us persuade her more..."* Diesirae brought her hand down and arrows flew again.

Daijiro kneeled forward, knocking away the arrows that aimed themselves towards Sulwyn and the Validus in front of her. Sulwyn stood up quickly; it didn't matter if she couldn't feel her body—she knew how to move, and she would force it to do so.

She pushed Daijiro aside and stood in front of him. But suddenly a small row of fire-tipped arrows came towards her. The Validus knocked most away, but Sulwyn slipped, an arrow scraping past her thigh and the fire catching on her clothes.

"Move back!" yelled Daijiro to the Validus, and without warning, he placed his bare hand onto the fire. Instantly it diminished and instead grew within his own palm. They looked at each other. Both astonished. But the flame faltered and disappeared into tiny balls of light before fading away completely.

"What happened to the great prince?" jeered Diesirae stepping forward. Daijiro and Sulwyn faced her. Sulwyn tried to stay focused, but Daijiro braced her back with one of his hands.

Daijiro turned to look at Galahad and Zalika, "Newcomer, I'm warning you now. Drop it."

Sulwyn turned to Daijiro, his hand warm on her lower back. The heat of it kept her steady, like the fire was still in his hands, but she looked past him to see his glare on Zalika while Galahad looked utterly lost. Though fear crossed her, Zalika huffed and let go of Galahad. Instantly he looked up to find Sulwyn's eyes. A strange cloud of confusion dropped from his expression, soon replaced with fear and anger.

"Honestly, I expected more from both of you," grumbled Daijiro impatiently before facing Diesirae and her group. The sun had set completely, leaving only a half moon's light in the sky. The purple haze continued to float around them, keeping this attack away from the watchtowers of the Empire.

"We do not mean any harm. We have come to negotiate," said Diesirae, arms up. Sulwyn noticed the thick bandage wrapped around her stomach, but she seemed to be doing quite well. Whoever the Devinal was, they were powerful.

JOIN US, PRINCESS…FOR AN EVOLVED EMPIRE…

WE ARE ON THE SAME SIDE.

Sulwyn froze, the voice pulled at her far stronger than it had the first time. It was still distorted, but it had a sort of calm, honey-like feeling.

And it felt right.

They did fight for the same cause. They had strength, something she needed more of if she wanted to take back the Empire. The numbness was overbearing, and the pain in her shoulder and thigh burned from the poison of Diesirae's clan.

She was tired. But somehow, she felt clearer, the explosion in her mind easing.

"Sulwyn," called Daijiro as she started to walk forward.

She lived in the Empire. She couldn't trust anyone there. Just like she couldn't trust anyone here or the voice. But then that made them all the same, didn't it? She would just have to make sure to survive and use this group for their power. How was this any different?

"You are a good girl…" whispered Diesirae. She stepped forward, holding her arms out for Sulwyn.

"Sulwyn!" yelled Galahad, his voice echoed alongside Daijiro's. She could hear the panic in Galahad's voice and the anger in Daijiro's. But they were the same. People she barely knew.

Yes, this was the same.

It didn't matter where she stood so long as it was against the Empire.

XXX

A Fallen Star
| SULWYN |

DIESIRAE stepped closer to Sulwyn, her arms ready to embrace. "Oh? Did you always have two different coloured eyes?"

Sulwyn could feel herself walking forward. Feel her tiredness ebbing through her. Voices called to her, but just like the haze they were behind, it came through in broken tones.

"See? I knew I liked you from the start. Kione was right to trust you," said Diesirae just as Sulwyn stepped in front of her. Sulwyn lifted her head to meet Diesirae's gaze.

"No!" barked Sulwyn, reaching for one of her oldest daggers. It had two blades joined by a piece of metal, creating two points at the end. Created for quick kills. Sulwyn quickly jabbed forward, but Diesirae stepped back. Sulwyn only managed to scratch her neck, though deep enough for it to bleed a trickle.

"Payback for that cut on my neck. You think Kione will be happy that you are doing this?" said Sulwyn as she tried again, but Diesirae dodged and pulled on the arrow that protruded out of Sulwyn's shoulder.

Sulwyn screamed, as the flesh caught on the head of the arrow. She kicked weakly, creating space between them, and then she reached up and snapped the shaft of the arrow.

"You will not tell Kione anything because you will not want to cause him pain with the knowledge of this," she tutted. "You are a reckless girl. Just like your mentor."

Sulwyn threw the wooden shaft of the arrow at her, "I learned from the best."

"I'm tired of this," called Daijiro suddenly. Controlling her, Daijiro quickly moved Sulwyn back to his side, meeting her halfway.

"Sulwyn…" said Galahad, but Sulwyn shrugged him off.

"Do not touch me." She growled. The irritation was low now, but she finally understood what had happened. Zalika was also a Velyūn, and they both played into whatever power she had. She expected herself to fall for it, but Galahad had spent years with Daijiro. Shouldn't he have been desensitized? He looked at her with regret but didn't try to touch her again.

"Bring her to our side," called the disembodied voice around them. Daijiro stood in front of Sulwyn, Galahad moving beside him. Instantly the Validus moved to stand behind them, flanking them on either side.

"You do not think you can actually fight us?" asked Diesirae. "We outnumber you. And prince, there is no one here from your clan to side with you. Your princess is injured, and the eyes of the Empire cannot see us. If you do not want this to get messy, I suggest you do as we ask." She smirked.

Galahad made to unsheathe his sword, but Daijiro held him back, whispering, "It's night now, I don't have your eyes." Galahad eyed him in shock. "I will be the distraction, you will take our Cailín and leave this haze."

Sulwyn looked at them, unable to fight any fault in his plan. They had no choice. They were at a severe disadvantage. Just then the heat rose in her again all at once. Throbbing pain and flashes of images she couldn't comprehend flew through her mind. She let out a scream that echoed around them, unable to hold it back, falling to the ground.

঵঵

| GALAHAD |

"What's wrong with her?" said Daijiro. Even Diesirae looked on in slight confusion, keeping her people back.

Galahad bent forward, lifting her lids, her eyes changing slowly from grey to green and back again. He touched her skin and it burned against his. He looked at Daijiro.

"She had a fever before the arrow hit her," said Daijiro suddenly.

"No…" He could hear the fear in his own voice, Taru's words in his mind. Daijiro turned to face their enemies.

"That is quite the look…" said Diesirae. "I do not know much about you, Leader of Uferor Divi. Are you going to play with me?" She smirked, but it faltered when Daijiro suddenly smiled widely.

"What is this?" she called out in panic, eyes narrowed, realising she was unable to move.

"Oh, the tiger panics, does she? You seem pretty fierce, got a nice group following you around." Daijiro walked forward, arms crossed "What happens when I prostrate you to them?" Daijiro held his palm out and flicked a finger down. Diesirae grunted, falling to her knees.

"So you can control people at your will?" she gritted, but Daijiro laughed and pointed his fingers up.

"Unfortunately, you'll wish that's all it was." He motioned a twist with his hand and instantly Diesirae screamed, hers louder than Sulwyn's. He slackened his hand and Diesirae dropped forward, her face in the grass. The other members of her group stared in fear.

"Attack him. However you like!" choked Diesirae, forcing herself up. But she faltered at the ecstatic look on Daijiro's face.

He held both hands forward, holding the movements of all the people in front of them. None of them could move and only terror etched its way onto their faces. "Haven't had this much fun in a while."

"Daijiro!" called Galahad, turning away from Daijiro and looking down. Sulwyn was convulsing.

"Take her, the rest of you cover him," demanded Daijiro. Galahad picked up Sulwyn, holding her tightly against him, but she continued to shake, her skin growing cold.

"Demir!" he called, just as Ki came forward kneeling in front of him. Demir helped him lift Sulwyn onto the horse. Galahad sat behind her and unsheathed his sword.

"Wait!" called Zalika, but Galahad didn't turn to look at her. How had it taken him so long to realize that she had similar powers to Daijiro?

"Join Demir, move fast, or you will be left behind," said Galahad, urging Ki forward.

"How fascinating!" said another voice suddenly. They all looked forward. A man appeared from out of the haze and stood next to Diesirae as if he had been there the whole time.

He was rather tall, with broad shoulders and long limbs. Dark blue and black hair fell to his waist, held up in a high ponytail decorated lavishly with long thin ropes of purple and silver. His angular bright violet eyes stood out in contrast to his hair and his golden skin seemed to shine in the moonlight. He was regal, with a confident poise, and when he smiled, his eyes were ecstatic.

"You have a rather *fascinating* power..." said the man with a honeyed tone. Galahad turned to Daijiro.

❦

| DAIJIRO |

"You're the Devinal, I assume?" said Daijiro gruffly, keeping his hold on the others. Should he attempt to control him too?

"You're quick. I'd expect nothing less from a man of the Empire." The man jeered.

"Galahad." Daijiro's voice was low.

"I'm ready."

"As a man of the Empire I am a lot of things," said Daijiro. He walked forward until he was in the middle of their no man's land. "But I do not have the time to list it off for you."

"Daijiro..." Sulwyn breathed deeply. Daijiro and Galahad looked at her, her eyes mixed with grey and green. "Don't kill Diesirae..."

Daijiro's face softened a little. "If you've asked it of me, Cailín..." he sighed in defeat, and laughed, "but it's still going to be painful." Daijiro curled his fingers in slowly, and all the people and Diesirae screamed in pain. The sound of cracking echoed amongst them.

"I didn't forget about you, Devinal." Daijiro maintained his hold on the others but used one hand solely dedicated for the man in front of him. He wasn't sure what it was about him, but he seemed familiar and different. And he looked genuinely surprised that his power could reach him.

"Interesting." He grunted until he too was clenched in pain, though he barely showed it. Daijiro clapped his hands together and every single member fell to their knees. He could break bones and tear muscle, but his most favourite thing to target was the nerves. Though he could not physically damage those, the pain he could create was more than enough.

ào∞

| GALAHAD |

Galahad took off and guided Ki far around the people on the ground. The Validus followed suit, taking off at a gallop. Though they had been about an hour away at their leisurely trot, at this pace they would reach the Empire in no time. In a few minutes, the faint moonlight and the stars shone over them as they exited the haze, but too soon another haze was before them, disguised as low clouds. The Validus faltered, and Galahad let his eyes change.

After suppressing his abilities for so long, when power seeped into his eyes, it burned like grainy dust. But with each change, the sensation became weaker and weaker, until now he barely realised it was happening anymore.

"We have no choice but to go through!" he beckoned, but looked down; Sulwyn coughed out blood. "We need to move fast, Ki," he whispered to the horse. They galloped quicker; running in front of the others, but inside the haze, Galahad could see about fifty more people.

"There are enemies in the haze!" he warned, and swung his sword down, impaling a man as he passed. Galahad was the only one who could see clearly and could only hope that the other men could make it through. But soon the haze dispersed in a flash, small dust sparkling in the reflection of the stars and floating around them, stunning the people hidden within; but they fought on.

"Galahad! Leave them, go and raise the alarm!" yelled Daijiro in the distance. Galahad turned to see him galloping quickly towards them but looked past Daijiro to see Diesirae and the rest slowly charging after him.

Galahad looked forward, the high black walls in clear view. The watchtowers should be able to see them now. He slashed through a few more people, unsure if they were male or female until he was finally close enough.

"The Empire is under attack! The Blood Princess is injured!" bellowed Galahad, but he knew they had already started to move. Massive, mirrored torch lights flooded the front of the Empire walls, a horn sounding throughout the night. The gigantic black walls opened, sliding to the side to reveal a hundred or so Néosan and Captains alike.

They parted, letting Galahad and the other Validus through, Daijiro coming from the rear. The Néosan closed their ranks, blocking them from the enemies, and charged to the threat. Galahad turned back to see the enemy fall back, escaping on horses hidden in the tall grass. He was sure Diesirae and that man had already escaped, leaving those people behind.

⤙⚬⤚

"What is wrong with her?" called Arsinone in Galahad's mind. He expected her and focused all his attention on her voice instead of the stares from all the Privileged as they galloped past in the still busy night.

"Bring Nori to Eques," said Galahad.

"Artaxiad will be coming," warned Arsinone, but Galahad knew he would have been the first alerted to the situation.

They reached Eques swiftly. The other Validus, getting off their horses, immediately went to gather medical supplies. Hurriedly they came out along with others from inside the castle, holding out a fabric stretcher. Ki knelt to the ground as others assisted Galahad in bringing Sulwyn slowly and carefully off Ki, lowering her onto the stretcher. Galahad noticed Zalika use that moment to slink inside Eques quietly, but he would deal with her later.

"Artaxiad's doctor is on the way," said one of the Néosan who had come out to help, watching Zalika pass with mild curiosity.

"Thank you. Please give us space," Galahad turned to the men who had travelled with them. "You deserve rest as well. Get yourselves fixed up with the doctor in Eques." They saluted him but worry seemed to leave with them.

"Sulwyn!" called Nori. Eztli, Arsinone, and Nori had all come on one horse, Kione arriving just after them.

"Before Artaxiad gets here, heal her a bit," said Galahad quietly. Nori shot him a look of fear before glancing at Daijiro. "Don't worry about him, please," begged Galahad.

Daijiro walked towards Sulwyn, grabbing some of the bandage wraps from the bag the Néosan had brought. "Magic girl." She looked at him slightly harassed and terrified, but Daijiro lowered his voice further. "That wound is not a normal one. It won't heal properly, so don't put too much energy into it."

Galahad and Daijiro exchanged looks as Kione came forward. "What happened to her?"

"Classified information, nominee," said Daijiro, but even though his tone was joking his eyes were in chaos. Galahad considered Kione for a moment but soon turned his attention back to Sulwyn. Carefully they cut her tunic; the wound on her shoulder from before had reopened, the new one going deeply through it.

"We need to get the arrowhead out first," said Nori hurriedly. They poured alcohol over her wound, washing the blood away. The skin was swollen with dark purple bruising and a yellow festering infection.

"I'll remove it," said Daijiro, his voice strained. Galahad looked at him apprehensively, but Daijiro smirked, holding up a hand. "It's not only you that has all the tricks."

He dumped the contents of the medical bag, grabbing one of the smaller forceps. Concentration laced his features, and a spark flashed between the points. Galahad narrowed his gaze. Nori and Eztli staring at Daijiro.

Arsinone and Kione stood back, waiting on guard for when Artaxiad would come close to her range of hearing.

Another spark flashed until finally, a small flame erupted and engulfed the metal. Slowly Daijiro pushed the forceps into the wound. Sulwyn flinched, trying to curl into a ball, but Nori and Galahad held her down as Eztli quickly shoved a cloth into her mouth for her to bite. Galahad watched the flames maintain shape around the forceps and around Daijiro's fingers without burning his flesh. He looked at the gash and soon, Daijiro managed to pull the arrowhead out.

"This should clean the infection that started. It's cauterized on the inside." Daijiro flinched, the fire going out. He dropped both the forceps and the arrowhead onto the ground. "Do your thing, magic girl." He stood, shaking his hand and massaging it.

Nori immediately whispered a few words, placing her hand over the wound. Soon she managed to slow the bleeding but was stopped. "You can't heal it any more than this. Artaxiad will know," warned Galahad. Nori stifled a cry, forcing herself to stop and wipe the blood from her hands.

Arsinone turned to them frantically, "Galahad. I can't hear her!"

"What? What does that mean?" said Galahad.

"I thought ya knew ya couldn't hear her anyway," said Eztli, bending closer to Sulwyn.

"No, not like that. She barred me from reading her soul, but I could still hear random thoughts or emotions. But now I can't hear anything. Nothing. Up until a moment ago I could hear fleeting things, but even that's gone!" cried Arsinone.

Galahad leaned closer to Sulwyn, touching her neck. She was no longer cold. He could feel her pulse beat slowly but strongly. He placed his hand near her nose, and her breathing was normal.

"Move," said Daijiro roughly, pushing Galahad to the side, and he knelt next to Sulwyn, by her head. Gently he placed his forehead to hers and stayed silent for a moment.

"Shit." He punched the ground hard, running his hands through his hair. The rest looked at him in alarm.

"Daijiro…" said Galahad.

Daijiro turned to him, eyes furious. "Tell me about her fevers!" demanded Daijiro, grabbing onto Galahad's shoulders.

"Don't tell me…" said Galahad, jaw clenched, not bothering to push Daijiro away.

"She's in a coma. What are those fevers?"

"She's in a coma?!" exclaimed Kione suddenly from his corner.

"Artaxiad is coming!" said Arsinone suddenly, within a few minutes they could hear the galloping of hooves. They all remained silent and still until finally, Artaxiad and his guard arrived before them.

Anger radiated around him as he dismounted. His personal guard walked along just a few steps behind. But before any of them could say anything, Galahad pushed Daijiro aside and stomped towards Artaxiad.

Just like Daijiro had done to him, Galahad grabbed the ornate black collar of Artaxiad and pulled him forward. The guards prepared to advance, but Artaxiad waved them down.

"This is your fault," growled Galahad.

Artaxiad had no smirk or smile. He looked past Galahad at Sulwyn's unconscious form on the ground, blood surrounding her.

"You sent us to that town, you knew about Tiergan and what kind of monster he was. Her condition is on you." It took everything in Galahad not to rip out the heart of the man in front of him and destroy him once and for all. Everything not to reveal himself in front of the man who had destroyed his life and the lives of those around him.

"Galahad," warned Daijiro somewhere behind him.

"I accept your blame. I didn't only send you for that purpose. You were also the group that could handle the rumours of murders and solve them. But this wasn't in my calculations either," said Artaxiad. "Blame isn't going to change what's been done. I see this as an attack on the Empire. An attack on her is an attack on us. Chaos will be born from this, and we will need to cut it down." He stepped forward, closer to Galahad. "I maintain order. I maintain rule. And I maintain your fear. I'm not ignorant to your strength, Galahad, but I went too far this time. There was another enemy I didn't account for. The few men that were caught outside our walls have already killed themselves to maintain secrecy. And this is now *all* of our problem."

Artaxiad placed his hands between Galahad's and pushed him off, straightening his clothes and waving his men to retreat. "What is her condition?"

Galahad waited for the guard to leave before he spoke. "Coma."

Artaxiad narrowed his gaze. "That…"

"Do not ask me to stay away from her again. I have already made enough sacrifices for you, and I returned, didn't I?" he barked.

"Your eyes…" spluttered Artaxiad.

Galahad stepped back, his eyes wide, but Daijiro was next to him in a second. "Look at you. You tell me to calm down…It's only at the edges…" Daijiro whispered, looking at Galahad. Artaxiad looked at them in genuine shock, but Daijiro stepped right in front of Artaxiad.

"My king, if you would just…" Daijiro reached forward quickly and tapped his index finger against his forehead. Artaxiad stared blankly before Daijiro quickly stepped back and behind Galahad. "Clear your eyes, prince."

Artaxiad shook his head for just a moment, facing Galahad again, and spoke. "Stay with her. It doesn't concern me. So long as she awakens. We have been attacked. This is treason and it will be dealt with."

Artaxiad glanced at the maids in afterthought. "You are close to her. Stay in this castle and help her recover." He looked closely at Eztli. "We'll switch you with the head chef here. My doctor will be here shortly."

Artaxiad turned to leave, glancing at Kione for just a moment before mounting his horse and galloping away.

"What did you do? Why do you have so many arbitrary powers?" said Galahad, rounding on Daijiro. But Daijiro just put a finger to his lips, smirking. Kione marched forward and aimed to punch Galahad. But he dodged quickly, making space between them.

"What's happened here?!" he yelled, visibly shaken and confused at the whole ordeal, atop the fact that he had just attacked the prince.

"Sulwyn is in a coma due to an attack on us," started Galahad, but Daijiro stepped forward, a glint in his eyes.

"He needs to learn the truth sooner or later."

"Daijiro stop…Sulwyn—"

"I know what Sulwyn would want, but this is *my* vengeance," hissed Daijiro. Galahad looked at him curiously.

"Need to know what?" said Kione cautiously, looking between them.

"That wound on her shoulder will heal slowly. Do you know why?" whispered Daijiro, stepping dangerously closer. Kione glanced at Sulwyn just as Nori and Eztli wrapped her in a blanket.

"There is a clan that embeds blood into their weapons…ever heard of it?" asked Daijiro. Kione's eyes widened. "On our mission these past few days, we met a group of *fascinating* people. You see, there is a cult of some kind sacrificing the innocent once a month to drink their blood for power…something that derived from your clan maybe?"

"I don't understand what you are talking about. We had no such clan. The only things done with blood were our weapon ceremonies and blood purification to send the dead to the Land of Hope," said Kione, clenching his fists.

Daijiro shrugged. "It's not really any of my concern. Instead, guess who decided to try something new to gain power?" purred Daijiro, now inches away from Kione's face. "Your sister."

Kione's eyes were wide with shock but soon narrowed in distrust. "Lies."

"I do not lie. When Sulwyn awakens, she will tell you. She would have told you in a nicer way, I am sure. But I am not nice. In fact, I am furious. And I am warning you." Daijiro bared his teeth, his crimson eyes begging for blood, pushing Kione back. "Choose the right side to stand on, or I will kill you."

XXXI

Not Your Enemy
| GALAHAD |

THE rest of the night passed slowly and in silence.

The nurses and head doctor in Eques set up Sulwyn in one of the spare rooms in between Galahad's and Daijiro's. The five of them watched Sulwyn's still form lying atop the softness of clean sheets. After carefully looking her over, they determined that despite the injuries she had sustained, her life was not in danger. But they could not give an answer as to her state of mind.

"Though we are not under the king's eye here, we still have to attend to our duties in this castle in the morning," said Eztli. She looked at Daijiro and Galahad a little uneasily. Galahad nodded to her in understanding as she, Arsinone, and Nori bid them good night.

Silence stretched between them, their breaths and the sound of a clock somewhere in the room ticking the seconds past. Galahad looked at Sulwyn with overwhelming guilt. Had he not been clouded by whatever it was Zalika had done to him, would he have been able to prevent this?

"Tell me about her fevers, Galahad," said Daijiro suddenly, standing up and bringing his chair closer to his. Galahad looked at him, the dim firelight reflecting in his eyes. Something had changed in him during this trip. Something Galahad never thought he would see in Daijiro.

If he was honest with himself, he had always admired something about Daijiro as well as feared him. And there was a pain in his eyes. Was it always there or did it just start to show now?

"Why does it matter to you?" asked Galahad quietly. How much could he trust him? *Could* he trust him? But Daijiro had his chance, multiple times over the last several days, to not only expose him to Tiergan but to destroy him in front of Artaxiad. Destroy everything he had been hiding. And instead, he helped him.

Daijiro glanced at him and in that moment, Galahad realized they were the same. Though he didn't know much about Daijiro at all, there was something similar about them, a shared pain that struck them both deeply, changed them completely. Galahad knew what caused his darkness, but what caused Daijiro's?

"Sulwyn has the ability of premonition," Galahad said, watching Daijiro carefully as he narrowed his eyes.

"That's not unheard of. But what does that have to do with her fevers?"

"There is a man I know. He can read the history of a soul. I took Sulwyn to him when we were in the fog town. She is a descendant of a certain clan of Seers. The fever is a defence. A novice Seer becomes vulnerable during the moment of premonition. According to him, the fever and heightened ability come in a short burst in hopes that the Seer can find safety, probably for protection. Sulwyn almost always loses consciousness during a vision and usually forgets it. But she was warned that if the vision is ever interrupted…"

They both turned to look at Sulwyn. Bruises and scratches covered her face atop thin fading lines of old scars. Her eyes were still. Dreamless. She could have passed for dead if it weren't for the subtle notes of her breathing.

"This is far from over, Galahad. If she doesn't—"

But Galahad cut him off with a glare. "She will wake up."

"We need to talk about this town and what going there truly meant," finished Daijiro.

Galahad looked down, his own mind a mess of memories blocked out for so long. "Tiergan brought us to the fog town, using the men he convinced to gallivant as Néosan to bait Caldwell. But when that was not enough, he pushed it forward by telling Artaxiad that people of my clan were in his town." The firelight burned lower now, the shadows growing around him like the suffocating darkness that was ebbing into his tired mind.

"Artaxiad made me step back from Sulwyn with this information. He knew about the town but didn't know where it was. If there is anything I know about Artaxiad, it's that he hates being led. Hates having someone use knowledge over him. I believe that's why he personally went out to find it. But because of the fog, there is no way he would have found it if Tiergan didn't want him to, and he must have met him halfway."

"Then Tiergan and the Devinal must know each other and wanted us there for a reason."

"They have to; there's no way Tiergan would have found someone like Diesirae on his own. He's been hiding this entire time since he betrayed us. I thought he was dead. He wouldn't risk himself to an alliance with a group he knows nothing about." Galahad paused for a moment, thinking. "Sulwyn said the magic over Valens felt the same as the magic used to hide that cave and create the fog."

Daijiro leaned back a bit, closing his eyes. "It does."

"I can't sense magic well, so I don't really understand what she meant."

Daijiro cocked his head to the side. "You're admitting a fault?" He smirked, but Galahad scowled. He chuckled. "The magic is the same. It feels like syrup. But it's thin. Whoever cast it here and there is well versed in it, able to fade it out so far into the background that most people don't notice it."

"Artaxiad hates Devinal," whispered Galahad.

"Then it must be someone they don't know…but regardless, whoever aided Tiergan is within the Empire, close enough to mask its castles with magic, probably to hide within it," said Daijiro, standing. "Are you staying with her, or should I?" He smirked again, but Galahad stood up as well. Daijiro conceded. "Let me know when you get tired."

"Daijiro…" started Galahad just as Daijiro reached the door. "What I experienced earlier on the way back to the Empire…"

Daijiro turned to face him properly. Galahad could see he was guarded but maintained impassiveness. "What about it?"

"You know of my secret. What is yours?" Though he asked it like a question, the demand was there. The underlying notes of wanting to trust, having to trust. Maybe if he had done this with Caldwell, he could have saved him. Though Daijiro was far from needing to be saved, he was definitely someone that their side needed.

"You don't look it, but you're as perceptive as our Cailín." He waved towards her sleeping form that was completely unaware of the conversation happening right beside her.

"Zalika has the same kind of power as you." Galahad could see the glare flash across his expression.

"Do not compare my power to someone as lowly as her. But you are not entirely wrong."

"What are you?"

Daijiro considered him for a moment, the same weight of this conversation hovering over him. But Galahad knew he was right. Something had changed and it was because of Sulwyn. He felt a prickle of jealousy go through him but pushed it down.

"A Velyūn." Galahad's eyes widened. "Based on your reaction you know what that is. A clan such as yours would be aware of ours." Daijiro clenched his jaw. "Since we're sharing a moment and bleeding our hearts out, I *was* surprised when I saw her. I thought I was the only one in existence. But maybe that was naive of me."

Galahad knew their conversation was over. Daijiro turned to the door once again but stopped when Galahad whispered, "Thank you."

Daijiro was still for just a moment, but soon he exhaled, opening and closing the door behind him.

⁎

Galahad was awake before the door opened.

He had fallen asleep with his head resting against the side of Sulwyn's bed. He looked at her. Her body had been still throughout the night. Eztli stepped into the room, a tray of clear soup in hand. She set it down, bustling through to open the curtains and windows. She looked down at Sulwyn for a moment, tears welling up but not falling. She began to massage Sulwyn's arms and legs. Eztli sighed, beginning to speak, but Daijiro walked in.

"Oh, perfect," she said upon seeing him. Daijiro had bathed and changed from his battle-worn clothes. Something Galahad had yet to do. "He looks befitting for a new day. Ya best get to it, prince," said Eztli a little nervously. Galahad looked at her in confusion. "Ya both have been summoned."

"Summoned?" asked Galahad, standing up and wincing. He had ignored his own injuries and sitting on that chair all night had not helped the situation. He stretched out, cracking limbs and shaking them out.

"The queen…" she said quietly, "she's coming to ya."

"She's coming here?" said Daijiro quickly. "She rarely comes here. She always demands that we go to her."

"She's a bit funny according to the other maids in Valens," said Eztli uneasily. "They said she's been strange all night. Best be ready before she gets here." She nodded to Galahad. She fixed Sulwyn's sheets and pillow, propping her up a little, before picking up the bowl of soup to try and feed her. She ignored them completely.

"I think the maid is angry at us," said Daijiro, but Galahad just looked at him.

❧

Daijiro stayed in the room by Sulwyn's side while Galahad left to get ready, and Eztli left after feeding her half the bowl.

Pandora was to arrive at noon, but it would be better if they were in the meeting room before she got there. Galahad re-entered the room to see Daijiro absentmindedly stroking the side of Sulwyn's head to no response. He paused when Galahad stepped in but continued anyway.

"I'm not doing anything I shouldn't be," said Daijiro, his emotions closed off to him. "And we are technically engaged." But Galahad continued to stare until finally, Daijiro stood, turning to face him.

"That engagement is just a title, Daijiro. Something to control you and Sulwyn with." He stepped forward. That pang of jealousy was coming forward again, but he still pushed it down. "If you ever harm her…" started Galahad, but Daijiro stepped right up to him.

"I can say the same to you, prince. As much as it annoys me to admit it, we obviously have a lot of things in common." Galahad was stunned by his words, but soon a small smile graced his lips as he realised they had the same thoughts.

A clock in the distance marked the hour of twelve, bringing them back to the main matter at hand. Quietly they both walked out, shutting the door on Sulwyn's sleeping form.

Daijiro and Galahad walked along the upper halls, down the many stairs, and towards the room they had had countless meetings in before. They had already messed up, failing to be in the room before her. Upon entering, the fireplace was alight despite the pleasant weather outside.

Galahad hated meeting Pandora. All year round she had a fire going. But even still, Daijiro and Galahad announced their presence, bowing before her seated form at the head of the wooden dining table.

Her eyes were closed, her head leaning against the tall back of the chair, a crystal glass of water by her side. Eztli was right, something was different about her. She seemed a little on edge but soon gestured for them to take a seat at the table. Quietly they did so, her eyes never opening.

"Our king has taken it upon himself to find the people who dared knock on our front door. You can rest assured that the weakest of this group will be dealt with immediately, but it will be up to you to aid us in finding the ones in charge." She wasted no time with pleasantries or empty words. "I want you to explain in detail what happened," she demanded. Her voice was low, almost bored. But something was strained within it.

Galahad's fists clenched under the table, Daijiro throwing him a glance. Before Daijiro could speak, Galahad asked, "Why did you send us there?"

"You know what your mission was."

"You sent me purposely to torment me. My people have been tortured enough by your games and your whims," said Galahad angrily, all calmness gone. He knew this was a dangerous road to tread but somehow seeing her sitting there so calmly raised his anger to the surface.

"Partially. You wanted to see your clan, so we let you. You are ours, Galahad. And you have been too free-willed as of recent. It's only natural to reel you back in if need be. As content as I am with you recklessly killing those who displease you, I will not have the Empire see you as a loose cannon. You have our title on your head."

"I never asked for it," he growled; his fists clenched tighter drawing blood that he felt seep under his nails. Daijiro glanced down.

"Prince…" he whispered, but Galahad paid him no attention.

"I will tell you the details, but I want answers first."

"Always a debate with you. Ask and I'll decide if I want to answer," she purred, her eyes still closed, arms folded across her chest.

"Did Tiergan lead you to my clan all those years ago?" His voice was low, but he would not let it waver.

"He gave the instructions, yes. But it was a fool's errand. He was tainted by madness. Spoke about you with hate and inconsistency. Said you were powerful in the eyes of your clan, but he knew otherwise. But if an entire clan believed your power, then it must be true. Either way, we used him to get to you as well as remove a possible threat."

"I want your word that anyone else with the eyes of my clan will be pardoned from this crime. They had nothing to do with it. Tiergan was the one who created the imposters to lead that cult group to the town, placing my clan members among them. He used them, as he always does, to get your attention and to get mine on a whim. Because of him, innocent people died."

"What cult group?" she asked, sitting upright and opening her cold grey eyes, piercing them.

"That…cannibalistic blood-drinking cult," said Galahad, irritated though he tried not to show his surprise. He was angry. Angry at them for sending him to the town. They could have sent anyone. It wouldn't have mattered, despite what Artaxiad said. Galahad wanted to know if it was intentional on their part. But all he could see was that Pandora and Artaxiad wished to open an old wound. If they didn't know about the cult, then they weren't in on the whole plan.

"Are they cannibals if they are only drinking blood?" asked Daijiro but Galahad just glared at him. Daijiro shrugged.

"They took sacrifices for their ritual. Drank the blood of the innocent, and their own, once a month to gain powers to counter the Empire, or so they believed. That is who Tiergan was aiding," spat Galahad.

"Their own blood...?" muttered Daijiro, but Galahad ignored him.

"This is the first I've heard of this. We assumed the murders and disappearances were tied with the imposters. Tiergan was a snake. It doesn't surprise me that he'd align himself with a group plotting against us. But that was not in our deal. Who leads this group?"

For once Galahad's anger faltered. Kione would be in danger once they realized the connection. He looked at Daijiro, who nodded to him. They would learn soon enough. Galahad continued. "A woman named Diesirae."

"Diesirae...Diesirae?" A sort of recognition crossed her face.

"As well as a powerful Devinal," said Daijiro.

Pandora's expression grew dark at the mention of this news. "Devinal?" she whispered, and for the first time, they both saw an expression of disbelief on her face. "Did you see the Devinal?"

"It was dark, but he was a tall man with long hair and violet eyes," said Galahad. But as soon as he spoke the words a cold trickle of foreboding struck him, creeping its way through him.

"Are you positive?" she whispered. They both nodded, watching Pandora process this information. She looked at them carefully, her expression switching from mild confusion to impassive. "What happened to Sulwyn?"

Galahad found it strange for her to ask about Sulwyn at all, but soon told her of the events regarding Sulwyn, leaving out almost everything about his clan, Sulwyn's premonitions, Daijiro, and what had transpired.

"You're not telling me everything." Her voice was cold. Galahad stayed silent, but she turned her attention to Daijiro. "Demir reported that you injured her as well?"

Daijiro looked at her fiercely. "Not intentionally...but yes."

Pandora stood up suddenly, the chair falling behind her as she banged her hands on the table. "How dare you?" she hissed out. She looked almost feral, and Galahad realized she looked strikingly like Sulwyn did when someone she cared for was harmed.

Daijiro was taken aback by this response but stood up, bowing. "It was an accident. Sulwyn intervened in my punishment of Tiergan. But I'll accept retribution if that is what you wish."

Pandora suddenly hurled the small crystal water glass towards Daijiro, missing by just an inch. It smashed somewhere behind them. Daijiro did not look up from his place when the glass whizzed by, but Pandora's next words shocked him enough to do so.

"No one else is allowed to touch her besides me. I will destroy her by my own hand when the time comes. No one else can bring her harm." she seethed.

Galahad and Daijiro stared. She was completely unhinged and neither of them knew what the cause was.

"Once your king is back and Sulwyn awakens I am sure he will want to hold the bi-monthly trials before we hold our Waning Summer Gala," she said. The topic completely shifted. "I will investigate further based on what you have told me. And Daijiro, you have been warned." Pandora swept her flowing red hair back behind her and adjusted the folds of her sweeping black dress. She stood poised again before seeing herself out of the room.

"He's here again," whispered Nori to Eztli. The sun had set, bringing night around them. It now marked the beginning of three weeks since Sulwyn had fallen into her coma. Though all of them took shifts to sit with or attempt to feed Sulwyn, Galahad had been hanging around the most, neglecting his duties and taking out his irritation when training the Néosan, training them until exhaustion.

Galahad had been sleeping at the edge of the foot of the bed, fatigued from lack of sleep and food, refusing to leave in case someone came after her or something happened to her while she slept. He kept his eyes closed as Nori and Eztli proceeded to quietly change Sulwyn's nightclothes and wipe her body down with a wet towel. A knock sounded at the door.

"Daijiro!" hissed Eztli, throwing the sheets over Sulwyn's bare body.

"What? Galahad is allowed in here while she lies naked, but I'm not?"

"He's sleeping, it doesn't count. Be respectful."

"Put a sign on the door then. Cleaning the unconscious princess." Eztli pelted a pillow at Daijiro.

"You're all very shameless around me recently, aren't you?" growled Daijiro, stepping forward. Galahad stirred, turning and opening his eyes. The torchlight around him blinded him momentarily, but he squinted up to see them all staring at him. He looked at the girls in the process of bathing and hiding Sulwyn.

"Let's go for a walk, prince. So they can attend to our lovely lady," said Daijiro smoothly. He glared at Eztli, but she stuck out her tongue at him.

They exited Eques, talking a walk through the open fields where the horses were trained behind the castle. The moon shone brightly over them, illuminating the fields in a strange whitish glow.

Daijiro pocketed his hands, looking at Galahad. He could feel the lack of sleep that hung under his eyes. "I understand we have a sort of...bond? Brotherhood? Happening between us."

"Don't call it that," said Galahad gruffly. He took a seat in the middle of the field, the grass cool under him. Daijiro joined him.

"Don't be shy. Anyway, as much as I love doing all your duties for you, the way you are right now, you'd be the least trustworthy person to protect anyone, let alone Sulwyn, if anything were to happen."

"Are you underestimating me?" he snapped, but Daijiro just punched the side of his ribs. Galahad was too slow to react, the wind knocked out of him.

"Lack of sleep can be man's greatest weakness, as I have just displayed. Get your shit together, Galahad. You make the title 'Prince' look bad, whether it is here or with your clan."

Galahad sighed, nodding reluctantly. "This isn't the only reason you're here?"

"I've let Zalika loose in Valens and in the main city." He smiled evilly. "The effect is great. So great that we have a dinner to go to tomorrow. I am in attendance as Sulwyn's fiancé. You are in attendance as a possible match for Zalika, as convinced by several of the higher council."

"What?!"

"Pandora has lost her mind. The talk going through Valens and Eques between all the servants is she has been fixating on something no one can see. She walks the castles at night muttering constantly. Artaxiad is arriving tonight. He's captured the pawns of that bitch and the Devinal. I'm not sure if this will make it better or worse. But they said she keeps muttering about treason."

"What does Zalika have to do with this?" grunted Galahad.

Daijiro looked at him carefully, almost hesitantly. "You're smart. Without realizing what I was or capable of you knew vaguely that I can…allure people into my bidding. Zalika's power is different. It preys on the hearts of only men, makes them see only her if women are of interest. But if there is someone in that person's heart the effect is stronger. And if the person in their heart is a woman with reciprocated feelings…that woman is driven to irrational jealousy. As I'm sure you realized with Sulwyn, though the result wasn't as strong. She has fantastic will."

Galahad looked at him, surprised by what he said but also a bit wary. "Sulwyn wasn't only jealous because of me."

Daijiro smirked wickedly. "It must pain you to be so perceptive."

"But it doesn't affect you?" asked Galahad, ignoring his comment.

"I am far more powerful than that tripe could ever dream of being. Her power could never touch me. But my power can affect her, unfortunately for her. She's aware of it but has no way of denying it, further showing where we stand regarding hierarchy."

"You said you thought you were the only Velyūn in existence, shouldn't you be more…happy for her? Attentive to her? Nice?"

"Just because she is one of my kind doesn't mean she is a good person. As I'm sure you understand."

"Are you a good person?" asked Galahad seriously, but regretted the words as soon as he said them. Though he and Daijiro had started a sort of "brotherhood" as Daijiro would like to call it, he was still secretive about himself. Galahad knew they were each on guard with the other, trust not fully there. And if it weren't for Sulwyn, they may have never gotten this far.

"I've been reminded recently of many things," said Daijiro quietly. "Memories I had forgotten or given up and the real reason I came to the Empire in the first place. I am by far not a good person. But I am not your enemy."

Things Change Quickly

| GALAHAD |

"I think they make a lovely pairing," said Artaxiad from above his wine glass. He looked pointedly between Galahad and Zalika. Since his return to Valens, he had been in a good mood. And it wasn't a secret as to why.

He and his guard brought back twenty-five of the people who had attacked the Empire three weeks before. However, none were part of the intimate group that surrounded Diesirae. But a win was a win no matter how small, and Galahad knew Artaxiad would use them as an example for the rest of the group.

Artaxiad turned his attention to Zalika, who had found a rather revealing dress of dark blue. Her hair, a darker shade of red compared to Pandora's, stood out against her bronze skin. Pandora had yet to speak a single word since they sat at the large dining table in Valens.

Galahad remained quiet while Artaxiad continued to compliment Zalika. Though he had just been exposed to her, the result was hard to miss. She pulled Artaxiad in with ease, though it wasn't hard with the way she looked and acted. Now that Galahad was aware of how it worked, or maybe because Sulwyn wasn't there, Zalika's power did not work on him anymore.

"I'm not sure, my king," stated Daijiro, eying Zalika down. Galahad sat next to Zalika, Daijiro directly across from her. "Her background is a little…"

"Background can change the perception of someone around you, but it doesn't always mold the person you become. We cannot judge her for living a hard life. We all came from unfavourable backgrounds and worked our way up," said Artaxiad sensibly.

"He is correct," said Pandora suddenly. "It isn't the background, it's what you do with what you learn and experience. But in my eyes, she doesn't stand out beyond any of those silly women in the Empire or elsewhere. Just another woman with a mouth."

Zalika turned her eyes on Pandora. Her flirty gaze and demeanour hardened. "It's my mouth that helped me survive these parts, my queen."

"I don't doubt it," said Pandora coldly. The servants cleared their empty dinner plates, soon replacing them with small cakes and fruits to go alongside their tea and coffee.

"Is this…coffee?" asked Zalika excitedly.

"It is, my dear girl. Have you tried it before?" asked Artaxiad, pouring the black liquid into a small cup and adding sugar and milk. He stirred it, gently handing it to her personally. Daijiro and Galahad looked at one another briefly.

"No, Tiergan mentioned it to me before, said it smelt like…a sort of burn or roasting of dry sweetness." She took a sip, and Galahad could tell she was shocked by the bitterness. But if it was distasteful, she didn't show it. He had to admit, she seemed to be in her element here.

Though he really had no idea what could come of this or why he had to sit through it in the first place, it was clear what Daijiro had said. She is at least powerful enough to tie men to her without missing a beat. But what was striking to him was Pandora's response…or lack thereof.

A loud knock resonated off the wooden doors. They all paused, turning to stare, but only Artaxiad looked up not in surprise but anticipation. One of the maids scurried to answer it, pulling the heavy door forward. A tall pale man dressed in dark greys, with short brown hair and round dark brown eyes behind square glasses, stepped in. He bowed ever so slightly, smiling as he looked up.

"I hoped I wouldn't be too late, but it looks like you are already on dessert." His voice was smooth and somewhat pleasant to listen to. Artaxiad stood up, holding his hand out for the man to clasp, Pandora standing as well. Daijiro looked towards Galahad, who also stood, though a little slower than the others.

"Gwydion, it's been a while," said Pandora, walking towards him. He took her hand in his, kissing the top gently before leading her back to her seat. Gwydion took his place next to Daijiro, who looked at the man in slight confusion.

"Daijiro, this is Gwydion, one of the Triarchy," said Artaxiad as a maid came to make the others their coffee. Gwydion held his hand out for Daijiro to take, but Daijiro just looked at him indifferently. Gwydion smiled, inclining his head to him instead.

"Galahad, it's been a long time since I've seen you. You've grown well, it seems." He accepted his cup of coffee, holding it up in a polite toast before sipping. Galahad stared, nodding silently.

Daijiro looked between them both and then looked at Zalika. "This will be a huge bi-monthly trial, I'm assuming."

"Nero was also supposed to be in attendance along with the Gala coming up," stated Pandora, "but he's been tied up by his post and an ongoing investigation. But yes, it's a big one, and I think you've proved yourself. You should come as well, Daijiro," said Pandora.

Galahad and Daijiro looked at her; her mood improved with Gwydion's arrival, but her expression had become impassive. She kept glancing at Artaxiad and Gwydion, making eye contact with neither, until finally, she was only looking at Gwydion. Galahad and Daijiro exchanged looks again, but a rapid knock on the wooden doors gained their attention. Instead of waiting for them to be opened, they were pushed forward, Eztli entering the room.

"How shameless of you to just step in without our approval!" snapped Pandora, standing up again. Eztli looked at them in fear but bowed deeply and stayed bowed.

"I'm sorry, I beg your forgiveness. However, I have urgent news," started Eztli. Galahad stood up quickly, Daijiro following suit.

"Is she okay?" asked Galahad.

Eztli took that chance to look up, nodding. "The Lady Princess has awakened!"

∽∾∽

| SULWYN |

The door burst open, Galahad and Daijiro stepping into the room. Sulwyn was propped up against a stack of pillows. Arsinone and Nori were removing the last of her bandages before Nori brought forward a large glass of water.

"Drink it slowly," she muttered, helping Sulwyn to tip the water into her mouth. Her arms were weak. Most of her muscle mass had diminished during her sleep, and she had lost weight as well. Her monthly bleeding also came and went, without her being able to take the herbal tea Wilkson had created and given her to pause it. Not the ideal time. She would need to drink that soon.

She turned to look at them as they entered in a flurry, Eztli scurrying past them with a small tray of clear soup. Sulwyn smiled softly. "Well look at you both..." Her voice was hoarse from weeks of silence. Galahad and Daijiro had healed up well just as she had, but she noted the dark circles under both of their eyes and frowned.

"Your eyes are grey again," noted Daijiro, recovering faster from the shock than Galahad. He walked in, pulled up one of the chairs next to her bed, and sat in it with one leg over the other.

"That's good to know. I didn't feel like having two-coloured eyes... No offence, Arsinone." She smiled back at her before her eyes widened.

"None taken... What? Are you in pain?" said Arsinone, suddenly looking at Sulwyn.

"No. Galahad, did you tell her?" said Sulwyn suddenly, and Galahad too had come forward into the room with them.

He placed a chair next to Daijiro and the bed. Taking a seat, he shook his head. "It completely slipped my mind."

Sulwyn turned to Arsinone, who was looking at them both a little skeptically. "You both are being really weird."

"On our mission, Galahad introduced me to an old friend of his. His name is Taru," said Sulwyn happily. Arsinone's eyes were wide until tears slowly began to fill them.

"Taru? Really? Did he have two-coloured eyes? Did he talk to everything?" she asked excitedly, her voice getting higher and higher. Sulwyn, nodding and looking at Galahad, smiled wider. Arsinone looked at him, waiting for his nod as well. She burst into tears, jumping onto the bed and tackling Sulwyn, almost knocking the glass out of her hand.

"Arsinone!" reprimanded Eztli, pulling the soup away in time.

"Did you tell him about me?" she asked through thick tears, Sulwyn just held her closely.

"I did, he was just as happy as you are. You two will see each other soon enough, I'm sure." She patted Arsinone's indigo hair softly.

"Okay, enough. She needs to start getting some real food in her. I've been feeding you small amounts of this horrible soup. Hopefully, this will be the last time," huffed Eztli. Arsinone nodded, getting off the bed.

Time passed quickly to Sulwyn, the sun already setting. She listened to what had happened after she lost consciousness, and about Pandora's sudden spiral into madness. About Artaxiad's feat, Zalika—begrudgingly—and the upcoming bi-monthly trial and Gala. She had a lot of catching up to do, not only physically but mentally as well. Her body was sore and bedridden. Her muscles felt stiff and useless; even her bones hurt. Despite not doing anything for three weeks, she felt more tired than she thought she should. Soon everyone stepped out of the room except Daijiro and Galahad.

"So…this partnership…" said Sulwyn.

"Brotherhood," corrected Daijiro, leaning back into his chair, arms behind his head. Galahad rolled his eyes but nodded all the same. Sulwyn smirked.

"Brotherhood…it's nice. Can't say I expected it. What changed both your hearts?"

"Nothing really," mumbled Galahad, but Daijiro chuckled.

"He's shy to admit that this is the friendship he always wanted with me. I must say, I'm not disinclined to it."

"Well, if you can trust each other, then I can trust you both," she muttered, looking down at her hands. In the three weeks she had been in a coma, a relationship she never thought to start blossomed right in front of her. And she knew it was for the best. There wasn't anyone else in the Empire aside from herself and Galahad who could give more assistance to their cause than Daijiro. But Daijiro wasn't like Caldwell. He carried death in his pocket, waiting for the excuse for a fight, and did not feel the threads of guilt tying him down. What was Daijiro's purpose in this?

She looked back at them, both watching her quietly. "Where is Kione?" She narrowed her eyes at their silence, "Did you tell him?"

"I wanted to wait until you woke up..." started Galahad but Daijiro stood up, fire in his eyes.

"Don't suck up to her. You know as well as I do that it was in his best interest to tell him then and there."

"*How* did you tell him?" Her tone was low, dangerous. She couldn't blame them for telling him. They didn't know how long it would take for her to awaken, and the sooner he knew, the better; but she didn't want to hurt him.

"He showed up as we were treating you. Saw the state you were in. His sister caused this, he needed to know," growled Daijiro, but he stepped back slightly. Sulwyn tossed the sheets off, slowly shifting onto the edge of the bed, her legs hanging off.

"Sulwyn..." said Galahad, but she glared at him too.

"He was innocent. He needn't have found out like that. You could have told him after..."

"After? After what? After what could have been months?" Daijiro said angrily. "He isn't a child, Sulwyn. The sooner he knew, the better. There are things he will need to prepare for too, no matter what side he chooses. And either way, he's in danger. We did him a favour," he spat.

"You still could have told him without the blood and the threats. Don't think I don't know at least that much about you." She stood up, the pain in her unused muscles screaming at her, her head wavy; but as she moved, she started to feel better. She knew they wanted to say something about it, but the challenge in her eyes silenced them. "I need to get up to speed. What is the most important thing that needs to be addressed?"

"The bi-monthly trial is tomorrow. Artaxiad moved it up a few days given the circumstances," said Galahad, still sitting. Daijiro sat back down, anger still present.

"And what exactly is wrong with Pandora?"

Daijiro and Galahad glanced at each other. "We chucked Zalika into the castle, let her run wild. But it's not affecting her the way we planned," said Daijiro, but Sulwyn just laughed dryly.

"That woman has no heart. I don't know what you guys thought you would achieve," said Sulwyn bitterly. An awkward silence passed between the three of them, none wanting to address the thoughts she knew crossed all their minds. Zalika had affected Sulwyn, but not only towards Galahad. She cleared her throat.

"However," said Daijiro, his eyes never leaving hers, "since Gwydion has come into the picture, Pandora has become pretty suspicious. Just as we left, they left together."

"So they're getting it on then, how is that suspicious? Again, she has no heart." Galahad just looked at Sulwyn a little oddly.

"Are you scandalized?" chuckled Daijiro, kicking Galahad in the shin. Galahad shot him a glare. They turned their attention to Sulwyn again, as she stretched vigorously. The taut pull of her muscles brought uneasiness to her.

Something about this whole conversation made her agitated, but she didn't know why. Maybe it was her embarrassment for falling for Zalika's power? Or her disgraceful downfall at the hands of nothing but her own ability. Or how she thought for even a fraction of a second that going to the Devinal side was a good idea.

How had she messed up so much? She didn't even remember much of her vision besides yelling and flashes of red and green, none of which made sense to her. On the battlefield, something like this happened to her. What if it happened again? What if she didn't wake up next time? She needed to learn how to keep her consciousness from now on. No matter how hard it was or how much it hurt.

"Sulwyn!" called Galahad, his voice so far away, face swimming before her, the dark ceiling behind him. She was on the floor.

Sulwyn sat up suddenly, the room tilting around her. Without warning, bile rose in her and she got up as quickly as she could. She had never been in this room, but the layout seemed similar to the ones in Valens.

She dashed across the bedroom, going outside the room to the sitting area and through a door that thankfully led to the bathing room, just making it to the toilet and vomiting.

Sulwyn leaned her head against the toilet seat, the coolness of the porcelain bringing her rising temperature down. This wasn't a fever preluding a vision. It was sickness, and rightfully so. She was wrong to have moved so quickly so soon after waking up. She looked towards the door, seeing the shadows of both men standing just outside the frame, giving her privacy.

"You need to take it slow," said Galahad lowly, peeping his head in. He went to step forward, but Sulwyn turned away.

"Leave me, please," she whispered. She knew they were exchanging silent words and glances. Something like fear rose in her. She had a bad feeling, raw and unstoppable. Almost like panic and edginess. She had been in this Empire too long and it had been too quiet. Something was coming.

XXXIII

Your Team. Your Family.
|SULWYN|

SULWYN insisted on riding with Ki to the Proelium Terra, but Daijiro and Galahad followed her closely. Since she had passed out right in front of them the night before, they refused to listen to her about feeling "okay" and "not bad." They thought she was lying.

She definitely was.

But the Empire had kept moving along without her while she was in her coma, and after a restless sleep, she realized that was why she felt this fear. The threat was not gone. It didn't settle when she was unconscious. There was no way around it besides through it and she needed to plan something drastic soon.

She had gotten into the Empire, no matter the means. It was her responsibility to use this chance to wreak havoc. She just needed to figure out how. She looked up to the skies, the Proelium Terra looming above them as they all trotted into the tunnels. The Privileged were excited, today more so as the rumour spread about the large catch of rebels against the Empire. As always, they wanted blood.

Soon everyone had assembled, Galahad, Daijiro, and Sulwyn all going to where she had sat the first time with Caldwell. Galahad's ban from the trials forgotten. In the adjacent row from them sat Gwydion. Sulwyn looked him over for a moment. He looked like a scholar as Galahad had called him before, a philosopher of some kind. His eyes connected with hers, and he inclined his head in a polite bow.

The gong resonated around them, bringing their attention to Artaxiad and Pandora. Instantly Sulwyn could tell something was wrong. Though they sat in their regular ornate chairs, Pandora's body language was closed off and tense. Her eyes furrowed, throwing glances between Artaxiad and Gwydion. Although Daijiro had mentioned she was acting bizarre, she didn't think it was like this. This Pandora lacked the usual graceful edge. She looked a little mad but not weak. If anything, she seemed more dangerous.

"We have a special trial for you all to witness today!" called Artaxiad, his arms open wide to the people in their seats. In unison, everyone started to stomp their feet. The gates opened and out trudged the people Artaxiad and his guard had captured and brought to bear their punishment. The Néosan lead them forward, pushing them to go faster, some tripping over their chains. Sulwyn could see some were bleeding or bruised. They had already received beatings.

To her understanding, these people showed up in a second barrier of haze, hidden from them, as an assault. A cheap move, the same kind she thought they would pull in the fog town when they left. Instead, they did it much after. But how much did they know? Did they even know Diesirae or the Devinal, or were they hired down the chain for a cause they didn't fully understand? They were people against the Empire, but they weren't part of her cult. So did they belong to the Devinal?

"These men and women before you attacked the Empire in an open assault. We must applaud their bravery. Their rashness. Their belief that their small power and ideals could make even a dent in our stone walls. In our force and in our will. And what do we do with men and women such as them?" he called, and the people spoke. Their hisses and taunts filled the seats around them, echoing into the distance like a horde of strange animals.

"Exactly. They must be brought to justice, made an example of," he finished.

One Néosan stood behind each attacker. And one after the other, in order from the start of their roughly laid-out rows, each Néosan brought their sword across the back of the prisoner's neck, cutting them deeply and letting them fall. They did as such so the others around them could watch in fear of their uncontrollable impending doom. This wasn't even a trial. It was just a live viewing of their mass murder of people who threatened their version of peace. Sulwyn clenched her hands into fists, anger and despair running through her, bringing waves of nausea all over again.

"What was the point of this?" bellowed Sulwyn suddenly. "You could have kept them alive for questioning. They could have aided us!" The last man fell to the ground, his blood pooling around him, soaking into the wide berth of red that seeped into the dirt ground. Artaxiad looked towards her, his smile twisting wider.

"We did question them, Sulwyn. But not only did they try to attack us, they brought a direct attack onto you, leaving you in a coma that you might never have awakened from. This is capital punishment, and their end is suitable to the lifestyle they chose to live."

Pandora stood up suddenly, touching Artaxiad's hand for attention. He stepped down, sitting back into his chair as she took over.

"They were not a threat. They were easily handled, but the one who herded them to us, the one who dared try and gather men and women to stand against us, she is our enemy. She is our threat. And like a coward, she left her people to take the fall. So instead, we must bring the fight to her wherever she may be," announced Pandora, and instant dread flooded Sulwyn before she saw Kione being led out.

"I asked you where he was!" panicked Sulwyn, looking back and forth between Daijiro and Galahad, but the shock on their faces proved they were in the dark just as much as she was.

Kione was yanked forward, his arms and legs bound in chains as he was forced to walk amongst the now-dead men and women, his feet dragging through the blood.

"This Common One, this man who believed he could step with us, is the brother of the woman who led these people, causing their death," Pandora called.

Kione was pushed onto his knees, looking at the Privileged with hate until he found Sulwyn's eyes. The look of relief, pain, and anger crossed his expression, all directed towards her. She clenched her fists tighter, the strength of it sending pain through the muscles of her arms and hands. The yelling roared around her, all of them directing their hate to him. She looked at Pandora, who looked down at him in contempt, relishing in his visible anguish.

"What—" started Sulwyn, but the man named Gwydion spoke at the same time, his voice louder than her own.

"What proof do you have that this man is involved with the woman you claim to be the leader?" Though his voice was loud enough to carry over all the cries of anger, it was calm and almost quizzical. But the challenge was there, and it was directed solely at Pandora.

Everyone in the Proelium Terra tensed. From what Sulwyn had learned, it had been several years since Gwydion had come to a bi-monthly trial, let alone back to the Empire. He presided over half of Guāngcǎi, with Nero in charge of the other half. But he held respect here in the Empire, having made his connections deep amongst the people.

Pandora turned towards his voice, her eyes wide. "The records of when they came to the Empire and registered to be official sellers in the Common One Residency. They are listed as siblings. Right under our noses, they plotted treason against us. After we let them have the opportunity to build a life here."

"What life?" demanded Sulwyn. Though every muscle in her body ached, she forced herself to stand and vault over the stone walls like she had done all those months ago. Her landing was unsteady, her knees bending into the ground. But the anger fuelled her. How dare they? How dare they force this new threat onto an innocent man? For what?

"Sulwyn!" called Daijiro. She turned to see him stand, but Galahad pulled him back down.

"This man is under MY protection!" she announced, earning the stares of everyone around them, including Gwydion and Pandora. Artaxiad stayed silent, watching. "I vouch for his innocence. To question him is to question me! Whatever his sister has done, or is part of, has nothing to do with him. He is my nomination and is under my guard. I will not allow you to condemn him like you have these people." She gestured to the dead around her, walking straight through the blood and standing next to Kione. Sulwyn turned her glare onto the Néosan, daring them to make a move against her.

"The princess seems to feel strongly about the innocence of this man, my queen," said Gwydion, his gaze never faltering. Who was this man that he felt confident to question Pandora like this?

Pandora's eyes were livid despite her cool demeanour. "If you both are so sure that this man has nothing to do with this woman named Diesirae, then you are both responsible for finding her and presenting her to me."

"With all due respect," interjected Daijiro, standing even though Galahad tried to stop him, "the Lady Princess has suffered quite enough at the hands of this woman, almost being sacrificed to their insane rituals. I don't think she needs to prove herself further in this state. I vouch for Kione as well, as does the prince. We have already agreed to let him take part in the trials to become a Leader. He has worked well as a Protector at the Solus. If anyone should oversee finding Diesirae, it should be the man who governs with deep trust over our people." He gestured to Gwydion. Sulwyn looked up at Gwydion, a sort of impressed yet bewildered expression crossing his face.

"I can't fault his logic," said Artaxiad suddenly, standing as well and agreeing with Daijiro. "Gwydion should be charged with the task of finding and delivering this woman to us."

"If it is this woman at all. We never received any solid proof," Gwydion chided.

"I am the proof," growled Sulwyn, but Gwydion smiled gently.

"Be that as it may, I am a man who deals with solid fact. I will find out the truth and those behind it," said Gwydion with a note of finality, standing.

Pandora gave them all a sweeping glance before she turned and exited the precipice without a second look.

☙❧

"How dare she," muttered Sulwyn angrily. She beckoned one of the Néosan back. "Unlock him." He looked at her like she was crazy, but she stood up straighter. "Don't make me repeat myself."

The Néosan still didn't move, looking back at the many people leaving. After Pandora walked out, the gong sounded, marking the end of what Sulwyn barely considered a trial. Artaxiad thanked them all for attending, announcing that in the next few days the Waning Summer Gala would be held, and they would celebrate her awakening and this triumphant feat together. But he soon took his leave after Pandora. Gwydion stayed back, sitting and watching them.

Sulwyn stepped forward and unsheathed the Néosan's sword, pointing it at him, the blade heavy and pulling at her wrist. "I am the princess. I do hold some sort of command here, do I not?" she demanded.

"Of course, my lady."

"Go back to your post," said Galahad suddenly as both he and Daijiro walked towards them. Sulwyn turned to Galahad.

"Why would you send him back?"

"He doesn't have the keys. They don't have the keys for someone like this, regarded as a high suspect," said Galahad, pulling out his own keys.

"I forgot you literally have the keys to everything in the Empire," she huffed, earning a laugh from Daijiro.

"Except the Solus, Cailín," said Daijiro, raising an eyebrow at her.

"Why did you help me?" asked Kione, but regret laced his words as soon as Sulwyn whipped her head around to face him. He flinched, while Galahad unchained him. As soon as he was on his feet, Sulwyn slapped him. The hit was harder than she thought she'd be capable of in her state, and it hit home. He looked at her, terror finally flooding his face and eyes.

"Sulwyn, what has happened, why has she done this? Look at all these people!" he whimpered, stepping towards her. "I never knew, I didn't think she would do this. I know she hates the Empire, but this isn't justice. She's just as bad as they are!" he hissed, panic growing, his breathing rapid.

"I don't know...Kione, I'm so sorry," muttered Sulwyn, pulling him forward into a tight embrace. Though he was much taller than she, he bent forward, crying into her shoulder. She looked at Daijiro, who had directed his attention to Gwydion. The seats were all empty, and he was the only one left in the Proelium Terra along with them.

"That was brave of you, princess," he spoke, ignoring Daijiro's stare. She turned her attention to him. Something about him bothered her. More than Pandora and Artaxiad, who wore their intentions on their sleeves for the most part. This man was strange. He seemed too calm for this lifestyle, yet everyone listened to him. Even she found a sort of solace when he spoke.

"Bravery is not needed to protect someone important to me," said Sulwyn.

"You are a rather strong woman. I'd love the honour of getting to know you better." Before she could respond, Daijiro stepped in front of her.

"She's already betrothed to me. I'm so sorry." But his tone was far from it. Galahad too had taken his stance in front of her, both blocking her from Gwydion's view. She could hear him chuckle.

"You've got yourself quite the fan club, princess. I'll see you at the Gala." She heard the folds of his clothes rustle, his shoes against the ground, until soon he too had left.

"You must vacate your home..." whispered Sulwyn, rubbing the back of Kione's head. "I thought you would have left the Empire after hearing about Diesirae."

She felt him shake his head vigorously, hugging her tighter. "I wanted to. I started packing. I know Diesirae...or well, I thought I did. But I know that if she doesn't want to be found, I won't be able to. The only one who I could trust to ask questions was in a coma by my sister's hands. I could not leave. Not when I didn't know if you would be okay."

"Okay, enough," said Daijiro, pushing his arms between them. "She's not going to tell you that you're hurting her. This isn't the time for crying."

"Daijiro, his sister is all he has, he has the right to react how he wants," snapped Sulwyn, but he was right. Kione's embrace had brought on more stiffness to her chest and arms. She just wanted her body back up to speed.

"Gwydion is in deep waters," said Galahad suddenly, but did not speak further as servants entered the Proelium Terra to dispose of the bodies and turn the earth.

"You're coming back with us," said Sulwyn, taking Kione's hand in hers. She led the way out and the four of them rode back to Eques.

∂∾∾

"I feel like this group keeps growing," said Eztli upon entering Sulwyn's room.

Before returning, Galahad went with Kione to help him gather his belongings and close shop. Kione had given away most of the things he had made to the other Common Ones around him but brought a handful of the handmade jewellery.

"Take one as payment…or better yet, for friendship," said Kione to all of them. Though Sulwyn already had one, she picked up another bracelet similar to the one she had but with a blood-red stone. She was so simple minded; her heart beat quicker as she pocketed it before anyone else realized what she had picked. Her heart was in turmoil, but that was another problem for another day. Sulwyn turned to see Eztli eyeing her, but she stayed silent, choosing a necklace of light and dark blue beads.

Galahad considered one as well, looking at the selection. "These are rather incredible." He picked up a bangle of reds and oranges, inspecting it.

Sulwyn had almost forgotten that Galahad rather liked fashion, a smile growing on her lips as she watched Galahad interact with Kione more about the process to make these. In the end, Nori chose a delicate choker of purple and black. Galahad, a thick-strapped leather bracelet with metal twisting along the length. Daijiro picked nothing but Sulwyn watched him fiddle with the necklace he always wore; an expression she couldn't read crossing his face. Arsinone didn't choose anything for herself but for Taru,

something that took her longer to do because she had to make sure whatever it was looked like it had a charming personality.

"I feel like this is your team, Sulwyn. A family of unique individuals
all trying to find the same purpose in life," said Kione suddenly, leaning
against the bed in her room. He pulled out a handful of black metal rings,
some broader than others. "I think to bring us together, to have something
that reminds us of each other. Maybe we should all wear one?" He held
out his hand.

All six of them looked at each other and at Kione. But Daijiro broke the
silence, "He basically just called us all weirdos," he sighed. "I'm surrounded by a bunch of sentimental babies." But he was the first to pluck a ring
from the pile of others. He put it on his right index finger, admiring it for a
second before gesturing for all of them to do the same.

In the end, everyone chose to wear one on the same finger and with it
vowed to protect each other and Vartugaul as they went down this path to
restoration.

"To make myself clear though, I don't really care that much about all of
you," said Daijiro with a smirk.

҈

Soon it was night, and she was alone, or so she thought until her eyes found
Galahad's. He was sitting in one of the side chairs, his expression solemn
and his body tense. Sulwyn sighed, continuing out of the bathing room,
drying her hair.

"I don't want your apology, Galahad," she said, sitting on the edge of
the bed. He faced her in silence, taking her actions in, his eyes trying to
hide what he was thinking. She didn't like it. She knew of the guilt he carried. She didn't want him to carry anymore.

"Look at me. This wasn't your fault. If anything, it was mine."

"How was it your fault? You were the victim, they wanted you.
If I hadn't been blinded…" but Sulwyn put her hand up, silencing him.

"I don't need saving. You forget I trained and lived with Raghnall my
whole life, and sometimes we didn't go on the same missions. It was my

mistake for never training myself to accept these visions. Had I learned to stay conscious and been able to evade, then this would have been avoided.

"Zalika is a power we've never experienced. I don't understand much, but I know she's—" Sulwyn stopped, looking up at Galahad. She didn't want to expose Daijiro.

"I know what she is," he said. "I know what Daijiro is now, too," he whispered. Something like irritation flickered past his face but soon it was gone, and he was looking at her once again. Galahad stood up, taking the towel from her hands and sitting next to her. Wordlessly she turned and he continued to softly dry her hair.

"He explained her power to me a few weeks ago. It's similar, but not as powerful as his. Well…according to him. She stirs jealousy in partners or those with another in their heart and can beckon men towards her."

"Fascinating…" she mumbled, reaching up to take the towel back and draping it across her legs.

She could feel his eyes on her, unspoken words and emotions passing between them, pressing on her. But Sulwyn didn't want to address this now. She had bigger things to think about than what was or wasn't between them.

"Where did you guys take Kione?" She kept her back to him and felt the bedding move as he gave her more space.

"There is another empty room down the hall. He can stay there for now. But we need to be vigilant." His tone was hard, making Sulwyn look back. "Gwydion directly defied Pandora for whatever reason. And in front of their Empire no less. She will want blood."

⁂

As each day passed, Sulwyn could feel her strength returning slowly but surely. She had started to join in on the Néosan training and quickly learned that even though she was healing she could still at least perform better than them, further proving to her that they only won because of quantity, not quality.

Eztli, Nori, and Arsinone had explained everything that transpired during her coma, and the odd friendship between Galahad and Daijiro intrigued her more than anything else. As Sulwyn walked back to Eques from the training grounds, a movement from the side of the walls gained her attention. Bracing herself, Sulwyn stepped forward but was met with a messenger.

"Lady Princess, I have a message from our king." He bowed elaborately, and she waved him to continue. "They would like you and your betrothed to attend dinner with them tonight."

"Why? Tomorrow is the Gala."

He shrugged nervously, "I'll tell them you're in agreeance. Sundown, proper dress please."

Sulwyn rolled her eyes but continued. By the time she reached Eques she only had a few hours to prepare for what she had hoped would be one of the last dinners she would have to endure with Artaxiad and Pandora for a while. Ever since the trial with Kione, she had felt unrest. Nothing good would come from a maddened queen.

Sulwyn climbed the many stairs to the top of Eques where her room sat between Daijiro's and Galahad's. She walked down the hall to where Kione was staying, his door closed to all of them. She raised a hand to knock on the door, but thought better of it, her hand falling back against her thigh. It was her fault he was in this mess. She turned back, a sound gaining her attention. Walking towards her room, she saw Daijiro's door was open. He had just returned from the Solus.

Her heart quickened, but she dismissed it, stepping forward and knocking on the open door. He turned to her, not surprised, but a gentle smirk greeted her.

"You're a mess," he purred, but she just raised an eyebrow.

"As are you. It's 'proper dress' tonight." She crossed her arms, the dirt rubbing against her skin. She was most definitely a mess, but she was in far better shape than when she first woke up from her coma. Maybe she should raise the bar and practise with a better challenge. She stepped forward, bracing her stance and watching Daijiro carefully as he rubbed the back of his golden blonde head and then his chin.

"As much as I like a fight, I can't in good conscious do it with you as you are now, Cailín. Plus, as you said, we have a dinner to get ready for." But she saw the tension rise in his shoulders as he braced himself. Unlike the first time they had fought, he seemed to take her seriously.

"This is the castle for sparring. If I want to get better faster, I think I need a real challenge." She smiled widely before running straight at him. Daijiro pulled his hands from his pockets and took her head on, blocking her punch and bracing against her kick. Quickly she aimed another punch to his gut, but he caught that too, both struggling. The heat of his hands seeped through her skin, and she shivered involuntarily.

"You aren't at a hundred percent," he noted lightly, but she could hear the underlying tone of worry. Though she had learned a lot about Galahad during their trip to the fog town, Daijiro's behaviour and change in attitude were what surprised her most, and she wanted to know where it came from.

"I don't need to be to fight with you for a little bit of practise." She pushed forward more, trying to use his weight against him, but he was more agile than she and turned her move against her. He pulled back quickly, and she stumbled forward, her balance and coordination still off.

Sulwyn cursed but brought her leg back, kicking wildly and connecting with his leg. Daijiro's knees buckled. She turned quickly and kicked his leg again, making him fall forward. But the speed of her attack threw him off and he stumbled awkwardly into the corner of a short wooden bookshelf. The side of his forehead scraped across the edge, drawing blood.

Sulwyn hesitated, feeling the air shift around her. She had messed up. Sulwyn watched his back straighten stiffly, bringing a hand to the side of his face. Blood coated the tips of his fingers and he wildly turned, his eyes flashing red with instant bloodlust. He held his hand out, paralyzing her movements and restricting her breathing. But this time, she noticed his eyes were unfocused. So his bloodlust wasn't something could control at all, even if he had changed. How did he become like this?

"Daijiro..." she struggled to speak, fighting against his hold. She managed to step closer to him, but soon he was knocked over to the side and onto the floor from a hit of rage. Galahad stood in the doorway looking at them both in fury, eyes bordering on black.

"Galahad, stop!" breathed Sulwyn, bending forward and gasping for air. She looked at Daijiro bent over on the floor, his head in his hands, breathing just as heavily as she; he looked unsettled if not traumatized. That was new.

"His instinct is to kill or be killed," said Galahad solemnly "You aren't in perfect shape to handle him and how he may change. And you," he rounded on Daijiro, "you should know better. You aren't a child, and if you care at all, you will work to control yourself better."

Sulwyn sighed. "I'm sorry I challenged you and made you bleed."

Daijiro looked at her with an apologetic smirk, but there was a deeper sadness in his eyes. "I'm sorry I wanted to kill you, but I seriously didn't mean it."

Galahad sighed, rubbing a hand over his face. "There is a dinner to attend. Get dressed."

XXXIV

Who Needs Shoes?

| SULWYN |

EZTLI alone had come to help her get dressed quickly for dinner before scurrying back to Valens to prepare for tomorrow's events. Nori and Arsinone had been moved to different sections to help all around in getting ready for the upcoming Gala that Sulwyn didn't even understand the point of. She insisted Eztli needn't worry about her dress, but was slapped with a hairbrush. "Ya know full well, if we left ya, you'd just show up in your battle wear."

Galahad left before them to begrudgingly escort Zalika to Valens while Daijiro and Sulwyn went together. She looked up at his forehead, seeing faint traces of the cut from earlier. Though they had said proper dress, Sulwyn could not be bothered with the heavy dresses they all liked to wear and instead opted for a light and silky pastel lilac dress that covered her chest and arms in decorated lace. Daijiro, in turn, wore a much fancier version of his usual unique style, with a silky long-sleeved tunic and pants, all in black, and a red scarf tied around his waist.

As they arrived in front of the familiar wooden doors to the dining room, they both froze hearing Galahad's raised voice.

"Caldwell had no ties to that impersonator group! We already discussed that they were a ploy sent by Tiergan."

"Since when do you defend Caldwell? You never showed anything but hostility towards him," scoffed Pandora.

Sulwyn didn't bother to knock, bursting through the doors, pushing them with more strength than she intended as they flew open. Sulwyn's eyes were set in a glare, taking in the guests at the table. Pandora was early and had sat in her regular seat at one head of the table. Galahad and Zalika were across each other on Pandora's left and right, respectively, and Gwydion was somewhere near the other end. But Artaxiad was not there even though he had called for this dinner.

Daijiro held his arm out for Sulwyn, who took it in an effort to look formidable as well as classy. He winked at her, his thoughts clearly the same, and led her to the chair beside Galahad before taking a seat across from her next to Zalika.

Zalika stiffened once he sat next to her, her expression disgruntled. Her primary target wasn't here, but somehow Pandora seemed more on edge. Who was Gwydion to her?

"It is only logical that it was Caldwell, as he was who led you all to those tyrants in Antac in the first place," continued Gwydion, giving Sulwyn but a glance of attention. "He had access to many towns and villages. Was rather gifted even. It wouldn't be beyond him to orchestrate this group and that cult."

"He was led there just as much as we were. You know damn well that Diesirae is behind that group. My wounds are from her. Caldwell is dead. And hiding behind a group with radical beliefs was below him," spat Sulwyn.

She paused when the maids came out with their dinner. Somehow silence fell over the table, but emotions rose high amongst them. The only one that seemed relatively calm was Gwydion. Sulwyn glanced at him every so often, and he returned those glances with curious stares.

After a few moments passed and they were well into their dinner, Gwydion spoke again. "I am in the process of proving that it was Caldwell. Isn't that better for both of us, Lady Princess? It will clear Kione's name."

"And taint another. Kione didn't choose his family, and he has nothing to do with Desirae's sick plans and whatever her goal is with that Devinal."

Gwydion sat up straighter. "What do you know about Diesirae and this Devinal? If you could tell me your side of the story, it may help me find the right person."

"I've told my story to the queen. I will not tell it again," said Sulwyn stubbornly.

"There is treason in this, no matter if it is Caldwell or Diesirae," said Pandora, her eyes boring into Gwydion's. Sulwyn looked at him, seemingly returning Pandora's gaze in mock innocence. The hairs on the back of her neck rose, a tingle of foreboding going through her.

"We shouldn't spend this dinner talking about negative things. It makes the food unpleasant," he suggested, but Pandora kept her eyes on him all the while.

"Was there a purpose to holding this dinner? The king is not even here," asked Sulwyn.

Gwydion considered her for a moment, "It was for me. Many things have changed since I've last been here. I had to make it my duty to meet you personally, Lady Princess." He bowed his head. "I'm sure your journey here was not a good one, but it's good to see you amongst the ones you belong with."

"I belong with the people who need me most," said Sulwyn.

"I adore your spunk…you are rather charming, taking after both your father and mother. Ah, does that bother you?" He faltered for a moment when Sulwyn shot him a glare, but she stayed silent. She wouldn't engage in his prattle.

The dinner ended far quicker than Sulwyn expected, and her suspicion of Gwydion only grew during this event. Zalika didn't even try to force her way into the conversation. She had toned down her actions quite a bit since the last time, especially when they noticed it didn't work on Gwydion as much as they would like. He seemed beyond her power, his mind far greater than they expected or he had nothing in his heart.

"Do not be wary of me, my queen," started Gwydion as he stood. "Our king has asked me to watch over you and this castle until his return tomorrow from his own investigations. Come, let us discuss further my plans to reveal who is truly at the head of this issue. I've already got a head start." He bowed slightly to Sulwyn, nodded to Galahad, and only glanced at Daijiro with an unknown humour playing in his eyes.

As they left, Zalika leaned back into the chair. "If I die because of you…" she turned to Daijiro, but he had no playfulness in his eyes as he regarded her.

"You will do as I will it because you have already caused enough chaos. You came to the Empire knowing full well that it is not an *ideal* place," he hissed. This silenced her. She stood suddenly in anger, taking her leave. Galahad, Daijiro, and Sulwyn stayed where they were, watching as the door closed behind her.

The maids came out to clean their plates and cups, sensing the mood and trying to leave as quickly as they could.

Sulwyn was furious.

First Kione, and now Caldwell, who couldn't even rest in death. He was by far not a good person, but how could Caldwell have any involvement? Even if he did, she knew it was only to find information. Not partake in it. But based on what he had told her, he was not even aware that there was something more than just that incident in Antac. He was just looking for his sister.

Suddenly a rising wave of nausea coursed through her, forcing a shiver. Galahad turned to her. She had been so lost in thought she didn't realize Daijiro and Galahad had been conversing together until that moment. Heat rose in her all at once, quicker than when they were leaving the fog town. She stood suddenly.

"Sulwyn, what are you feeling?" asked Galahad, standing with her, but she just shook her head and pushed out of the chair. Quickly, she kicked off her heels, hefted up the skirts of her dress, and ran towards the heavy oak doors, pulling them open haphazardly and dashing through them swiftly. The energy from her vision pushed her faster down the halls, ignoring her lingering pain, but where she was going, she had no idea.

Until she found her way in front of Galahad's original bedroom door.

But it was locked, and she was running out of time; this vision was coming on far stronger and faster. His room was the last one in the hall, but she spotted a tall ornate pedestal with some sort of bronze vase atop at the end. She ran and hid, crouching down behind it and leaning against the cold stone, forcing herself to stay conscious. But this time it was excruciating.

Sulwyn wanted to scream from the knives that coursed through her body and into her brain. This was not normal. This was the price she paid for surviving her vision and her coma. Sulwyn bit into her arm hard, trying to stifle her cries and calm her ragged breathing. Was this how it would always be from now on?

But the heat burned through her, rising higher still, higher than she normally felt. She could feel her head falling forward and her eyes rolling back, her mind fading in and out of consciousness. Suddenly a cool hand touched her forehead and another her wrist. The pain eased slightly from the hand on her forehead, but before she could register who it was, she was lifted off the floor and cradled.

"Is this your room?" said Daijiro, his voice a distant echo. "You like to collect dead plants?"

Sulwyn wanted to laugh and wasn't sure if she managed it or not because the pain coursed through her again. The hand was over her forehead once more, but she could feel it flinch at the touch of her skin.

"This is far hotter than the last time," said Daijiro, pulling his hand away, "I can't subdue her pain anymore."

"Let it run," said Sulwyn hoarsely.

Galahad placed her atop one of the large couches, and she could vaguely smell the scent of dry and musty leaves. But that couldn't distract her from the heat and knives of pain that thrummed through her very veins. She didn't know if it was better to crouch into a ball or flail or grip the edges of the cushions. So she did all three.

"No one can hear you in here," whispered Galahad, stroking her sweat-soaked hair. The messy bun had fallen out of its style and onto her shoulders, her dress just as sweaty, sticking to her skin. She groaned until her blurred vision of the ceiling was black and a scene unfolded before her.

This vision was different not only in the pain and the heat but in its clarity. She felt as if she were right there as it began to play in front of her. At first, the sounds were muffled and her vision unfocused, but soon she saw Pandora in a vacant room, music streaming under the door from a distance. Sulwyn looked around, recognizing this as one of the spare rooms for servants. They were in Valens. But Pandora was furious, fierce, and mad all at once. She rushed forward in a tangle of blue and purple silks that flowed around her, a concealed dagger in her hands.

"How dare you try to play me as a fool!" she hissed, the recipient of her fury stepping into the moonlight. Gwydion looked down at her with a smile playing wickedly across his lips.

"I admit, Diesirae is more than an acquaintance. Though I never intended for the group to grow as much as it did. We just wanted to test a theory of blood. She has a way with words like Artaxiad does. And she has aided you. Diesirae helped me bring Raghnall over. You know I can be persuasive, but even I needed help convincing someone such as he."

"Don't compare us to her! This is treason! You are trying to unravel everything we have worked hard for!"

"I want nothing to do with treason. I want to maintain peace, same as you and Artaxiad. You are hysterical, and you need to calm down."

"And who is it that made me this way?!" shrieked Pandora, her skin tinged with panicked sweat. Gwydion gave her a strange look, comprehension dawning over him.

"You chose your path, Pandora. Do not put the blame on me. Place it where it lies. Had you never given birth to Sulwyn you might have kept your sanity, you would never have become the way you are." But Gwydion's head turned to the side, contemplating, looking where Sulwyn stood unseen to all. For just a moment she thought she saw violet in his brown eyes, but then it was gone, and he was looking at Pandora.

"You do not speak of her. And I am not the only one who holds secrets, Gwydion. I've kept yours as well. What do you think will happen when Artaxiad finds out about you?"

Sulwyn watched Gwydion's expression melt from the teasing, slightly baffled look to one of cold and impassive hatred. He took a step forward.

Suddenly the colours and sounds of the room melted away until Sulwyn felt blackness and nothingness press against her eyes. A loud, clear voice erupted around her, both male and female or none at all.

"Young Seer. It is an honour to meet you. But with it comes our warning. We cannot always pull one of our own out of the darkness. You are lucky to have survived. You have proven your worth and with it, we have granted you stronger sight. You may have visions more frequently if danger is near. But there are consequences, as you have felt. Be cautious, young one, and believe and harness your gift so that you will rise stronger than before."

⚬⚬⚬

Sulwyn shivered, the coolness of clean sheets over her arms. She opened her lids slowly to the sun filtering through the vines—the only living plants in the room now. As she rubbed the sleep away, she noticed the trees had lost most of their leaves, and the smaller bushes and plants had shrivelled to dust, making a mess along the bedroom floor.

She tried to bring the sheet closer, to wrap herself more, and noticed she had been changed out of her dress and into a plain blue nightgown. Pain shot through her arms with movement and with it, memories of her vision.

Already surprised by the fact that she could even remember it, she marvelled at the clarity and then remembered the voice or voices of what must have been all the past Seers. She needed to be careful but now knew what to expect. Sulwyn pushed that aside and concentrated on her memories of the room.

Suddenly, there was a light knock on the door and Galahad gently pushed it open, carrying with him a tray with a bowl of something she realized was soup once the smell hit her.

But she sat up, the memories of her vision slamming into her all at once, "Galahad!" He looked at her in concern. "I think Gwydion might be a Devinal. The one with Diesirae."

Galahad looked at her first in shock, but then it changed to something darker. "Are you sure?"

Sulwyn hesitated. Gwydion looked nothing like the man they had described to her, but if he was a Devinal, then that would make sense. He had been hiding his true appearance all this time.

"What did you see?" he asked softly.

Sulwyn was taken aback. "You didn't hear me say it?"

Galahad crossed the large sitting area of his room to the bed, placing the tray down next to her and taking a seat at the foot.

"We both feared you had fallen back into a coma until you started crying at the end. But you said nothing, you only screamed, until at one point you were utterly silent and still. It was eerie."

Sulwyn could see the fear in him. With every movement, the pain from the night before eased. She reached forward, taking his hand in hers.

"Gwydion said he knows Diesirae and the group, though he didn't expect it to get that far, something about a theory of blood? And he had enlisted her help to meet with and persuade Raghnall with whatever it was they promised him or said." As she said this the old pain of betrayal and confusion passed through her, but with it something else. If Gwydion was a Devinal and Diesirae with her talent had difficulty reaching Raghnall, then there might be more to this than she initially realized.

"Sulwyn?"

She looked up at him carefully; she would keep this to herself for now. "They mentioned me, about me being the cost of Pandora's sanity. But Pandora cannot be threatened. She threatened him in turn with a secret of his. The look he gave her at the end..."

"But Artaxiad hates Devinal. How is it that Gwydion was employed as one of the Triarchy if this is true?"

"He doesn't know…which would make her threat that much more powerful. It's not just revealing him to the Empire, it's revealing him to *Artaxiad*."

"And Pandora kept this a secret? What could she possibly gain from keeping something like this from him? I don't know about you, but I don't think Artaxiad would see Pandora in a light of glory if she told him. That means she's been lying to him for the last thirteen years, or however long it's been since she found out the truth."

Sulwyn paused, remembering her first few encounters with Caldwell. "Caldwell mentioned that Pandora had Devinal connections…did he know about Gwydion?"

"It's possible…" Galahad took his hand from Sulwyn before gently pushing her knees down so he could lay the tray across her legs. He motioned for her to eat. "Caldwell was talented in stealth. And Gwydion knew enough about him to want to try and use him as a scapegoat for Diesirae. If Caldwell knew the truth, then it would be in Gwydion's best interest to put the blame on him."

"But he's already dead. Dead men tell no tales. What is the point of this?"

Galahad shrugged. "Maybe if they can denounce his credibility then if there is anyone he had told, they would question it. But that's stupid. Anyone who knew Caldwell knew he didn't make friends or allies."

"But he did talk to prisoners…" said Sulwyn suddenly. She looked down at her soup before scarfing it down completely. Galahad gave her an incredulous look as she bounded off the bed and ran to the bathing room. A few minutes of washing later, she was out wearing whatever she could find.

"Those are my clothes," said Galahad, a tinge of pink in his cheeks.

"Yes, well this is your room. Eztli brought all of my things to Eques. And it's either your clothes or I go gallivanting through Valens in a nightdress. Though it wouldn't be the first time." Sulwyn hiked up the pants, her feet peeking out from the bottom. The door opened again and Daijiro walked in, stopping to stare.

"Why do you wear that sash around your waist?" ask Sulwyn suddenly, shuffling over to Daijiro.

"Style? And I use it as a scarf when I get cold."

"It's summer," said Galahad.

But Daijiro tutted, "For one who grew up in the snow, you don't understand how cold it is."

"I didn't grow up in the snow any less than you and it's not cold around this time," Sulwyn deadpanned but still shuffled closer to him. Daijiro stared at her as she stepped right in front of him smiling mischievously.

"It's not cold right now. I'm borrowing this." She quickly untied and removed the black sash from around his waist, her arms wrapped around him.

"No, it's not cold right now." He mumbled down at her. Sulwyn tried to ignore the heat radiating off him as he obediently kept his arms up.

She used Daijiro's sash to hold up Galahad's pants, which in turn helped bring some shape to the overlarge tunic.

"You're wearing green, princess," noted Daijiro, refusing to make eye contact with her.

"I know." She smiled wider, then ran out of the bedroom door before they could berate her about not wearing shoes.

XXXV

So Many Tarts & Not Enough Plates

| SULWYN |

SULWYN dashed out of the room. The farther away she got from Galahad's secluded room, the closer she got to the hustle and bustle of every servant in Valens, and probably Eques, preparing for tonight's events. As she passed, wide eyes followed her, perhaps because someone other than Galahad was wearing green and that someone happened to be the Blood Princess.

Sulwyn pressed on until finally, she made her way to the kitchens. The door swung open just as she arrived, forcing her to duck down, tuck, and roll in as it closed behind her. Quickly she surveyed the area, watching the cooks and helpers run about. Stoves were cooking and boiling stews and soups, smells of baked goods and meats wafted everywhere, and steam rose to the ceiling. No one noticed her while she crawled along the old, polished wood floor, her limbs protesting. To her right she could hear Eztli giving orders, and to the left she heard the man she was looking for doing the same.

She stayed low until finally, she was just behind the cold metal counter that he stood at. Zander looked down just as she looked up, shock evident on his face. Sulwyn shushed him and pointed to one of the larger pantries. He looked around him, nodding, and beckoned her to follow. She watched him lead the way, noticing how much better he looked since the time she met him in the Solus. His light brown eyes seemed brighter, and his face had gained some weight. He opened the door wide enough for her to shuffle in, closing it quickly.

"If you wanted to draw even more attention to yourself, wearing green was the best idea." His face was laced with confusion, disbelief, and admiration all at once.

"I didn't have a choice. Looks like you fit right in though," said Sulwyn standing, giving him her hand to shake. He took it, shaking it heartily.

"You have a reason for coming here like that. We don't want to be discovered so go ahead." He smiled lightly but as she stared, a sense of recognition passed through her again, his face so very familiar.

"Have we really never met? Before the Solus, I mean," she asked, looking closely into his eyes and at the lines of his face. He considered her for a moment, but a raised voice outside the door brought them back to the task at hand.

"Never mind, I wanted to ask if Caldwell ever talked to you, or anyone you know, about anything at all." Zander hesitated but soon relaxed.

"He did a few times, asked if I had seen a certain girl during my travels. Asked how I learned to cook, just mundane things really. After a while, he stopped asking anyone anything. More reserved than anything and then well, you know what happened."

"Did he ever mention anything about..." she dropped her voice further still, "...Devinal or magic?"

He furrowed his brows, "Not that I can think of...at one point he told me that the Solus felt like mud and that Valens felt the same way, but then he looked as if he had said too much and never mentioned it again. I never understood what he was talking about."

They both turned, hearing muffled voices outside the door. Sulwyn sighed and ducked back down onto the floor, attempting to hide behind a barrel, just as the kitchen light flooded their dim pantry. Galahad was outside the door, his hand on the large brass handle. He looked on in confusion before Daijiro peeked in, smiling mischievously. "Well, well, well, Cailín. Looks like you know how to get on your knees."

Sulwyn stood up immediately, her entire body prickling in embarrassment as Daijiro roared with laughter. Galahad just sighed and waved her out, looking curiously at Zander, his eyes narrowed. Sulwyn kicked Daijiro but followed them out of the kitchen.

"Who is he?" asked Galahad once they were out of earshot and walking through the halls, servants too busy to give them more than passing bows as they passed. She had only heard of the Waning Summer Gala, but no one outside the city besides other elites was ever invited. No one knew what it was like or what they boasted. But after being in the Empire for half a year, she realized it was definitely bigger than anything she had seen or attended yet.

"I met him at the Solus…he was let out because he's supposed to be a really amazing chef, and based on that lunch we had a while back, I believe it," said Sulwyn.

"I caught him and put him in the Solus," shrugged Daijiro. Sulwyn glared at him.

"Did he at least give you a reason for running off?" asked Galahad, ignoring Daijiro.

"Caldwell used to talk to prisoners for information to find his sister. If he knew anything about Gwydion, I thought it would help us figure out why he's so hell-bent on making Caldwell out to be the culprit, but I guess it's because it's easy."

A loud bell resonated in the background, causing them to pause on their way towards Galahad's room. The bell chimed five times, signifying that there were five hours left before the Gala.

⤬

Sulwyn sat, soaking in the warm water of the bath and letting the soreness ebb away. Galahad gave her a mix he created from various herbs to soothe the body that dyed the water green. She wished she could stay in it forever but knew she needed to get on with this night.

Lost in thought, parts of her vision came back to her. The vividness of it still surprised her, and the message from the Seers still stuck in her head. She kept that bit to herself. She didn't need anyone to worry about when she was getting a vision and what it might cost. She just needed to be more vigilant.

Moments from their dinner replayed in her mind as well, until Sulwyn found herself standing suddenly just as one bell chimed in the distance.

"Sulwyn?" called a voice from the bedroom.

Quickly she got out of the tub, drying her skin and letting her hair down. Pulling on a robe, she stepped out to find Nori looking around until she spotted her—smiling, a pile of dresses in her arms. The room had been cleaned earlier, the dead leaves and ashes of plants swept away, leaving only bare trees and wild vines.

"I'm here to help you get dressed. Eztli can't leave." She gestured for her to sit, but Sulwyn could tell she needed to be quick. This Gala seemed even busier than she thought it would be. Probably since they had spilt so much blood—a sign of their believed success.

"Are the Galas always this busy?" asked Sulwyn, shifting through all the dresses, but soon huffing at the number of choices. Nori smiled shyly and rifled through them, taking some out.

"I know they used to throw grander parties often back when they had those battles and when the Triarchy was finally established. Stuff like that. Since they only have this one once a year, they usually make it rather showy." She now started holding up dresses to Sulwyn and throwing them in two different piles.

"Oh, so they don't just make a scene for every little thing."

"They want them to be special. How do you feel about this one?" asked Nori, holding out a deep scarlet one. The dress reminded her of the one they first made her wear when they had presented her to everyone in the Proelium Terra all that time ago. Except this time, the lace only decorated the top of the dress, the rest a slightly fitted silk with an adorned bodice of tiny jewels. Instead of long sleeves, it was shoulder capped in lace as well, in a way that could be worn somewhat lower and off the shoulder. It gathered around the hip area and cascaded down in folds, but she spotted a slit for easy walking. It was rather beautiful and rather ironic for her to wear something similar to the first dress. She nodded.

As usual, Nori's way of dressing was modest and simple. She kept Sulwyn's hair down for the most part, but brushed it to the side with tight curls and an elaborate red jeweled hairpin of leaves to keep it back. Nori fixed her makeup to match the night. Darker and bolder in her eyes with dark browns and golds lined in shadowy kohl, and deep, red-tinted lips. Even though she kept it modest, it was far fancier than any dress or make-up she had done thus far. It made her a little uncomfortable.

"Thank you, Nori, for helping me...I could never achieve this on my own, nothing like it." Sulwyn looked herself over in the tall mirror, admiring everything down to the high gold heels with just as many tiny jewels as her dress, if that were even possible.

"My pleasure," she smiled, giving her a light hug before she ran away to attend to last-minute business. Once Nori had taken off through the doors, Sulwyn ran back to the bathing room to gather her thigh holster. As much as she would like to just wear her belt, she figured that wouldn't bode well given that this was a celebration. She already stood out enough as it was.

Sulwyn used the folds of the long dress to hide the knives and only then did she feel lighter. This weight that bore down on her leg gave her the strength to deal with this night no matter what it would bring.

꙰

Sulwyn had to hand it to them.

They put on quite the festival.

Sulwyn entered the Gala alone, escorted by no one, as Galahad and Daijiro both had to see to extra security around the entirety of not only Valens but of the entire Empire. This was a night when both the Privileged and the Common Ones alike had permission to attend. Though the Common Ones weren't allowed to enter Valens itself, they were allowed to gather in the large gardens that surrounded the back as well as directly in front where the stores in the streets transformed into a festival for the night.

She didn't want to think about where the resources for such an evening had come from, nor the impact it would have or always had on the rest of Vartugaul. Even though Artaxiad hated anything to do with magic, no other word could describe the feeling the Gala gave off.

Magical.

Sulwyn was currently in the same ballroom used for her coronation. It had been transformed and decorated with heavy velvet hangings and tons of tiny candles strung along the ceiling beams or hanging from small candleholders. All the doors to the ballroom were open so that guests could spill in or out to enjoy the festivities from both ends.

There were no tables that could fit any more than three to four people standing at each. All were set with food and drinks. The night was meant for dancing and entertainment. And entertainment they had.

Aside from the symphonic band that played light tinkling music, there were various talented people strewn around. From fire eaters to jugglers to actors and actresses flitting about, engaging in shows with the guests.

There were no official entrances this time. Everyone arrived at the predetermined time and began the festivities right away. Sulwyn spotted both Artaxiad and Pandora greeting guests at either end. She looked at them for a few minutes, unsure of what to do with herself until a shadow crossed her own in the doorway. She looked up in hopes of finding someone she knew, only to see Gwydion come stand beside her.

He had shaved his face and combed back his short brown hair. His tailcoat was a deep rich brown to match his black pants and shirt underneath. He cleaned up well, looking a few years younger, though she placed his age around Pandora's. He turned his brown eyes to hers, eyes smiling as he smiled, but something about them unsettled her.

"Good to see you here, Lady Princess. I understand it's your first Waning Summer Gala?"

"Obviously," muttered Sulwyn, going to make her way down the stairs. However, he stepped in front of her, stopping her in her tracks.

"It would be rude of me to let you continue down these stairs unescorted. The pleasure is mine." He held out his arm for her to take. Sulwyn glanced around her, aware of the many eyes that watched her every move. She had to maintain her patience.

Sulwyn smiled lightly, taking his arm. It was far warmer than she expected, though she didn't know exactly what she was expecting.

"You seem to be highly distracted; is this not to your liking?" he asked, leading her down the stairs until they were level with everyone else. Seeing all the forms of entertainment and guests alike this close overwhelmed her slightly; even the smells of food and something like pine and honey wafted over her. So many people and things. Far more than her coronation.

"Would you care to dance? It may rid you of those nerves, though you shouldn't feel so nervous. These are your people, and you fit in perfectly. Do enjoy yourself." He spoke calmly, his voice glossing over her. He had delicate tones that made her want to listen to him all day.

Hesitantly, she took his hand and let him lead her to the centre of the dance floor. Quite a few people were already there, excited to dance more than anything. But once she stepped into the middle, they gave them space, some continuing to dance, others watching. Was it because of her or because of Gwydion?

Galahad said Gwydion had come to the Empire thirteen years ago, already on the good side of many of the Privileged, and knowledgeable enough to impress Artaxiad. People flocked to him in times of need or advice. Though she found this a little odd, she still couldn't exactly understand why he was so revered.

"You dance well, princess." He spoke low near her ear, pulling her closer.

"I had a great teacher…" said Sulwyn, much quieter than she intended, pulling away a bit. Who was he to be so nervous with? But then she looked up into his eyes that peered into hers and saw her own reflection.

He was the person trying to frame Caldwell.

She stepped back suddenly, and as luck would have it, the music had a moment of pause just before a new song started. "I'm sorry, I think I need to go mingle with the others. Princess duties and all." She curtsied stiffly, but he made no qualms against it. He tipped his imaginary hat to her.

"I will see you again soon. We have a rather enthralling presentation to make later in the night. It will benefit us all, I think." He smiled again and Sulwyn noted the slight twitch in his brow. The smile was a smile, but somehow Sulwyn knew this was not his real smile. She didn't even know if he could make a genuine one. What she did know was that it was not reassuring at all. She felt even more uncomfortable.

"I'm sure it's befitting for this gathering," she nodded, taking off towards one of the emptier tables in a far corner and feeling a little dizzy, her mind lacking concentration for a moment, a subtle buzz in her ear.

Soon she was distracted by the food. Last time she had barely eaten, but this time she found herself marvelling at the different types offered from table to table. The one she was at held small meat pies, colourful potatoes, small cubes of cured meat, and cheese. A part of her felt terrible that probably most of this food was stolen or allocated to the Empire instead of the other towns and villages, but another, suddenly stronger part was too fascinated by what she saw to let that guilt linger long. Food was important if she was planning to endure this night, and she wanted to indulge. She desired everything in front of her.

"Glad the food is to your liking," said a deep voice. She turned to see Zander smiling sheepishly at her enjoyment. All the servers of the night had worn their most formal uniform of greys and blacks, and as he was the head chef, his uniform was a mix of red and black, crisp and almost military but in a different sense.

"I've never had food like this…this is quite amazing. Are these your recipes?" She had taken one of each on her plate, intending to probably take one of each of everything from every table. What was wrong with her?

"They are. The other staff follow quickly though, so it wouldn't have been as good without their help. And Eztli is a genius in the making. I'm sure she'll surpass me soon enough."

Sulwyn smiled brightly at the compliment as if it were given to her, and just then she spotted Eztli in the same red and black uniform rearranging another table in the distance. She caught her stare, smiling and winking.

"That means a lot coming from someone of your talent. Where did you learn to cook?"

"My parents used to cook for the High City," he muttered quietly.

"You used to live in the castle?"

"Once upon a time. As I started getting into cooking, I travelled to better my skills. That was why I was away during the fall. But my parents were killed that night by our queen."

Sulwyn looked at him, wide-eyed, "Pandora killed your parents?"

"This isn't something we should discuss. But I can promise that if you ever need my assistance, just ask for it. I must go now. Enjoy the night. Besides, there is someone that I think needs your assistance." She watched him point to their left. Sulwyn turned to see Kione skulking in the corner, just as unsure of what to do as she had been. Unlike her, he was cast in a negative light.

"Thank you," rushed Sulwyn, putting the plate down with a little regret. She dashed as gently as she could through the tables, people, and dance floor without drawing attention until she stopped suddenly. A few of the elite Privileged who resided in Valens had stepped up to Kione.

"You must have a lot of confidence to step into this Gala, Common Filth," spat one man. Kione stood straighter, his unique orange and brown clothes rustling around him, watching them carefully, but Sulwyn could see he was shaking either in terror or anger—she wasn't sure which.

"How dare you set foot in the king and queen's home after what you have done?" said a haughty woman.

"Now, now, you know the Common Filth aren't very bright. He was drawn in by the colours and sound. Would you like some treats?" said one of the men, who had been a prospect for her hand. The one that didn't get banned. Maybe she should have made a bigger scene at the time. The man stepped forward and tossed some bite-sized tarts at Kione's feet.

"Maybe if you're a good boy, you'll get more—HEY!" he snarled as he was pushed forward.

Sulwyn was absolutely seething, trying her best to reel her emotions in, but pushing him did nothing to ease it. As soon as the man turned to her, he paled.

"My lady." His eyes scanned her entirety and it just reminded her of the dinner with him.

"Apologise," she demanded, watching his face fall into confusion as well as fear.

"I beg your pardon?" He tried to laugh lightly but the longer she stared at him, the more he faltered, and with it the more she could see his anger in being cornered like this. So she pressed him further, something inside her egging her on.

"Apologise and pick up the food you threw onto the floor," said Sulwyn calmly, standing taller. Somehow watching his fear and anger mixed within brought her a kind of elation she had never cared for before, knowing full well that he needed to be careful of how he acted, but also wanted to fight back.

"Oh, that? That food slipped from my plate is all, we have help for messes like this." He laughed, looking at the others around him to join in. But she had never met these people and they had never talked to her. First impressions were everything, so they bowed and curtsied respectively to her but took steps back.

People started to notice the Lady Princess and another man were having a sort of standoff. More eyes joined them, and she could see the man's anger and fear rise in his eyes. "Are you questioning what I saw? The food did not fall."

"I apologize for my rudeness." He bent down in front of Kione, picking up the food and putting it back onto his plate. He turned to her, an apologetic smile on his face, but defiance was now in his eyes. And somehow that goaded Sulwyn to do more. She desired nothing more than to humiliate him.

"Now eat it." She crossed her arms, watching him. All eyes were on him, and he shifted restlessly.

"Lady Princess, surely this is enough?"

"I believe I said to eat it. This isn't food to waste, throwing it at people. Throwing it at my nomination, of all people. It took time and effort for food such as this to be prepared and served to the likes of you. Now I'll ask you again. Nicely. To. Eat. It. Or would you like me to force you?"

"Sulwyn, that's enough…" muttered Kione. She had almost forgotten he was there. She frowned. Was she finally being enticed by the lavishness of the Empire? She looked at the man in disgust, but it was for her own actions. Sulwyn pushed past him, reaching for Kione's hand, leading them away to the gardens outside.

She was mildly distracted from her actions when her eyes met the decorations outside. More entertainers of all kinds flitted about; paper lanterns hung around and within the trees. The large fountain in the centre had been decorated in lights as well, all reflecting in the water making it look like stars on land and in the water itself.

"Are you okay?" she asked Kione, the air clearing her mind a bit.

The lines in his jaw clenched. "Can't say I didn't expect it. This is the first time I'm here within Valens and without my sister."

"The more people see us together, the more they will stay away from you," muttered Sulwyn just as Eztli came forward in a bit of a rush.

"I saw what happened, sweetness, and you," she addressed Kione strongly, "I think we need to get some food in ya, yeah?" She smiled widely and led Kione away to the outside tables that were larger and more spaced out than inside.

Sulwyn waved them off, looking up to the sky. It was a clear night, the multicoloured stars shining over them brightly. As she walked along the garden walls, some people came up to her to engage; others just wanted to look at her before they went away. Every head turned as she walked past, and she wasn't sure if that was because she was the princess or because of her outfit or both.

She stood straighter and continued walking. In the distance, where space was more open, servants were setting up a sort of large bed of wood. She looked past the area and saw Gwydion walking with Pandora, deep in conversation. He looked up as if he sensed her gaze and smiled, waving politely. Sulwyn turned to walk away only to crash into someone…or two.

"Sulwyn…" started Galahad, appraising her quickly before his eyes found hers.

"He actually wants to tell you that you look rather stunning tonight," said Daijiro, who shoved Galahad over, taking her hand and kissing it.

"You both took your time." She suddenly felt flushed but tried to will it to fade away. Her previous emotions disappeared, focusing instead on the men in front of her.

Daijiro smirked at her, passing a hand through his slicked blonde and white hair that seemed to shine under the lights that surrounded them. He wore similar clothing as their most recent dinner with a black shirt and pants and a purple sash. But the deep plum jacket with many brass buttons down its centre had been tossed over his shoulders like an afterthought. The collar of his shirt was low, exposing the delicate necklace, a shining rainbow in the night.

"There were a few drunken riots that needed to be dealt with," said Galahad somberly. As always, he wore green, though it was only his jacket, similar to Daijiro's with brass buttons and zippers; the clothes under were a dark brown and black. His now longer hair had been fixed back and tousled to the side. Lost in a trance, she suddenly realized that they both had weapons on them. She cursed.

"What?" asked Galahad, looking around them suspiciously.

"I could have kept my belt!" she huffed, lifting the ruffles of her dress much to both of their surprise. She flashed the thigh holster with three knives.

"We have weapons because we are still on guard. You wouldn't have been able to wear your belt," said Galahad, nonplused, but Daijiro only laughed.

"This is a party, not a test. We should enjoy ourselves for a bit, no?" asked Daijiro, but before she could respond, he whisked her away to the open space. A temporary area of flat wood had been built for dancing in the middle of the garden in front of the fountain. Sulwyn glanced back at Galahad, but her attention was turned to Daijiro when he touched his fingers to her cheek.

"I deserve a little attention," said Daijiro, his eyes gentle. "It's been quite the week, with your awakening and all that. I never got to tell you something important."

Sulwyn watched him carefully, aware of the grace he carried through the dance floor and the way he held her to himself. As they turned, she spotted Galahad who had been intercepted by Gwydion, Zalika, and Artaxiad. Though she understood the reason for Gwydion and Artaxiad, she really didn't see the purpose of Zalika.

"Jealous?"

Sulwyn looked back at Daijiro. "No, I just don't like her around. The more I think about it, the more suspicious she becomes. I don't know why we even brought her along. Tiergan wasn't a man who deserved a wish to be granted. And though not as powerful as you, she is still a Velyūn. I think she's trouble, but I don't know what kind yet."

The music changed from the fast-paced beat of spinning and wide steps to something slower and more intimate. Daijiro held her closer still and she made no effort to move. Silence spread between them until finally he whispered closely to her ear, "I'm sorry."

Sulwyn faltered in her steps, making them both stop; but he kept her hand in his and his arm around her waist. He looked at her with eyes as vulnerable as the time he told her what he really was or when he had hit her by mistake. He brushed the side of her forehead, where the scars had healed enough that only faint white lines could be seen if one looked closely.

Daijiro was forced to let go of Sulwyn as an actress and an actor extravagantly stepped between them. The woman took Daijiro's hand in hers and placed the other around her waist.

"Now, we should add a little spice to your night!" Her face was half covered by a dark blue mask, and only her bright pink lips and dark brown eyes could be seen. Daijiro regarded her with annoyance, holding her much further from himself than he had Sulwyn.

But Sulwyn was now distracted by the man in front of her. He had taken her hand in his and pulled her close. He too was hidden by a black mask, his bright blue eyes and thin lips the only things visible. "It is an honour to dance with you, Lady Princess. I hope my group's acting and talents are up to your standards!" He spoke excitedly in hisses and yelps. She wondered if he was on any sort of hallucinogens.

"It's lavish enough, befitting the king and queen. I didn't expect them to be into something such as this."

"The king is a man of the people. Always likes to bring some excitement for us to enjoy. We have been working with our king as well as Sir Gwydion for some time now...I think he has something prepared!" He twirled her, and she felt dizzy once again.

Suddenly she felt a quick prick to her hand, pulling it back and out of the man's grasp. She steadied herself, ready to confront him, when a slight wave of vertigo passed through her. But he had already bowed and switched to another woman on the dance floor. At the same time, Daijiro's partner had curtsied, moving along to an overly excited man. Daijiro looked at the woman with disdain before turning back to Sulwyn.

She looked at the back of her hand, a tiny red dot in the centre, but was brought out of her thoughts when Galahad hissed out her name from the sideline. She walked back towards him to see he was alone again, pointing in the distance, urgency laced in his expression. Daijiro looked as well, where a crowd was gathering in front of the bed of wood Sulwyn had seen earlier.

The music dwindled softly until it stopped completely. Everyone crowded around the area in the middle of the garden in ample open space. Néosan had been stationed to keep a circled perimeter around, stopping guests from getting too close. Validus called attention to a makeshift stage just behind the pile of wood that hadn't been there before.

The three of them gathered behind others, but once they got closer, the other Privileged moved out of their way, letting them get right to the front.

Gwydion stood atop the centre of the makeshift stage, his eyes surveying everyone around him. Sulwyn looked around to find Pandora and

Artaxiad somewhere off to the left, their expressions in contrast to each other. While Artaxiad was elated, Pandora seemed dark and rather upset.

Soon she spotted Eztli, Kione, and Nori, who were beckoned to join along with the rest of the Common Ones. Before she could spot Arsinone, Gwydion called them all to attention. His voice called everyone over like a gentle embrace, pulling them towards him.

"On behalf of our king and queen, I thank you all for attending our annual Waning Summer Gala. As many have noticed, they put a lot of extra care this time given the multitude of things that needed to be celebrated." The way he spoke was different from how Artaxiad or Pandora addressed the people. It was quiet and patient, yet it seemed to bring everyone into his words and his actions. He was calmer, more stoic, with a brief smile here and there, but he gave off the feeling of understanding and warmth. A shiver ran through her but she couldn't bring herself to look away.

"To further add to this night, I have concluded the search on who was the real cause of the attack on our Empire, and who threatened the peace in one of our important towns, Antac."

They watched as a pair of Néosan gingerly carried a large, bound bundle onto the bed of wood. Dirt coated the sheet, black spots seeping through. But Sulwyn could spot a few dried blue and white flowers that clung to the ropes. Hot anger ran through her, head spinning. She stumbled slightly on the spot. She looked at Galahad, her fear confirmed in his eyes.

"Caldwell. Our past Leader of Uferor En was a traitor," he called, to the gasps of many. "A man sworn to treason in hopes that the Empire would fall; his connection to others like himself, as well as filthy Devinal, further slandered his person. Fortunately, his life was taken at our princess's hand. Unfortunately, he never truly paid for his crimes and with his death let his followers roam free and attempt to wreak havoc on our land."

Sulwyn moved forward, the rage rising. Did they discard the bodies of the family as they rummaged around for Caldwell's? How dare they defile their grave! How dare they disturb his soul after death and run his name through the mud? Everything he had worked for was as if he didn't even exist as anything more than a pebble on their grand, elaborate path. In that moment she felt like she could only see Gwydion and the lies he spewed, her desire to destroy his slandering face rising despite herself.

"How…" started Sulwyn, until she turned back to Daijiro and Galahad, quickly looking around, something cold growing in her suddenly.

"You need to stay calm," said Galahad, but Sulwyn pushed his arm away.

"Galahad, how did they know where he was buried…" she continued, the fear and foreboding she had been feeling rising in her once again, crawling through her, keeping the anger at bay.

Until it hit her.

When was the last time she had actually *seen* Arsinone?

XXXVI

| SULWYN |

"IT is our Lady Princess who battled this threat and killed him before he could reach in and try to destroy us all. And as a message to the group he founded, it is in our best interest to show that even in death you cannot cross the Empire," continued Gwydion quietly. Everyone around them waited with bated breath until they all agreed with his words. There was more to Gwydion than she fully realized, but he wasn't important at this moment.

Sulwyn turned to leave, but a few Validus held her arms, forcing her to face Gwydion. She resisted for just a moment, but they removed their hands quickly, too many eyes watching. Sulwyn found herself looking towards Pandora and paused.

Pandora looked furious.

At least she did to Sulwyn, because Sulwyn knew, though she wasn't sure if anyone else realized it—that if Pandora was angry, truly angry, then there was no sass. There was no smirk or poisonous tones and words. Her face remained impassive, accepting, a mask for the fury within. Just like Sulwyn's did.

"Princess," Gwydion called to her, distracting her thoughts yet again, "it would be an honour..." He beckoned one of the Validus forward to pass him a lit torch. Gwydion signalled for Sulwyn to come and accept the flame.

Sulwyn stepped towards him, her own face impassive, a mask of fury within. She originally should have burned Caldwell and spread his ashes, not buried him. Burning him the way she had with the family in Antac and the lady in the lower dungeons. At least that way it would have been private and personal between them and Galahad. But this. This was humiliation. Trespassing on his afterlife.

She reached for the torch even though every fibre, every nerve in her body wanted to lash Gwydion with it. She gripped it tighter still, watching his eyes on her with a hint of humour she didn't understand.

Without a word, Sulwyn stepped onto the makeshift stage and behind the bed of wood. She looked down at the covered remains of his body, the putrid smell mixing with the scents of the night, remembering his face and pain despite what they had gone through.

Gwydion stepped up next to her, bending low to whisper in her ear. "If you want me to tell you where she is, you will finish what you have started." His cool breath on her exposed shoulder sent an uncomfortable chill through her.

Rage roared in her as she dropped the torch onto Caldwell's body, the smell of pine and honey wafting around her alongside burning rot. Cheers engulfed them just like the flames engulfed Caldwell's remains.

Caldwell was right. In death he was free, but death wasn't meant for any more of them. Sulwyn turned around to look at Gwydion, his coy smile disturbing her until he pointed back to the east entrance. Her desire to find Arsinone beat her desire to push his face into the flames.

"If you run far enough, you might *hear* her." But he soon stepped back, the crowd's cheer waning as Pandora rushed forward suddenly, her blue and purple gown and its many folds rustling around her in a fury.

"You have disgraced me long enough! How dare you question my authority? Enough of this! I do not approve of your actions!" growled Pandora with a hint of hysteria. But Sulwyn couldn't care less about the fight that was about to start. She used that moment to dash off the stage and past Pandora, who didn't so much as glance at her.

No one else seemed to understand what was happening and if they should look at the queen or the princess, but either way Sulwyn did not stop. Slowly the guests parted for her until she made it back into the east entrance of Valens. She ran through the ballroom and back up the stairs, calling out.

"Arsinone? Arsinone! Where are you?" she yelled, running down the empty halls. Would it be better to yell out loud or in her mind? For extra measure, she did both.

"*Sulwyn...*" She stopped. Arsinone's inner voice was feeble. Her own anger started to ebb away, leaving only fear in its wake.

"*I know, it must be hard. But I need you to guide me,*" said Sulwyn gently. But something was wrong with Arsinone. Sulwyn could feel her thoughts trickle in. Had they drugged her? How much did Gwydion really know about her?

Soon images filled her mind, guiding her, taking her back to the upper dungeons. Sulwyn dashed to a path she had tried to forget. Through the first iron door, then the second, as she climbed the stairs until she was facing the very hall she had woken up to, where fate had brought her. The smell was worse than ever, fading with the closing door.

In the same cell she had been in, a small, battered form was tucked in the corner, the torchlight barely touching her.

"Arsinone? Are you okay?"

"Sulwyn!" called Galahad from behind her, the door closing again. She hadn't even realized he followed her but thanked her luck for it. She wouldn't have been able to open the cell door without him.

"Galahad, what did they do to her? Why did he target her?!" cried Sulwyn. His eyes were solemn as he walked towards her and handed her the keys. Sulwyn quickly found the old, large one she had used all those months ago and opened the cell door.

It was as cold as she remembered. Black streaks were engrained onto the ground and the walls. Gwydion had whipped her, torturing her for the location of Caldwell's grave. Sulwyn bent down, cautiously approaching her. The last thing she wanted to do was startle her. In this state, her power could harm them all.

"Sulwyn..." mumbled Arsinone weakly. Cuts covered her arms, legs, and face. Her eyes rolled and her body was unable to move.

"He drugged you?"

"He?"

"Gwydion. A man with glasses, brown eyes, and short hair?" asked Sulwyn gently, picking her up and cradling her in her arms. It wasn't like she hadn't seen it before—young boys and girls who had been beaten at the hands of the Empire just like Arsinone. But it didn't mean it was easy to see. It was never easy to see, no matter who was on the receiving end.

"Oh, he only came once...at her request...the drugs were from him..."

"Her request?" Sulwyn's hands were numb, as cold as Arsinone felt from lying on the stone ground.

"The queen's..."

Arsinone became silent, but soon images seeped into Sulwyn's mind, fuzzy and a little dim.

Pandora's main office came into view, the corner of girl's dolls sitting creepily in the firelight. "Caldwell is a dead man! Stop covering for Desirae and admit your alliance to her!" shrieked Pandora.

"My queen, he was a talented man. And with this, we can put the people's minds to rest. How can we say that two Common Ones who have lived amongst us were the start of this? The panic that would ensue!"

"I don't know where his body is. The girl was fond of him, despite killing him," said Pandora scathingly.

"Then I'm sure we can get his location from someone she is close to...?"

Pandora considered him. "There is a young one she has taken to. To my understanding, she's not worth more than I initially thought."

"How so?" he inquired, his lips turning up in a crooked smile.

"She was blamed for the murder of her town, but I see no signs of that ability. But I'll need to have her incapacitated, just to be sure."

The scene switched again, this time flashes from Arsinone's own eyes. She could see the flowing, long plum dress and the whip that Caldwell had used on her. Arsinone looked up farther to see Pandora standing over her, something like terror and anger reflected in her eyes by the firelight.

"Sulwyn," warned Galahad, but Sulwyn couldn't hear him. She couldn't hear anything besides the feeble breathing of Arsinone's battered form.

Her mind was dizzy and clouded. She didn't care who Gwydion was and what his alliance was to Diesirae. She didn't care that the elite of the Empire was just outside the walls of Valens and how reckless this would be. All she felt was vengeance and the unmistakable yearning for it.

"She knows enough about you, you don't have to hide. Please heal her, just a small amount is fine until we can get her to see Nori," said Sulwyn quietly. But she couldn't hide it from him, or anyone for that matter. Her entire body shook with rage and the unknown desire to act building in her.

"This ends tonight, Galahad. Before we left, Pandora confronted Gwydion. It's tonight they fight, and that is enough for me to kill her and put the blame on him."

"That is a ridiculous plan. Everyone saw you run out; that won't go unnoticed."

"It doesn't matter, they won't assume I'd kill her. Not after that. Whatever is happening led Pandora into a shrieking rage. And everyone was a witness to that. I've done nothing since coming here; this is the opportune moment I've needed."

"How will you find her?"

"I can," whispered Arsinone.

"I can't ask you—" but Arsinone made a face, cutting her off.

"As long as I'm conscious I can always hear…there's no yelling right now, but there is a scene. My radius has grown since coming here, but I can't hear it well from this distance. They are still outside."

"Can you heal her and walk?" whispered Sulwyn. Galahad took Arsinone into his own arms, signalling for Sulwyn to lead the way.

As they stepped out of the dungeons and back into the main parts of Valens, Arsinone was able to hear almost everything.

"Gwydion is trying to pacify her but it's mocking. I think she's aware of the scene she's making…" mumbled Arsinone. With Galahad's help, she was already starting to look a bit better. Sulwyn watched Galahad breathe out, fatigued.

"That's enough, Galahad, thank you," said Sulwyn as they made their way back towards the ballroom.

"Wait, they're moving inside…"

"What is Artaxiad doing exactly?" asked Sulwyn, stopping in the middle of the desolate hall. She found his behaviour just as odd as Pandora's. She didn't expect him to come to her aid, but he usually sided with her.

"They are going to the servant's quarters far from the gardens and the Gala…Artaxiad…is brushing it off and addressing the crowd. Zalika is around him, distracting him. I'm sorry Sulwyn, I can't stay awake…" And with that Arsinone passed out.

Sulwyn turned to Galahad, brushing some of Arsinone's hair back. "Get her to Eztli."

"You can't go alone," countered Galahad, but whatever look she was giving him, silenced his next words.

"It's best if there aren't extra people around. I'll find her. You just make sure Artaxiad finds us when the time is right."

Galahad's lip was thin. She knew he wanted to say more but decided against it. He took off towards the Gala as Sulwyn continued to the servant's quarters. But she turned when he called to her.

"Sulwyn…Pandora may be your blood, but she was never a mother to you."

⁂

Sulwyn slowed to a light jog, passing by every door until finally, the music that streamed through the distance aligned with what she had heard in her vision. She walked slower, hovering by each door, careful not to let her shadow crawl under, until finally she heard Pandora's raised voice and Gwydion's passive tones. A shiver ran through her.

Sulwyn reached for the longer of her knives, wishing she had something other than small daggers. But as she held the hilt in her hand, feeling the rough leather grind into her skin from holding it too tight, her rage and sadness flooded her, coursing through her in mad hot waves, and as thick as the vile toxic waters in the fog town. Somehow, she felt justified, but at the same time she felt tainted and dirty. Only a slight buzzing in her mind soothed her. And then she heard Pandora yell out and instantly all she could feel was the desire to end that voice.

"Cailín…" whispered Daijiro behind her.

Sulwyn visibly jumped, turning and pointing the dagger under his chin. He held his arms up, but his look was one mixed of surprise and devilishness.

"I convinced Galahad to stay. I'm all kinds of reckless, but I'm not stupid and neither is he. You can't expect Gwydion to stand still and watch you murder. That's where I come in." He smiled, putting his arms down. "Galahad will bring Artaxiad, using your cook friend as a witness."

"Eztli? I can't involve her!" hissed Sulwyn. The music in the background now matched exactly what she heard. Gwydion would step up to Pandora soon with the dangerous look in his eyes. What if he was planning to kill her? Would he?

But Pandora was her prey. She couldn't let someone else do it for her.

"The other one, the man. He sought us out after the debacle outside. Said he will do whatever you ask when the time comes, says he owes it to you. You seem to trust him, so we agreed to his involvement," shrugged Daijiro. She watched him tense slightly. But she didn't have time to question Zander's sudden involvement. If his story was true, then he wanted revenge on Pandora as well.

"Can you do this without being seen?" she whispered even lower.

"I just need to hear him, make him say something so I can pinpoint him." His face concentrated, and she knew hers mirrored it. He placed his hands on her shoulders, looking at her carefully before letting go, the buzzing faded slightly but her rage was still there.

Sulwyn took a deep breath. She had killed before. Blood was on her hands, the blood of the innocent, blood of the guilty. But this blood…a crash inside made Sulwyn leap into action.

She pushed the doors open, watching just as Gwydion caught Pandora's wrist, holding back the dagger she had seen in her vision.

They both turned to her, Pandora in shock and something else she couldn't read, and Gwydion with his eyes cast in suspicion.

"Princess...this is a very compromising thing to walk in—" he froze, his grip on Pandora's hand slackening. His eyes darted to the other side of the wall instantly, comprehension and something like irritation flashing in his face. But it was quickly exchanged for amusement.

"If looks could kill, Sulwyn..." whispered Pandora, pulling her arm away.

Sulwyn had heard that line before, she wracked her memory for who had said it, but the way Pandora was looking at her distracted her from that. She was no longer holding her mask of anger. Instead, she looked cunning and poisonous like the queen she had always heard about.

Pandora dropped the dagger, standing calmly as if Gwydion had not been in the midst of assaulting her. She faced her fully for the first time, looking at her directly in the eyes. Unwavering. She didn't give Gwydion a second look, uncaring at his immobility.

"I warned you and Artaxiad, if you touched any one of them..." Her voice was barely a whisper; she was beside herself with fury.

"This was an unavoidable situation, Sulwyn. You're old enough to understand that. I did what I had to."

"You don't even believe what he's been saying! You just took it out on her, and she's a child!" yelled Sulwyn. But she couldn't drag this out, so why was she hesitating?

Pandora seemed a little unsettled at how Sulwyn knew this, but that moment of emotion was wiped off her face and replaced with disdain. "Are you here to kill me? Do you think you can? For what? A girl of no importance? A child with no meaning in this world? You would take the chance and risk what you've managed here to have your vengeance?"

Sulwyn stepped closer, wrath and desire to kill this woman rising. But something else she couldn't place was clashing within her. Instead, she smothered it with her fury.

This was why she was here. She was trapped in this castle, biding her time until she could slowly take them apart and rebuild Vartugaul from scratch in honour of the High City. Wasn't that always the plan? How could she not take this opportunity?

"You look just like us, Sulwyn. That hate within your eyes and the confidence that you have the power within you to kill anything that displeases you. Believe it or not, I feel a sense of pride in that, and in you for honing it."

"How long did you torture her?" whispered Sulwyn, disregarding everything she said and watching Gwydion, who was seemingly relaxed despite being held against his will, anticipating even.

"She broke fast. Faster than I thought she would. Maybe because of the drugs, maybe because you don't have her trust. That's why you should keep your heart to yourself, girl. Trust doesn't come for free."

"You know nothing of trust. This ends now, Pandora." Sulwyn rushed towards her, hands cold, barely able to feel the knife she held so tightly in her hands.

She slammed into Pandora before she could guard herself, throwing her back and onto the floor.

Sulwyn hovered over her, one knee against the wooden floor, the other astride her. She propped up her knife arm, keeping herself steady. The blade pressed against Pandora's neck.

This was not like her other kills.

This one had been in the back of her mind since she learned about them all those years ago.

In her hands and veins anytime she saw the destruction and death caused by the Néosan.

In her heart since she had been born.

Sulwyn could hear her pulse thrumming in her ears, and a rush went through her. But another hidden desire was building in her, starting to form into words, and before she could help herself, they came out in a rush and a whisper: "Why did you leave me for dead?"

XXXVII

The Queen Of Vartugaul

| SULWYN |

PANDORA'S eyes widened, taking her in carefully. Staring at her as the seconds between their breaths felt like hours and days and centuries.

Sulwyn couldn't believe she even asked that question, and it looked to her like Pandora was just as surprised. But then she smirked.

"Weakness, Sulwyn. Even I had my moments. So, I cut it out and left it behind in hopes it would rot. But you grew like a fungus and spread your spores on everything we've created, leaving us with annoying sores. Nothing more. You were not a threat. You could never be. The Steel Warrior raised you with too much compassion. Why haven't you killed me yet?"

Pandora raised her arms and pulled the edges of Sulwyn's dress, bringing her closer. The blade dug into Pandora's throat, but her smirk remained, and her eyes were bright and relentless and full of fire, something Sulwyn had never seen. Something that tied their resemblance that much more.

"I don't know how you know the truth about him," she whispered, barely audible, "but I'm sure you know more than you're letting on. You're taking too long. Whatever hold you have on him won't last, in fact, I'm sure he's playing into your game. He loses nothing if I die," she spoke so quietly Sulwyn had to strain over the music streaming into the room to hear.

But then she continued speaking loudly again. "The girl screamed endlessly because of you. How does that make you feel? Close your heart, Sulwyn. Don't endanger the people you think you trust. I am your enemy and it doesn't end with me. Artaxiad is just as terrible if not worse. He will come after them all, one way or another. And after him..." she faltered, struggling with something Sulwyn couldn't see, "there are more..." she breathed the last part, glancing behind her where Gwydion stood immobile.

Pandora pulled her even closer, until Sulwyn could feel Pandora's hot breath on her, feel the erratic beat of her heart through her chest. "Or are you too weak? All those years spent hunting us down, fighting our army... You have me in your hands, and you can't do anything. Don't think I don't know what game you've been playing."

Pandora dropped her hands from Sulwyn's shoulders, quickly grabbing the dagger that she'd dropped onto the floor earlier. Pandora stabbed Sulwyn in her arm before she could block it, and at the same time, Sulwyn's fury and sadness and confusion reached their peak and she drew her blade across Pandora's neck without any more hesitation. Warm blood coated her hands instantly.

Pandora's eyes grew wide, her grip on her own dagger slackening. She reached to her neck, which was gurgling and bleeding profusely around her hands. Sulwyn started to move out of the way, but Pandora pulled her back down with strength she didn't think she had, closer than before, her lips to her ear.

"I knew..." she choked in barely a whisper, her eyes full of anger and tears and pain. "Raghnall had been tracking us before you were born." Pandora looked away and behind her, quickly pushing Sulwyn back and off her, creating space.

But before Sulwyn could register what Pandora had done, Gwydion was in front of Sulwyn, grabbing her by the neck and lifting her off the ground. He gave her no chance to breathe as she watched Pandora's eyes on hers, her brows knitted in frustration and anguish.

But it wasn't Gwydion anymore, or at least not what he had looked like just a few seconds ago. Sulwyn realized the song in the background had just changed; only a few minutes had transpired between her and Pandora. She looked into the man's angular violet eyes—glasses removed—his hair, longer than hers, flowing delicately around him. His entire face changed into someone else. He had been hiding his true self with magic.

The door crashed open, revealing Galahad, closely followed by Artaxiad, who froze at the scene. The transition was quick—his face grew from confusion to fury then madness within a second. Gwydion dropped Sulwyn onto the ground, his hands up, a smile playing along his lips.

"It's Gwydion…he's a Devinal," choked Sulwyn, pulling the dagger out of her arm. She got up quickly and, against every fiber in her body, forced herself to run towards Artaxiad and embrace him as if she were terrified.

Gwydion shot her a look of frustration. "Clever girl…"

Artaxiad accepted her as if it were the most natural thing between them, pulling her to his side.

"How dare you…" started Artaxiad, his voice low and dangerous, and for the first time Sulwyn actually felt fear and relief that it was not directed at her. "Years we had a partnership…Is this what you really look like? Did Pandora find out you were Devinal filth? Is that why you killed her? To silence her?"

"I did not kill her, nor would I ever raise my hand against her with the intention to do so," spoke Gwydion. His entire tone and demeanour had changed and Sulwyn could see that Artaxiad was unsettled. Everything he knew about this man was a lie, and that was perfect for her. This was going perfectly.

Daijiro stepped through the door, taking in the blood and Pandora, who lay still. He lingered on Gwydion, a look crossing his eyes that Sulwyn didn't fully understand, and then he looked at her. But before he could move, another person stepped in from behind him.

Zander walked in, his eyes lingering on Pandora briefly until he turned to Artaxiad. "I had also heard them talking in this room before. He threatened Pandora, drove her into a corner with magic, and bid me to silence. When she ran out of the Gala, I felt strongly that something terrible was about to happen…so I followed to the best of my ability…"

"And you are?" asked Gwydion lazily.

"Pandora's brother. Our king is already aware of this fact since my arrest, though it was kept secret." He bowed before turning to find Sulwyn, her eyes wide.

Did Pandora know he was her brother? But more than that, Pandora had killed her own parents too? Cold flooded her. The vengeance fulfilled, the odd buzzing settled, and the desire was put out like water to a fire with the vague smell of pine and sweet rain wafting around her.

Many pairs of feet could be heard marching through the hallways until a small platoon of Validus stood outside the room. Daijiro was handed a couple of chains, stepping forward and shackling Gwydion with them as Artaxiad reported to the Validus.

"Don't think these can hold me for long," she heard him whisper to Daijiro, but he was thrilled at the challenge.

"Don't think I can't use powers of my own to keep you long enough to kill you," whispered Daijiro, flicking his hand. Gwydion fell to his knees, clenching his teeth in silence.

"Take him to the Solus. He will stand trial tomorrow," announced Artaxiad, dismissing the Validus. He removed himself from Sulwyn's side, ignoring them all. Passing Gwydion without a second glance, he bent down to Pandora's still body, closing her eyes.

ȣ

"Sulwyn?" whispered Galahad as they walked, but she couldn't hear him.

Pandora had killed her parents. Her actions mirrored her own. She had never felt more similar to her before that moment. But then…"What have I done?" choked Sulwyn, looking down at the blood on her hands. She looked down at herself and realized that even though the blood was drying, it was only a few shades darker than her dress. Melding into the fabric as if it had always been part of it, the blood that ran through her veins decorated her clothes.

Tears had fallen from Pandora's eyes, and she initially thought it had been from the pain. But even Sulwyn rarely cried from pain, so she didn't think Pandora would either. And all she could hear were her words, banging against the inside of her head.

Sulwyn didn't know where she was going. No one knew their queen had died. The Gala was still happening despite the turmoil she was in. As she walked farther and farther away from the room, from Pandora and from Gwydion, a rise of different emotions erupted within her. The strange buzzing desire that had pulled at her before was now in the background, fading and fading until finally, there was only despair.

Had she been wrong? Had there been more than she realized? Pandora knew Raghnall was tracking them. And Raghnall had mentioned once that the placement of the fire in the house when he saved her always bothered him, but he passed it off as luck.

Had Pandora left her alive with the intention of Raghnall finding her?

But that changed everything.

Or did it?

Even if that were the case, she had still been abandoned, and Pandora and Artaxiad were still dictators. Even if Pandora planned it out so that she could be saved, it didn't change the fact that they had killed thousands either by their own hand or by their lead. Pandora deserved to die, just as Artaxiad did and would also.

But there were others besides Artaxiad? Who was she referring to?

The more Sulwyn thought about it, the more she felt as if Pandora hadn't said anything without reason. There had been warnings, things she said in hopes that Gwydion wouldn't hear; why? And at the end, she looked at Gwydion before pushing her away. Was she trying to give her time? That couldn't be possible...

Sulwyn was outside, barely aware of Daijiro and Galahad following closely behind her. She was back in the garden of the Gala, but she couldn't stay there.

She needed to leave.

To run and run and run and...

"Sulwyn!" hissed Galahad. She turned to him, her face and hands and body grew colder still at exactly what she had just done. As if her own blood was draining out of her body.

Suddenly a loud, long resonating bell tolled in the distance.

A cold, foreboding sound.

It rang out four times before the last toll vibrated into the distance, bringing with it a dead silence. Sulwyn watched as all the Privileged and the Common Ones alike immediately got down onto their knees wherever they were standing. Shock evident on some faces, confusion in others.

Daijiro pulled her down to follow suit. "Four long bells for death…" he whispered, pointing towards the entrance.

Sulwyn looked over and saw the procession of not only Validus but the maids and manservants who worked close to Pandora. They walked out with dark red and black flags parting the way through those on their knees. Soon the procession split and Artaxiad walked through them carrying Pandora's body draped in deep blue silk, her blood trailing along the ground.

Waves of horror and surprise rose around them like hisses of steam, but Artaxiad carried on, not seeing those in front of him. If Sulwyn didn't know better, she would have mistaken him for someone in mourning. And maybe he was. Just a part of him, saddened that the person who had helped him reach the Empire was now dead after all these years. But she knew most of it was rage that bordered madness. Rage that the enemy had been so close to them, right under his nose, and that he had lost this battle. Rage to his shamed pride.

Bile rose in her. The dry blood was still on her hands. She looked down at it, coating her palms thickly; if anyone saw this…

But soon Nori was crawling to her side with a damp cloth. "They explained it to me." She wiped her hands clean. "Arsinone is being cared for by Eztli now, she's fine."

By the time she finished, the cloth was soaked in red like her dress. Daijiro took it from her quickly, setting fire to it with a touch of his fingers; it disintegrated in mere seconds.

"I've been meaning to say…that's not magic," said Nori a little shakily.

"I don't really know," he admitted, but then they all faced the front as Artaxiad reached the same wooden bed that Caldwell's ashes rested on. He placed Pandora carefully onto the surface, uncovering her face and moving her hair back before looking up.

"A night meant for celebration has been tainted with darkness. After this moment, the Waning Summer Gala will never be held again in honour of your fallen queen." He spoke loudly, clearly, but his eyes were dead and broken.

The people remained silent despite the confusion stirring around them. Tremors went through her. A million things ran through her mind. But one thought began to surface faster and stronger than the others, one that should have risen above all the others tonight.

Gwydion was a Devinal, the same one working with Diesirae. The same one who managed to get Raghnall to betray her to the Empire, who managed to fool Artaxiad for years. There was no way they could keep him locked in the Solus, not with the power he held. It was only a matter of time, and if Gwydion had this power, what was stopping him from getting Artaxiad to submit to it and use it to return the rightful blame on her?

The fact that the Blood Princess killed her mother; the queen of Vartugaul.

This was her worst plan.

The most reckless one.

Raghnall always told her that if she didn't stop, she would get herself killed. But somehow, this time she couldn't fight against it, or maybe she could have but chose not to. Being still for too long in the Empire must have driven her mad. How could she have thought this would be a good idea?

"Our queen has been taken from us by the same hands you all revered. Gwydion." The whispers turned into cries of shock and disbelief. There was no way that Gwydion of all people would do that. It must be a mistake! It must have been someone else! But who else could manage to get close enough save for someone in his position?

The people started to turn their attention to Sulwyn, looking at her with eyes of sadness, yet some with eyes of distrust. But the stares were too much for her, and she stood up, needing to run.

"Sulwyn, come before me," called Artaxiad as soon as he saw her. Sulwyn froze, looking up at him in fear. She looked down to Galahad, Daijiro, and Nori, all of them looking at her the same way she looked at Artaxiad.

Sulwyn moved forward, aware of all the eyes on her, and somehow the panic rose within her more, bringing with it tears that streamed lightly down her face. She walked up to the makeshift stage for the second time that night. Where once she stood there with hate and fire, she now stood there with dread she didn't know she had. Doubt and despair for the fact that she may have made a huge mistake.

"It is your honour as well as mine to have you set her soul to rest," he turned to her, watching her with eyes that didn't really see her. But then he raised his hand and touched the tears that kept falling down her cheeks. And with it, her fear grew deeper.

Artaxiad called for two torches, handing one to Sulwyn. "There are no words to describe this feeling of loss. The Empire has lost a magnificent leader to the hands of someone we trusted. Alas, some take for granted what they have been given. Tomorrow, Gwydion will stand trial and receive the judgement he deserves. But tonight, we have dug into this box of despair and reached hope that this will not be in vain." He looked to Sulwyn, who followed his hand as they both set a torch down onto the blue silk sheets around Pandora's still, cold body. Her face calm for the first time since Sulwyn laid eyes on her.

The flames rose, higher and higher, the smell of burning flesh and blood filling her nose and lungs and weighing her down further and further.

⁂

The participants of the Gala cleared out once the fire burned down to ash. Cries and tears carried them into the late night. Pandora's ashes were gathered in a fine vase and were meant to be scattered across the land of the Empire. Sulwyn remained silent the entire time after she lit her mother's body, and hadn't even realized when they reached Eques.

"Sulwyn…" whispered Galahad, and it was only then she noticed that she was back in her room, still sitting in a dress of blood. Daijiro left to attend to the Solus, and Galahad sat her down on the bed, eyes full of concern.

"Tell me what happened," he asked softly. She looked up; his multicoloured eyes were tired but alert.

"Pandora…" started Sulwyn, but even saying her name set the thoughts all in motion again. And none of them made sense. She shook her head, moving back from him. He looked at her, his concern turning into worry.

Sulwyn took a deep breath. If Pandora knew they were being tracked, and purposely left her in a way that she could be saved, then she should have anticipated the chance that Sulwyn would grow up and come after them. But why? And if that was the case, then that meant Pandora had even more faith in Raghnall than Sulwyn had right now.

"That doesn't make sense," said Sulwyn out loud, standing up. She knew the answer she was looking for was deep inside, evading her the more she thought about it. But just as she felt like she was scraping the edges, a loud knock sounded on the door.

Galahad crossed the room, opening the door roughly. Demir faced him, his face pale.

"The king would like an audience with the princess, and you if she allows it."

"At this time? Why?" Galahad asked, annoyed. Demir backed up a bit but keep his back straight, poised.

"I'm not in any position to defy his orders a second time." He looked at Sulwyn pointedly, but faltered when he saw her.

"We'll be there shortly," Galahad dismissed him, closing the door behind him.

"He's found out…he knows I did it. And that's it. I can't fight him now, not right now. It's only been a week since I woke up. Even if I tried to kill him now and succeeded, the entire Empire would be against us," said Sulwyn, panic erupting in her. Galahad looked at her in confusion and fear.

"Tell me now, Sulwyn, what happened? Why are you like this? Is it because she was your mother? I told you…" But she silenced him with a look of anger.

"She left me alive, Galahad. Knowing full well that Raghnall was on their trail."

"That…" but Galahad was at a loss for words. And she knew he understood now, where she stood.

"But that doesn't change what they've done," he said.

"I know that! I know. But what if there is more to all of this?! Was this a mistake?"

"No," he said firmly, "but we need to go now before Artaxiad becomes suspicious. We'll deal with that tomorrow. After this, you can rest and give yourself time to think. Okay? We'll deal with this together. You aren't alone." He took her hand in his and pulled her into a warm embrace. She felt her nerves calm slightly, but too soon they were riding back to Valens.

Midnight finally settled over the Empire, everything darker than normal in her eyes. When they got to the main entrance, a Néosan was waiting for her, casting a glance at Galahad. Something about his look threw her into doubt. But her mind was cloudy, and heavy with the weight of what she had done and what everything could mean.

They were led to the throne room. A room Sulwyn had heard was used once a year when they opened Valens up to the public to deal with the politics of Vartugaul that went beyond the Triarchy. The large black doors were pulled open for them, but Galahad was told to stay back by the entrance as Sulwyn walked farther in.

It was a large, white open space. The floors were tiled in white and grey, while red stones were speckled throughout them like drops of blood scattered across the surface. The walls had been draped in dark reds to commemorate Pandora, and her seat was covered in black silk. Artaxiad was sitting on his own thrown, a tankard of what must be wine or ale in his hand.

But his eyes were dark.

"Sulwyn...how saddened you must be. As am I..." he whispered, but his eyes never left hers. "However, the Empire must always continue. We must always continue to lead and guide those in our care. Alone I will be targeted. Riots will start once news breaks that we have lost our queen. They will assume us weak and think an uprising possible. History does have a way of repeating itself, despite my efforts...But with you..." He stood up, placing the tankard aside and descending the few stairs from his seat.

"We still have power, Sulwyn. I still have you." He smiled widely, and before Sulwyn could move, ten men—Captains—came towards her from out of the folds of the red velvet hangings.

"Sulwyn!" yelled Galahad, she turned to see Validus and Néosan, far more than ten, apprehending him and holding him back. But he didn't make it easy. Just as the Captains grabbed her, holding her still, she watched him make quite a few steps towards her, stretching his arm to reach her. The Validus pulled him back, gripping him hard around the waist as she too tried to stretch towards him.

Suddenly fire burned in her nose through a dark cloth, the same poison that Raghnall had used on her, but far stronger and more potent.

Her mind swam, the colours of red flowing around her until his green eyes were in front of her, melding into the red just like her vision in the haze. "Sweet, young, Sulwyn..."

"Artaxiad! Let her go!" roared Galahad, but Sulwyn watched one of the Validus bring the hilt of a sword to the back of his head, hard, stunning him but not knocking him out. He stumbled to his knees, fighting to stand again.

"Impressive...I knew it would be hard to subdue you. But you will not get in my way. Not this time. I am not ready to stop being king just yet." He turned to face Galahad, his eyes wicked. "Galahad, you are banned henceforth from having contact with Sulwyn. You are not to speak to her, approach her, or even see her unless I permit it. You are forbidden entry into Valens."

"Galahad..." breathed Sulwyn, forced to her knees, head spinning, threatening to fade, but she willed and willed herself not to pass out. Artaxiad turned back to her, kneeling before her. The look in his eyes was evil, broken, and unfocused. The smell of pine and honey lingered.

"You are mine now. As the new queen of Vartugaul, you will rule beside me." He took her chin roughly between his fingers, looking at her.

She could barely focus on him, and she didn't want to. She tried her hardest to look at Galahad, trying to make eye contact with him, until Artaxiad forced a kiss onto her lips.

"I WILL KILL YOU!" roared Galahad, but Sulwyn found Galahad's wide eyes. His eyes that threatened so much to turn black. All she could manage was to shake her head until blackness coated her eyes and mind.

∂∾ᕟ

Ten men mixed of Captains and Validus alike stood guard around a special cell used for Artaxiad's personal use, far from the lower and upper dungeons.

Torch lights lit the hallways, but the light barely managed to penetrate the dark corners of the cell. A lone figure sat within, legs curled onto the floor and bound by chains. A dress as dark as night draped her body, embroidered with fine silk, ribbons, and gold. But it was not long enough to cover her legs, leaving most of them exposed, showing the scars and bruises that covered her. Her hair was left to hang loosely, covering her face as she breathed deeply, unconscious. Her arms were chained to the wall above her head.

Sulwyn—the new queen of Vartugaul.

TO BE CONTINUED IN

THE BONDS THAT BIND US

BOOK II

The Corrupted Prince

Names, Words and Terminology of Vartugaul:

Characters: *Note: This is how I pronounce them.**

Sulwyn*: SUL-win – *our main protagonist, daughter of Queen Pandora and King Artaxiad.*

Raghnall: RAE-N-aeL – *The Steel Warrior, former High Captain of the High City and Sulwyn's saviour and mentor.*

Galahad: ga-la-Had – *the adopted prince of the Empire and Leader of Validus Uferor San.*

Daijiro: die-JEE-rOH – *Leader of Validus Uferor Divi and Interrogator of the Solus.*

Artaxiad: ar-TAX-ee-ADD – *King of the Empire.*

Pandora: PAN-do-RAH – *Queen of the Empire.*

Caldwell: KAWld-wel – *Leader of Validus Uferor En, the first Uferor group founded.*

Eztli: ezz-li – *A maid and head chef in Valens Muros.*

Arsinone: ar-SE-non – *A maid of Valens Muros and Soul Reader.*

Nori: NO-ree – *A maid of Valens Muros.* | **Duri:** DOO-ree – *The alter identity of Nori.*

Kione: KEEY-on – *A Common One and Protector in the Solus.*

Diesirae: DEZ-ah-ray – *Sister to Kione and Common One.*

Tiergan: tEAr-gin – *The spokesperson in the fog town.*

Taru: TAA-roo – *A whimsical old man and Soul History Reader.*

Zalika: ZA-li-Kaa - *A servant of Tiergan's.*

Gwydion: Gwid-ee-ohn – *Member of the Triarchy and scholar.*

Nero: NEE-row - *Raghnall's younger brother and founder of the Triarchy/Diarchy.*

Ildri: iLL-dree - *Prisoner in the Pain Cells of the Solus, also known as number Thirty-Six.*

Eleri: eL-lar-REE - *Prisoner in the Pain Cells of the Solus, also known as Twenty-Seven, Raghnall's second in command during the High City reign.*

Names, Words and Terminology of Vartugaul:

Places

Vartugaul: var-TU-gaal - *The name of the entire land.*

Antiqua: an-tee-gwa - *The continent where the Empire resides.*

Guāngcǎi: gang-kai - *The largest continent in Vartugaul. Where Nero and Gwydion govern.*

Mortui Gemma: more-too-ee gem-mah - *The snowy continent, harsh winter conditions all year round.*

Uhuru: oo-who-roo - *The sandy continent where Kione, Diesirae and Ildri are from.*

Antac: an-TAAK - *The town responsible for making weapons out of Neuore.*

Tranquillum Forest: tran-QILL-um forest - *The forest that boarders all Vartugaul.*

Valens Muros: VAL-eez moo-rose - *The main castle of the Empire where the King and Queen reside.*

Eques Muros: eh-qwess moo-rose - *The secondary castle where all military personal train or live.*

Proelium Terra: pRO-eel-i-UM tear-RAH – *Colosseum like structure dug out of a mountain to hold trails and battles or major announcements.*

the Solus: the SOUL-Uh-s – *The prison of the Empire built by the High City.*

The Fog Town: *A mysterious town hidden from the Empire.*

Names, Words and Terminology of Vartugaul:

Titles:

Néosan: NAY-oh-san – *Artaxiad's Army, lowest level.*

Captains: CAP-tins – *Above Néosan, lead large platoons of fifty or more.*

Validus: vAL-ee-doS – *Above Captains, smaller platoons of ten.*

Uferor: U-for-er – *Consists of four Validus and one Leader in teams of five.*

Leaders: Leed-eers – *Higher than all army personal, only five.*

Protectors: pro-tek-tours - *On par with Validus, govern over the Solus.*

Triarchy: try-arr-key - *Group of three that govern over Empire business.*

Races, Clans and Tribes:

Devinal: dee-vine-all - *People born with the ability to hold magic.*

Kuvuli: coo-vuu-lai - *An honourable tribe, with old history from Uhuru.*

Kurome: coo-row-meh - *The clan of black eyes.*

Velikat: vel-ee-cat - *Race of elite humans that evolved sometime after the Lost World.*

Velikai: vel-ee-kai - *The term used for female Velikat.*

Velika: vel-ee-kaa - *The term used for male Velikat.*

Velyūn*: veel-yuun - *The term used for a Velikat half-breed.*

| ACKNOWLEDGEMENTS |

Vartugaul has been a piece of me since I was fifteen. I got into reading later in life compared to all the other writers I read about who started when they were three years old. I just never found a book I liked despite my mom's efforts. She tried to get me to read Nancy Drew and the Hardy Boys. And while, I didn't really mind them, they just weren't for me. I was ten when Harry Potter and the Goblet of Fire came out. At that point, everyone was already obsessed, so I figured there had to be something about this book. And that was where my love for reading happened. Since then, things have happened, but I want to believe the Harry Potter books have taken a life of their own in the hands of the fans. After that I started to read a lot, until I happened across Eragon. This is the book that made me feel like I needed to write my own book. And so, I did. When I was fifteen, there weren't many books with strong, female protagonists in the same kind of setting like Eragon. Though my initial ideas started out with a boy, I quickly turned it into a girl, and thus, Sulwyn was born.

At the beginning of this book, I added a dedication to myself. I did this because this story has been my best friend and enemy for seventeen years. Despite my struggles with mental health, I managed to finally put this story out into the world, and for that I am proud. It took a while to get here, but I'm here and I'm staying. Hoping to bring more stories and adventures to you, and of course, more books in the world of Vartugaul. But with that, I want to thank so many others.

Thank you to my husband, Steven. My other best friend, soulmate and partner in mediocre crime. You have been there since you stepped into my life almost fifteen years ago, and I couldn't have made it this far without you. You challenge me and try to keep my dream afloat when I want to sink it with my own hands.

To my daughter, Theodora, who is almost two, and has no idea how to read. I want this to show you that you can do it. Whatever it is. You can do it. And I hope nothing holds you back. I've never known love the way I do now since meeting you. We've cried, laughed and lost a lot of sleep together, but I wouldn't have it any other way. I love you so, so much.

To Alex. You convinced me not to stop writing one devastating night after hours of texting way past our bedtime. Since high school you read all my atrocious words and still encouraged me. Without context or questions, you answer all my questions regardless of how spontaneous they may be. For being my second, third and forth opinion, I thank you!

Katie Judy. You, my friend, are someone I wish to keep in my life for the end of time. Despite the fact that we live in two different countries, you've been there for me and all my ramblings. You are a queen, and I love you. I really hope we meet in person one day, but until then, we'll just have to continue our really long voice notes to each other.

There are a bunch of you over the years who took my unedited monster of a manuscript and read it. Be it the original version or the versions after. Thank you, Ludovica (buzz buzz), Ashley (who read everything I have, even unfinished stories). Allison (who was the first person to call Galahad a cinnamon roll), Michelle, and Kristen. My beta readers Katie Judy (yeah, you get double thanks! Who is the best hype women. The writing community on Instagram is phenomenal and so are you!) Brittany, Chelsea and Insiya (who took the time during her studies in England to read, then returned home and reread it again!) And to all my ARC readers, who have gone out of their way to help me. Special shoutout to Susan from Grendel Press for signing me and taking me one step closer to my dream!

To my parents who kept me weird, getting me into all this fantasy stuff in the first place.

It's been years since I started this, and there are many others who have encouraged me along the way, so I thank you too.

To the reader, if you've made it this far and want to continue this story with me, I thank you and hope to hear all you have to say about the world of Vartugaul. This world is my second home, and I am so excited to share it with you.

And to all of us who struggle with mental health.

Don't let the voices deny you your dreams. Don't let the darkness and suffocation keep you from fighting your way through. It's hard. I know it's hard. But every day you survive is another day you can dream and work towards anything you want to do. You are your greatest enemy, but you are also your biggest fan. I see you. You are safe. We got this. So go do the thing!

Thank you.

S.A. Gonsalves is a Canadian author from Ontario.

While The Blood Princess is her debut novel, it is not the only book she has planned. She can't wait to bring more of the world of Vartugaul to you along with tons of other stories that bang around in her head just waiting to get out.

In her spare time if she isn't writing (which doesn't happen often with a toddler at home), she tries to junk journal, paint, design, catch up on her ever-growing TBR list, anime list and game list. While also trying to balance mom life and fitting in dates with her husband when they aren't just sleeping instead or being potatoes on the couch and rewatching Naruto.

www.sagonsalves.com

Follow her unorganized process on Instagram:

@writer.stepfanie

www.ingramcontent.com/pod-product-compliance
Lightning Source LLC
Chambersburg PA
CBHW032102310726
48972CB00001B/69